A New Leaf

A New Leaf

A Cape Light Novel

THOMAS KINKADE
& KATHERINE SPENCER

DOUBLEDAY LARGE PRINT
HOME LIBRARY EDITION

BERKLEY BOOKS, NEW YORK
A Parachute Press Book

This Large Print Edition, prepared especially for Doubleday Large Print Home Library, contains the complete, unabridged text of the original Publisher's Edition.

A Berkley Book
Published by The Berkley Publishing Group
A division of Penguin Group (USA) Inc.
375 Hudson Street
New York, New York 10014

This book is an original publication of The Berkley Publishing Group.

ISBN: 0-7394-4007-1

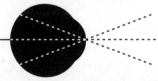

This Large Print Book carries the Seal of Approval of N.A.V.H.

A LETTER FROM THOMAS KINKADE

A *New Leaf*: The title of this Cape Light book suggests a fresh start, a new beginning. As a painter, I love new beginnings. One of my favorite moments is when I put my brush to a blank white canvas to begin a new painting. The precious newness of the moment is a thrill that is difficult to describe, but when people hear me say that, they often ask, "Don't you feel daunted by the blank canvas in front of you? Doesn't the task ahead ever seem too difficult, even frightening?" Truthfully the answer is no, for one simple reason: I have learned that no canvas is ever really blank. Every painting, every stroke of my brush, every glowing dot of light carries with it a little bit of me, everything that has come before. My task, and my joy, is to not hold back, to let the canvas fill with everything I have learned and seen and felt. My raw materials are not the paint and brushes and canvas cloth. My raw materials are my family, my friends, my joys, my sorrows, my faith in God, everything that makes up the color and form of my life. If I can embrace all of that, I know the painting will emerge.

For me, all of life is like that—a painting that we create and change and shape for all our years on earth. As you will soon see in *A New Leaf,* several of Cape Light's residents are facing a new white canvas. Some will feel the elation of love and others the sadness of parting. Some are hesitating to pick up a brush to let their new paintings take form. New relationships are begun and old relationships undone. Others are looking back on the canvases they have already filled and hoping to make sense of what they have created. But as they turn their new leaves and begin to allow their new paintings to emerge, they will certainly come to understand and appreciate anew the fullness that is a life lived on God's earth.

So join us now. Jessica and Sam, Dan and Emily, Sophie and Gus, and Molly are ready to welcome you to Cape Light. And I welcome you, too, with my thanks. Thank you so much for saving a small corner of the canvas of your life for the people of Cape Light.

—Thomas Kinkade

A New Leaf

CHAPTER ONE

Molly Willoughby ran down the hallway, a radio tucked under one arm, a bucket of cleaning supplies dangling from the other. The vacuum followed like a dutiful pet, coming to a sudden stop beside her in the middle of the empty room.

She checked her watch. Nearly four and she had the whole second floor to finish: three bedrooms and two baths. Large rooms, too. And dirty. She'd never expected the place to take this long. The kitchen had been a nightmare. Scouring the stove and refrigerator had taken hours and worn out two sets of gloves.

She propped the radio on a window

ledge and turned up the volume loud enough to be heard over the vacuum. The station was her daughter Lauren's favorite, one Molly usually avoided. But it was good cleaning music; the frantic beat kept her moving.

She covered the room in big strides, shoving the vacuum in all directions over the blue carpet, thinking how she'd never even wanted this job. She wanted to give up housecleaning altogether, but here she was, once again breaking her neck to finish on time.

Why do I let myself get talked into these things?

Because you need the money, a small, familiar voice answered.

True enough. Sometimes she felt like a hamster in a cage, racing endlessly on its wheel but never making any progress. There was the housecleaning, errand jobs, cooking for private clients, baking for restaurants. If someone offered her work, she couldn't afford to refuse. She took the job first and figured out how and when she would do it later. She worked hard to support her girls, though ironically, she knew they sometimes felt neglected. As if she didn't give them enough of her time and attention.

Well, maybe I don't, she admitted. If her ex-husband, Phil, would just grow up and help support his children in some consistent fashion, maybe she'd have some extra time to spend with them.

She hoped when they were older they'd understand. She thought she was doing a good job so far raising them. Hopefully, she'd send them to college someday. That was her real goal.

So they won't end up like me, racing from job to job, just to make ends meet, constantly juggling work and their needs, not to mention the often complicated child-care arrangements.

Her parents helped a lot, watching the girls while she worked. But Molly came from a large family, and her five other siblings needed help at times as well. Her parents were in Florida now with her younger sister Laurie who had recently given birth to twins. Her mother had called with a full progress report the other night, adding that she and Molly's dad planned to stay a few more weeks. Even though the babies and her sister were doing well, two infants at once were quite an adjustment. Molly remembered making some appropriately cheerful reply. She couldn't blame her parents for spending more time with their new grandchildren. And who wouldn't want to escape the New England winter? Though it was the last week of February, the cold and snow hadn't let up one bit. It felt positively endless. Still, Molly was unhappy to hear she'd have to get by without her mother for a few weeks longer than expected.

Her older brother Sam had always pitched in with the girls and still did, even though he had married a few months ago. Sam's wife, Jessica, had the girls now. Molly knew Jessica wouldn't mind if they stayed until she finished here. But Molly had promised her daughters pizza and a movie at the mall, and she didn't want to disappoint them.

I'll work until five, then come back real early tomorrow and finish up, she decided. *That should give me plenty of time to be in and out before the tenant arrives.* Fran Tulley, the real estate agent who'd handled the rental, had mentioned that the tenant wasn't due until noon.

Dr. Harding's arrival had been a hot topic

around town. The village had been without a general practitioner since Dr. Elliot had retired last spring, almost a year ago now. Molly had heard Dr. Harding was a widower and a friend of Ezra Elliot's, and she pictured the new practitioner cut from the same mold, an elderly Yankee with a dry wit and a pragmatic manner.

She had never been a huge fan of Dr. Elliot, not like some in Cape Light. He was kind enough, in his way. But something about him had always intimidated her. He moved in a different circle, with the Warwicks and the rest of them, the kind of families in the grand old Victorians who might hire her to cook or clean but rarely acted as if she were their equal.

The window molding was coated with dust. She would need the brush attachment to get at that. The window panes needed to be sprayed and wiped down, too. Molly shut off the vacuum and looked for her spray bottle. Now the radio volume seemed deafening, and she rushed over just as the song was ending.

"*. . . Our love's down the drain. Ain't it a shame? You call to complain. . . .*"

Molly clicked off the radio, relieved at the

sudden silence. "Give me a break. I'd complain, too, if I had to listen to you all the time."

"Me, too," a deep voice agreed.

Molly spun around to face the doorway. A man stood there, staring at her. Her heart jumped in her chest, and she took a sudden step backward. She had taken a self-defense course once, and her mind raced to remember the helpful tips. Don't scream? Or was it, scream your head off?

Hey, pal, I have a vacuum cleaner attachment here, and I'm not afraid to use it!

"I'm sorry. . . . I didn't mean to startle you," the intruder said gently.

"That's okay. I'm fine." *Good move. A stranger just broke into the house, and I apologize to him.*

"I called up the stairs to you, but I guess you didn't hear me."

"Apparently not," she agreed.

He had nice eyes, dark brown, and thick brown hair with a few silver-gray strands blended in, though he didn't look much older than she was.

Why was she even noticing this?

"I'm just bringing in some boxes. I know

it's the country out here, but you shouldn't leave the doors unlocked."

"I thought I locked it," Molly replied.

Okay, he's a delivery man. Or at least, that's what he says. Jeans. Work boots. A sweatshirt and a down vest. That's what they wear, right?

He wasn't exactly brawny, she noticed, but he did look fit.

He smiled again, then stepped back, raising both hands in a gesture of surrender.

"I'll back out slowly now, if you promise to lay down your weapon."

Molly didn't understand him at first, then realized she'd been brandishing the vacuum attachment in a menacing fashion.

"Oh, sorry." She slowly let it slip down to her side but didn't let go altogether. She glanced at him again, still feeling uneasy at the way he was looking at her.

"Are you finished down there, yet?" she asked.

"Hardly. But don't worry. I can handle it."

She suddenly got it. Since the doctor was older, he probably needed help with items he didn't trust to the movers, which explained this guy. Well, that wasn't her problem. She already had enough on her plate cleaning up the place.

"I wasn't offering to help. I have plenty left up here to do, and it's almost five."

He looked surprised at her answer, then showed a neutral expression. "Sure, I understand. But maybe you can keep the music down a few decibels?"

"No problem," Molly returned, echoing his tone. "Would you mind wiping your feet as you go in and out? I just finished down there. I don't want to do it all over again."

He gave her a surprised look again, then nodded. "The place looks great. I'll be careful to keep it that way."

"I hope you're through soon. I need to lock up before I go." Molly turned and sprayed cleaner on the window. "The tenant won't be here until tomorrow, and I'm responsible for the place until then."

"The tenant?"

"Dr. Harding, from Worcester. Those are his boxes you're delivering, aren't they?"

He paused a moment, his expressive features warming with a slow smile of understanding.

"I *am* Dr. Harding."

Molly opened her mouth to reply, then

abruptly shut it. Then she said, "Oh, I thought you were a delivery man. Actually I didn't know who you were."

He looked as if he were about to laugh, but he was too polite to embarrass her. She felt her cheeks grow warm and red. Then she felt like laughing at herself, too.

"One false move and I was going to brain you with the vacuum-cleaner pipe."

"I had a feeling that was your plan." He smiled again and then leaned forward to offer his hand. "Nice to meet you. I'm Matt Harding."

"Molly Willoughby." She met his gaze as they briefly shook hands, and she felt her knees get rubbery. She quickly looked away.

He's either really good looking, or I don't get out much, Molly thought, clearing her head.

"The real-estate agency hired me to clean the house for you," she said in a more professional tone.

"Right. They said they were sending someone over. You must have been working hard. It looks a lot better than when I was here last time."

"That's my job." She forced a smile. "I'm

sorry for the mix-up. Someone told me you were a friend of Dr. Elliot. I guess I pictured you . . . differently."

He laughed. "Old and cranky, you mean?" When Molly didn't reply, he added, "I've known Dr. Elliot since I was a boy. He and my father are good friends."

"I get it." Molly nodded, feeling silly.

"I guess I'll go down and get the rest of the boxes."

"Sure. See you later." Molly looked away, suddenly engrossed in the contents of her cleaning bucket. But once she heard his footsteps disappear, she ran into the small bathroom that adjoined the bedroom and shut the door.

She stared at her reflection and gave a silent shriek. Her ponytail had exploded, and long, dark curls sprung out in all directions. A streak of oven grease marked her cheek and the tip of her nose. The mess trailed down her worn-out sweatshirt, which would not have been an entirely bad thing, Molly thought, if only the stains had blocked out the ridiculous saying printed across her chest: *Save a Chicken's Life. Eat a Lobster.*

Unfortunately, they did not.

For heaven's sake, he must think I'm a complete idiot, she thought mournfully. *And why did I wear these jeans today? They look terrible.* She surveyed her rear view and yanked the sweatshirt down over her hips, only to watch it immediately rise up again.

I've got to lose some weight. Get back in shape. I just never seem to have the time. . . .

A long dark curl flopped across her face, and she blew it away like a feather.

Oh, well. What's the point? He's a doctor, not a delivery man. He isn't going to be interested in someone like me.

Molly wearily pulled out her hair clip and quickly combed out her hair with her fingertips, then rinsed the grime off her face and patted it dry with some tissues.

That will be enough primping for Dr. Harding, she decided.

The room had darkened with late afternoon shadows. She couldn't wait for spring to come. She was so tired of the short, dark winter days. Molly checked the time. A quarter past four. She considered staying longer, but her surprise meeting with the new tenant had thrown her off. She decided to ask if she could finish the rest of the work tomorrow and hoped he wouldn't mind.

As she came downstairs, she saw Matthew struggling through the front door with a stack of boxes. She ran down the last few steps and plucked a package from the top of the pile to help him.

"Oh, you don't have to do that." He set down his load and looked up at her.

"That's all right. It looked like it was about to slip. Is there anything else out there?"

"That's the last of it." Molly followed his glance to an impressive stack of boxes piled against one wall of the living room.

"The movers have the rest. There were some fragile things I didn't trust in the truck. Some medical instruments. And some family china that my daughter Amanda already has her eye on. I'd never hear the end of it if any of that turned up broken."

The tender note in his voice made her smile. "How old is she?"

"Fourteen . . . going on forty," he noted with a wry smile.

"I have one of those at home myself." He looked surprised, but Molly was used to that reaction. She had Lauren less than a year after graduating high school, and some people said she looked even younger than her age, which was now thirty-two. She kept talking, hoping he wouldn't make the usual comment. *Gee, you look too young to have a teenager. . . .*

"Lauren is my fourteen year old, and I have another who's eleven, Jill."

"Amanda is my one and only. I have it easy, I guess."

"Oh, I wouldn't say that. I think in some ways one is harder. With two, they have each other for company, so they go off on their own, and they're not always bugging you. And you have the older one to practice on, so you know what to do when the second one acts out."

He nodded. "A practice child. That's an interesting theory. I don't think I've ever heard that one before."

He seemed amused, and the way he kept gazing at her made her feel nervous again. She smiled, controlling the urge to tug on her sweatshirt.

"I guess I would have liked more kids myself," he admitted, "but life doesn't always turn out the way you plan."

"I know what you mean." She remembered he was a widower and guessed from his serious tone that his thoughts had suddenly turned to his loss. She glanced away, thinking of her own disappointments. "I hope coming to Cape Light works out for you. We're a little off the beaten track. But it's a nice place once you get used to it."

"Have you lived around here long?"

"All my life. That sounds horribly boring, doesn't it?"

"Not at all. I grew up in Worcester—which isn't nearly as scenic, I must say—and only left for medical school."

"But now you've come here."

"I have a sister in Newburyport, and I've always liked the area. Then word came through Ezra that he'd retired and the village needed a general practitioner, so here we are. It was time for a change, I guess." Matthew smiled but didn't say anything more.

Molly sensed that the decision to move had been hard for him, and he'd come with mixed emotions. She didn't know what to say. Then her phone emitted a long, shrill beep, saving her from having to make a reply.

"Excuse me. I think that's mine." She

found her big black tote bag at the bottom of the staircase and dug out her cell phone.

Matthew turned his attention to the boxes on the other side of the room, sorting them into two piles.

"Molly! Thank heavens I caught you! I'm in a total panic. I had a closing today that was absolutely endless and now everyone will be here in two hours and I haven't even set the table or taken a shower and the mousse is a disaster—"

"Calm down, Betty. It's going to be all right," Molly said, soothing her.

It was her friend Betty Bowman, the town's leading real-estate broker and foremost female entrepreneur. Molly admired her tremendously, but Betty was easily the most domestically challenged person Molly had ever met. Their friendship had grown primarily from their common ground as single mothers and from episodes of Betty begging Molly to rescue her from some cooking or entertaining catastrophe.

Betty had a dinner party planned for that night for just four people, including herself. But that was more than enough to throw Betty, even though Molly had already cooked most of the meal and Betty was buying the rest prepared. All Betty had to do was fix the dessert, chocolate mousse. Betty was set on making that herself to impress her new suitor, Richard Corwin, since she knew it was his favorite.

"I followed your instructions exactly, but it looks like, well, like brown clay. I can move the spoon through it. That can't be right."

"Um, no. You shouldn't be able to stir it." Molly tried not to laugh.

"Could you run over for a minute and take a look? I don't even have time to run up to the bakery. . . ."

"Sure. Just for a minute. I'll be right over." Molly said good-bye and glanced over at Matthew.

"Something wrong at home?" he asked politely.

"No, thank goodness." Molly shook her head and smiled. "But I do need to run, if it's okay with you. A friend of mine is having a little crisis with some chocolate mousse—"

"—And you have to make a house call?" he finished.

"Something like that."

"You must be a great cook. I mean to get emergency calls on your cell phone."

Molly felt a warm flush creep into her cheeks again.

"I have my moments," she said lightly. His smile encouraged her, and she continued, suddenly wanting him to know she wasn't just a housecleaner. "I actually have a cooking business. Well, sort of a business. I'm just starting out really. But I bake for some restaurants in town and for private parties. Things like that . . ." Her voice trailed off quietly.

It didn't sound like much, she thought. Not very impressive compared to, say, saving someone's life.

Still, he nodded at her thoughtfully. "Sounds like you keep yourself busy."

Was he really impressed or just trying to be nice, she wondered.

"Your husband is a lucky guy, being married to a professional chef," he added in a teasing voice.

"He *was* a lucky guy . . . until I divorced him." She laughed at her quick reply but also heard the subtle note of anger there. "It was a long time ago," Molly added with a shrug.

She started to pull on her jacket and felt Matthew politely helping her. He met her gaze for a long moment, then stepped back. The room was dark enough now that she could barely read his expression.

She pulled out her bright blue wool gloves and matching hat and tugged them on.

"I'd better get going. I'll come back early tomorrow and finish up. You won't even know I've been here."

"Don't rush. Come whenever you like. Why don't you bring your girls? I know Amanda would love to meet Lauren. Then she'll have a familiar face in school on Monday."

Molly appreciated his offer. Most clients didn't welcome her children, and she hadn't quite figured out what she'd do with them tomorrow. Lauren sometimes watched Jill on her own, but it wasn't Molly's ideal arrangement, especially on a Saturday.

"Okay, I will, if you really don't mind," she said brightly as she pulled open the front door. "Thanks for the offer."

"Not at all. I'm looking forward to meeting them. See you tomorrow, then."

"See you." Molly smiled and walked quickly down the path to her car. He stood in the doorway and watched as she got into her aged hatchback. As she pulled away from the curb, she saw him wave and she waved back.

He was a nice man. An attractive man. Easy to talk to, she thought. Not at all what she'd expected. They seemed to have something in common, too, once they'd started talking about raising teenage girls.

And attractive, she noted again. *No doubt about that. I wonder when his wife died? Fran said a few years ago. I wonder why he's still single? He must have somebody,* she decided. *But if he does, why did he move here all the way from Worcester? Maybe he is unattached.*

But it could never work. He's a doctor and I'm just a jill-of-all-trades, master of none.

Don't even give it another thought, Molly, a sour little voice advised her. *He's out of your league.*

Ten minutes later Molly pulled up to Betty's house and parked in the driveway. Betty had a lovely home, a classic Federal-style Colonial on one of the best streets in town. Originally built for a ship's captain in the early 1800s, it was now a registered historic site. Molly secretly dreamed that one day she, too, might own a house like this. It wasn't just that the house was beautiful and spacious. More than that, it was a symbol to her of Betty's independence and success, the essence of what Molly aspired to.

Betty greeted Molly at the door dressed in a pale blue silk bathrobe with hot rollers sprouting from her short blond hair.

"I followed your directions exactly," Betty declared as she led Molly into the kitchen. "Maybe the chocolate was stale or something."

Molly peered into the makeshift double boiler and prodded the brown, sticky mass. "Looks like water from the boiler got into the chocolate. We have to toss it."

"Oh, drat. Is there time to make more?"

"We'll manage. I stopped at the store just in case." Molly opened the shopping bag and took out a box of chocolate, then found a clean pot.

"You're a pal, Molly. I owe you one." Betty stood at the counter and watched as Molly started cooking. "What can I do to help?"

"Just stand over there." Molly pointed to the far side of the room. "I don't want you anywhere near this stuff until it's time to eat it."

"Oh, you're mean." Betty laughed, shaking loose a roller. "Where were you when I called before?"

"At a cleaning job. Fran Tulley's rental on Hawthorne Street."

"Oh, right. The new doctor. Fran said he's quite good looking. And single," Betty said.

Molly slowly stirred the melting blocks of chocolate, vigilantly searching for lumps. "He's not bad," she finally offered.

"You saw him? He's not due to move in until tomorrow."

"He stopped by the house to drop off some boxes. I didn't know who he was. I almost hit him on the head with a vacuum-cleaner pipe."

Betty sighed. "Sounds about right. Go on."

Molly shrugged. "There's not much to tell. He sounded a little sorry to be moving but said he needed a change. He has a sister in Newburyport and a daughter who's fourteen."

"Same age as Lauren," Betty pointed out.

"Yes, we covered that." With a deft twist of her wrist, Molly cracked an egg, separating the white from the yolk with one hand, then picked up another and cracked it.

Betty looked on in fascination. "I just love the way you do that thing with the egg."

"It's not hard. I'll teach you sometime."

"Deal, but let's get back to this doctor. He sounds like a possibility to me."

A *romantic* possibility, Betty meant. Betty had somehow deemed herself Molly's relationship coach, determined to find Molly a man despite her complaints of not having time to date. Molly always gave her a hard time when she slipped into this mode, but she had to admit, Betty often had some good advice.

Concerning Matthew Harding, Molly thought it best to shut Betty down from the start.

"He's not my type. Honestly." She beat the egg yolks with a fork and added a dash of vanilla.

"He sounds like anybody's type to me." Betty gave her a puzzled look. "What's going on with that guy Micky, your brother Sam's friend? Still seeing him?"

"No, thank goodness." Molly rolled her eyes. "He's nice enough, I guess. But he's just so dull. All he ever wanted to do was call out for pizza and watch sports on TV.

One night he lost the remote, and I had to dial nine-one-one."

Betty started laughing. "He did not. You're making that up."

"How could I make up something like that? It was the end of the Super Bowl and the channel switched somehow, and he couldn't find the remote. He got so upset, he started getting dizzy and short of breath. I thought he was having a heart attack. The fireman said it was just a mild panic disorder."

Betty could hardly stop laughing. "I can see why that didn't work out."

Molly carefully poured the yellow ribbon of egg yolk into the melted chocolate and beat the mixture together with a wire whisk. "I'm glad you agree. My brother Sam thinks we were a perfect match. He claims I'm too picky."

It stung that Sam didn't think she could do any better than boring old Micky. But she didn't confide that part to Betty.

"You're the one who has to decide if it's right or not." Betty patted her shoulder. "It takes courage to drop a nice but boring guy. It's like clearing out your closet and giving all the dull, old clothes to charity.

Now you've made room for something new and exciting."

Molly glanced at her and smiled. "Does that mean if I clean out my closet, I'll get a new wardrobe *and* a new boyfriend?"

"You never know." Betty stuck her finger in the satiny chocolate pudding, then popped it into her mouth. "Mmmm. That's scrumptious."

"I think you can take it from here." As Molly untied her apron, she reviewed the last steps of the recipe with Betty, who looked alarmed to be sent on alone.

"You can do it," Molly promised her. "Besides, you want to tell Richard you made it. You wouldn't want to fib about that."

"Me? I'd never do that. What a thing to say."

Betty grinned at her. Before they had become such good friends, Betty had often taken credit for Molly's cooking with dinner guests. They were close enough now to laugh about it.

"Who else is coming over?"

"Just Emily and Dan. Things are moving along for those two. I have a feeling they may have a big announcement soon. Emily doesn't say much, but I think they're going to get married."

"Wow! I didn't realize it was so serious. How nice."

Molly felt odd, even a little shocked, though she didn't know why the news should matter. She knew Dan by sight and Emily only slightly better. Dan had run the local newspaper most of his life and recently handed it down to his daughter. Emily Warwick was the town's mayor, and she was now related to Molly by marriage, as the older sister of Sam's wife, Jessica.

If there was ever a woman who seemed content with a solitary life, it had to be Emily. But now she was in love and might soon be married. Molly felt happy for her . . . and for some strange reason, sad for herself.

She picked up her bag and hitched it over her shoulder. "Got to run, Betty. Don't worry. The party will turn out fine."

"Oh, I hope so." Betty nervously plucked a few rollers from her hair and stuck them in her bathrobe pocket. "Thanks again, Molly. I owe you one."

"I'll collect." Molly was sure it wouldn't be long before she was asking Betty for some advice or favor. It was good to know she had a friend like Betty.

Molly left Betty's house in the village and quickly found her way through the side streets to the Beach Road. Driving beyond the town, she raced along to the turn that marked Sam and Jessica's house, which was hidden, even in winter, by trees and brush.

Molly had known Jessica Warwick since high school. She had always thought Jessica was Little Miss Perfect and a snob, just like her mother, Lillian, who had acted like a queen in exile since the Warwick family fortune was lost years ago. Jessica had gone away to college and then taken a banking job in Boston. But after Lillian had a stroke, Jessica moved back to town temporarily to help care for her mother. When Sam started seeing her, Molly was sure that Jessica was just using him for a summer fling. Even after the two became serious, Molly urged Sam to break off the engagement.

Okay, so she could be a little stubborn and narrow-minded at times. She'd be the first to admit it. But now that they were married, Molly had to confess Jessica was not exactly what she expected.

Despite her privileged upbringing, Jessica was happily married and content to live in this remote spot in a lovely old house that seemed a never-ending renovation project for her carpenter husband. Jessica also showed a real interest and affection for Lauren and Jill. Her hours at the bank made it easy for her to watch her nieces after school, and Molly had come to depend on her help, which was also a surprise.

As Molly walked up the path, the front door swung open. Jessica greeted her, wearing an apron over her office clothes, a satin blouse, slim-fitting skirt, and heels. An appetizing cooking smell drifted in from the kitchen.

"Lauren and Jill are upstairs getting their things together. Sam isn't home yet, though. Want to come in and wait for him?"

Molly was relieved to hear she'd miss her brother. She had escaped defending her decision to dump his friend Micky. This time, at least.

"Thanks but we'd better get going. I promised the girls a movie at the mall tonight, and I want to make the early show."

"Yes, I heard all about it. They can't wait."

Jessica turned and called up the stairs. "Girls, your mom is here."

"Lauren, Jill, I'm waiting," Molly added in her "Commander Mom" tone. "Thanks again for minding them. I was in a pinch today."

"No problem. I love having them." Jessica smiled, and Molly felt her words were sincere.

As if on cue, Lauren and Jill galloped down the stairs, carrying their jackets and knapsacks. Jill jumped off the steps, hurling herself at Molly in a flying hug.

Molly grunted in reply. "Thanks, honey. I needed that."

"Hi, Mom." Lauren came down the last few steps more sedately. Molly kissed her on the cheek. Lauren was too old now to act so uncool, Molly thought with a secret smile. She watched as they both showed good manners, thanking Jessica, and each gave their aunt a hug.

"Sam will be sorry he missed you. But we'll see you on Sunday, right?"

Molly had almost forgotten. Jessica and Sam were taking the girls ice skating so she could work. Looked like she would have to face complaints about Micky and more advice about her life then.

"That's right." Molly nodded. "Well, thanks again. Tell Sam I'll call him."

"Bye, girls, see you soon." Jessica watched them from the doorway and waved as they all walked to the car.

Visiting hours had officially ended long ago. The hospital rooms were dark and the corridor nearly empty. Reverend Ben Lewis stood beside Gus Potter's bed. Gus gripped Ben's hand, his head resting on a pile of pillows. His skin was as pale as the white pillowcase, and it appeared almost translucent.

His blue eyes were bright, though, and his grip still surprisingly strong. He looked far happier than a man in his condition ought to, Ben thought. Far calmer, too, though he must realize what's happening to him. His wife, Sophie, knew only too well, and Ben could see her struggling to keep up a brave front.

"Thanks for coming, Reverend," she said. "You didn't have to trouble yourself. You'd better get home. Carolyn must be wondering what's keeping you."

"Carolyn is used to my late hours by now."

"How is she feeling?" Sophie asked with interest. "Is she still in therapy?"

A few weeks after Christmas, Carolyn had suffered a stroke and gone into a coma. That was over two months ago now, Ben calculated. He had nearly lost her. But she'd finally woken with few ill effects and was coming along with the help of medication and physical therapy.

"She's doing very well," Ben reported. "She still has some weakness in her left arm, though, and can't play the piano yet. But she wants to get back to her students soon. Maybe at the end of next month."

"Glad to hear it," Gus said. "Tell her we were asking for her."

"Yes, I will. Maybe she'll come with me next time I visit. I guess you'll be home again by then."

"The doctor said I can take him home in a few more days. Monday or Tuesday," Sophie said brightly.

She met Ben's gaze a moment, then rested her hand on her husband's shoulder.

An array of tubes and monitors was attached to Gus's body, and Ben averted his gaze from the tangled paraphernalia.

"These doctors don't know anything." Gus waved his hand weakly. "Listen to them, and you'd be working on my eulogy right now, Reverend." Ben forced a smile at Gus's quip but swallowed hard. He knew he'd face that task soon enough.

"I'll spring right back. Always do. This is just another false alarm. I'd get up out of this bed and walk home right now if they'd let me."

"He must feel better. He's getting rambunctious," Sophie said with false cheer.

"Yes, very," Ben agreed wistfully.

They all knew the truth. The prognosis was grim. Gus's great and generous heart was finally giving out, his other vital organs rapidly failing. All the doctors in the world couldn't do much more for him. Sophie and Gus had decided that he would spend his last days at home on the orchard, in his own bed, rather than in a sterile hospital room.

Ben gave Gus's hand a final pat. "Bless you, Gus. I'll keep you in my prayers."

"Thanks, Reverend," Gus said. Sophie's

eyes misted over. She nodded and blew her nose on a tissue.

A nurse briskly entered the room and picked up Gus's chart from the end of the bed. "How are you doing tonight, Mr. Potter?"

"Just fine. And yourself?" Gus sounded genuinely interested in her reply, Ben noticed. As if he was in the middle of a church picnic instead of a critical-care unit. Some people were just born with a certain buoyant spirit that didn't desert them, no matter what. Sophie was the same. They were made for each other and had lived together happily for nearly fifty years. They had that to look back upon at the very least.

"I'm just going to walk the reverend to the elevator, dear," Sophie told her husband. Gus, who had a thermometer in his ear, nodded and waved good-bye.

Sophie walked beside Ben, lost in thought. Ben waited for her to speak first. At times like this it was imperative for him to hold his peace and listen. Offering comforting words was important, of course. But listening, that was paramount.

"He's had a good day," she said finally. "His spirits are up. Did you hear the way he was talking?" she asked, shaking her head. "But he knows. He just acts as if it's all going to be okay. Like he can lick this somehow. Of course, he won't this time."

She pressed a tissue to her eyes. "Once I get him home, well, it will be easier for everyone. He'll have his family around him, and he'll have the orchard."

"That will be a great comfort to him," Ben agreed.

"I'm going to spend every minute with him from here on in. Luckily the TV show people have given me a break until the spring. We taped a bunch of shows right after Christmas, and they told me they're set for awhile." Sophie released a long breath and shook her head. "Lucky for me. I wouldn't have the heart right now to get up in front of a camera. I might not go back after Gus goes," she concluded.

Ben swallowed hard. Sophie was talking about the cooking show she did for a local cable station, *A Yankee in the Kitchen: New England Cooking and Crafts with Sophie Potter.* The producer had spotted her at a fair on the village green last fall and the show had been a great success so far. Ben was sorry to hear she might abandon it. It would be a distraction for her after Gus passed on, he thought.

"It's probably best not to make any decisions about that now," Ben said gently. "What about the coming days, when Gus gets home. Do you have enough help?"

"My daughter Evelyn's made all the arrangements for the visiting nurse and home-health aid," Sophie said, mentioning her oldest child who lived in the area. "She and Una are taking turns helping with the housework. My son, Bart, should be in from Boston for a quick visit this weekend, and his daughter, Miranda, is coming in from New York. It should be a full house on the weekends. I hardly know where everyone's going to sleep."

It sounded like the typical Potter family reunion. But this time the gathering was for the most serious reason of all. If Sophie's entire family was coming together to spend time with Gus, she clearly didn't expect him to last long. Ben felt a sharp pang in his heart, and he reached out to take Sophie's hand in both of his own.

His gaze met hers, and her eyes filled with tears. "You'll get through this, Sophie. One step at a time. You have your family and all your friends. You have me," he reminded her. "Most important, you have the Lord."

She nodded. "Yes, I know. I'm grateful for our time together. Our blessings. I just wish sometimes . . ." Her voice caught and she couldn't go on. "It might be wrong to say it, Reverend, but I'm older than Gus. I always thought I'd go ahead. I didn't imagine living on without him. I know it's wrong to second guess, but I wish the good Lord had taken me first."

Ben didn't answer immediately. "I felt the very same way when Carolyn was sick," he said finally.

When Carolyn had been in her coma, there were a few days when it seemed unlikely she would survive, and Ben had entered the chilling dark places where Sophie now wandered. But of course, not fully, since the Lord in his mercy had spared him that irrevocable blow, the loss of his life partner. Barring a miracle, Sophie would not be spared.

"I felt . . . afraid. The greatest fear I'd ever known," he admitted. She glanced at him, then looked down at her hands. He knew he had voiced her deepest feelings.

"Yes. I am afraid. Terrified." She nodded her head. "I haven't said that many times in my life. But this . . . this is different."

"Very different," Ben agreed.

"It's as if my whole world is being pulled out from under me like a rug." Her voice held a note of amazement mingled with sadness and fear.

Ben didn't know what to say. Her whole world *would* be torn away once Gus was gone. Once a widow, she'd probably be forced to give up the orchard.

But first things first. She would face that road when she came to it.

"When Carolyn was sick and I felt the most afraid, there was a certain Scripture that came to mind and helped me through it. 'Be strong and of a good courage, fear not . . . for the Lord thy God, he *it is* that doth go with thee; he will not fail thee, nor forsake thee.' "

"Yes, I remember." Sophie nodded thoughtfully. "Deuteronomy. That's what Moses said to the Israelites when he knew he was going to die soon, and they'd go on without him."

Ben nodded and squeezed her hand.

"He will not fail me," she quietly echoed.

"I know that's so. Thank you, Reverend. And thanks again for coming by tonight."

"No thanks necessary, Sophie. You know that." Ben hugged her briefly, then stepped back. "Don't hesitate to call me at any hour, night or day. Even if you just want someone to talk to."

Sophie nodded. A small smile appeared on her lovely moon-shaped face. "I'll be all right."

He prayed that she would be. The elevator bell sounded. He stepped inside and hit *L* for lobby. Sophie stood watching him, framed like an image in a photograph. Then the elevator doors closed, blocking her from view.

Ben felt a heavy sadness nearly overwhelm him. He wished there was more he could do, more he could say to bring some comfort to Sophie and Gus at this dark hour. And there was so little. He'd counseled many families losing a loved one and knew that only too well by now. But he always wished there were more.

He pushed open the heavy glass doors of the hospital entrance and hurried to his car, feeling the stinging of cold air on his skin and in his lungs. The temperature hovered somewhere around twenty, he guessed. This was the toughest stretch of the winter, especially in New England. The holiday cheer long gone and so much cold and darkness to get through before spring.

But spring would arrive, Ben thought as he began the long drive home. Gus Potter wouldn't see it, though, his body returned to the earth, his soul hopefully home in heaven, well before the world grew warm and green again.

"Do we *have* to go with you?" Lauren whined.

"Yes, you do," Molly said curtly. Molly somehow managed to get the girls home by nine-thirty after their pizza and movie at the mall. Getting them in bed with the light shut off was another matter entirely.

"We won't be there long. I just need to finish the second floor. And you'll get to be the first one to meet Amanda. She'll be new at school on Monday, but you can tell everyone you've already met her."

Lauren sat back against her pillows, her arms crossed over her chest. The cat, Jasper, jumped on the bed and climbed into

Lauren's lap, but Lauren barely looked at her. "I really need to go to the library and start my science project."

"Don't worry, we'll start the science project. Did you pick a topic yet?"

Nothing too ambitious please, Molly silently wished.

"The effect of electromagnetic fields on mealworms. This kid did it last year. It's really cool."

"Yuck! That's gross." Jill made a gagging noise.

"Come on, cut that out. It's science, for goodness' sake. Now get in bed," Molly coaxed her.

Worms? She secretly agreed with Jill and hoped she didn't have to handle any of the subjects.

"We'll go straight to the library right after Dr. Harding's house. I promise." Molly picked up a stray sneaker and set it next to its partner, then bent over to kiss Lauren good night.

Lauren didn't seem persuaded, Molly thought, but she had given up arguing at least.

Once the light was out in the girls' room, Molly went into the living room to fold a basket of laundry. When she was done, she peeked in again. They had both fallen asleep, and the cat was curled up in a snuggly ball at the foot of Lauren's bed.

Molly pulled up Jill's covers, gave her another kiss as she slept, then did the same to Lauren. They did her heart good, these girls. She loved them so much, sometimes it actually hurt. When she watched them sleeping like this, she didn't question working so hard and going to the limit to give them a good upbringing. Her daughters were everything to her. Maybe making up for a lot that was missing right now, Molly reflected as she left the room. But what could she do? This was her life. She had to make the best of it.

In the kitchen, she filled a bowl with her favorite ice cream, chocolate chocolate chip, then carried her treat into her bedroom. She picked up a thick paperback and stretched out on the bed. The book was a predictable but satisfying mix of romance and suspense and the ice cream, a guilty pleasure. She knew she shouldn't have it after promising herself just this afternoon to start dieting. Especially right after eating pizza.

But she was so tired and felt she deserved some reward after such a long day. Besides, she didn't need to squeeze herself into any Saturday night date clothes this weekend, she reminded herself, thinking of boring Micky and of Betty's pep talk.

When you got right down to it, Molly decided, men may come and go, but a good romance novel and some premium ice cream never disappoint. With a smile and a satisfied nod, she turned the page and savored another cold, sweet spoonful.

The drive from Southport Hospital to Cape Light took more or less an hour. Ben found little traffic on the highway and knew the ride would be faster than usual.

In the dark, humming silence he mentally worked on his sermon for Sunday's service. He often found he got some of his best inspirations driving late at night on empty roads. The trouble was remembering them. His theme for this Sunday was connection, the web of friendships and family ties that supports us throughout our lifetime. He considered using the parable of the Good Samaritan, then remembered he would have that Scripture reading the following Sunday when he was going to talk about compassion. He would find some other Scripture to illustrate this Sunday's theme. He had noted a few already on a pad in his office. He'd stop off at the church tonight and pick it up so he could finish the sermon at home tomorrow.

Once off the highway, he drove down the Beach Road and into the village. Main Street was deserted, the old-fashioned gaslights casting a glow in the frosty night air. He'd lived here over thirty years but still found his attention captured by the charm of the Victorian homes, vintage storefronts, and the harbor view ahead. It was a timeless place, yet somehow ever changing, reflecting the mood of each season or hour of day. You'd have a hard time finding a prettier place to live—although the picture-book setting gave no one here immunity to life's challenges and sorrows. That was for sure.

At the end of Main Street, the blue-black water of the harbor stretched to the opposite shoreline. By Memorial Day, the inlet would be so full of boats, one would barely be able to see the waves in between. But the harbor was nearly empty right now, ex-

cept for a few hardy, unadorned vessels be-
longing to the fishermen who worked year
round. Still in a partially frozen state, the oc-
casional boat stranded out in the ice looked
like an odd decoration on the top of a
frosted cake.

Ben turned on Bayview Road, which ran
along the village green. At the far side of the
green Bible Community Church stood,
silent and dark, the steeple cutting a sharp
silhouette against the clear, starry sky. Ben
pulled into the lot behind the church and
parked at one of the rear doors.

He unlocked the door and headed down
the long dark hallway, past Sunday school
classrooms. There was no need to turn on
lights; he could find his way blindfolded.
But just as he reached his office, he heard a
strange sound. A muffled moan, distinctly
human. Ben stood stone-still, his body
tense and alert. There it was again, coming
from the all-purpose room.

He approached cautiously, stopping in
the doorway to turn on a light. "Is anybody
in here?" he called out.

No one answered, and he glanced
around. Then he heard movement coming
from the kitchen area, a small room in the

corner with a pass-through window. He wondered for a moment if he should call the police. But what if someone was hurt and needed help? Precious time might be wasted.

Ben walked slowly toward the kitchen, not knowing what he would do if the intruder was aggressive or carrying a weapon. He wasn't scared, though, feeling sure that the Lord would protect him.

"Is there anyone here?" he asked again at the closed kitchen door. "I'm coming in now."

He slowly pushed the door open and then felt it obstructed. Wedging his upper body through the opening, Ben saw a man's body sprawled out on the floor. The man was curled on his side, his arms clutching his stomach, his body quaking with chills. A booted foot blocked the door, but Ben managed to squeeze inside.

The man was filthy, his pants torn and his dirty coat ragged. Ben couldn't see his face, only a mass of long greasy hair and a full beard.

Ben knelt beside him, holding his breath against the stench, and touched the man's shoulder. Whatever the stranger had found to eat in the kitchen cupboards hadn't stayed in his stomach for long.

"Can you hear me?" Ben asked.

There was no movement at first, then the man slowly turned his head. His dark eyes met Ben's. One shoulder lifted, as if the man were trying to get up, but he crumpled back to the floor at once.

"Steady, my friend. It's okay." Ben touched the man's shoulder with his hand. "Don't be afraid. I'm going to get help."

Ben rose and removed his overcoat, then placed it over the stranger. He gently rested his open hand on the man's brow. "Don't try to move. I'll be right back."

The intruder stared up at him a moment, then closed his eyes. His chest rose and fell in a labored effort to breathe.

Ben ran to the phone in the far corner of the all-purpose room, dialed 911, and asked for an ambulance. After checking on the stranger, Ben went outside to wait for the ambulance. Though he was wearing only a shirt and wool vest, he was unmindful of the cold. He stared up at the cross on top of the church steeple, starkly outlined against the blue-black sky, then bowed his head in prayer.

Dear Lord, please help this stranger. Please let him get medical treatment in time.

The ambulance arrived a few minutes later, and the EMS workers followed Ben inside.

"He's back here. I'm not sure if he's fully conscious. He's having trouble breathing." Ben led them to the little kitchen and then stood to one side while they examined the stranger.

A few moments later, one of the workers opened a portable stretcher while the other spoke to Ben. "Hard to say what's going on. He definitely needs care. We're going to take him to Southport. I can't find any identification. When I asked him his name, I think he said, 'Carl Jones.' Are you sure you don't recognize him, Reverend?"

Ben shook his head. "I don't believe so."

He leaned over and took another long look. The room was fully lit now, and the man lay flat on his back. Ben stared at the stranger's face, just about to repeat that he'd never seen him. Then Carl Jones opened his eyes and looked up at Ben. His dark eyes were filled with anger and fear, like a wounded animal, angry at his captors and at himself for being too weak to get away and fearful of what would come.

Something clicked in Ben's mind. He knew this man. Or did long ago. Just about everyone in town would remember him.

But no one would ever imagine he'd dare to return.

CHAPTER TWO

Tucker Tulley gazed out the kitchen window, his thoughts wandering as he waited for the coffee to brew. An icy glaze, glistening in the early light, coated the shed and bench near the birdbath. Just enough ice to be a nuisance on the road this morning, Tucker gauged. He'd be called out for some fender bender before that stuff melted down. As a senior police officer, he didn't often pull Saturday duty. But ranks were thin because of a flu bug traveling around, and every officer left standing was pitching in.

He poured himself a mug of coffee and turned to the window again. A bank of blue-gray clouds fringed the eastern sky, a pale orange light barely visible where they parted. A few birds swooped down from the bare branches and flapped around the feeder. It was a dull winter morning, and he envied anyone still snug in his bed, like his wife and two children upstairs.

The phone's shrill ring broke the stillness. Tucker turned quickly to pick it up before it woke anyone.

"I'm sorry to call so early, Tucker," Reverend Ben said. "But something important came up. I thought you should know about it right away."

"That's all right, Reverend. What is it? Are you okay?"

"It's not about me. I'm fine. Last night I found an intruder in the church. A vagrant, I guess you'd have to call him. He broke in and collapsed in the pantry. He was very sick. I called an ambulance, and it took him to the hospital in Southport."

"That's too bad. Would you like me to stop by so you can file a report?"

"I'm not going to report it. That's not why I'm calling you." The reverend paused. His silence made Tucker nervous. He sensed bad news on the way but couldn't imagine what it was.

"The man gave his name as Carl Jones. I didn't recognize him at first," Reverend Ben said. "Then later, I realized . . . well, I'm pretty sure he's your half brother, Carl."

Tucker blinked and took a deep breath. He felt as if someone had just slugged him in the stomach. "That's impossible. I mean, how could it be? Even if he's still alive, why would he ever come back here?"

"I asked myself the same question. I don't know why he'd come back here." The reverend's reply made Tucker feel relieved for a moment. "But I feel fairly certain he has. He's in terrible shape, too. I went to the hospital to make sure he was admitted. I'm going to call later this morning and find out how he's doing."

Tucker hesitated. Did the reverend expect him to drop everything and run down to Southport?

"I'm on duty today. I'll look into it, though, Reverend. . . . Maybe tonight, when I get off."

"All right, Tucker. I thought you should know."

The reverend's tone was mild, but Tucker felt the heavy burden of his unspoken assumptions. He knew the reverend expected him to visit this homeless man and find out for sure if it was his half brother. That was the right thing to do, the Christian thing to do. But if it *was* Carl . . . what then?

"Thanks for the call," Tucker added half-heartedly.

"That's all right. See you tomorrow." Reverend Ben said good-bye and hung up.

Tucker rubbed his forehead and took a deep breath. He felt a dull ache deep in the center of his head, the start of one of his tension headaches. Just what he needed today. He found a bottle of pain relievers and shook two tablets out into his hand.

Why in heaven's name would Carl come back here? It didn't make sense. It couldn't be Carl. *There's no reason to get so worked up,* Tucker told himself as he swallowed the medicine. *The reverend is mistaken. This is all a false alarm.*

Tucker hadn't spoken to his brother now in what—over twenty years? The last time he'd seen Carl was through a bullet-proof slice of Plexiglas in the visitors' room of the state penitentiary where Carl was serving fifteen years for manslaughter.

Once a month on visiting day Tucker would take the long drive across the state to see him. But Carl didn't want his visits or his letters. Tucker would show up, and Carl would meet him with cold indifference or acid bitterness. For a while Tucker kept going, out of pity or guilt maybe. It certainly wasn't out of love. The younger brother's hero worship he'd once felt for Carl had long since vanished.

"Forget about me," Carl had ordered him. "Don't come here anymore. I won't come out to see you, understand?"

Finally, Tucker gave up. But he'd never quite forgotten about Carl, the image of his renegade half brother always lingering on the edges of his memory.

Now he heard Fran's slippers scuffing across the floor, and he turned to see her standing in the kitchen doorway. She blinked sleepily at him, then walked over and kissed his cheek.

"Who was that on the phone, hon?"

"Reverend Ben." Tucker watched her pour a cup of coffee. She took a seat at the table and looked up at him.

"Is there a problem at the church?"

Tucker wondered for a moment if he should even tell Fran what the reverend had said. She'd get excited and worried, maybe over nothing. But finally he decided he had to tell her. Married couples shouldn't keep secrets from each other. It wasn't right.

"The reverend found a homeless man in the back of the church last night and checked him into the hospital. The man said his name was Carl Jones, but Reverend Ben thinks he recognized him. He thinks it's my half brother."

"Your half brother?" She set her coffee mug down on the table and shook her head. "That's impossible. The way he drank and carried on, I doubt he's still alive. Even if he is, why would he ever come back here?"

Fran's frank appraisal took him aback. But she was probably right. Of course, it wasn't Carl. "That's what I told the reverend. He thinks I should check though. Just to be sure."

"Oh, dear. I'm not so sure that's a good thing to do."

Tucker heard the note of worry in his wife's voice and realized that he didn't entirely disagree with her.

"Did this homeless man ask for you?" Fran peered at him over the edge of her cup.

"No. I just told you, he gave his last name as Jones."

"That should tell you something." Fran shrugged and took a sip of coffee. When Tucker didn't reply, she added, "I just mean, if he wanted to see you, wouldn't he give his real name? Maybe he's ashamed to get in touch. He doesn't want you to see what he's turned into. It might be kinder not to bother him."

"Maybe," Tucker said. "But I can picture Carl giving a fake name for any number of reasons. Maybe he felt guilty about breaking into the church. Maybe he came to town intending to get in touch but feels awkward after all this time. Maybe . . . maybe anything."

Fran took a deep breath and hooked a wayward strand of brown hair around her ear. When she spoke again, her tone was softer. "I'm sure whatever the reverend said made you feel responsible, honey. Of course you feel bad, thinking it might be Carl. Anybody would. But it's probably just some stranger. Nobody's seen Carl in years. How would Reverend Ben even recognize him?"

Tucker considered her words. "I don't know. He didn't say."

"Well, all I'm trying to say is that I don't see any point in stirring things up. I really think you ought to leave well enough alone."

Tucker sat down at the table across from her and sighed. Stirring things up was one thing Fran didn't like. He knew that by now. She was a wonderful wife and a loving mother. But she liked her world orderly, predictable. It didn't take much to get her worried or even frightened. That cautious side was what attracted him to her when they were younger. When she'd get this way, he'd find himself filled with an urge to soothe and protect her.

But by now Tucker knew her anxious nature sometimes made it hard for Fran to see things clearly. A person needed to put her fears aside and get some distance to sort out a tricky situation like this one, he thought.

"I don't know what I'm going to do," he told her honestly. "But it's not so simple. I'm not exactly overjoyed either to hear Carl might be back. But I don't know if I can just ignore it."

Fran sighed. She met Tucker's gaze and then rose from the table. She took a carton of eggs and the butter dish out of the refrigerator and placed them purposefully on the countertop. "Do you want some breakfast?"

"No thanks. I'd better get going. I'll grab something later at the diner. So what are you up to today?" He got to his feet and picked up his jacket from the back of the chair.

"Michael has basketball practice, and Mary Ellen has a party at the skating rink. I'll drop them off and run into the office for a while, then check on the rental on Hawthorne Street. That new doctor I told you about is moving in today."

"Oh, right. Don't forget his welcome basket and coupon book." Fran had gone back to work a little over a year ago at Bowman Realty. Tucker was proud of her, though he still had the urge to tease her about it from time to time.

"Don't be silly." She placed a frying pan on the stove and lit the burner. "Will you be home for dinner?"

"I'm not sure. I'll call you later." Tucker thought of the homeless man in the hospital again. If he didn't go to see him, what would he say to Reverend Ben tomorrow?

Tucker slipped on his jacket, buttoned up the front, then straightened his silver shield. He was a law officer, a father, a husband, a deacon in the church while his brother was an ex-convict and probably a homeless vagrant.

And there, but for the grace of God, go I, Tucker thought sadly. Life was strange. He knew the Lord had a plan for every one, but sometimes it just didn't seem fair the way things worked out for some people and not for others.

Molly arrived at Dr. Harding's house by nine, cleaning supplies, vacuum, daughters, and all. While the girls worked on their homework downstairs, she worked on the second floor. The entire house was clean and ready by noon as she'd planned. Then she quickly made some repairs on her own appearance, changing into a blue velour top that was too good to wear for cleaning but didn't look that obvious, she hoped. She dabbed on some lip gloss and eyeliner, then combed out her long curly hair and pulled it back from her face with a thin tortoiseshell band.

Not bad, she thought, checking herself out in the mirror. She pulled the long top down in the back, wishing she hadn't indulged in that ice cream last night. She hoped the girls wouldn't embarrass her by shouting out something like, "Hey, Mom, why did you change your top and put on all that makeup?"

Why did I? Molly wondered. *Maybe just to feel more at ease around this guy, since I looked so awful yesterday,* she told herself.

Yeah, right. Tell me another one.

She heard someone pull into the driveway, and she walked to the window. It was the moving van, followed by Matthew's SUV. Molly felt her stomach do a flip, and she took a deep breath. *Get a grip, Molly. You're just the cleaning lady, remember? Say hello, help the man a little with his moving day and be on your way.*

Matthew parked his Land Rover in front of the house to leave the movers room to unload. He turned to Amanda and forced a smile. "Here we are, honey. We made it."

Amanda pursed her lips and fumbled with her seat belt without answering him. She didn't even look up at the house, he noticed. She'd already seen it once, about a month ago. But that was before it had been painted and cleaned up.

"It's a nice house, don't you think?" Matthew looked up at their new house, an ordinary but neat Dutch Colonial, newly painted in pale yellow with black shutters and white trim. "I mean, it's fine for now. Until we find something permanent."

"It's n-nice, Dad. It's fine." He could hear her speech faltering, a definite sign that she was nervous. Years of speech therapy had nearly rid her of a frustrating stammer. But whenever she was stressed, it cropped up again. A hard way to start off in a new school, he thought sympathetically.

"I w-wish Aunt Erica had come," Amanda said.

"I know. I do, too. But they needed her at the library. She couldn't get the day off."

Amanda sighed and leaned toward the backseat to get her backpack. He got out, opened the gate, and unloaded their suitcases. When he looked up at the house again, he saw Molly Willoughby on the porch, flanked by two girls, both with beautiful long dark hair, just like their mother's.

She smiled down at him and waved. "Welcome home," she called out. "You made it."

He smiled back, feeling instantly brighter. He'd almost forgotten she'd be here. And forgotten how pretty she was. Especially when she smiled like that. He was glad he'd asked her to come.

"Who's that?" Amanda turned to him, looking puzzled and even more nervous.

"That's Molly Willoughby, the woman who cleaned the house for us. She has a girl your age, and I thought you two should meet. It will be good to have at least one familiar face at school on Monday, don't you think?"

"I guess so," Amanda said doubtfully. She hoisted her knapsack to her shoulder and picked up a small duffel bag.

Matt thought Molly and her daughters were just what he and Amanda needed today, the perfect distraction from their moving-day blues.

Matt reached the porch with his bags and put them down near the door. "Well, here we are," he announced. "Amanda, this is

Molly, and these lovely young ladies must be her daughters." He met the gaze of the older girl who looked determined not to blush at his gallantry.

"You must be Lauren." She nodded, and he turned to the smaller one. "And you're Jill."

"Wow, you're good," Molly said. She turned to Amanda and held out her hand. "Nice to meet you, Amanda. I hope you like Cape Light. It might seem tame compared to Worcester, but there's a lot going on at school. Lauren is going to electrify some poor defenseless worms for the science fair."

"Mom!" Lauren gave her mother an adolescent gasp of humiliation.

"Well, you are, aren't you? What did I say?" She glanced at Matt, who was struggling not to laugh, then turned to her daughter again. "Why don't you guys find some place to talk and you can tell Amanda about school and all."

"Okay." Lauren shrugged. She didn't look that excited by the idea, Matthew thought, and he felt himself tense, worried about Amanda. He knew he tended to worry about her too much, especially since his wife had died. But this was one of those days when he couldn't help it.

Then he noticed Amanda's expression brighten. "I like your hair weave. It's cool," she said, complimenting the bright threaded braid in Lauren's long hair.

"Thanks. They do them at the mall. There's this booth."

"I know. We had one in Worcester. But my dad won't let me do it," Amanda said, casting an exasperated look at Matt.

"Don't worry. I'll work on him for you," Molly promised. "I want to get one myself. I'm saving up my allowance."

The girls laughed, and Lauren rolled her eyes. "My mom is a little weird sometimes. Don't give her too much attention. It only makes it worse."

Amanda met Lauren's knowing grin. Matt noticed how the girls' smiles mirrored each other with glittering mouths full of braces.

"Which is going to be your room?" Matt heard Lauren ask as they walked into the house.

"The one in the front. Come on, I'll show you." Amanda started up the steps and Lauren followed.

"Wait, I brought my CD player. I'll bring it

up." Lauren raced back down the stairs and soon returned with her own knapsack. She ran around the adults and Jill like a light-stepping doe and bounded up the staircase again.

"Can I go?" Jill quietly asked Molly.

"Sure, go ahead, honey. I'll tell Lauren it's okay." Jill ran after the older girls, and Molly called up the stairway, "Lauren, your sister is coming. Don't be mean."

Molly looked over at Matt. "Well, let's get to work. What can I help you with?"

He stared down at her, feeling as if a mini-tornado had just breezed by. Did she have those big blue eyes yesterday? It was so dark in here, he hadn't noticed.

Although, to be honest, he really hadn't noticed women in general since his wife died. Not like this, anyway.

A moving man stumbled by, carrying two large boxes on a handcart. "These are for the kitchen, right?"

Matt glanced at them and nodded. "Back there, to the left."

"I can start unpacking the kitchen stuff," Molly said, turning to follow the moving man.

"Unpacking? I thought you were here to clean upstairs."

"Oh, I finished that. I can help you down here for a while."

"You don't have to. You probably have things to do today. I don't want to keep you." While he appreciated the offer, he didn't want Molly to feel stuck here, helping him unpack. She had only been hired by the Realtor to clean. He'd find a way to pay her extra for her trouble. He'd insist on it.

"I don't have anything special to do except work on Lauren's science-fair project, which I am *not* looking forward to. How did I ever get talked into helping electrify a bunch of mealworms?"

Matthew laughed. "Well, in that case, I guess the kitchen is a good place to start."

"Is there any special way you'd like me to organize things?"

"Whatever you think makes sense."

"Okay. See you later," Molly said brightly.

He followed her with his gaze until she disappeared, feeling strangely light-headed. The scent of her flowery perfume lingered in the air.

"Where would you like this, sir?" a moving man grunted, bumping into him. Matt turned to see two men staggering into the house, a long leather couch held up between them.

"In here, against the front windows. That's a good place," he said, hoping he was right. It had been a long time since he'd set up a house on his own.

The next two hours flew by as the movers emptied their truck into the house. Finally, they were gone and the rooms seemed strangely quiet. Matthew stood in the middle of the living room, staring around at the piles of boxes and the overall chaotic mess. Why had he done this? It seemed like a big mistake. He felt the sudden urge to cry, and he blew his nose hard on a hanky.

Then he heard Molly humming in the kitchen, a sweet, soothing sound. He took a deep breath, feeling suddenly calmer. He couldn't let her see him falling apart like this.

He picked up a box that read, "Kitchen," and carried it to her. He found her sorting out the silverware and arranging it in a drawer. She turned and smiled when he entered. "Don't mind me. I'm a champion hummer with a tendency for show tunes."

"I like show tunes. Perfect for humming. Who can ever remember the words?"

Molly laughed. "Not me, that's for sure. I could never be on Broadway."

Matt smiled. "Did you ever want to be?"

"Nope. Broadway star was never one of my job titles. Though there have been a lot of them, I must say."

"Really? How many?" He pulled open the box and pulled out some wadded-up newspaper.

"Oh, I don't know. Twenty or so at least since high school. I don't think I ever counted."

"Twenty jobs?" He looked up at her. She didn't seem the flighty type. "I don't know if I've ever met anyone who's had that many jobs. I'm not sure I believe you," he teased her.

"Well, let's see, I was a cab driver, a school-bus driver, a waitress, a check-out clerk at the supermarket, worked in a doctor's office filing and answering the phone. That was deadly boring," she added, shaking her head. "I had to go back to the supermarket job after that."

Matt laughed. "Go on. That's only five."

"I'm counting the market twice. But never

mind. The car wash, the dog groomer, the fast-photo place, the fast-food place, the slow-food place, baker's helper, mother's helper, hamburger helper—"

"Hamburger helper?"

"I just tossed that in to see if you were really listening." Her eyes sparkled, framed by thick dark lashes. He hadn't noticed those dimples before. Very fetching.

He looked back down at the box and cleared his throat. "Go on. I think that's twelve."

"Okay, let me see. I have more." Molly squeezed her eyes shut, thinking. "I nearly forgot, hostess at the funeral parlor." He shot her a puzzled look. "You know, arranging the flowers, showing people which room to go in, that sort of thing. I didn't really have the personality for it. It was the only time I was ever fired before for smiling too much on the job."

"Quite ironic," he agreed, with a grin.

"The delivery service, the shoe store, the movie theater, the answering service, one of those women in a department store who squirts you with a bottle of perfume. I had to quit that one before lunch hour. I had a monster allergy attack."

"That must have been rough," Matt said sympathetically.

"No great loss." Molly shrugged. "It was on to bigger and better things, the giant hardware warehouse—paints and floor coverings. How many is that?"

"Nineteen," he said, feeling awestruck.

"Oh, yes, census taker. That was actually fun. Once you get some people talking, it's hard to make them stop."

"I'm sure they must have enjoyed talking to you," he said sincerely. He caught her blushing again, and she turned back to the silverware.

"You have quite a résumé."

She shrugged. "That's what happens when you don't go to college. That's what I tell my girls. You have to stay in school. Get a good education. Find a real career. Don't end up like me."

He could see she was sensitive about the topic and felt self-conscious with him now. She had no need to be. He didn't think any less of her for not having a college degree. Her persistence and willingness to try just about anything to earn a living was impressive.

"From what I can see, your girls would do very well to end up like their mother."

She glanced at him over her shoulder. "Thanks," she said quietly. "Oh, dear . . ." Molly stared down into the box she was unpacking. "I think something broke."

"My fault probably. I'm not a very good packer, I'm afraid."

Molly drew out the broken article, handing it to him with a look of concern.

It was a framed photo, one taken years ago when his family vacationed in San Diego, about a year before his wife got sick. Amanda looked so different then, like a little girl. They were all smiling brightly, the white-capped waves of the Pacific in the background. Were they happy then, he and Sharon? It was hard to remember now. Were they ever really that happy with each other?

Even on that trip, he remembered now, he was at a conference and had to attend meetings. Or he thought he did. Sharon wanted him to go sightseeing with them, but he let them go alone. She was mad at him after. He hadn't been a good husband to her. Not really. There was no making up for it now.

"It's just the glass. You can have it repaired in town," Molly suggested. He looked up at her. He'd almost forgotten for a moment that she was there.

"Oh . . . sure. I'll have it fixed." He wrapped it in another sheet of newspaper and put it aside. He felt Molly quietly watching him. She didn't say anything, but he felt that the light mood between them had suddenly shifted.

"I guess that's it for the kitchen. Let me show you where I put everything."

"Sure, fire away." He tried to concentrate but knew he wasn't going to remember half of it. The cupboards and drawers looked so neat and orderly, though, that he felt as if half the work of moving in was done.

"Thanks. This is great. It would have taken me a month to get it looking so organized."

Molly shrugged but he could tell she was pleased by the compliment. "No problem. It's just a kitchen."

The doorbell rang. Matthew was surprised. "I wonder who that is?" he murmured, stepping over a mound of newspaper as he went to answer it.

He pulled open the front door to find Dr.

Elliot holding a large green potted plant decorated with a ribbon. "Welcome to Cape Light," the doctor greeted him.

"Ezra, come on in." Matthew felt happy to see his father's old friend. Happier than he would have expected.

"Well, looks like you've landed, bag and baggage," Ezra said, gazing around.

"It's a mess. But I'll get it sorted out."

"Moving—what a headache. I could never face it. I guess that's half the reason I stayed put so long."

Matt smiled. "What's the other half?"

"Oh, that's a secret," Ezra said, with a twinkle in his eye. "Everybody needs at least one to keep life interesting."

"I'll remember that," Matt said, grinning.

"Enough philosophizing. I just stopped by to see if you got in okay. Here's a little something to brighten up the place," Ezra added, handing him the plant.

"Thanks. Very thoughtful of you."

"Don't mention it. That's a philodendron, by the way. It can survive all kinds of neglect. A popular choice for waiting rooms, I might add. But you keep that one here. I've already put one in your office, which, I might add, is shaping up nicely."

"Yes, I know. I stopped by quickly yesterday. It looks great. Sorry I didn't get to call you."

Ezra had been kind enough to oversee the work on Matthew's office while he was still in Worcester. Matt knew the older doctor was eager to bring a new physician to the town. Still, his help had gone well beyond the call of friendship. Matt was starting to think that going out of one's way for a friend or neighbor was not the exception but the rule around here.

"That's all right. I'm glad you're pleased. What else does a fellow like me have to do? I like to make myself useful when I can," Ezra insisted.

Molly came out of the kitchen carrying a plastic bucket. She looked surprised to see Ezra, Matt noticed, and not very happy.

"Molly Willoughby, I didn't know you were here," Ezra greeted her. "Working hard as usual, I see."

While Matthew was sure Ezra's comment was innocent, maybe even a compliment, he could see Molly felt stung. She glanced down at the bucket with a tight smile.

"That's me. Have bucket, will travel. How are you, Dr. Elliot?" she asked politely.

"Fit as a fiddle. How are the girls? No colds this winter, I hope."

"Very well, thanks. You can see for yourself. They'll be down in a minute." She turned to Matthew. "I guess I'll go now," she said. "Unless you need more help. I can work upstairs on the linen closet or make up the beds."

He felt sorry to see her go but didn't want her to do more unpacking. She'd already been too generous with her time. "That's all right. Amanda and I can do all that. Would you like to take a coffee break, though? If I can find the coffee," he added with a smile.

She looked about to agree, but then he saw her reconsider. "Thanks, but I really should go. The girls have a ton of homework, and Lauren has to do some research at the library."

"Oh, yes, the electrified worms. Some other time, okay?"

"Sure, some other time." Molly nodded and dropped her bucket at the door. "Jill, Lauren, time to go," she called up the stairway.

The three girls quickly appeared, galloping down the stairs. To his amazement Amanda looked cheerful and relaxed. He'd

envisioned their moving day as being difficult, even traumatic for her. Somehow it
had turned out quite the opposite.

As Amanda swung by he noticed a long
thin braid in her hair, a colorful bead fas-
tened to the end. It wasn't exactly like the
one Lauren wore but a homemade varia-
tion. He met Molly's amused expression, realizing she noticed it as well and had decided not to say anything about it.

As Molly said her good-byes and shep-
herded the girls toward the open door,
Matthew found himself at a loss for words.
He felt he should say something more than
the usual, but what?

He suddenly spied her vacuum cleaner
on the porch and jumped to pick it up before she could. "Here, let me carry that for
you."

"Oh, thanks." Molly glanced at him,
sounding surprised. They walked out together toward her car, a worn-looking blue
hatchback. He loaded the vacuum into the
trunk, then stood by Molly's open door.

"I know I keep saying it, but I really appreciated all your help. And talking with
you, of course. I'll see you around town, I
hope."

He inwardly cringed at his own words. As Amanda might say, how lame was that? Wow, he was rusty at this stuff. He hadn't had a date in decades. This was harder than he remembered.

"It's a small town. You won't be able to avoid me," Molly replied, with a wry smile.

"Right. Of course. Well, I wouldn't want to." He stared at her for an awkward moment, then realized he was holding on to the door and she wasn't able to close it. He let go and took a step back. "Well, good-bye now. Thanks again."

"Bye, Matt. Good luck with the rest of the unpacking." Molly smiled at him, closed her door, then quickly pulled away.

He stood on the sidewalk and watched her drive off, sure he'd forgotten something important he needed to tell her. But he couldn't think what. Once in the house, he shut the door, then noticed the bucket by the stairway where Molly had left it.

He picked it up like a prize, realizing he now had the perfect excuse to call.

The Clam Box was nearly empty by the time Tucker found his usual seat, a stool at the counter behind the grill. He'd purposely taken his lunch break late to miss the rush, but so far Charlie had been busy in the kitchen with some emergency, and Tucker hadn't spoken to him.

He ate a bowl of chowder, paging through a copy of the *Cape Light Messenger.* He stared at the front page, fantasizing for a moment that the headline read "Ex-convict Returns to Town, Breaks into Church," but he knew he was just being paranoid. Even if the paper reported the incident, they wouldn't word it quite that way.

They wouldn't need to, he thought grimly. That news would travel around town in no time.

Charlie appeared and set a dish down in front of him. "Are you sure I got this right? I've never seen you order a grilled chicken sandwich before."

"Fran's been after me to watch my cholesterol. Says I eat too many cheeseburgers."

"Well, you've got to eat something tasty. What's the sense if you don't enjoy your food?"

"Good point." Tucker stared at the sandwich, which did not look at all appealing.

"This would go down a lot easier with a few slices of bacon on top."

"Coming right up." Charlie turned and arranged bacon slices on the grill, then set the metal press on top of them, making them sizzle.

"Listen, I had some news I wanted to tell you about," Tucker began. "A homeless man broke into the church last night. The reverend found him and took him to the hospital in Southport. Says he's real sick. The guy gave his name as Jones. But Reverend Ben thinks he's my half brother, Carl. He wants me to go down and see him."

Charlie turned and stared at him. "Your brother, Carl? That's a wild one." He shook his head.

Tucker knew Charlie wasn't much of a churchgoer and didn't have a high opinion of the reverend. Not the way Tucker did. But that was another matter.

"Well, what if it is Carl? I'm thinking I ought to at least find out."

"What the heck for? You don't owe him anything. All he's ever given you is trouble and aggravation." Charlie turned briefly to flip the bacon. "I thought you washed your hands of good old Carl years ago."

"I did. In a way," Tucker admitted.

"When did he get out of jail? Do you know?"

"A fellow I know in Paxton called me when Carl got out on parole. I guess that was about ten years ago."

"He never tried to get in touch with you, all that time?" Charlie asked, glancing back to check on the bacon.

"No, none of us ever heard from him. Not a word. I tried to find Carl when the old man died, but I didn't have any luck. I can't say I really blame Carl for not keeping in touch. The old man was too hard on him. I wouldn't treat a dog the way my father treated Carl. That was a lot of the problem right there."

Charlie laughed harshly. "Plenty of boys don't get on with their fathers. Plenty got disciplined with a belt or the back of a hand. But they didn't turn out like Carl. You can't blame your old man. Carl was a bad apple from the word go. Always in trouble at school. It's amazing he didn't wind up in jail long before he killed that man."

"Yeah," Tucker agreed. "He was always pulling some stupid stunt, and people always looked the other way, gave him another chance. Until he found a mess he couldn't talk his way out of."

"But how about the time he broke in here and emptied the cash register? You consider that just another stupid stunt?"

Tucker met Charlie's eye and looked away. "You know it was never proved Carl did that. It was just your father who suspected him."

"Everyone in town suspected him, Tucker. Except maybe you and your mother. Carl was just lucky there was no evidence and that the police back then were too lazy to follow up."

The bacon sizzled noisily, and Charlie turned again to check it. Tucker considered Charlie's words and decided it was wiser not to reply. This debate was decades old, and he knew he'd never win it.

Charlie was referring to the time years ago when the Clam Box was robbed. Tucker and Charlie were just kids, and Carl was in his teens, already known as the worst kid in town. There wasn't much in the till, so it wasn't a great loss that way. The police were never able to figure out who had broken in, but Carl had already been caught once that summer breaking into a house with his gang of friends, though he hadn't actually stolen anything. Otto Bates, Charlie's father, was convinced that Carl was the culprit. Otto had no evidence, just a gut feeling and a deep distrust of Carl. He'd told everyone in town that Carl was to blame, and everyone believed him. It was nearly as bad as if Carl had been arrested and convicted.

Charlie set the improved sandwich down in front of Tucker and disappeared to take a phone call. Tucker pushed the sandwich away, his appetite suddenly gone. It was easy to sit here and bad-mouth Carl. Other memories came to mind, though, images of his tough, older half brother scaring off a bunch of kids who were bullying Tucker after school. Or Carl tossing a game-winning pass on the high-school football field.

Due to their seven-year age difference, their relationship was never a close one. But they still spent time together, especially when their mother—who was actually Carl's stepmother—worked at the cannery and Carl was left in charge.

Tucker remembered now how he had once broken the windshield of his father's car when a baseball bat had slipped out of his grasp. He must have been about nine and Carl, who was pitching, about sixteen at the time. Tucker had been so terrified imagining their father's reaction, he'd thrown up on the spot. Carl calmed him down, saying he'd take the blame as long as Tucker would keep the secret. Tucker gratefully agreed. But when he saw his father lash into Carl that night, he couldn't keep the pact. By then, his father was in a mindless, drunken fury and hardly heard a word Tucker said. He felt grateful to this day for Carl's selfless action . . . and still a little guilty.

Tucker had looked up to Carl as a little boy, that was for sure. Then later, when he saw Carl's flaws all too clearly, he felt embarrassed by his misplaced admiration. Still, there was some spark of feeling left for his half brother, if only a sense of shared history and duty.

Charlie returned and started working on another order. Tucker watched him a moment before he spoke again. "Come on, Charlie. He wasn't all bad. The way he played football, we thought he was something else. Scouts from all the big schools came to check him out. They came as far away as Chicago," Tucker reminded his friend. "He had some arm. Could have made pro."

"He was good," Charlie acknowledged. "But they all knew he was trouble. Carl had a self-destructive streak a mile wide. You talk about your father mistreating him, but he gave Carl his fishing ticket," Charlie went on, referring to the lobster-fishing permit. "Would have set him up with a nice income if he worked at it. Carl managed to mess that up, too."

"Nobody ever proved Carl was poaching." Tucker found himself coming to Carl's defense again. "He was accused. It was never proven."

"Accused is as good as proved in my book. The state permit board seemed to think so, too. He lost his ticket, didn't he?"

Tucker didn't answer. Everything Charlie said was true. Carl's losing his lobster-fishing license wasn't the worst thing he'd done, but it was the beginning of the end, Tucker thought now.

The waters in New England were crowded with lobster men and the waiting list for a license was long. The valuable lobster-fishing permits were handed down from father to son. Each lobster fisherman marked his traps with a colored float, uniquely his and registered with his license. The float's design stayed in the family for generations, like a crest. The Tulley float was yellow with a white stem striped with pink, black, and green. When Carl lost his license, the colors were given to another fisherman. Losing the permit and the float for poaching—or even the accusation of it—was a family disgrace. That's the way Tucker's father saw it. His threadbare relationship with his firstborn finally reached an end. As far as Tucker knew, Walter Tulley gave up on Carl that day and never spoke to him, or of him, again.

It wasn't long after that, Tucker recalled, that Carl got into a fight in a bar that ended when Carl felled his opponent with an unlucky punch to the head. The man died in a hospital a few hours later, and Carl was arrested on charges of second-degree murder. He claimed he acted in self-defense, that the man had been coming at him with a knife. But eyewitness testimony was shaky and the case was prosecuted by an aggressive D.A. who was trying hard to win convictions and make a name for himself in the county. Tucker had tried to get Carl a good lawyer, but his brother had stubbornly chosen the court-appointed attorney who was well-intentioned but sorely inexperienced. Foregoing a trial, Carl entered a guilty plea. He was sentenced to fifteen years in jail and drew parole in ten.

Sometimes it seemed to Tucker that Carl had always drawn the bad breaks. Sure, he was responsible for his actions and the consequences, just like anyone else. Still, it seemed as if his half brother had been handed a heavier load than most and asked to walk a far tougher road. *If I'd been treated the same, constantly told I was worthless and would never amount to anything, maybe I would have turned out like Carl, too,* Tucker thought.

"You're awful quiet." Charlie scraped the grill with his metal spatula. "Strolling down memory lane?"

"I was just thinking how Carl and my father were exactly alike." Tucker shook his head and sipped his coffee. "Always angry, always blaming someone else for their troubles. Turning to drink when things didn't go their way. Always with some grand scheme that didn't work out. Ever notice that?"

"I know what you mean," Charlie agreed. "Meanwhile your old man ran around saying he wasn't even sure if Carl was his son."

"Oh, that old story." Tucker shook his head. "My father could never swallow the way his first wife ran off and left him with a baby. He couldn't get back at her, so he had to blame it on Carl. Carl was his boy, all right, when he was out on the football field scoring a touchdown. But when he got into trouble, my father would disown him. Walter Tulley was a hard man to live with. He was lucky my mother stuck with him."

"She was a good woman. She did her best by Carl, too. She tried to help him." Charlie wiped a spot on the counter with a rag and rearranged the napkin holder and sugar shaker.

She did try, Tucker thought. She always told Tucker that Carl was his brother, period. Never mind the "half" part. Tucker knew his mother would have urged him to go to the hospital tonight and help Carl if he could.

"It might not be Carl. I might be worried over nothing," Tucker said, thinking out loud.

"Maybe. But if it is Carl, the only reason

he'd come back is because he needs something, and he's got no one else to go begging to. He probably wants money or some place to crash awhile. It certainly isn't because he wants to visit with your wife and kids and see how your life is coming along."

Tucker had already come to this conclusion. He nodded and stirred a spoonful of sugar into his coffee.

"I'm telling you, Tucker. Don't get involved. Don't let that pushy preacher tell you what to do, either."

Tucker shook his head, his patience wearing thin. This conversation hadn't helped him one bit.

"So it's okay for *you* to tell me what to do but not Reverend Ben. Is that it?"

"Come on, pal. You know what I mean. I'm trying to give you some friendly advice. Some practical advice."

"You're not getting it, Charlie. I know Carl is trouble. I don't need you to tell me that. But what if it's him in that hospital?"

Charlie shook his head. "He'll just sucker you in. Mark my words. I know him and I know you."

A slow burn went through Tucker. He'd

come to Charlie for some friendly sympathy—not to hear his brother's disreputable
history recounted and then to be insulted.

He tossed some bills on the counter and
pulled on his hat. "I've got to get back to
work. See you."

Charlie looked surprised. "You hardly ate
a bite. Want me to wrap this up?"

"No thanks," Tucker said, as he walked
away. "The bacon didn't turn out to be such
a good idea after all."

"Do you think they'll let me be in a few of
Lauren's classes?" Amanda tugged her corner of the quilt, helping her father make up
her bed.

"We'll ask the guidance counselor on
Monday," Matt promised. He watched
Amanda pick up a towel and her toothbrush
and head for the bathroom. "Are you nervous about starting school?"

"A little," she admitted. "But at least I
know Lauren. She's really nice. So is her little sister and her mom."

"Yes, they're a very nice family," he
agreed. Amanda left the room, leaving him
alone with his thoughts of Molly.

Molly was more than nice. She was bright and funny and a good mother, too. He thought she was beautiful, though he could see she felt awkward about her weight. She didn't have that starved, aerobically tortured look women seemed to think was ideal. But he didn't mind her curves. Not at all.

She was the first woman he'd really noticed since his wife's death, and he wasn't quite sure if his strong reaction to her was simply because Molly was so intriguing or because he was changing. Maybe something inside of him was waking up again.

But he wasn't sure he could handle dating. He had so much to do, getting Amanda adjusted to this new place and setting up a new practice. No, it wasn't the right time to start dating again, he decided as Amanda emerged from the bathroom. He wasn't ready.

With her face scrubbed clean and her long hair pulled back, Amanda slipped under the quilt. Matthew sat down on the edge of her bed.

"We got a lot done today, and we still have tomorrow to work on the house. We might be in pretty good shape by Monday."

"I guess so," she said. "Everything seems like such a big mess, though."

"We'll get there," he promised. "I thought we'd go to church tomorrow. We can try the one on the green, Bible Community Church. That will be a good way to meet more people, too, don't you think?"

Amanda nodded. Matt had never been very religious. He'd always left churchgoing to his wife and Amanda. But when Sharon got sick, he found himself more aware of his spiritual side and of his own mortality.

"Would you like to say a prayer together?" he asked.

Amanda nodded, then folded her hands and bowed her head. "You start," she said.

"Um, okay." Matt thought for a moment and then began, "Dear Lord, thank you for helping us find this new place to live and for a good moving day. We only found one or two things broken so far, despite my sloppy packing," he joked. "Please help us get settled here. Help Amanda make friends at her new school and help me with my practice." He turned to Amanda. "Anything else?"

She glanced at him, then lowered her gaze again. "Please bless Mom and keep her safe with you in heaven. We hope she knows we're thinking of her. We know she's watching over us."

Matt couldn't speak for a moment. "Amen," he said finally.

He stood up and kissed Amanda good night, then left the room.

Downstairs in the kitchen, he unpacked a sack of groceries. He found a bundle wrapped in newspaper on top of the refrigerator and opened it: the family photo, with the broken glass. He'd stashed it up there this afternoon to get it out of the way.

He stared down at the picture, thinking how unhappy his wife had been with him. She said he gave everything to his patients and left nothing for his family. They were often angry at each other, distant. They could never work it out and had nearly separated right before they found out about her cancer.

He'd tried hard to be a good husband to her then, but it was too little too late. When she died, he was left with a kind of grief that was like an overstuffed closet. Nothing had ever been resolved, and three years later, he still couldn't quite close the door.

He wrapped up the picture again and set it on the kitchen table so he'd be sure to take care of it. His own regrets and shortcomings were much harder to repair. He knew he was a good doctor, but maybe Sharon had been right. Maybe he couldn't be a good doctor and a good husband at the same time. Maybe he just wasn't cut out that way. He thought he'd done well with Amanda since her mother passed away, though he still had to be careful not to get lost in his work and shut her out, which was his automatic way of coping whenever things were difficult.

How could he think of dating again? Especially someone like Molly Willoughby. She was the type who would be looking for a serious relationship. Not just dinner and a movie on weekends. Matt couldn't imagine marrying again.

No, it would be better not to start anything. He'd drop off the bucket with an extra check for her, at the real-estate office. Like she said, it was a small town. If and when he was ever ready, he'd know where to find her.

The man asleep in the hospital bed looked nothing like Carl, Tucker decided. This had all been a huge mistake. A false alarm.

A huge wave of relief washed over him. He watched the man sleep, breathing heavily, an oxygen apparatus hooked to his nose. His battered face told the story of a hard life, the heavy dark folds around his eyes, a squashed-looking nose that appeared to have been broken a few times, a jagged scar on his cheek. Carl was about fifty by now. But this man looked much older, in his sixties, Tucker would guess. Under the loose sheet Tucker caught sight of a swollen leg, puffy and discolored.

It wasn't Carl, thank God.

He took a deep breath and began to walk away. But then he felt as if he were being watched. He quickly turned and saw that the man in bed was looking at him. They locked gazes for a second and the sick man closed his eyes again, his expression unaltered.

But it was too late. Tucker knew. He felt his heart turn to lead. It was Carl. From somewhere down in that wreck of a body his half brother peered out with a familiar light. He'd been pretending to be asleep, waiting for Tucker to go. That was exactly the kind of thing Carl would do.

Tucker stood at the foot of the bed,

tempted to walk out the door and never look back. Who would ever know? He wasn't even sure why he'd come in the first place. Still, he'd driven all this way. Might as well go through with it.

"Are you awake?" He waited.

Finally the sick man opened his eyes. "Who are you?"

"You know who I am. And I know you're not Carl Jones."

The man drew a raspy breath and glanced to the side. "I don't have any idea what you're talking about, mister. I ought to know my own name by now."

"Get off it, Carl. We're both too old for games."

"If you say so." The man sighed heavily and closed his eyes. Tucker waited for him to speak again, and Carl let him wait nearly five minutes before saying, "I tried to let you off the hook. But you never could take a hint, could you, Tucker?"

"Still playing the tough guy, huh?"

"Why not?" Carl shrugged. "You're still playing the Eagle Scout. Still got the uniform, I see. I didn't want you to come here. But I guess you couldn't help yourself."

Tucker took a step closer, feeling

strangely immune to Carl's insults. Nothing Carl could say had the power to hurt him anymore.

"Why did you come back? Were you looking for the old man?"

"Are you crazy? What would I want to see him for?"

"He died about three years ago. I tried to get in touch with you before the funeral, but I couldn't find you."

Carl took another labored breath and shifted against the bed. "Doesn't matter. I wouldn't have come."

"So what are you doing here?" Tucker persisted. "I don't get it."

"There's nothing to get. I was on my way up to Maine to see this friend of mine in Portland. Figured I'd stop in Cape Light, see what's become of the place. I didn't plan on making any social calls."

"I see," Tucker said, wondering whether Carl was really passing through with no intention of getting in touch or whether this was yet another of Carl's stories.

Carl began coughing again, a choking cough that sounded as if he couldn't catch his breath. "Do you want a nurse?" Tucker asked quickly.

Carl shook his head and waved his hand. "It'll pass. Just let me be."

Tucker sat in the chair near the bed, his hat in his lap. The coughing abated, and Carl turned to him. "So, you found me. You've done your duty. You can leave now."

Tucker ignored him. "I heard when you got out. A guy I know called me. What've you been doing all this time?"

Carl grinned, showing a row of stained, jagged teeth. "I'm a big shot on Wall Street. Can't you tell?"

"I mean besides that," Tucker said, without smiling.

"Making my way. What difference is it to you? I kept myself out of jail, if that's what you're asking me."

Tucker felt weary. Weary and sad. He'd rarely seen a man who had done such a poor job of making his way in the world.

Carl started coughing again; this time the violent spasms forced him to sit up. His face grew beet red; his bloodshot eyes bulged. It sounded as if Carl were about to cough out his insides. Tucker quickly leaned over and pressed the call button for the nurse.

He stood up and touched Carl's shoulder. "Easy now. The nurse is coming."

"Water . . ." Carl managed.

Tucker poured out a cupful from the plastic pitcher near the bed, and Carl took it in a shaky hand. Only a few drops reached his mouth, the rest spilling on the sheet and hospital gown.

The nurse arrived, and Tucker stepped aside. "Just lay back, Mr. Jones. I'm going to turn up your oxygen. Just try to relax," she coaxed him, pulling the curtain around the bed. "The patient needs some privacy," she told Tucker. "You can wait in the hall if you like."

"I was just leaving."

Tucker tried to catch Carl's eye, but it was too late. The curtain was closed. He heard Carl continue to cough violently on the other side.

Finally he turned and left the room. Carl was in bad shape. He might even die. *That would let me off the hook real fast,* Tucker thought. Then he felt horribly guilty. He didn't want anyone to die. He just wished Carl hadn't turned up here after all this time.

Maybe Charlie and Fran were right.

Maybe he should never have come here. He should have left well enough alone.

Tucker sighed and punched the button for the elevator. He had a problem now, and he didn't know what to do about it.

CHAPTER THREE

"I like the quiet church before the service begins," Ralph Waldo Emerson once said. But Ben often thought of the quote as the service ended and he stood in the back of the sanctuary while the choir finished singing its response to his benediction. He loved the quiet in the church at that moment, as the voices harmonized and held one last note, the congregation standing with heads bowed having just received a final blessing. In that silent moment before the bodies began to stir and make their way back into the world, he felt the indescribable peace of the Lord, invisible yet tangible, filtering down on them all like shafts of colored light through the stained-glass windows.

Then the notes of the postlude sounded and the worshipers began to leave their pews, lining up to say good-bye.

He saw Tucker Tulley approach and greeted him.

"Thank you, Reverend, that was a fine service," Tucker said appreciatively.

"You're welcome, Tucker." Ben leaned closer, talking in a more private tone. "I was wondering, did you have a chance to check on that man in Southport?"

Tucker nodded. "I went down there last night. It was Carl, just as you thought. We talked a few minutes. Then the nurse shooed me out."

Tucker's tone was not encouraging. Ben could see his brother's return was going to be a challenge for him—a great challenge. Ben hoped Tucker would turn to him for help. Yet he didn't want to press and have Tucker shut him out.

"Maybe you can visit again sometime. It sounds to me like he'll be in there awhile, from what the doctor said."

"I didn't get to speak to a doctor. What exactly is wrong with him?"

"Oh, a number of things. Emphysema, to start," Ben began. But before he could go on, Fran Tulley appeared. She quickly greeted him, then turned to her husband. "Excuse me for interrupting, honey, but I was just going out with Michael for those cartons for the food drive. Could you give us a hand when you get a chance?"

Each fall and spring, the church gathered donations of nonperishable food items and stored them in a pantry that was available to those in need. Reverend Ben now recalled that Fran was in charge of the spring collections and doing an impressive job.

"More donations?" Reverend Ben asked, pleased. "This could be the best drive we've ever had."

Tucker smiled at his wife with pride. "Fran's really put her all into it, Reverend. She's sending out flyers, knocking on doors. She even went up and down Main Street and got donations from all the restaurants and merchants."

Fran blushed, looking embarrassed by her husband's praise. "Oh, it's not such a big deal. Everyone's been very generous."

"Thanks to your efforts, Fran," the reverend put in. "We all appreciate it."

"No thanks necessary. I enjoyed doing it, honestly. Oh, there's Michael coming in with a box. I'd better show him where to go. See you later."

"I'd better go help them," Tucker said. "See you, Reverend."

Ben said good-bye to Tucker, feeling it was unfortunate that they hadn't finished talking about Carl. But if Tucker was truly interested in his half brother's diagnosis, he could surely find out on his own. Ben wondered if he would make the effort.

Sophie Potter stood next in line. Her oldest daughter, Evelyn, and next born, Una, had brought her to church today along with another young woman whom Ben guessed must be a granddaughter. Sophie had so many, he could never keep track.

"Lovely service, Reverend," Sophie said. "I appreciate you mentioning Gus. I'll tell him what you said."

After asking the congregation to remember in their prayers those who were sick, Ben had talked about Gus Potter—his work for the church and his place in the community. He hadn't said much but Sophie had been deeply moved.

"I'll tell him myself. I'm coming to see him this afternoon. Can I bring anything?"

Sophie patted his arm and smiled. "You're the best tonic for Gus, Reverend." She turned to the young woman standing beside her. "This is my granddaughter, Miranda, my son Bart's girl. She's an actress in New York," Sophie confided with pride.

Ben noticed Miranda blush. "More of a wanna-be," Miranda amended. "I'm mainly an office temp right now."

"If pretty counted for anything, she'd be in Hollywood, for goodness' sake. Why, just look at her," her grandmother insisted.

"Absolutely. She looks a lot like you, Sophie."

Now it was Sophie's turn to blush, but Ben thought it was true. Miranda had been blessed with the same lovely round face and reddish gold hair that had now gone white on her grandmother. Yet unlike Sophie, who was short and compact in build, Miranda was close to six feet tall. And she wasn't the wispy willowy sort that was in danger of being blown over by a stiff breeze. Miranda Potter looked strong and fit. She had the kind of looks they used to call statuesque.

"How long will you be visiting?" Ben asked.

"I can stay as long as I'm needed," Miranda said carefully. "Grandpa is coming home from the hospital, and there'll be a lot to do, a lot of visitors."

Miranda put her arm around Sophie's shoulder and met Reverend Ben's gaze. Her eyes were gentle, sea green in color. In her gesture he sensed her love and respect for her grandmother and realized that the Lord had a way of sending angels when they were most needed.

"I'll see you again then, Miranda."

"I'm sure you will." Miranda smiled and walked on with Sophie.

When Ben turned he was confronted by a new face, a dark-haired man with a teenage girl. Father and daughter, judging by their resemblance. He'd spotted them earlier, sitting off to the side, and wondered who they might be.

"I'm Reverend Ben Lewis. Welcome to Bible Community Church."

"Hello, Reverend. I'm Matthew Harding. This is my daughter, Amanda."

"Nice to meet you both." Ben shook

Matthew's hand and then Amanda's. "Are you visiting us today?"

"More permanent than that, I hope," Matt said with a smile. "We're new in town. Just moved in yesterday. I'm a doctor. I'm going to open a practice here."

"You must be Ezra Elliot's friend," Ben said. "I do hope you can stay for the coffee hour. There are a lot of people here who are looking forward to meeting you."

"I'd like that very much." Matthew smiled agreeably. He seemed a modest man, Ben thought. Not like some physicians he'd met.

"Well, here's a good start." Ben spotted Emily Warwick nearby. "Let me introduce you to our mayor . . . if I can catch her attention."

Emily stood with her mother, Lillian, whom she brought to church every Sunday. But today Emily was also accompanied by Dan Forbes, Ben noticed with surprise. He'd never seen the former newspaper owner and avowed cynic in church before. Of course, it had something to do with Emily. *Everything* to do with Emily from the looks of it. *God moves in strange ways indeed.*

Ben finally caught Emily's eye, and she

approached with a wide, winning smile. "Good morning, Reverend. Did you want to introduce someone?" she asked, turning to Matthew and his daughter.

Ben made the introductions. Emily and Dan, of course, welcomed Matt warmly. Lillian, however, appraised Matthew in her usual manner. "You look a bit young," she said, fixing him with a sharp, critical gaze. "I won't go to a doctor under forty. Not nearly enough experience. I won't have physicians learning by trial and error on me."

Matthew smiled mildly. "I think that there are good and bad doctors of any age," he said diplomatically.

"That's just my point. You can't be too careful when it comes to choosing one, can you?"

"I'm sure there's no question about Dr. Harding's abilities," Emily said, casting a warning glance at her mother. Dan stepped up beside her and deftly steered the conversation on to other topics, and within minutes Matthew was soon surrounded by a circle of welcoming parishioners.

Digger Hegman and his middle-aged daughter, Grace, stood to one side, looking on. "What's going on here? A political rally in the church vestibule?" the elderly ex-fisherman asked Ben.

"Hush, Dad. That's not polite." Grace shook her head. "It's the new doctor, Matthew Harding. Emily's just introducing him around."

"Hmmm . . . well, he looks like a decent fellow," Digger allowed. "I don't need to meet any more doctors, though. I think I'll wait to introduce myself if and when the need arises."

"That seems reasonable to me," Ben said, with a smile. All in all, he thought, Cape Light was going to be a good place for Matthew Harding and his daughter.

"Come on, girls. Your uncle will be here soon." Molly sifted through the open duffel bag on Lauren's unmade bed, checking the contents. "How about those waterproof mittens? Are they in here?"

Sam and Jessica were taking the girls ice skating and then entertaining them until the evening so Molly could catch up on her orders. She had a sudden increase in business, which was very encouraging. But now she needed to bake the entire day and into the night to make the deliveries on time.

The doorbell rang, and she started out of the bedroom to answer it but stopped as she saw Jill standing in front of the mirror, her hairbrush hopelessly tangled in her long hair. Molly groaned at the sight. "Lauren, help Jill with her hair, will you, honey? I think there's some detangle spray in the bathroom."

"Got any dynamite?" she heard Lauren mutter.

Oh, boy. That one is starting to sound just like me, Molly thought, as she left them alone to sort it out.

She pulled open the front door, expecting to find her brother, Sam. But instead it was her ex-husband, Phil Willoughby. Feeling shocked, her breath caught in her throat. Then she felt her anger rise.

"Hi, Molly." He smiled widely. Too widely, Molly thought, for a man with his track record. If he had any sense of decency, he'd be hanging his head in shame.

"What do you want?" She stood in the doorway, blocking his view. She didn't want the girls to catch sight of him. Then she'd really have a problem.

"Well, it's Sunday. I'd like to see my daughters." His calm tone annoyed her; he sounded as if he should have been expected and she was the one acting oddly.

There was a time, long ago, when Sunday afternoon was Phil's regular time with the girls. But in Molly's book, he'd long since forfeited that privilege.

Molly glanced over her shoulder, then stepped out into the hallway with him, closing the door behind her.

"You have some unbelievable nerve, I'll say that for you." Her tone was hushed but fierce.

"Molly, come on now. I thought about calling, but I knew you were going to act this way. You would have just hung up on me."

"You got that right."

He paused and looked her over. "You look good. Did you lose some weight or something?"

"Phil—" She shook her head, not knowing whether to laugh or scream. "You never change, do you?"

"Wait. Just stop right there, okay?" He reached into the front pocket of his jeans and pulled out an envelope. "Here, this is for the girls. I've got a good job now selling cars and trucks. It's a big dealership in Peabody. I'm living around there, too, now."

Molly considered this information. Peabody was about thirty miles southwest of Cape Light. The drive was mostly on the interstate, though, which was often loaded with traffic. He might get tired of that real quick, she thought.

"I made top salesman two months in a row," he added proudly.

"How nice for you, Phil." Her tone was flat and sarcastic, her expression blank. She took the envelope but didn't open it. She could guess a check was inside. "Fine. But it's a drop in the bucket, pal. You owe me so much child support at this point, I can't count that high."

"I'm going to make it up to you. Every cent," he promised. "That's just a start."

He'd said all this many times before, but Molly didn't bother to remind him of the fact. "Okay, you're going to start paying the child support again. Thanks a bunch. Do you think after all this time you're just going to buy your way back to see the girls?"

"Now, come on, Molly. That's not it all.

I'm just trying—" He tried to explain, but Molly cut him off.

"What are you trying to do, Phil? Do you even know? Trying to disappoint them again? To confuse them and undermine their self-confidence, their sense of trust? You can't just walk in and out of their lives. I won't let you. Not for all the checks in your checkbook."

Phil nodded, his head bowed. "You were always like a mother lion with those girls," he said softly. "I bet if I tried to go in there, you'd claw my eyes out."

"You got that right." Molly felt like crying, but she didn't know why. She kept her hands crossed tightly across her chest and took a deep breath. She couldn't look up at Phil. She knew what she'd see. He wasn't a bad guy, really. Not deep inside. He'd never meant to hurt her or his daughters. But somehow, he always did.

"What do I have to do? Just tell me, and I'll do it. I want to see my girls again. I know I messed up, but it's different now." He paused, watching for a reaction while Molly tried hard not to show one.

"How is it different?"

"I've been thinking about things. I feel . . .

older or something. I don't know." He shrugged and stared down at her. "I can't really explain it right now. But I promise, this time is different. It really is."

Molly took a breath. She hadn't seen him in months, not since last summer. He didn't look any different; Phil was still a big, broad-shouldered lumberjack type with blue eyes and thick blond hair. It wasn't hard to see why she fell for him in high school. His clothes looked a little finer, she noticed, the shearling jacket, for instance. But that didn't mean anything. Phil never minded blowing an entire paycheck on himself if some expensive piece of clothing caught his eye.

"I can bring you back to court, Molly. I have some rights, too," he reminded her quietly.

Now there was a threat she hadn't heard for a while. *He really must be planning to keep up the child support,* she thought, *or he wouldn't have the nerve to spring that one.*

But before Molly could decide how to reply, the door behind her swung open. She turned to see Lauren standing there with Jill still attached to a hairbrush, crying her eyes out.

"Mom, we really need some help here," Lauren moaned. Then Jill looked up and noticed her father.

"Daddy!" She immediately stopped crying and jumped into Phil's arms.

"Hello, sugar pie." Jill was big now, but Phil was still much bigger, Molly realized as she watched her ex-husband lift Jill off her feet in a tight hug, the brush dangling from her daughter's hair.

Lauren hung back, looking shy of her father, Molly noticed, or maybe just distrustful. But Phil smiled warmly at her and stretched open his free arm. "Get over here, Lauren Marie," he coaxed her. Molly saw her waver for a moment, then move toward him. He soon stood hugging both girls, one under each arm in a giant three-way embrace. Molly stood back, feeling invisible.

"Wow, I missed you girls so much," he said.

Right, so why haven't we seen you for months? And why just a five-minute call on Christmas? Molly wanted to say. But she bit her tongue. She didn't want to dash the happy reunion with cold water. She wasn't that mean-spirited. Part of her did believe that Phil was sincere. He was inconsistent and irresponsible, but in his own way, he still really loved them.

"Why don't we go inside," he said, ushering the girls through the door. He glanced at Molly over their heads, and Molly had no choice but to let him in. She closed the door and suddenly smelled something burning.

She raced to the oven and yanked open the door. She grabbed some pot holders and pulled out the pans of muffins.

"Blast! Double blast!" She hated for Phil to see her out of control, but she couldn't help her reaction. The muffins were over-cooked, too brown outside for her customers. She had to start over again with this batch. It was all Phil's fault for distracting her, of course. No doubt about it, the man was trouble.

She turned to him, feeling angry all over again.

"Something wrong, Molly? You look upset."

"No problem. Everything is under control," she insisted. She pulled off the oven mitts and tossed them on the countertop.

The girls were still hanging on him, and Phil looked awfully smug, his repentant attitude apparently wiped away with their greeting.

"Why didn't you tell us Daddy was here?" Jill's tone held a note of reproach. "We thought it was just Uncle Sam."

"I wanted to surprise you," Phil replied, and Molly didn't bother to contradict him. "How would you like to go out for the day? Do something special with me?"

"Yes!" Jill jumped up and clapped her hands. Lauren glanced at Molly. She could tell from her older daughter's expression that she wasn't totally buying this.

"Sorry, they already have plans. Sam and his wife, Jessica, are taking them out."

"Sam has a wife?" Phil shook his head in amazement. "I didn't know there was a woman alive that could hook your brother."

"Every man meets his match." Molly met his gaze for a moment, then looked away. She had once thought Phil was her match, but she'd discovered her mistake the hard way.

"Sam won't mind if the girls go out with their father," Phil said, gazing at Lauren and

Jill again. "Just give him a call. He'll understand."

Sam and Phil had been friends in high
school. Sam had been angry with him on
Molly's behalf, but she knew her brother still
had a soft spot for his old buddy Phil. That
was just the trouble. It was hard for anyone
to stay mad at Phil for very long.

"Please, Mom?" Seated on Phil's lap, Jill
turned to Molly with a pleading expression.
Lauren didn't say anything, though, and she
looked a little sullen, Molly noticed.

"I can't call him. They're coming straight
from church," Molly said curtly. "And you
guys aren't even ready. Maybe you can see
your father another time. You go finish up,
and the adults will talk."

Jill got a grumpy face and didn't move
from Phil's side. He gently patted her back.
"Oh come on now, Molly. Have a heart. I'm
here now. What's the point of making a big
deal out of this?"

"The point is, you can't just fall out of the
sky and expect us to drop everything. Especially since no one's heard from you for
months. That's just like you, Phil." Molly
heard her voice rising, but she couldn't help

herself. "You say you've changed. This time is different. Well, that's no different."

Phil stared at her, his expression unreadable. Jill sat with a stricken look on her face. Lauren bit her nail, trying to look unfazed, but obviously disturbed as well.

Molly felt vaulted back through time, when her arguments with Phil left the girls frightened and confused. How did she fall into that trap again so quickly? She was ashamed of herself.

"A person has to start over somewhere, Molly. For pity's sake. Just give me a chance." Phil's voice was quiet and calm, a stark contrast to her own.

Molly looked at the girls again. She was between that old rock and hard place. If she let them go with Phil, they might end up painfully disappointed and she'd be left to soothe their hurt feelings. But if she held the line and made him go, they would be mad at her, and she'd feel guilty for depriving the girls of a rare chance to see their father.

"Please, Molly? I'm going to toe the line this time. Honestly."

Jill turned to him and put her arm around his shoulders. "I believe you, Daddy."

"Thank you, sweetie." Phil smiled at Jill,

then looked over at Molly. She knew she was beat. He always knew how to get his way, didn't he? No wonder he'd finally found his calling as a car salesman.

"All right. You can take them out. Just have them back by eight so they can get to bed on time."

"Yes!" Jill ran back into the bedroom, hairbrush flipping. Lauren turned and followed. "Should we bring that bag of stuff for ice skating?"

"Sure, I'll take you skating if you want. We can do lots of things." Phil came to his feet, all smiles again. "Thanks, Molly. I appreciate this."

"Don't thank me. Thank your girls. Just don't mess up this time, I'm warning you. There are no more chances after this one, Phil. I'm not kidding."

"I hear you." Phil nodded his head. "I won't need any more chances. This is it."

She gave him a look but didn't say anything. The girls rushed back into the room. Jill had managed to untangle the brush and had bunched her hair in a big clip. It looked a little funny, but Molly didn't have the energy to make any improvements.

The girls quickly kissed her good-bye

while Phil looked on from the hallway. Lauren didn't look nearly as elated as Jill about the unexpected outing, but she didn't complain about it, either.

Once they were gone, Molly went inside and shut the door. The silence in the apartment seemed oppressive. She couldn't quite believe what had just happened, and she couldn't quite believe Phil had gotten his way, after all. The realization made her mad at him all over again.

She pulled Phil's envelope from her pocket and opened it. As she'd expected, it contained a check. But the sum, several thousand dollars, was far greater than she'd ever imagined, even as a peace offering. Phil owed her much more, of course. But this was an impressive start.

Molly sat down at the kitchen table and stared at the check. For most people she knew, this wouldn't be a lot of money. It wasn't exactly a lottery jackpot. But she could do a lot with this money. Buy the girls a good computer. Get some badly needed new tires for her car. Pay off the lingering bills from Christmas. Catch up at the orthodontist. Have a little money stashed in the bank for a rainy day. . . .

Did it make her think better of Phil? Only slightly. Did it make her trust him? Not one bit. If anything, it made her more wary. He was clearly trying to buy his way back into their lives, and she didn't want to play right into his tricks.

But he did owe her the money for child support, fair and square. And she did need it. So she folded up the check and put it in her purse so she could take it right to the bank tomorrow.

The doorbell rang, and Molly realized it had to be Sam and Jessica. She'd forgotten all about them.

She pulled open the door and let them in. "Hi, Moll." Sam leaned over and gave her a kiss on the cheek.

"Gee, it smells good in here," Jessica said, following him inside. "What are you making?"

"I just charred a bunch of banana muffins. They look awful but still taste pretty good. Anybody hungry?"

"No, thanks. We're fine. Are the girls ready?" Sam said.

Molly glanced at him. "They're not here, actually. I know you won't believe it, but they went out with Phil."

"Phil took them out? I didn't even know you were speaking to him again." As Molly expected, Sam looked amazed and confused by the news.

"I'm not. I mean, I wasn't. He just showed up here and wouldn't take no for an answer. Then the girls found out he was here, and Jill almost started crying when I said, 'No.' I'm really sorry you had to come all the way over, but there was no way to reach you."

"I get the picture." Sam shook his head. "A sneak attack. That's Phil." He glanced at Jessica who had taken a seat at Molly's kitchen table and opened her gray wool coat.

"He put you in a difficult position, asking right in front of the girls," Jessica offered.

"Exactly," Molly replied, feeling Jessica understood the situation perfectly. "What could I say? He claims he's changed. It's all going to be different. He even gave me a check." Molly pulled the check from her purse to show it to Sam.

Sam looked impressed when he read the amount. He handed it back to her. "That's a lot of money. Looks like he's serious this time."

"Or just feeling more guilty than usual,"

Molly noted. "I just hope he doesn't pull one of his vanishing acts. I'd never forgive myself for giving in to him. I told him this was his last chance. If he fails those girls again . . . well, he'll be sorry. Very sorry. I'll figure out some way to teach him a lesson."

"Molly, please," Sam coaxed her. "I know Phil wasn't the model husband—or the model ex-husband, for that matter. But he's not a monster. Maybe you should just relax a little and give him a chance. Maybe he's finally ready to grow up and face his responsibilities. Some guys are a little slow. But it can happen."

"Right, like snow in July," Molly said cynically. "I've heard all this before, Sam. Do you honestly think Phil Willoughby can ever change? I don't."

"Anyone can change, Molly." Sam shook his head. "You're so negative sometimes. Especially about men. We're not so bad, you know."

Jessica glanced at him. "Molly's been through enough this morning, Sam. She doesn't need a lecture about man bashing. She has every right to be concerned about the girls. Phil's been totally unreliable. Why should she believe him now?"

Molly was surprised to hear Jessica speak up on her behalf. Since the two had been married, she'd never heard Jessica and Sam disagree except about minor issues such as what color to paint the hallway. She'd never expect her brother to take Phil's side and Jessica to defend her.

Sam looked equally surprised. "No reason. Except to give the guy a break. That's all I'm saying. Is he going to pay his child support again?" he asked Molly.

"He says so. He has a new job selling cars or something."

"And apparently he's doing well at it," Sam added, nodding at the check.

Molly and Jessica shared a doubtful look. "It shows he made some extra money lately and he was feeling guilty," Molly said.

Sam sighed. He stuck his hands in his pockets. "I guess we all just have to wait and see."

Molly nodded. "I guess so."

She wished her brother was more sympathetic to her side of the situation. But Sam was like that; he always gave a person the benefit of the doubt. Even someone like Phil. It was a good trait in general, Molly thought, but awfully annoying at the moment.

As if guessing her thoughts, Sam reached over and gave Molly's shoulder a reassuring pat. "I guess we ought to go. You have work to do. Come on, honey," he said to Jessica.

Jessica stood up from the table and joined her husband. "Okay. But we ought to stop over at my mother's now for lunch."

Sam frowned. "I thought we ducked that invitation."

"Looks like it boomeranged." Jessica took her husband's arm as she turned toward Molly. "Emily brought Dan to my mother's today after church. She could really use some reinforcements."

"Have some sympathy, Sam. Sounds like Dan is going to be your new brother-in-law," Molly said.

"Yeah, poor guy. I do feel sorry for him."

"Honey, please. My mother's not that bad." Jessica stared up at him.

"No comment. Especially since we were just in church." Sam grinned at Molly. He didn't have to say anything more.

Jessica's mother was a tough old bird, notorious for her sharp tongue. She had thoroughly disapproved of Sam and had put so much pressure on Jessica, it had nearly broken up the match. The fact that Sam was able to joke about Lillian was actually to his credit, all things considered. Lillian Warwick would be more accepting of Dan, Molly thought, because of Dan's stature in the town. Then again, she'd probably give him a hard time on sheer principle.

"So long, Molly. Good luck with your work." Sam touched her arm as he walked out.

"Call if you need me to watch the girls this week, okay?" Jessica said.

Jessica gave her a quick hug, and Molly found herself hugging back. She felt as if Jessica had understood how much Phil's appearance had shaken her—understood and sympathized with her. That was the second surprise of the day.

Molly worked all afternoon and into the early evening without taking a break, mixing up batches of muffins and pies, running between two apartments to check on the cooking. Her next-door neighbor often went away on weekends, and she let Molly use her oven when she had to do a lot of baking.

It wasn't a perfect solution, but it was the only way she could even attempt to fill such big orders. If she wanted to go into this business full-time, she'd definitely need some other arrangement. Right now she didn't seem to have enough business to warrant renting out a real bakery or setting up a shop. But if she didn't get a larger, more professional work space, she'd never be able to handle more business. It was a circular puzzle she couldn't quite figure out.

She didn't have time to figure it out today, either. She didn't even have time to eat a real meal, but she sampled her wares so often, it didn't matter. She made a delivery to the Clam Box and another to the Beanery, a hip urban-style café in the village. Her last stop was a new client, the Pequot Inn, a fancy restaurant just outside of the village.

Back home again, she worked on an order for a dozen quiches with different fillings, which she would somehow manage to fit into her refrigerator tonight and deliver early tomorrow morning to the Beanery.

All the while she worked, Molly's stomach was twisted into a knot. She worried about facing Phil again and what would happen next. Sam had advised her to give her ex-husband time to prove himself. But all Molly could think about was all the times in the past that Phil had hurt and disappointed her.

Since they'd divorced seven years ago, Phil had never been a consistent presence for the girls or even consistent in sending support payments. He'd make an effort for a month or two, then the novelty of being a dad would wear off. He'd start missing his visits, calling at the last minute or, sometimes, not even calling at all. There were several times when they didn't hear from him for months at a stretch, and he seemed to move around so much that Molly was never sure of his phone number and address. Once they didn't hear from him for almost a year. Molly had learned through the grapevine that Phil had moved to Connecticut and tried to start a car-repair business with a friend. Again, he'd come back, insisting he'd changed, and he started visiting the girls and giving Molly support money. That was last winter. A little over a year ago, Molly realized.

By the spring, his old pattern prevailed,

and he'd stopped visiting and sending checks, though he did call to say hello to the girls from time to time. He'd called on Christmas, though he did not send them any gifts.

He had probably taken them to the mall today, Molly thought. It would be typical Phil to try to make up for all the missed occasions in one extravagant shopping spree. The girls ought to be too old by now to fall for that tired trick. She was curious to see if it had worked this time. Curious and nervous. She didn't like the feeling and resented Phil for still being able to upset her like this.

Finally at a quarter past seven, she heard the doorbell ring, and she rushed to let them in. Lauren and Jill greeted her happily. They kissed Phil good-bye and went to their room.

"Good night, girls. I'll see you next week," Phil called after them. He met Molly's gaze. "That is, if it's okay with you."

Molly was relieved to hear Phil already making plans to see the girls again, but she remained wary. "What did you have in mind?"

"Well, a regular schedule, I guess. Two nights a week and every other weekend?"

"You are trying to make up for lost time, aren't you?"

"Yes, I am," he admitted. "If you'll let me."

Molly's first impulse was to answer in anger. No one had been stopping him all these months from seeing his daughters any time he pleased. But she remembered Sam's words and held her tongue. It was hard to give Phil another chance, but she didn't see that she had any other choice here.

"Did you open my envelope?" he asked her carefully.

She nodded. "I did. Thanks."

"I know it's not everything. But it's a start. I'm doing pretty well now. I can give you more than the regular amount as a sort of back pay, okay?"

Molly nodded again. "That sounds all right."

"Listen, when we were talking this morning, there was something I forgot to tell you."

"Oh? And what was that?" She felt her nerves jump into emergency alert. Was this the part where Phil announces that he's leaving for Australia in a few weeks? Or something equally impulsive and thoughtless, proving that he'd gotten the girls excited over nothing.

"I wanted to tell you that I know now that I really screwed things up. I'm sorry for the things I did, the things I said to you. I was just . . . a fool. A total fool. I'm really sorry, Molly. I hope someday you can forgive me."

Molly was shocked by his admission and apology. But it would take more than remorseful words to heal the wounds from their marriage. Digging up their unhappy past was the last thing she wanted to do tonight.

"That's ancient history, Phil. It doesn't matter to me now one way or the other."

He was quiet for a moment. At first she thought her harsh reply must have upset him, but when he spoke, she could tell he wasn't mad—just ashamed of himself.

"I know you don't trust me anymore. I guess I deserve that. But I promise, I won't let you down this time."

"Don't worry about me. I'm immune to you. Just don't disappoint Lauren and Jill."

"I understand." He dipped his big blond

head. "Good night, Molly. Good to see you again."

"Good night, Phil." She stood at the doorway and watched him walk down the hall. She couldn't say that it had been good to see him. It had been a shock, though. A real earthquake.

Molly heard the girls in the bathroom getting washed up for bed. She knew they would bubble over in describing their day with him. Though she was curious to hear how it went, Molly wasn't looking forward to hearing the girls sing his praises or show off all the presents he had bought them that she normally couldn't afford. Alone in the kitchen, she stood by the counter and mindlessly ate a banana-chocolate-chip muffin, one of the rejects from the order that had overcooked this morning. The cat appeared from wherever she'd been sleeping and twined herself around Molly's legs.

Molly was so tired, not to mention tense and angry. Why should Phil be able to drop down out of the sky and pick up where he left off? It shouldn't be so easy for him. It didn't seem fair. She knew she shouldn't still be mad at him for the way their marriage had ended. But she couldn't help it.

The check would come in handy, but she felt mad about that, too. Mad at herself for feeling bought off. She wished she didn't need Phil's money and could just rip up that check and toss it in his face.

But the truth was she did need it. She was sure he could see that as soon as he walked in, but he was too smart to say anything. She was working hard but not doing all that well on her own. What was all this muffin baking and quiche making and back-breaking work adding up to anyway?

Molly sometimes imagined herself having her own shop, with loads of people working for her. She'd sit up front and be the boss, organized and smartly dressed. But that was just a fantasy, an imaginary carrot dangling just beyond reach that helped her get through the drudgery. It gave her some hope, some inspiration. But it would never come true. Who was she kidding? She could never start her own business. She never went to college. She just didn't have what it takes, the smarts and the confidence. Success took more than just making a good chocolate cake.

Jill walked into the kitchen, dressed in her nightgown. "Look at what Daddy bought me." She held out her arm, showing off a silver bracelet with a dangling heart charm. "He got one for Lauren, too. And some CDs and some other stuff. Want to see?"

Molly forced a smile. "Sure, honey. I'll be right in."

She put a dirty cup in the sink and shut off the kitchen light. Maybe she was lucky Phil had surfaced and would help out now. *I'll never do any better than this,* Molly thought sadly. *I'm a fool to try.*

CHAPTER FOUR

"Are you sure you're up to it? You can see just as well from the window in the kitchen." Sophie stood by her husband's wheelchair, which was parked in the living room, right next to his favorite armchair. He had the newspaper spread out on his lap, but it obviously wasn't holding his interest this morning. Miranda, who stood nearby, cast Sophie a concerned look over her grandfather's head.

"I need some fresh air. *Real* air," Gus insisted. "I've still got that blasted hospital smell in my nose. It's driving me crazy."

Sophie felt worried. He had only come home on Tuesday, the day before yesterday.

Since then he had spent most of his time in bed. But this morning he'd asked to get dressed in his real clothes, his trousers, suspenders, and flannel shirt. That was a good sign, she thought. Except for his sallow complexion and hollow eyes, he almost looked his old self. But going outside? She didn't think that was a good idea. She glanced over at Miranda, who seemed to have the same reaction.

"It's cold out, Grandpa. It looks like it might snow any minute."

"Oh, that's nothing. A little flurry maybe. Bundle me up like a mummy, you two, if it makes you feel any better. I don't care. I want to go out and get some air."

Sophie sighed. Meeting her husband's watery gaze, she realized they had come to a point when she couldn't refuse him any request, no matter how extreme. Anything to please him now, to make the days he had left happier for him.

"I'll get his parka and scarf. Give him a thick sweater. That gray one on the chair in the bedroom should do."

Miranda nodded and disappeared to find the sweater while Sophie fetched the parka, scarf, and gloves from the mudroom. They soon had Gus bundled up beyond recognition in his wheelchair. Sophie heard him chortling under the layers. "Where do you think you're taking me, girls, on an expedition to the North Pole?"

Miranda reached up and loosened his scarf. "Is that better?"

"A little," he conceded. "Okay, ready to roll." He jauntily patted the side of the chair.

Miranda pushed while Sophie went ahead and opened the doors. Gus was too weak to walk even the short distance from the bedroom out to the back porch. She could hardly believe it and willed herself not to cry.

Once outside, Miranda turned the chair to give her grandfather a sweeping view of the orchard and, in the far distance, the village below and the sheltered harbor. The sky above was heavy and low, gray clouds promising snow.

Miranda looked at Sophie. "Call me when you're ready to come back in, Grandma. Don't stay out here too long."

Sophie nodded. Her granddaughter understood that she and Gus needed some time alone right now. There were things to talk about, important things, with no time left to procrastinate.

"Warm enough?" Sophie pulled up a chair and sat beside him.

"Warm as toast," Gus replied. He held out his gloved hand, and she took it in her own. "We're sheltered from the wind back here, facing east. I see the snow coming down, though. It's just starting."

Sophie saw it, too, fat white flakes that slowly drifted down from the sky as if shaken loose from a flock of doves.

"I missed this place. It's good to be home. I don't want to go back to that hospital again."

"I know, dear. I don't think you'll have to," Sophie said honestly. The best they could hope for now was that Gus would be able to die right here in the comfort of his own home.

"In all the years since I came to live here, I don't think I ever spent more than a night or two in a row away from the trees. Or apart from you."

"Not a handful, by my count. We were never big on vacations, were we?" She smiled at him. "There was always something to do around here."

"We didn't need to go gallivanting around, honey. This was our world. God gave us plenty. As near to perfect as it gets, if you ask me. I couldn't ask for more."

"Me, neither," Sophie agreed. Born on the orchard, she had been living here so long, she sometimes imagined she would wake one morning to find roots sprouting out of her toes, like one of the apple trees. She often thought people must pity her, thinking she never did much with her life. But she knew in her heart she'd had a rich life—full of hard work and challenges, joys and sorrows.

If she died tonight, her spirit would leave this earth with a feeling of satisfaction; she had peace in her heart at a job well done. She glanced at Gus, his once strong profile worn down by sickness and age. But in his gaze there was a peaceful light, as peaceful as a calm blue summer sky. *He feels the same,* she realized. *He's not afraid of dying.*

"I've had a good life with you, Gus. You're a wonderful husband and father. My best friend and the love of my life. . . ." Sophie felt her throat tightening, and she paused to take a breath. "I don't know what I'm going to do without you. I don't know how to keep going without you."

"Hush now, sweetheart. None of that." Gus leaned over and put his arm around her shoulders. "I was the lucky one. Everyone knows that. I didn't know up from down until I met you. You gave me children, this orchard, the kind of life a man could be proud of. You didn't even want me at first, remember?" he teased her.

"Oh, it wasn't like that. I liked you right away. I just couldn't see what you wanted with me. I'd been thrown over. I was practically a spinster."

Sophie's first love had left her at the altar, a public humiliation she had somehow survived. With her failed wedding day and the scarcity of eligible men after the war, she had lost all hope of finding another who would want to marry her.

"Prettiest spinster I ever saw." Gus laughed softly and shook his head. "I'll never forget that day your brother brought me here. I came to ask for a job and saw you, up in a tree, your arms full of apples. I felt my heart just jump out of my chest, I swear it."

He rested his hand on his heart and

smiled. Sophie smiled too, remembering. Gus and her younger brother, Fred, had just come home from the army and neither had jobs. Tall and lean with a head of black wavy hair, Gus looked liked a movie star standing there in the dappled sunlight. She nearly fell right off the ladder the first time he spoke her name.

"You proposed pretty quickly, that's for sure. My brother said you were just after my property," she reminded him. "Tell the truth. It can't make any difference now. Was that your intention?"

Gus laughed and hugged her. "Yup, a gigolo. That's what I was. But you reformed me. A man needs a woman to improve himself, you know."

"I did reform you ... almost." She sighed. "That feels like it was yesterday, doesn't it? Where did the years go?"

"They flew by. Season to season. Around and around we went. It felt like it would never end. Spring will be here before you know it. The trees will green up and the blossoms will come."

Sophie nodded, staring out at the orchard with him. She could almost hear that low hum of the bees right now and smell the moist earth coming alive again. Even the snow flakes clinging to the branches started to look like white blossoms.

"Every one will get to work again. Even your bees." Gus's voice held an optimistic note as always.

But they both knew he would not be out in the orchard working this spring. He would be gone by then. *Long gone from my side,* Sophie thought.

Her vision of spring suddenly melted before her eyes, and she began to cry. Gus patted her shoulder.

"There, there, sweetheart. I'm not going so far. It will be as if I'm sitting right here on the back porch, watching you."

Harder than that for her, Sophie thought. But she didn't disagree. There was a heaven, Sophie felt sure. And she was just as sure that Gus would be up there.

But where would she be? Away from the orchard by then, probably, if their children had a say in the matter.

"The kids don't think I should stay without you. Evelyn and Una had a little talk with me while you were in the hospital. Bart called and said the same thing, too."

"What do you want to do?" he asked her softly.

"They make some sense; I'm not saying they don't. Still, I can't imagine leaving here. I know it won't be the same without you. I might just hate it. But I was here on my own when we met, and I think I can do it again. I'd like to try, at least."

Gus didn't answer for a moment. He sat staring straight out at the trees and the low falling snow.

"I hate to think that my dying will force you off, Sophie. After all the times we struggled to hang on to this place when it wasn't easy. But I guess I'm worried about you, too. I don't like the idea of you out here all alone. We're not young anymore."

"Oh, let's not talk about that now. Worrying is a waste of time. It says so right in the Bible," she reminded him. "The Lord doesn't want us to worry. He'll show me the right thing to do, I'm sure of it."

"I know He will. I just love you so much. And I promised I'd always take care of you." He wiped his gloved hand across his eyes, which were glassy with unshed tears.

Tears started trickling down Sophie's cheeks again. She couldn't help herself.

She leaned over and wound her arm through his and put her head on Gus's shoulder.

"We'll be all right," she said finally. "He'll take care of us both."

"Mom, how do you spell *horrendous*?" Jill sat at the kitchen table doing her homework, while Molly stood at the counter, chopping a pile of parsley. She paused, thinking, then shook her head.

"I'm not sure. You need to look it up in the dictionary. There's one right on your desk in your room."

"Never mind. I'll just say, 'It was really horrible.' "

Molly wanted her to get into the habit of using a dictionary, but she didn't push it. Jill was hurrying to finish her homework before Phil came by. He was due to pick up the girls at six, but Molly felt sure that with the snow he'd be late. He hadn't called to cancel, though, which was a surprise. In the past Phil had always grabbed the slightest excuse to postpone his visits.

Lauren didn't seem to remember that Phil was coming tonight, Molly noticed. But she was distracted by an unexpected visit with Amanda. Matthew had called in the afternoon from Southport and asked if Molly could pick up Amanda after chorus practice since he didn't think he'd get home in time with the snow.

Molly didn't mind helping him out. She had to pick up Lauren anyway. He was also due to arrive shortly, and she felt undeniably nervous about seeing him again—and at the prospect of his visit overlapping with Phil's, though she didn't know why that should matter. Maybe because Phil brought out such a shrewish side of her personality? One she didn't want Matthew to see, that was for sure.

The sound of giggling came from the bedroom where Lauren and Amanda were holed up, supposedly doing homework. Well, that's how it was at that age. Somehow the homework got done.

Molly forced herself to focus on the task at hand. She had an important appointment tomorrow at the Beanery and was making several special dishes for the café owners, Jonathan and Felicity Bean, to sample. On Monday, when she had dropped off their order of quiches, they told her that they planned to expand their menu and asked if she could supply more lunch and dinner dishes. The order was potentially humongous, as Jill might say, and Molly felt both excited and nervous at the prospect. So nervous that she had only told Betty about the appointment.

Molly didn't want to get her hopes up, but she had already done some rough calculations, and if things worked out, she might finally be able to quit her cleaning clients to cook full-time.

Don't count your cupcakes until they rise, she reminded herself with a grin. But it was sure hard not to. Molly stirred a pot of seven-bean chili, a vegetarian entrée, and then checked the trays of beef empanadas and chicken pot pies that were baking in the oven.

Still feeling anxious, she went into the living room and glanced out the windows that overlooked Main Street. The snow was piling up out there. The forecast had predicted only flurries, but this was something more. Molly sighed. She had had enough snow this winter. When would it end? It was already the first week of March. She hoped this latest addition would melt quickly.

An SUV-style truck slowed down and parked across the street. It was Matthew's Land Rover. She watched him get out and head for the door to her building. Molly spun around and quickly surveyed the room. She found a pair of slippers, an empty glass, and a magazine on the floor. She dumped the glass in the sink and brought the rest to her bedroom. She quickly checked her appearance in the mirror, pulling off her apron and adding a dash of lipstick from the tube on her dresser.

She paused and took a deep breath. She was getting too nervous. Exactly what she didn't want to do. She would act relaxed and friendly to him, but she didn't want to seem too interested. After all, Matthew clearly wasn't interested in her. He hadn't called during the past week, and he'd had the perfect excuse as she'd left her cleaning bucket at his house. But Fran Tulley had called to say he had dropped off the bucket along with an extra check at Betty's office. To Molly, his leaving the things with Betty was an obvious message: He didn't want to get involved.

She knocked on Lauren's door before heading back to the kitchen. "Lauren,

Amanda . . . time to come out. Amanda's father is here to pick her up."

In the kitchen Jill looked up from her homework. "Is Daddy here?"

Molly shook her head as the doorbell rang. "It's Dr. Harding."

Then she turned and pulled open the door. Matthew smiled at her. His cheeks were red from the cold and his dark eyes were bright. Flecks of snow clung to his hair and coated his shoulders.

"Come on in," Molly greeted him. "You must be freezing."

"I'm all right. I'm used to the cold." He took off his gloves and rubbed his hands together. "Hello, Jill. How are you?"

"I'm good. Just doing homework. Do you know how to spell *cataclysmic*?"

"Hmm, that's a good one. I'm not really sure." He glanced at Molly with a helpless— and totally charming—smile. "Why don't you try the dictionary?"

"That's okay. I'll just say, 'It was really horrible.' "

"Right. And if you don't go into your room and get the dictionary, your grade on that story is going to be really 'horrible,' " Molly warned her.

"Okay, okay. I'm going." Jill sighed the- atrically and picked up her notebook.

"Don't mind her." Molly turned to check the chili. "She gets a little cranky when she's hungry."

"Don't we all. Low blood sugar," Matthew explained. "Gee, something sure smells good in here. What are you cooking?"

"Well, let's see . . . we have some vege- tarian chili up here." Molly gestured at the pot. "Some chicken and mushroom crepes in this pan, and beef empanadas and chicken pot pies in the oven." She pulled open the door and took a peek. "Oh, and some string beans to make sure there's something green."

Matthew stared at her wide-eyed, looking as if he wanted to laugh, but he wasn't sure if he should or not. "Quite a menu. Are you expecting company?"

"I have sort of an audition tomorrow. At the Beanery. They're expanding their lunch and dinner menus and asked me to bring some samples for new orders."

"Oh, I see. Well, everything smells so good, I can't see how you could miss."

"Thanks." Molly smiled at him and low- ered the heat on the oven. His expression peaked with interest, but he didn't say more. An awkward silence hung between them.

I'm sure I'll live to regret this, but what the heck, she thought glancing back at him.

"Would you like to stay for dinner? There's plenty here."

"Oh, no. We couldn't put you out like that. I wasn't hinting at an invitation," he added with a self-conscious grin.

"It's okay. I was going to ask you anyway. I need some more taste testers." That wasn't exactly true. But she was trying to make him welcome. "I can't trust anything the kids say unless the recipe involves pizza, peanut butter, or chocolate."

Matthew laughed. "Yes, the three major food groups as far as Amanda is concerned, too." He met her gaze again. "I'd be honored to be a taste tester. But I really don't want to impose on you, Molly."

"It's no trouble. You'd be doing me a favor, honestly," Molly insisted.

So much for her plan to act disinterested and not put herself out. But he looked hungry, and she really could use another adult opinion.

Oh, who was she kidding? She liked the

guy. More than she wanted, and here she was giving in to that feeling after promising herself that she wouldn't.

But Lauren and Amanda seemed to have hit it off so grandly, Molly thought. Whether she wanted to or not, she would be seeing a lot of Matthew Harding. It was probably smart to try to work out a friendly relationship. Even if it never amounted to more than that.

"Well, okay then." He sounded doubtful but was smiling. "I'd love to."

"Great." Molly glanced at the clock. "My ex-husband is coming at six to see the girls. I guess we'd better sit down right away."

"No problem, I'm starved. What can I do to help you?"

Matthew washed up, then set the table. Five was a tight fit in Molly's small kitchen, but it would work out all right, she decided. The Hardings weren't going to stay that long.

While Matthew rounded up the girls, Molly set the bowls and platters of the various dishes on the table, along with a green salad and a basket of hot cheese biscuits she had baked to go with the chili. She had taken a course in food presentation and tried to add a professional finishing touch, sprinkling finely chopped herbs on the platter rim.

She was pleased with the way the table looked and with Matthew's reaction. "Wow, it looks like a restaurant in here," he said, taking a seat across the table.

"A very small restaurant," Molly amended. She was about to sit down between Lauren and Jill when the phone rang. Before she could answer it, the answering machine picked up. "Hi Molly, it's me, Phil. I got stuck late at work, and the turnpike is creeping because of the snow—"

Here we go again, she thought tiredly.

Molly picked up as he spoke. "Hi, Phil. I heard your message. So I guess you're not coming tonight. Is that what you're trying to say?"

"It's my own fault. I got a late start. I didn't think the snow would be so heavy." He sounded sincerely apologetic and disappointed. "Tell the girls I'm really sorry about tonight, but I'll see them on the weekend, right?"

"Sure. That should work out." Molly had lots of baking to do again, so Phil's visit would be a help to her.

"Are they around? Can I say hello?"

"We just sat down to dinner. I'll have them call you later at home."

They said good-bye, and Molly hung up. As soon as she returned to the table, she realized everyone had overheard the conversation. Jill sat with a long face, suddenly looking too listless to eat. Lauren looked subdued as well, though not nearly as crushed as her younger sister.

"I guess you guys heard the news. Your father can't make it tonight. He got held up with the snow."

Lauren shrugged. "That's okay. I didn't want to go anyway with Amanda here."

"Will he come on Sunday?" Jill asked.

"He said so." Molly wished she could sound more definite, but she didn't think it was wise. What if he canceled again? It wouldn't surprise her.

Part of her felt vindicated for distrusting him, while another part felt upset for her daughters, especially Jill. The weather *was* bad though. Maybe Phil wasn't falling back into his old ways so quickly. She would just have to wait to see.

"You can call him after dinner," Molly added.

"I'm not that hungry. I'll call him now." Jill started to get up from the table, but Molly stopped her with a look. "We have guests, Jill. You can be excused when everyone is finished. Your father is still on the road. He won't be home for a while."

Jill sat sullenly, pushing chunks of the beef empanada around her dish with her fork. Molly felt embarrassed that Matthew had witnessed their little domestic drama but there was nothing she could do. She would need to talk with Jill alone later to soothe her hurt feelings. *See, it's already starting.* Molly sighed to herself.

"So how was school today, girls?" Matthew asked in a tone Molly thought determinedly bright. "How was chorus?"

"Mrs. Pickering drove us crazy," Lauren complained. "She made us sing the last bar of 'Oklahoma' about a million times. You know, that part when all the sections harmonize and get louder and louder. 'Oklahoma,   o-kay, o-kah-ay . . . *O-kaaaay!*' " Lauren stood up from her seat, singing, waving her arms, and getting carried away.

Molly blinked, watching her daughter's outflung arms narrowly miss Matthew's head. Luckily he ducked in time, quietly laughing.

"I remember!" Molly interrupted. "You don't have to give a live performance," she added, sharing a grin with Matthew.

"Then Cheryl Nielsen said she had to go, and Mrs. Pickering totally freaked. Cheryl acts like such a big diva and always misses practice even though she has a solo. And—" Lauren suddenly turned to Amanda. "Tell your dad what happened next."

Amanda seemed uncomfortable and wouldn't look at anyone. "You can tell," she said.

"No, *you.*" Lauren poked her friend with her elbow. "Go on."

Matt and Molly exchanged a curious glance. "What happened, honey?" Matt asked.

"It's no big deal," Amanda said, looking down at the table. "Mrs. Pickering got mad at Cheryl for talking back and said if she didn't stay, she couldn't sing the solo. It's in the finale, when we do this medley from *The Sound of Music.* Then Cheryl left anyway, so she picked me to do it."

"Wow! A solo part. That's wonderful. That's terrific news!" Matthew was beaming, and Molly felt happy for him. She wasn't surprised, though. Lauren said Amanda had a beautiful voice, despite her speech problem.

"When is that concert?" Molly asked. "Isn't it April something?"

"*Earth to Mom.* More like a week from Saturday?" Lauren reminded her tartly.

"Oops. I didn't realize it was so soon. Guess I'd better mark the calendar."

Matthew's eyebrows rose in surprise. "This is the first I've even heard about it. When were you going to tell me, Amanda? That day?"

Amanda gave him a casual shrug. "I just forgot. I wasn't even sure I'd be in the show since I just joined up."

"Well, sounds like you'll be there, front and center." Matthew paused and glanced at Molly. "Why don't we all go together, and I'll take everyone out to dinner after?"

Molly felt her expression freeze in shock and tried to quickly recover. "That sounds nice. But you don't have to take us out to dinner, Matt."

"I want to. I'd like to reciprocate for this . . . this absolute feast. I can't remember the last time I've eaten such delicious food. If the Beans don't hire you to cook truckloads of all this stuff, they're crazy, by the way. But I can't have you over to my house. I'm a terrible cook."

"He really is. You'd *better* let him buy," Amanda chirped up.

Lauren and Jill giggled. Matt looked about to reply then brushed it off. *I guess my feisty kids are rubbing off on Amanda,* Molly thought. *I hope he doesn't get annoyed.*

The girls talked more about the concert, and Matthew explained his frustrating delay in Southport regarding his privileges at the hospital. He'd thought that all the paperwork had been completed, and he would be able to sign in patients when necessary, but some form had been held up somewhere, and he'd spent the entire day there trying to figure it out.

"So finally, after about twenty phone calls back to my old hospital in Worcester, it was faxed over late this afternoon. I know I filled it out months ago."

"Sounds worse than the Registry of Motor Vehicles," Molly sympathized, but she was only half focused on the story. She couldn't stop thinking about his invitation to dinner next Saturday. The whole idea of it made her nervous—and excited. She started to reach for another biscuit, then folded her hands in her lap. *Get a grip,* she told herself. *The diet starts now.*

Don't make too much of this, she warned herself. *It's not a date. Not even close. He was just being friendly and polite, probably because he hasn't made any friends in town yet. And once he starts meeting people, he won't want to socialize with you. He's more the type for the other side of town, where Dr. Elliot and the Warwicks live.*

Matthew sat back and wiped his mouth with his napkin. "I know I said it before but I have to repeat myself. That was absolutely delicious, Molly."

Molly felt her cheeks flush. "Thanks. Glad you could join us." She rose to start clearing the dishes, but Matthew stood up and began clearing off the table, too.

"You sit. I'll clean up," he said.

Molly wasn't used to anyone telling her to relax and not work. She just couldn't do it.

"That's all right. It's getting late. The snow has stopped. You must be eager to get home."

"It's not late at all and I insist. I'm not going to freeload, then leave you with a huge mess to clean up."

I never met a man who didn't, she was tempted to reply.

But she didn't say anything, distracted suddenly by the sight of Matthew yanking off his expensive-looking silk tie and rolling up his shirt sleeves. He looked even more attractive somehow. It was downright annoying.

"If you're done with dinner, bring your dishes to the sink," he told the girls.

Molly picked up the dishes of leftovers to be stored away. "Did you guys finish your homework? I heard a lot of giggling in there before," she said to Amanda and Lauren.

"We didn't *exactly* finish," Lauren said. She and Amanda exchanged a secret glance, trying not to start giggling again.

"Why don't you get back to work?" Matt suggested. "We'll call you when we're done."

Jill brought her dish to the sink. "I'm going to call Daddy now," she said quietly.

"Sure, that's okay. The number is on the fridge," Molly told her.

"I know the number." Jill turned and headed for the phone in Molly's bedroom.

Molly sighed, and Matt glanced at her. "I guess she's disappointed that she didn't see her father," he said quietly. "Does he visit them regularly?"

"Not really," Molly murmured. "Well, he says now he wants to. But this is only the second time after a long break, and he's already messing things up again."

She didn't know Matthew that well. She didn't know him at all really. She felt upset about Phil but wasn't sure if she should confide in Matt.

"The snow really was heavy. I had trouble myself on the turnpike."

"I know. And I think he was telling the truth. But I hate to see the girls get their hopes up, thinking he's going to be a real father to them again and having it all come to nothing. I'd rather he didn't see them at all. I guess that sounds awful of me, doesn't it?"

Matthew wiped a dish with a soapy sponge. "You don't want to see them get hurt. I understand. I'm that way with Amanda. I get so overprotective . . . too much, sometimes. But it's hard not to be. You feel for them. It's only natural." He set the dish on the drain board and picked up another. "How long have you been divorced?"

"About seven years. We were married young. Things were always rocky between us. Then he met someone else. So we split up." Molly turned her back so Matthew couldn't see her expression.

Matthew didn't say anything for a moment. He rinsed off a dish and set it on the drain board. "What happened then? Did he remarry?"

Molly shook her head. "His fling didn't last that long. Just a way to get out of our marriage, I guess. He's still single. Moves around a lot. Changes his job a lot, too. He hasn't helped out much supporting the girls. He's around for a few months, then disappears. He always has some excuse when he comes back and makes big promises. The girls want to see him, so it's hard to say no."

"That's tough on you, too. I'm sure you don't want to be the bad guy and keep them away from their father."

"Tell me about it. Sometimes I think I should wear a T-shirt that reads, 'Big Mean Mom.' "

Matthew laughed. "I think you've got

something there. You could sell a lot of those. Some that read, 'Big Mean Dad,' too, of course."

"I could have used one this Sunday. Phil showed up unannounced. I didn't even want the girls to know he was here, but they saw him and that was that." She took out a container of cookies and arranged them on a dish. "I'm just afraid he's going to pull his famous disappearing act again."

"It sounds like you're in a tough spot. But I think you're doing the right thing. Even if he does disappear again, at least you gave him a chance. You showed charity." Matthew glanced at her over his shoulder. "Jill and Lauren will remember that. I don't think you'll regret it."

"Thanks. I hope you're right."

Molly started a pot of coffee, and Matthew turned back to the dishes. "You're a good mother, Molly. You've done a great job with Jill and Lauren. You should be proud."

"I am proud of them," she said honestly.

Still his compliment didn't sit that easily with her. She knew that there were so many times when she showed the girls exactly the wrong example. Especially when it came to Phil. By now, she should have for-given and forgotten all the slights, large and small, that had broken up their marriage. But the sore spots had never really healed, only covered over.

"So, how do you like Cape Light?" she asked, hoping to shift the conversation to less personal matters.

"So far so good. I'm really pleased to see Amanda adjusting so well to school. She's naturally shy, I guess, and her speech prob-lem makes it even harder. She's had a lot of speech therapy, but it never resolves com-pletely."

"That's too bad," Molly said sympatheti-cally. "I hardly noticed it, actually. It's great that she likes chorus. Lauren says she has a beautiful voice."

Matthew smiled. "She really does. I think you'll be surprised." His expression grew more serious. "I can't tell you how happy I am that she joined up. It must have to do with Lauren. She joined at her last school, then dropped out. She wouldn't say why, but she's always so tough on herself. Amanda has . . . well, perfectionist tenden-cies. I'm trying to encourage her to open up, to relax about life a little."

"It's hard for kids at that age. They're so self-conscious. If Lauren wakes up with a blemish, you'd think it was a world crisis. She actually begs me to let her stay home from school."

"Oh, yeah. I've heard that zit emergency myself. But this is different." He paused, and Molly sensed he was deciding whether to confide some deeper issue.

"My wife, Sharon . . . she was a good mother, don't get me wrong. But she could never really accept Amanda's speech problem. She could never just let it go. Sometimes I felt when she looked at Amanda that was all Sharon saw: that she stuttered when she was nervous. Not how bright and sweet and beautiful she is." He sighed and shook his head.

Molly didn't know what to say. She had imagined Matthew being married to someone who was perfect in every way. It was surprising to hear his wife had shortcomings and also to learn there had been friction in his marriage.

"I'm not sure how I would handle a situation like that," Molly admitted. "I guess there's a fine line between trying to solve the problem and paying too much attention to it."

"That was just it. Sharon kept finding new therapists, new treatments. I know she really believed she was just helping Amanda. But she couldn't see how she was hurting her at the same time. It made Amanda feel like something was horribly wrong with her. As if she wasn't good enough just the way she is."

Molly's heart went out to him. He loved his daughter so much. Strangely, she found she could also relate to Amanda, feeling she'd always been judged by her shortcomings and never her talents.

"I know this might sound a little crazy, but sometimes I think God sent Amanda into my life for a reason. She's made me a better person . . . and a better doctor. I think she's perfect just the way she is. I tell her that all the time. But I know she doesn't believe me."

Molly knew that feeling, too. If someone gave her even the slightest compliment, she couldn't help but contradict them.

"Keep telling her. Someday she'll believe you," Molly advised him.

Matthew stood drying his hands on a

towel. He gazed at her and smiled. His warm brown eyes held a tender light. Molly wanted to look away, but she just couldn't quite. She felt a tug of attraction. Foolish, she told herself, but undeniable.

Lauren and Amanda ran into the kitchen. "We're finished with our homework, and we definitely need cookies. Please," Lauren announced looking around. She spotted the dish of cookies on the table and headed for it like a chocolate-seeking missile.

"She's part shark, I swear. She has the most amazing sense of smell," Molly said in amazement.

"My mom made these. They're awesome," Lauren promised, handing one to Amanda.

"They do look awesome," Matt agreed. He started to reach for a cookie then stopped, staring at Amanda.

"What happened to your fingernails?"

Molly looked, too. Lauren and Amanda had pasted on fake nails and painted them alternating shades of sparkle blue, lilac, and silver.

"They're just for fun." Amanda stared up at her father with a wary expression. "I think they look cool."

"They come off with a little nail-polish re-mover," Molly explained. Matthew looked relieved but still disturbed. "They'll probably fall off while she's sleeping," she added.

"With any luck," he said, giving the daz-zling fingernails a resigned look.

"Would you like some coffee?" Molly asked politely.

"Yes, please." He nodded, unsmiling. The girls were uncharacteristically silent, munch-ing mechanically on their cookies.

"Milk and sugar?" He nodded again, and she stirred some in. "How about some nail-polish remover?"

He stared at her for a moment, then his face broke into a grin. She heard the girls laughing and hoped he didn't mind the joke at his expense.

"If you have an extra bottle, I'll take it to go."

"No problem." She set the mugs of coffee on the table and poured glasses of milk for the girls, then joined them at the table where the pile of cookies was rapidly dimin-ishing.

Jill walked in, sat at her place, and took a cookie. She seemed to be in a better mood,

Molly noticed. Her chat with Phil had definitely cheered her up.

A few minutes later, Matthew and Amanda were putting on their coats and saying good night. "Thanks again for dinner, Molly. And for picking up Amanda. Sounds like there's going to be a lot of chorus practice next week. Why don't we share the driving?"

"That would be a big help," Molly replied honestly.

"I'll call you tomorrow and we'll figure it out."

"Okay. Let me give you my cell-phone number. I'm always running around." Molly took one of her business cards from the basket near the phone and handed it to him.

" 'Molly to the Rescue. Cleaning, cooking, errands, and more,' " he read aloud. He looked up at her and smiled. "Not to mention the awesome cookies and sage advice."

"There's just so much you can get on a card," she said wryly. "Oh wait. Don't forget this." She grabbed the bottle of polish remover that Lauren had retrieved from the bathroom and handed it to him. He slipped it in his pocket, his eyes flashing appreciation.

They said good night again, and she closed the door.

So he was going to call her tomorrow. She'd be recharging the cell-phone battery tonight, that was for sure.

Tucker let himself in through the side door and paused in the mudroom to pull off his wet boots, hat, and jacket.

"Tucker? I was wondering when you'd be home." Fran came out of the family room to meet him. "Why didn't you call?"

"I left a message on the machine. Didn't you get it?" He kissed her cheek.

"You said you'd be a little late. It's after *ten.*"

"That late already? I didn't realize." Tucker walked into the kitchen, and Fran followed. "Are the kids in bed?"

"Michael's still doing homework, but Mary Ellen just shut off her light." Fran watched as he sat down at the table and stretched out his legs. Tucker's dog, Scout, trotted over and licked his hand. Tucker scratched his soft head.

"I saved some dinner for you. Would you like me to heat it?"

"That's okay. I grabbed something on the road."

"How about a cup of tea? I was just going to make some. You must feel chilled from the cold."

"A cup of tea sounds good. I'll have some with you."

Tucker knew Fran was wondering where he'd been all night. Well, he had nothing to hide. "I went down to Southport to visit Carl again."

He watched her expression as she filled the kettle and set it on the stove. "I had a feeling that's where you were. Why didn't you tell me?"

Tucker shrugged. "I don't know. I didn't really plan on going to see him. But I had to drive down to Hamilton at the end of the day to interview a witness on a hit-and-run. So I was halfway there anyway."

Fran didn't reply. Tucker could tell from her expression that it bothered her to hear he'd been visiting Carl. Well, he couldn't help that. He could visit his brother in the hospital if he wanted to. He didn't need Fran's permission.

The kettle's shrill whistle broke into his thoughts. He watched Fran pour the water into two mugs, place them on the table, then sit down in her usual chair.

Neither spoke for a moment. Fran stirred some sugar into her tea. "So, how is he coming along? You never even told me what is wrong with him," she said.

He hadn't told her, Tucker realized. Mainly because, so far, he hadn't gone into much detail about Carl; it seemed a subject best avoided.

"Well, let's see. He's in pretty bad shape. He has emphysema, a collapsed lung, an ulcer, high-blood pressure, phlebitis, and a touch of diabetes."

"That's too bad. Has he improved at all since the reverend found him?"

"A little. He looks better, and they've pulled a few tubes out of him." Tucker blew on his tea and took a sip. He wondered what Fran was thinking. She didn't look happy; her pretty face was drawn into a tight frown.

"You must feel sorry for him. It's only natural."

"Of course, I feel sorry for him. Don't you?"

"Yes, of course, I do." She looked up at him, her brown eyes open wide. "But he never took care of himself. He never lived a normal life. Now he's facing the consequences, I guess."

Tucker sighed. "Some people just don't fit with a normal life. I see it all the time. You can't really blame them. That's just the way it is."

"I wasn't blaming him, exactly." Fran looked away and sipped her tea. "When will they let him out of the hospital? Did his doctor say?"

"He'll be released on Monday. You know how it is. They don't keep you very long in a hospital these days, no matter what's wrong with you."

There was a basket of clean laundry on one of the kitchen chairs. Fran came to her feet and started folding the clothes. "What are his plans? Is he still going up to Portland? Maybe that friend of his has a job up there for him." Fran matched a pair of socks and rolled them into a tight ball. "You'll have to give him some money, I guess."

"I thought I'd give him some," Tucker replied. "But I'm not so sure now what to do."

Fran stared at him curiously, a bath towel

dangling from her hand. "What to do? What do you mean, Tucker?"

"The doctor says he's still pretty sick. Not well enough to work or travel around. I thought we should let him stay here a while. In the spare room. Just until he gets back on his feet."

Fran's eyes widened in dismay. "Stay here? But he's been in jail, Tucker. He *killed* a man."

"That was an accident, self-defense. You know that." Tucker tried to catch her eye, but she wouldn't look at him. "I'm surprised at you, Fran. I thought you'd be more sympathetic to the poor guy. You've been running all over town for the past month collecting food for poor people. Well, now's your chance to really help someone who's down on his luck. Not just give him a few free cans of soup."

Fran's fair skin turned a mottled pink color. "That's not fair! One thing has nothing to do with the other. It's not that I don't feel sorry for Carl. I do. But he scares me, Tucker. He killed a man, and you're talking about bringing him into the house with our children."

"Come on, he's not going to hurt anybody. Carl's not like that. He's my brother, for goodness' sake."

"One that you haven't seen in over twenty years. He's been in jail a good part of his life and up to God-only-knows-what since. We don't know him anymore. We don't know what he's like."

Tucker pushed back from the table. He wasn't used to arguing with Fran. They hardly ever disagreed. He was tired from work and driving in the snow. He didn't want to say something he'd regret, but he could feel his patience unraveling.

"Can't you make other arrangements?" Fran pressed him. "There are agencies and public programs and all sorts of places that can take him in."

Tucker had looked into the alternatives, but they all seemed too grim. Too cruel. He knew how dangerous the shelters were. Most homeless people desperately avoided them. Besides, Carl was too sick now for any of those places.

"Even if I could get him into a shelter that was halfway decent, he wouldn't stay. He'd find a way out and start hitching rides again, living hand-to-mouth until who knows what happens."

Fran shook out a T-shirt and laid it flat on the table to fold. "He's been living that way for years, as far as I can see. Do you think a few days in our guest room is really going to change him?"

"I'm not trying to change him," Tucker assured her. "I just want to help him get back on his feet. I'm not thrilled to have him here, either. But there really isn't any place else he can go. Not until his health improves. I've looked into this, Fran. I really have. If there was some other way, I'd do it."

He watched her pick up a white handkerchief and fold it into a neat square. Her face was drawn into a tight expression.

"Come on, Fran. You're blowing this way out of proportion. I don't see that it's such a great imposition. It will only be for a few days. You'll hardly know he's around."

"Of course, I'll know he's around." Fran sat down at the table again and held his gaze. "I just feel as if your mind is already made up. You're going to do this no matter what I say. My feelings about it don't really matter to you."

Tucker sighed, feeling tired and frustrated. Still, he couldn't deny Fran's point. Driving home from Southport tonight, he'd considered the options and had pretty much decided to take Carl in. He just hadn't figured on Fran opposing him so strongly.

"I'm in a tough spot, Fran. I wish you could be a little more understanding. I'm asking for some patience. For my part, I wish the guy had never come back. But he did and he's here and I feel obligated to help him."

"Because?"

"Because the alternative is that I turn my back and get a call in a week or a month or whenever saying that he's been found dead somewhere and I didn't help him. Now that's something I just couldn't live with."

Tucker had been careful not to raise his voice. But the look on Fran's face made him feel as if he had all the same.

He stood up from the table. His shoulders felt stiff from too much driving, and he rubbed the back of his neck.

Fran looked up at him, then just shook her head. "Will you at least think about it a little more? Make a few more calls to places that would take him? There's probably a social worker at the hospital you can talk to. I'll call if you want me to."

He took a deep breath and then another,

trying to use a stress-management technique he'd learned at work. Fran was quiet but doggedly persistent when she wanted something. Maybe that was why she was such a good salesperson.

"All right. I'll make a few more calls. I'll try to track down the hospital social worker. But I'm not so sure I'll come to any new conclusions on this, Fran." When she didn't answer or look up at him, he said, "I'm going upstairs. I have an early day tomorrow. Are you coming?"

She glanced at him briefly and shook her head. "I need to put the laundry away first. I'll be up in a while."

"Okay, then. Good night." He leaned over and kissed her cheek, but she didn't kiss him back.

It was going to be difficult around here for a while, Tucker thought as he climbed up the stairs. Carl wouldn't shower him with gratitude, that was for sure. And now he and Fran were at odds as well.

He'd made up his mind on the long drive home tonight that the only thing to do was take Carl in. Now he wondered if it was the right choice after all.

CHAPTER FIVE

Tucker sat near the back of the church, on the pulpit side, with Michael and Mary Ellen beside him. Fran didn't like to miss church, but she had to show houses today to a couple from out of town, and she had raced out to meet them at the train station while he and the kids were still eating breakfast.

The voices of the choir soared as they sang "Amazing Grace." The hymn was one of his favorites, but for some reason, the familiar lyrics failed to touch him this morning. Tucker's mind wandered, chewing over the same question about Carl and still feeling unsatisfied with the answer. Carl would be released from the hospital tomorrow, and a social worker had found him a space at a homeless shelter, a place run by a church down in Beverly. Tucker knew the shelter and didn't think it was so awful. A far cry from the comfort of his own guest room, but maybe not too bad for a guy like Carl.

He hadn't seen Carl since Thursday night so he couldn't say if his brother really planned on staying there or had only agreed to go in order to get released from the hospital. Maybe he didn't really want to know, Tucker realized. He'd told Fran on Friday night after dinner about his talk with the social worker and about Carl's plans.

She hadn't said anything at first. Then she dipped her head and said, "Well, that's good news, I guess. Maybe we could send him a care package or something. Some books and things he might need."

Her well-meaning suggestion had irritated him. Carl needed to rest up some place more hospitable than a shelter, Tucker thought. He didn't need chewing gum and a new package of handkerchiefs; he needed a good bed and a private room and some home-cooked food. But the look of sheer relief on Fran's face made it hard to open up the discussion all over again. She was genuinely afraid of Carl, no doubt about it, though it seemed clear to Tucker there was no reason in the world she should be.

Maybe it was just as well that Carl went to the shelter, that they didn't get any more involved, he had finally decided. Though that was back on Friday, and now, not even three days later, the decision didn't sit well with him, like something he'd eaten that just wouldn't go down.

Tucker focused again on the service. The Scripture readings had concluded, and Reverend Ben had started his sermon. Tucker shifted uncomfortably in his seat as he realized that today's Gospel was the familiar parable of the Good Samaritan.

"What is the reason Jesus even tells this story? He is first asked a question." Reverend Ben glanced down at the open Bible on his pulpit. " 'What shall I do to inherit eternal life?' " he read aloud. He looked out at the congregation again.

"In other words: How do we get to heaven? What do we need to do? Fair enough questions, I think. Jesus first answers that you must do two things: love God with all your heart and love your neighbor as yourself. Simple enough, you might think.

"But then the same man asks, 'Who is my neighbor?' " Reverend Ben paused, his gaze sweeping over his audience. "So in answer to this question Jesus tells the story of the Good Samaritan. A traveler is attacked by thieves and left on the roadside between Jerusalem and Jericho, half dead. Two men pass him, one of them a priest. Neither of them shows compassion or charity, neither of them stops to even see if the wounded man is still alive. Callous and indifferent, they move to the other side of the road.

"Then the Samaritan comes along. He binds the man's wounds and takes him to an inn, even though it means he has to walk while the wounded man rides. He then gives the innkeeper money, promising to pay for everything while the man recovers."

The reverend paused as if to let the words sink in.

"Is this wounded man a relative of the Samaritan? Is it his friend or someone from his town? No, of course not. The man is unknown to him, a traveler from Jerusalem, we are told. Yet, the Samaritan does what is necessary. He makes an effort, physically, financially, even emotionally, one might surmise. He puts himself out for this stranger. He doesn't fall back on all the excuses that seem to come so easily when we find ourselves in a similar situation. You know what I mean. We all do it, myself included." The reverend glanced around. " 'I'd like to help this man, but if I stop, I'll be late for my appointment. I really can't bother this time. Next time, I'll help.' Or, 'I don't really have much money myself right now. Someone else with more will probably help.' And here's a good one: 'Gee, I feel badly for the poor man, but what kind of person gets themselves into such a state? He should have known better than to drink, to gamble, to take drugs, to lose his job.' I'm sure you can fill in the blanks. 'I'd never get myself into a jam like that,' we tell ourselves. 'He pretty much got what he deserved.' "

Tucker sat up and crossed his arms over his chest. He felt his cheeks flush. He knew Reverend Ben hadn't written this sermon to send a message just to him—but it was starting to feel that way.

"Does the Samaritan ask the wounded traveler any questions? Does he try to figure out if the man is worthy of his aid? No. He finds a man in distress and immediately takes care of him. And so we find, at the end of the story, Jesus asks, 'Which now of these three, thinkest thou, was a neighbor onto him that fell among the thieves?' And of course the answer is, 'He that showed mercy on him.'

"So this then is the notion of a neighbor as set forth in this passage. A neighbor is the wounded one we find on the roadside, the one in distress who needs our aid without questions or judgments. Who needs our mercy . . ."

The reverend continued but Tucker stared down at the floor, hardly hearing another word. All through the story, he saw Carl's face on the wounded traveler. But he couldn't cast himself as the Samaritan. No, he was one of the men who had passed to the other side of the road. Or, rather, was just about to, he realized.

On Monday morning Tucker checked in at the station house, took care of some paperwork, then prepared to go out on patrol.

Just before leaving, he stopped in to see his boss, Chief Jim Sanborn.

"I need a few hours of personal time today, Chief. Say from about eleven to two?"

"Dentist appointment?" Jim glanced up at him and grinned.

"I wish. I'd rather have a root canal than sort out this piece of business."

The chief looked at him quizzically, then turned back to the papers on his desk. "Sure thing. Just tell Nelson at the desk so he knows you're off duty."

Tucker felt jumpy all morning but focused on his work. He was assigned to a speed trap near the elementary school. He ticketed a teenage girl flying through the stop sign and later stopped a guy in a panel truck doing close to sixty through the school zone. Tucker smelled the alcohol on his breath as soon as the trucker rolled down his window.

Tucker felt satisfied taking a drunk driver off the road. He had seen enough car wrecks to know that in a small but significant way, he had made the world a little safer today. But overall, day to day and hour to hour, he couldn't say he faced his job with the same eagerness he had felt years ago.

He'd never minded being a cop in a small town where the night police report often didn't amount to anything more ominous than raccoons rattling garbage cans. Lately, though, he'd felt restless. Bored perhaps by the sheer routine of ticketing traffic violations or taking down car-accident reports. He'd been on the force almost twenty years now and would qualify for early retirement in two more. He was starting to think he might be ready to quit the force by then, to do something else with his life, though he wasn't sure quite what. Being a policeman was all he'd ever really wanted to do. It was all he really knew.

At eleven o'clock he radioed the station that he was going off duty. With a sigh of resignation, he drove up to the turnpike and headed for Southport.

He wasn't sure why or how, but he had somehow decided to drive to Southport and see if Carl would come home with him. He thought about calling Fran at the real-estate office to give her some warning. *No,* he decided. *Better wait to see what Carl says.*

Despite his talk with the social worker last week and despite telling Fran that Carl was going to Beverly, Tucker had been see-sawing in his mind all weekend about the situation. Sunday morning in church, though, was what ended the indecision. Reverend Ben's sermon had gotten to him.

Tucker reached the hospital at half past twelve. As he crossed the lobby, the elevator doors opened, and he spotted his brother being wheeled out of the elevator by a nurse. Dressed in ill-fitting secondhand clothes, Carl held a bunched-up plastic bag and a new set of crutches across his knees. *All he has in the world in his lap,* Tucker thought.

Tucker hurried to catch up with the wheelchair, aware that if he had been a minute later, he would have missed him. He wasn't sure if that was a lucky break or an unlucky one. Carl saw him and a bitter expression came into his eyes.

"What are you doing here?" Carl demanded. "Can't you give me some peace?"

"Simmer down. Just let me talk to the nurse."

The nurse pushing Carl looked Tucker

over. "Are you here to pick up the patient, Officer?"

"That's right. I'm his brother," Tucker said. "Do I need to sign something?"

"Mr. Jones has to sign," the nurse told him.

"Hold up, here. I didn't give him permission to pick me up," Carl told the nurse. "You don't have to do what he says because he's wearing that uniform."

The nurse looked confused. She checked her clipboard, then looked up at Tucker. "The social worker has made arrangements for Mr. Jones to be transported to a shelter in Lowell. A van is coming soon to take him there."

"Lowell? I thought he was going to Beverly."

"There wasn't any room in Beverly. My travel agent had to switch my reservations." Carl smiled slyly at him.

Tucker didn't answer. The shelter in Lowell was awful, a real pit. If he'd had any doubts at all about taking Carl in, this clinched it. "Lowell is hours from here," Tucker said finally.

"What's the difference? You worried about visiting me or something?" Carl laughed, then coughed into his hand. "I've been to worse places than Lowell, believe me."

Tucker did believe him. That was half the trouble.

He paused for a moment, realizing that if he just let Carl go, all his problems would be solved. Carl hadn't asked him for his help. Quite the opposite. He was his usual surly, ungrateful self. But finally, Tucker just couldn't do it.

"You don't have to go there, Carl. You can stay at my house for awhile in the spare room."

"Your house?" Carl shook his head. "That's not for me. What do you think you're doing anyway? Swooping in here like Superman, saving the day? You make me laugh, Tucker."

Tucker glanced at the nurse. "Will you excuse us a minute while we talk?" She nodded knowingly and walked toward the front desk.

"Stop arguing with me," Tucker said wearily. "It's a long drive back, and I don't have that much time. Now just sign the paper and let's get out of here."

"I know why you're doing this, Tucker.

You can't fool me. You just feel guilty. Too much church, that was always your problem. You'd be just as happy to see the back of me than set me up in your spare room. Isn't that right?"

Tucker folded his arms across his chest. "Yeah, that's right. I'm not going to lie to you. But you have no money and nowhere to go, and the doctor says you're too sick to get a job or even travel. So either I can drive you to my house and give you a clean, comfortable bed and three meals a day or you can get on that van and go to Lowell," he stated bluntly. "What's it going to be?"

Carl stared straight ahead, his jaw set and a blank look on his ravaged face. He gripped his bag tighter. For a moment, Tucker thought he might choose the shelter just to spite him.

"All right," Carl said finally. "But I'm not staying long. A few days. Just until I get my second wind and this darn leg gets better."

"That's all I'm inviting you for. Just until you can travel," Tucker agreed, though he was sure it would take more than a few days.

"I'm due in Portland, you know. My friend is waiting for me."

"I know, I've heard all about it." Tucker wheeled Carl over to the information desk and found the nurse with Carl's release form. Carl scrawled his name in the designated places and grumbled his thanks to her good wishes.

"I don't need this chair. I can walk out of here on my own," Carl complained as Tucker pushed him.

Right, that's why they gave you crutches as a going-away present. Because you're ready for the Boston Marathon, Tucker was tempted to reply.

He looked down at Carl. "It's an insurance thing. They don't want you to slip in the lobby and sue somebody."

Out in front of the hospital, he left Carl sitting in the wheelchair in the patient pick-up zone and went to get his car. As he drove back, he spotted Carl from a distance, huddled into his worn clothes, clutching the crutches and the plastic bag. He might have been a stranger, Tucker thought, the kind you don't want to look at too long. Tucker felt a twist in his stomach. His brother was a pathetic sight, a ruined man.

Tucker took the bags and helped Carl out of the wheelchair.

"Nice wheels," Carl said, nodding at the patrol car. "Don't you want to read me my rights before I get in?"

Tucker ignored him and stashed the crutches and folded wheelchair in the trunk.

"You might be more comfortable in the back. You can stretch out your leg," Tucker suggested.

"Yeah, I usually ride in the back of these taxis," Carl replied. "Cops don't invite guys like me into the front seat very often."

Tucker could well imagine his brother's many rides in police cars. He opened the back door without comment, and Carl hobbled over and fit himself inside. He clamped his jaw down hard as he settled in, and Tucker knew he was in pain.

As Tucker began the drive back to Cape Light, the only sound was the police radio with the volume turned low. Carl was quiet, and Tucker thought he had fallen asleep until he glanced into the rearview mirror and saw that Carl was wide awake, staring straight ahead.

"This spare room of yours, is it up in the attic?" Carl asked.

"On the first floor. It's half of the two-car garage. There's no climbing. You've got a bed, a dresser, and a little table with a TV. There's a bathroom with a shower there, too. Fran's mother uses it when she stays over."

"Great. I bet it even has wallpaper with little flowers," Carl grumbled.

"Yeah, there's wallpaper. And wall-to-wall carpet," Tucker noted.

"Just like the Copley Plaza Hotel. Remember when I brought you there?"

Carl's hard living had scrambled his brains, Tucker thought. Then he did remember. Carl was right.

"Yeah, I do. My wedding night," Tucker said.

He and Fran stayed at the Copley Plaza on the first night of their honeymoon, before they left for Bermuda. It was one of the best hotels in Boston. Charlie Bates had been best man, but Carl was the one who had driven them into the city after the wedding. Tucker had been just a rookie cop then, fresh out of the academy. Carl had already lost his lobster fishing permit, his life quickly sliding downhill.

Funny to think of that now, all things considered.

*   *   *

Thursday night's snowfall was nearly melted, a sure sign that spring wasn't that far off, Molly thought. Unmindful of the slushy pavement beneath her high-heeled boots, Molly nearly skipped up the path to Betty's real-estate office. She stepped inside and found Fran Tulley working at her computer. Fran looked up when Molly entered, greeting her with a wan smile.

"Are you here for your bucket? I think it's in the back. Betty has that extra check for you from Dr. Harding."

"Oh, that. I nearly forgot."

"He was certainly singing your praises," Fran added. "He would be a good client for you, Molly."

"I might be phasing out the cleaning business soon," Molly announced breathlessly. "But I can recommend someone. Is Betty here?"

"She's in her office. You can just go on back." Fran looked at her curiously.

Molly knocked on Betty's half-open door, then walked in.

Betty was on a phone call, but she quickly excused herself and hung up the phone. "So? How did it go? Did you get the order?"

Molly nodded and couldn't help but smile. "It's a whopper, as we say in the business."

Betty leaned back in her bouncy leather chair and clapped her hands together. "Bravo! The Spoon Harbor Inn, that's a big deal around here. You've got quite the client list now."

"I wouldn't exactly call it a *list,*" Molly hedged. "More like a little lump of clients at this point."

"A list, a lump. What's the difference? You're really on a roll. So what about the cleaning business?"

Molly had mentioned to Betty last night that if she got a good order from the Spoon River Inn, in addition to last week's new order from the Beanery, she might be able to phase out house cleaning. But now that she had the order in hand, she was definitely getting cold feet.

"I'm not sure about that yet. I really have to rework the figures and check my expenses." Molly slipped off her good wool coat and left it folded on a chair. She wore black wool pants that she liked because

she thought they made her look considerably slimmer and a turquoise-blue sweater
set the girls had given her for Christmas. It
was her favorite appointment outfit and also
the only one she had in her closet.

"What about that money from Phil? That
should help right about now." Betty sat up,
talking excitedly, a bunch of gold bracelets
on her arm jangling as she gestured. "You
really need to take the leap, kiddo. You're
definitely ready."

Molly sighed. She knew Betty was right.
It was a now-or-never kind of moment when
you got right down to it.

"Well, timewise it looks as if something's
got to give," she admitted. "If I don't give up
the cleaning, I won't have enough time to
do the cooking and deliveries. So I guess I'll
have to give up cleaning in the next week or
so."

"Molly, that's great news." Betty popped
out of her chair and gave Molly a big hug.
"I'm so happy for you. I was hoping you'd
make this kind of change."

"I've been thinking about it for a while.
You know that."

And meeting Matthew had pushed her
over the edge, Molly admitted to herself.

Last week, when she'd first met him, she didn't want to tell him she cleaned houses for a living. It was odd; she'd never felt embarrassed about her work before. Even if nothing more came of their relationship, she'd always have him to thank for that sudden moment of motivation.

"I only hope I can get all this work done. I've bitten off a real big chunk here. I'm not sure I can do it."

"You have to hire a helper. This is just what I've been telling you. You're at the next level. You have to grow the business."

Molly laughed. "Thanks, but I don't think I qualify yet for business-school lingo."

"Of course you do," Betty insisted. "If you start thinking of your efforts as a real business, it will *be* a real business."

"How can I afford to hire someone? It's going to be a stretch just to stock up on all the ingredients."

"Find a teenager. You can afford that. Call up the high school. They have a list of kids who want part-time jobs. If you have some help, you can really increase your output and pay the helper from the profits, which should be double," Betty advised smoothly. "If it doesn't work out, you can cut back again. But it will work out. I feel really good about this, Molly. You're making a big move."

"I guess so." Molly had arrived feeling elated with her news, but now that they were discussing the practicalities, she felt a little overwhelmed. "I don't mean to sound like a wimp, but I'm scared. I don't know if I can do this. Maybe I should cancel the orders. . . ."

"Don't be silly." Betty put a settling hand on her shoulder. "Of course you can do it. You have to do it," she insisted. "If you want your life to be different, you have to make some changes, Molly. If you keep doing what you always do, you'll just get what you've already got."

"Who said that? Benjamin Franklin?"

Betty shook her head and smiled. "Another great American philosopher. Ann Landers. Oh, I nearly forgot. Speaking of profits, I have a check for you from that doctor. He couldn't stop talking about you. What did you do to that man?"

Molly felt herself blushing. "I just organized his kitchen, for goodness' sake. Besides, if he were really interested in me, he could have called and dropped the check at my house. He didn't have to leave it here."

"Some men are a little backward. They outsmart themselves. You know that. He may have dropped the check off here just because he *is* interested."

Molly did know. That was just the problem. Men were so convoluted sometimes. It hardly seemed worth the effort it took to figure them out. Molly bit her lip. She did want to talk to Betty about Matthew; she was dying to, actually. But she didn't want to make too big a deal about it. She could think of a thousand reasons why she wasn't right for him and it wouldn't work out. It was better not to get her hopes up, she thought.

"You could still hear from him. You never know," Betty said breezily.

That did it. Molly couldn't hold back anymore.

"I saw him last week. Thursday night. Lauren made friends with his daughter, so he came by to pick her up and ended up staying for dinner. You know, with the snow and all."

Betty's eyebrows went up in a knowing expression. "There wasn't *that* much snow."

"It was nothing. Just a last-minute invita-

tion. But the girls are going to be in a chorus concert on Saturday, so he asked me to
go with him . . . and we're all going out for
dinner after." She saw Betty's eyes brighten
at the news and quickly tried to discourage
her. "But it's not a date or anything, Betty.
Honestly. He's glad Amanda made a friend,
and he's just trying to be nice."

"Nobody's that nice, Molly. He wants to
spend time with you."

"It's not like that, really. Maybe he likes
me as a friend, but I don't think it's anything
more than that. He still misses his wife. And
I'm really not his type."

"Okay, it's nothing." Betty shook her head
and raised her hands in a sign of surrender.
But Molly knew her well. She could tell from
the soft expression on Betty's face that she
sensed her real dilemma about Matthew.
Molly was afraid. She had finally met a man
she really liked, but what if he didn't like
her? What if he didn't think she was good
enough for him? That would really hurt, and
she didn't want to get hurt anymore.

"So, I know it's not a date. But what are
you going to wear?"

Molly sighed, surveying her friend's slim

figure. "Hopefully something that makes me look ten pounds thinner."

"Molly, please. You have a great figure. Haven't you heard? Real women have curves."

"Yeah, they don't get more real than me." Molly smiled in spite of herself.

The phone rang, and Betty took the call.

Molly sat back, thinking that Betty was full of perky little sayings today. Not surprising from a former head cheerleader and high-school class president. Betty always managed to find a positive side to a problem and hardly ever seemed to let life get her down. Not that her success had been achieved without setbacks and hard work.

Maybe I should pipe down and listen more to Betty, Molly thought. *I could learn a lot from her.*

Betty hung up the phone and checked her slim gold watch. "Lunch time. Want to grab a bite?"

"Sure." Molly picked up her coat and her bag. "Where would you like to go?"

"How about the Beanery? We can grab a quick bite and then run over to that new store around the corner. They're having a big sale. I saw the perfect dress for you in the window."

Molly's first impulse was to refuse. She loved Betty, but she didn't need her to pick out her clothes. Even Lauren hated that by now. Then Molly realized Betty was only trying to help.

Maybe it's time I learned to accept a favor now and then, Molly thought ruefully. *It wouldn't kill me to see the dress Betty thinks is perfect. It might even be fun.*

"Okay, I'll take a look. You do have great taste."

"Yes, I do. Kind of you to notice." Betty smiled brightly at her as they swept out the door.

"Tucker? Can you help me with these groceries?" Fran called from the front door.

Tucker walked quickly to meet her. He took one bag from her hand and two others she had dropped just inside the door.

"You got home early," Fran remarked, dropping her load on the countertop.

"Where are the kids? I thought they'd be home by now."

"Michael has a game. I thought you were

going to drop by and catch the last quarter."

"Oh, man. I guess I forgot." Tucker rubbed his forehead. "It was a hectic day." Fran didn't know the half of it.

"The coach will give him a lift home. Mary Ellen is at chorus practice. She'll be there late a few nights this week—practice for the concert. Mrs. North is going to drop her home about six. It's our turn to drive tomorrow. Could you do it?"

"Um, sure. I can pick them up. Just write me a note or something so I don't forget."

He grabbed a box of rice out of a bag, confused for a moment about where it should go. He was relieved to hear the kids would not be home for a while, though if they were, it might help Fran keep her temper under control when he told her about Carl.

There was no good time for it. He really had to tell her. He had to do it right now.

"Fran, I have something to tell you, and I don't want you to get upset," he began.

She closed a cupboard and turned to him. "Did something happen at work? Are you okay?"

The concern in her voice was touching.

Fran always worried about him getting hurt in the line of duty, even though it wasn't very likely in Cape Light. Tucker almost wished he had been in some dangerous situation. It would be easier to tell her that than his real news.

"Carl is here. I picked him up at the hospital around noon."

"Tucker, you didn't! I thought he was going to that shelter in Beverly."

"That one was full. They were sending him to one in Lowell. That place is a real pit. I couldn't let him go there," Tucker insisted.

Fran stared at him wide-eyed, obviously not knowing what to say. She abruptly turned her back and pulled a can out of a grocery bag. "How did you even know that?"

"I went down to Southport on my lunch break."

"So you intended on taking him home all along, I guess."

"Yes, I did. But I wasn't sure he'd come," Tucker slowly admitted. "When I heard where he was going, I knew I had to."

Fran turned to face him again. Her dark eyes were shining. At first he thought she was about to cry, then realized she was furious.

"Why didn't you just tell me this morning that you intended to do this? You could have at least talked to me about it."

"I wanted to, Fran. But I couldn't. I knew if I did, you might make me change my mind again, and I didn't want to change my mind. I need to help him. I really think this is the right thing to do."

"There are other ways to help him, Tucker. He doesn't have to stay here." Fran placed a can of coffee in a cupboard and slammed the door shut.

"Quiet down, will you? He's asleep in the spare room."

"You put him in my mother's room?" Fran was aghast.

"That's the guest room. It's not just for your relatives. Where did you think I was going to put him, in the toolshed?"

"I didn't think you were going to put him anywhere." Fran's voice rose on a shrill note. "It's my house, too, Tucker. I should have some say in this . . . this situation."

"Hello, Fran. Nice to see you, too."

They both turned and saw Carl in the doorway, leaning on his crutches, smiling bitterly. Tucker watched Fran's face go white as snow.

"Carl . . . I didn't see you there . . ." Tucker said, feeling his own face flush scarlet with embarrassment.

"Doesn't matter. I heard everything. We don't have any argument, you and me," Carl said to Fran. "I told Tucker this wasn't going to work."

"Go back to bed, Carl. Fran and I will figure it out."

"I heard what she said. I don't have to stay here. I should have gone to Lowell when I had the chance. I can probably get a bus there tonight, if you'll lend me the fare."

"Just give us a minute to talk this through," Tucker told him. "Besides, you've lost your place there by now. You'll just end up sleeping on the street."

Fran didn't say anything. She pursed her lips in a tight line and stood staring at Carl. "There must be someplace for him."

"There is. He'll stay here."

"Didn't you hear her? Your wife doesn't want me around. I told you this wasn't a good idea, but you—"

Carl began to cough furiously. His face grew beet red, and he gasped for air. He tilted so far forward on his crutches, Tucker was sure he would tumble to the floor.

"Oh no! Oh my goodness . . . Tucker, do something." Fran covered her mouth with her hand, frozen where she stood.

Tucker ran over to Carl, slung his brother's arm around his shoulders, then half carried, half dragged him back to the guest room. He set him down on the bed, propping him up against the pillows. Finally Carl's coughing spell passed, and he sucked in wheezy breaths of air.

"You still need the oxygen. I'll get some set up here for you tomorrow." Tucker stared down at him. The coughing had exhausted him; Carl leaned back, his eyes closed.

"Are you hungry?" Tucker asked.

Carl shook his head. "Just leave me be. Go on inside and talk to your wife."

"She'll be okay. Don't worry about her."

"Tell her I'm going in the morning."

Right, in the morning. Maybe some morning a month from now, Tucker thought. But he didn't reply. He left the room and closed Carl's door behind him.

In the kitchen, Fran had started making

dinner. She glanced at Tucker, then set a pan down on the stove top.

"He's very sick. I told you he needs help."

"I can see that. He looks awful." She shook her head. "I would never have recognized him. How can a person let himself go like that?"

Tucker glared at her. "Quiet, Fran. He'll hear you."

Fran sighed. She put a bowl from the freezer in the microwave and set the timer. "I guess we're stuck with him for a day or two. But don't expect me to turn into Florence Nightingale."

He knew what she meant. He'd brought Carl here, and now Carl was his problem. She wasn't going to do much to take care of him.

Tucker heard the front door slam.

"I'm home. What's for dinner?" his son Michael called out.

"Hi, Mike. How was the game?" Tucker asked as his tall, rangy son came into the kitchen.

"It was okay." Michael took a banana out of the fruit bowl on the table and ate it in two large bites. "Coach has me playing forward."

"Pretty good. First season on varsity, and he's playing forward. Did you hear that, Fran?"

Fran nodded. "I heard. Very good, Michael." She spared a smile for her son, then turned back to the cooking.

"You'd better work on your fake shot," Tucker advised. "I think the snow has pretty much melted from the driveway. I'll practice with you out back on Saturday."

Fran glanced over her shoulder. "Go easy on him, Michael. Your father's not sixteen anymore."

Tucker shook his head. "Thanks, Fran. I almost forgot."

"This old guy? He's still got some moves." Michael slapped his father on the back as he passed his chair. "What's for dinner? I'm starving."

"Just some stew I had in the freezer. It will be about half an hour before we eat. Do you have homework?"

"Yup. I'll do it upstairs."

"Wait a second. Your father needs to tell you something."

"Sit down, Mike," Tucker said. "This will only take a minute."

Michael stared at him curiously. He

looked a little worried, Tucker noticed. "Am I in trouble or something?"

"No, nothing like that," Tucker assured him. "Why? Is there something you need to tell me?"

"No, sir." Michael looked at him, then up at Fran. "What is this about?"

"I've told you I have a half brother, re-member?" Tucker began carefully.

"Right, his name is Carl. I've never met him. He went to jail or something, right?"

"That's right." Tucker paused, wondering if he should explain Carl's crime to Michael. They had never really discussed it in great detail. "He got into a fight with another man in a bar—"

"Oh, Tucker, do you have to tell him everything?" Fran cut in.

"Yes, I do. He's bound to hear it from some kid in school, so he might as well hear it from me first."

"I did hear it," Michael admitted. "Carl killed someone, right?"

Tucker took a breath and gave Michael the full story, concluding with his finding Carl in Southport Hospital.

"So what happened?" Michael asked. "Did he die or something?"

"No, he didn't die. He's still sick, but the doctors said he could leave the hospital. So I brought him here."

Michael's eyes widened. "He's here? In our house?"

"He's staying in the guest room."

"Can I see him?"

"Sure you can. Well, he's resting now. Maybe later. I'll see if he feels up to it."

"He's not feeling well, Mike. He needs his rest. We don't want you to bother him," Fran added nervously.

"Okay, I won't. But that's really cool. A real convict is sleeping in our house!"

"He's my brother, Michael," Tucker said in a warning tone. "I expect you to treat him with respect, the same way you treat me. You might hear some kids talking in school about this, but I want you to just ignore it. Carl's a sick man, and he needs some help. I want you to be nice to him."

"I will. How long is he going to be here?"

"Not long," Fran said quickly.

"Until he feels better," Tucker said, casting her a dark look.

Michael looked at both of them. "Can I go upstairs now?"

"Sure, go ahead," Tucker said. When

Michael left the room he said to Fran, "See, that went okay."

But Fran just stirred a pot on the stove with a wooden spoon, and didn't reply.

Tucker got up from the table. "I'm going to bring Carl some dinner. He's got a list here of foods he's allowed to eat." He found the list on the refrigerator and glanced at it. "A bland diet, it says. Jell-O, applesauce, cottage cheese—"

"That's okay, Tucker. I know what a bland diet is. He can have some of these noodles." Fran shook her head. "There's some applesauce in the cupboard. We're out of cottage cheese, though. I'd better buy more tomorrow, I guess."

"I guess so." Tucker touched her arm gently. She had a right to be mad at him, he supposed, for not discussing this with her. But he thought it wouldn't take too long before she softened up about Carl. Fran could be stubborn but she wasn't heartless.

A short time later, he had assembled a tray and brought it to the guest room. Carl was awake, sitting up against the pillows. The radio on the bedside table was tuned to a sports news channel.

"Was that your boy that came home before?" Carl asked.

"You don't miss much, do you?" Tucker set the tray on the night table and sat in a chair by the bed.

"My body is shot, but the ears still work pretty good."

"Here's some dinner. I don't know what you like. I just picked some stuff off that list." Tucker eyed the bottles of pills on the nightstand. He'd have to check later to see if Carl was following his prescriptions. "You'd better eat something before you take those pills."

Carl glanced at the food but didn't move to eat it. "I heard you and Fran going at it pretty good in there. Why didn't you tell her I'm going tomorrow, like I said? I can't stay here."

"Look, let's not get into this all over again. I spoke to your doctor today, Carl. You need bed rest, and you have to go back for checkups and tests and whatever. You're going to stay here until you're fit and that's the end of it."

"Are you crazy? I'm not staying here that long. Your wife won't put up with it, for one thing," he joked bitterly.

"Don't worry about Fran. I'll work it out with her."

Carl turned away, facing the wall. "This wallpaper is making me dizzy."

"So stop looking at it."

Carl suddenly turned and met his gaze. "Sorry if I'm not oozing all over you with gratitude. But I never asked you to bring me here. You're doing it for yourself so you can sleep at night and face your preacher on Sunday. You don't have to phony up to me, Tucker. I see right through you."

Tucker's chin lifted, feeling the words like a slap across the face. It wasn't enough that neither his wife nor his best friend gave him any understanding or sympathy in this. Or that his own common sense was fighting him every step of the way. Carl had to fight him, too, paying back his kindness with bitterness, ingratitude, and contempt.

After twenty years his brother still knew how to push his buttons, he'd give him that much. Carl's words stung because they rang true.

"Tucker? Dinner's on the table. Everything's ready," Fran called from the kitchen.

"Wife's calling. You'd better run along

now." Carl's expression was set in a grim line, and then he closed his eyes.

Tucker stood beside the bed, watching Carl. He smelled the hot food and heard his children and Fran gathering around the table. Carl might scorn and mock him. What did it matter? The blessings in his life were like a coat of armor. He thanked God for all he had compared to Carl, the simple things in his life that he took for granted, even his health.

Tucker left the room and quietly closed the door, his heart heavy with emotion. It was hard to imagine having nothing and no one—no job, no place to live, no one who cared whether you were alive or dead. He couldn't think of anyone he'd ever known like that, though as a policeman he'd seen his share of derelicts. But this was different. This was his own flesh and blood. What choice did he really have but to take Carl in?

Chapter Six

Tucker stepped out of his house and took in the clear sky and the bright sun that had just begun its climb. The wind was sharp and chilly, but the patches of snow that clung to the ground in icy clumps would not last the day, he predicted. It was the beginning of March, and though there might be more snow, the cold weather couldn't hold out much longer.

Fran and the children were just stirring when he left. Carl was still sleeping heavily. Tucker had set a tray of breakfast by his bed and a number he could call in an emergency. He would find some time today while he was out in the patrol car to stop home.

He knew he couldn't count on Fran to help right now. But Tucker thought she might pitch in after a while.

He drove into the village and parked in front of the Clam Box. Main Street was nearly empty, the nearby bank and shops still closed. He usually loved this time of the day, starting off with breakfast at the diner and a chat with Charlie. But this morning his stomach grumbled acidly as he entered, his senses assaulted by the rich smells of coffee, bacon, and home fries on the grill.

Tucker had seen Charlie a few times since he'd told him he was going to see if the guy in the hospital was Carl, but they'd carefully tiptoed around the topic. Now that Carl was staying at his house, though, Tucker knew he had to be the one to tell Charlie—before he heard it from someone else in town.

Tucker took a seat at the counter. Charlie was nowhere in sight. But Lucy Bates suddenly appeared beside him, a wide smile lighting up her pretty face.

"Good morning, Tucker. Coffee, of course."

"Absolutely." Tucker smiled at her as she

filled his mug. "I haven't seen you around much, Lucy. Busy with school?"

"I'll say. I have some really tough courses this semester. The reading list is just killing me. Though, I must admit, it still beats working here," she confided, in a teasing tone. "At this rate, I'll need a walker for the graduation march, but I'm trying not to think about that too much."

"Come on, now. You'll be done sooner than you think. I admire you, Lucy. I hope you stick with it."

"I'm trying," she said with a wistful grin. "Now, what can I get you this morning?"

Lucy was suddenly all business, pulling out her pad and scribbling his order, but he sensed his words had pleased her. He was sure she didn't get much encouragement from Charlie, who had fought so hard against her wish to go back to college that the conflict had nearly ended their marriage.

"How's your brother, Tucker? Is he still in the hospital?" Lucy asked as she put in the order.

"He came out yesterday. He still has a long way to go, though. He's got a pile of medications to take and needs to see the doctor for a while."

"That's too bad. Where is he staying now?" Lucy had turned to pour two glasses of juice. Tucker paused a moment before answering her. He didn't know why it should be so hard to admit that Carl was staying at his house. But somehow it was.

"He's staying with me for now. Until he gets back on his feet."

Lucy glanced at him as she set the juice glasses on a tray. "That's good of you, Tucker. A lot of people wouldn't go out of their way like that."

"What else could I do?"

"What else could you do about what?" Charlie asked, coming up behind him.

Tucker hadn't even noticed him there, and he now turned in his seat to face his friend. Lucy hurried off with her tray like a small animal in the woods who had just heard a gun shot, Tucker thought.

Charlie moved to his place on the other side of the counter and stood facing Tucker, the look on his face still expecting a reply.

"We were just talking about Carl. He came out of the hospital yesterday." Tucker stirred his coffee. "He's staying at my place for a while."

Charlie's eyes widened. "You took him in? What did you do that for?"

"I didn't have much choice. I couldn't let him go to some shelter."

Charlie stared at him a moment, then turned to the grill, where he cracked open two eggs and set them to fry.

"I knew he would get to you. Like the frog and the scorpion. Remember that story?"

"No, I don't," Tucker said dryly. "But I'm sure you'll remind me."

"There's this frog about to swim across a stream. And there's this scorpion, sitting on a rock. He asks the frog for a ride across the water. Now the frog is a helpful guy. He doesn't like to see anyone else in a fix. But he's afraid the scorpion is going to bite him. So he says, 'All right. I'll give you a lift. But only if you promise not to sting me.' "

Tucker had an idea of where this was going and sighed. "Go on . . . and check on my eggs while you're at it. I don't want them cooked to rubber."

Charlie turned back to his cooking without missing a beat. "Well, the scorpion agrees to the deal, of course, and he jumps on the frog's back. Off they go, sailing across the stream. But once they get to the other side, the scorpion curls his tail and gives the frog a sting. The frog is dying; he doesn't know what to do. 'Why did you sting me? You promised not to,' he says." Charlie paused and flipped the fried eggs into a dish. "The scorpion just laughs. He says, 'Why did you believe me, you dumb frog? Because it's your nature to trust. That's why. And that's the same reason I had to sting you. I couldn't help myself. That's just my nature.' "

He set the eggs down in front of Tucker with a dish of rye toast on the side. Then he stood back, a satisfied expression on his face.

Tucker dug into his eggs and shook his head. "Okay, the scorpion stung the frog. It's a story about nature. What's that supposed to mean?"

"Don't you get it? If you let Carl ride on your back, you're going to get stung, my friend. He won't mean to. But he'll do it anyway. Mark my words."

Tucker stopped chewing, his mouth full of food. He tried to swallow, but it wouldn't go down. Charlie had some nerve, that was for sure. He was no stupid frog. And Carl . . . well, Carl could be nasty. But that wasn't the point.

"My brother isn't going to hurt me. That's ridiculous."

"That's what you think, Tucker. If you let Carl hang around, you're just asking for trouble. You think you're doing a good deed. But something bad is going to come from this." Charlie sagely nodded his head. "Carl Tulley is trouble waiting to happen. It's just who he is. And you should have wised up by now."

Tucker sat back and wiped his mouth on a paper napkin. "Thanks for the fable, Charlie," he said sarcastically. "But I can handle my brother. I'm not worried about it."

"Really? Well, what about your reputation in this town? People will be talking about him, Tucker. They'll be talking about you. You're not going to win any popularity contests around here by making it easy for Carl to stick around."

"That's all right, I'm not running for office. And you're no expert in that department anyway, as I recall," he added.

Tucker could tell in an instant his angry retort had hit its mark. Charlie had run for mayor last year against Emily Warwick and lost. The defeat had hurt Charlie badly, and now Tucker had rubbed salt into the wound.

Charlie spun around and attended to the grill. "If that's the way you feel, fine. Just don't bring him in here. I'll throw him out on his ear," Charlie stated flatly.

"All right." Tucker got up from his seat. "If that's the way you feel, I won't come in here anymore, either."

He pulled some bills out of his wallet and slammed them on the counter. Charlie flinched, but he didn't turn around. Suddenly Lucy appeared beside Charlie. Tucker could tell she'd heard everything.

"What is this now? Don't fight like that, you two. For goodness' sake, you've been best friends since kindergarten." She touched Charlie's arm, but he barely glanced at her. "You're two kids in a school yard sometimes. Come on, Charlie. Apologize to Tucker. You can't let him leave like that."

Charlie sniffed. He pushed at a pile of potatoes with his spatula. "He's the one who should apologize. I was trying to give him some advice, and he jumps down my throat and insults me."

Tucker stood there a moment. He met Lucy's pleading gaze, but he was too angry to even attempt to smooth things over.

"See you, Lucy," he said shortly. "I've got to go."

He walked to the door.

"Charlie, please," Tucker heard Lucy say again.

"Just let him go. Who needs him. . . ." Charlie muttered disgustedly.

The bells above the door jingled, the sound ringing in Tucker's head. The rest of Charlie's words were lost to him, but Tucker had heard more than enough.

He turned toward the station house and stopped. Reverend Ben was walking toward him. The reverend was another morning regular at the Clam Box, and running into him at this time of day was no surprise. Sometimes they even had a bite together. Tucker didn't feel like talking to the reverend right now, but he didn't see a way out of it. This was not turning out to be a good day.

"Tucker, I've been thinking of you," the reverend said in greeting.

Tucker forced a small smile. "Good morning, Reverend. What's on your mind?"

"Oh, nothing much. Why don't we talk inside?" the reverend suggested.

"I've already stopped in, thanks. I've got to get to work." Tucker shifted on his feet, impatient to go.

"Another time then." Reverend Ben nodded. "I was in Southport and tried to look in on your brother yesterday, but the nurse said he was gone."

"Yes, they finally released him. He's staying at our house in the guest room."

Reverend Ben smiled, but Tucker didn't smile in return.

"I'd like to visit him, if that's okay. How long will he be there?"

Tucker shrugged. "I'm not sure exactly. I thought he'd have to stay at least a week or two until he gets his strength back. But Fran . . . well, she really doesn't want him there. Even Carl has been giving me a hard time," Tucker admitted. He laughed sadly and shook his head. "It seems like I'm the only one so far who thinks it's a good idea."

"You're doing the right thing, Tucker. That isn't always easy. It seldom is, actually," Reverend Ben pointed out.

"Thanks, but the truth is, I'm not helping Carl because I really care for him. I don't even know the man anymore. I'm not even sure I like him," Tucker confessed. "I feel sorry for him, but it's not that either. Last night Carl said he knew I was only helping him because I felt guilty."

"Of course you do. He's family," Reverend Ben said quietly.

"But that's the *real* reason. The only reason. I know it looks like I'm a good Christian and all that, but I'm really just going through the motions. It's not in the right spirit . . . not like that parable you read on Sunday about the Samaritan." Tucker stared down at the puddles near his heavy black shoes. "I'm on shaky ground, if you know what I mean. So when Fran starts complaining or Charlie in there gets under my skin, I get confused. Why should I put up with all this aggravation? For what? What am I getting out of this?"

Reverend Ben reached out and touched Tucker's arm. "Frankly, hearing that you don't like Carl makes me think your actions are even more admirable, not less. It's easy to help people we like, Tucker. But to extend compassion, real charity, for someone we don't know or don't like, that's in a different league in my book."

"I'm not trying to show charity, Reverend. I just feel guilty, like I said. I know my conscience will get to me if I don't do something for Carl."

"I understand. But maybe pure motives are unrealistic. Like the idea of courage without fear. Think about it, Tucker," the reverend urged him. "If the world relied on pure motives for right action, I don't know where we'd be. Your intentions are good, and you're doing something to help. The results are the same and that's what really counts. Keep going. You might find the feelings you think you lack. I'm sure that sooner or later—maybe even a long time from now—you'll feel truly glad you helped Carl. No matter what Fran or Charlie or even Carl himself has to say."

"Thanks, Reverend." Tucker rubbed the back of his neck. "I'm going to think about what you've said."

"Good. I'm glad I ran into you. But not surprised, actually. Sometimes my Boss schedules appointments for me without marking them in my book." The comment made Tucker finally smile. "If you ever need to talk more, Tucker, call me, okay?"

"Yes, I will," Tucker promised. "I'd better get to work. You have a good day."

"It's starting off pretty well." Reverend Ben patted Tucker's arm again and headed into the diner.

Tucker stood on the sidewalk and watched the reverend go inside. As Tucker had predicted, the large yellow sun had sailed up over Main Street and the morning sky had turned bright blue, and he suddenly noticed the sound of snow melting all around him, running down the drain spouts and dripping from rooftops.

Talking to Reverend Ben had not made him totally settled and resigned about Carl. But it had helped, Tucker realized. It had helped a lot.

Molly woke up slowly, a tangled dream clinging to the edges of her mind like a cobweb in a corner. She turned in bed and checked the clock. Five after seven. Why hadn't the alarm gone off? The girls would be late for school.

Then she remembered it was Saturday. She rolled on her back again, feeling an ache in her shoulders and back. Her legs felt leaden and sore. She had been cooking and baking all week—pushing herself to fill the new orders—and still had more to do over the weekend. She couldn't drop all her housecleaning clients with so little warning, either. She didn't think it was responsible of her. Besides, the same people who hired her to clean might call her for a catering job someday. So on top of all the new work, she'd somehow managed to fit in a few cleaning appointments as well.

She'd been so busy all week, she had hardly had a minute to spend with the girls, clean her own apartment, or even to eat. Which may have been a hidden bonus, Molly thought, since she felt as if she'd lost a few pounds without even thinking about it.

She glanced over at the closet door where a new dress, covered in a plastic bag, hung from the door. It was the one Betty had spotted. She had a good eye for clothes, no denying it. Just as she'd promised, the simple, tailored style did wonders for Molly's figure, and the deep blue color brought out the best in her eyes and fair complexion. The price was right, too, and Molly knew she would have treated herself anyway, even if Betty had not threatened to keep her trapped in the dressing room until she agreed to buy it.

Molly tried to think of the dress as a necessary purchase for all her new business appointments. She didn't want to admit she had bought it specifically to go to the school concert with Matthew tonight. She was trying to be low-key about this, but it wasn't easy. Luckily she'd been so busy all week, she didn't really have the time or energy to work herself up into a full blown, first-date frenzy.

"Relax, just be yourself. And try to forget all the reasons you think he wouldn't want to date you," Betty urged her.

Still, Molly found herself thinking about Matt a lot. Too much really. She finally had to give up telling herself she didn't really like him. She did like him. More than any man she had met in a long time. Which made her even more wary of getting her hopes up.

Molly sighed and forced herself to stumble out of bed and start her day. *If nothing comes of it, I'll be all right,* she told herself. *I just have to be.*

The doorbell rang at precisely five-thirty, just as Matthew had promised. Molly had already spotted his car pulling up on the street and had raced to the bathroom to check again on her lipstick, a bright new color she'd bought to go with the dress.

"Could you get that, Lauren? It's Dr. Harding and Amanda."

She heard the door open and the girls greeting each other with squealed compliments. "Okay, pal. It's show time," she whispered to her mirrored image. She shut the light and took a deep breath, then walked to the kitchen to see her guests.

"Hi, guys," she greeted Matthew and Amanda brightly. "Ready to go?"

"You look great." Matthew seemed unable to take his eyes off her and hurried over to help her with her coat.

"That dress totally goes with your eyes," Amanda agreed.

"Thanks." Molly's heart skipped with secret glee as she smiled up at Matthew. Dressed in a tweed sports jacket and coffee-brown sweater, he looked great, too. But she didn't have the courage to return the compliment. Not in front of the girls.

She glanced over at Amanda. "You look very pretty tonight. I like the way you did your hair."

Amanda had gathered her long brown hair into a single braid down her back. "Dad helped." She suddenly grinned. "It took a while, though."

"Hey, I did my best. I had trouble getting this thing to stay on." He pulled a small clasp with a velvet flower from his pocket. "Amanda wanted to wear it, but it keeps falling off."

"Here, let me." Molly took the clasp, quickly fit it to the end of the braid, and secured it in a neat, tight bow. "That should do it."

Amanda peeked at the braid. "Thanks, Molly."

Molly patted her shoulder. "No problem. Are you nervous?"

Amanda shrugged. "A little."

"Don't worry. You'll do fine. Lauren says you sound just like Julie Andrews. A real showstopper," Molly teased.

"Thanks," Amanda said shyly. When Molly looked up Matthew gave her a beaming smile. A silent thank you for her attention to Amanda?

"I guess we'd better go. These performers need to warm up their voices, and we want to get good seats." He held up a camera. "I want to take some pictures."

"These school shows are always so crowded. We'd better go," Molly agreed. The group paraded out of the apartment and headed downstairs to the car.

Once at school, Lauren and Amanda ran off to join the chorus backstage. Matthew led the way into the auditorium, and they found seats down in front in the center section. Matthew sat next to Molly, and she was suddenly very conscious of his nearness, his broad shoulder brushing against her own smaller one and the spicy scent of his aftershave.

The house lights went down, the chorus filed onto the stage, and the music began. Although Molly loved watching Lauren and Amanda perform, she was finding it hard to concentrate on the show. Each time Matthew wanted to tell her something, he leaned close, his shoulder rubbing hers and his hushed words tickling her ear. Her senses befuddled, she somehow managed to say the right things in response.

Finally the show was drawing to a close. The chorus director, the infamous Mrs. Pickering, thanked the audience for coming. ". . . and for all your kind applause. Now, for our closing piece, a medley from *The Sound of Music.*"

Matthew straightened up in his seat, an anxious, excited expression on his face as he stared up at the stage. He didn't have to say a word. They both knew it was time for Amanda's solo.

The band swung into the bright notes of "My Favorite Things." Amanda stepped front and center, her strong soprano carrying the lilting verses, while the rest of the group sang a medley of other songs from the show in a soft harmonic background.

Amanda's voice rose powerfully on the final notes as the rest of the chorus went silent. Molly felt goose bumps on her arms, and she turned to see tears glistening in Matthew's eyes, his camera sitting untouched in his lap. He glanced at her a moment, then reached over and squeezed her hand, his gaze returning to Amanda.

The last note sounded, and applause suddenly roared through the hall. Matthew, Molly, and Jill all came to their feet, clapping.

"Wow!" Jill looked up at Molly. "I didn't know she could sing like that."

"Neither did I, honey," Molly admitted. Her eyes felt watery, and she quickly dabbed them with a handkerchief.

The chorus and their teacher took a few bows. The curtains closed and the house lights came on. Matthew turned to her, looking awestruck and very proud. Molly could see he was at a loss for words.

"She was wonderful. Really."

"I never heard her sing like that before," he said, sounding stunned. "She's really coming along. I wish her . . ." He stopped himself mid-sentence. Molly saw a faint flush cross his cheeks. "I wish I'd taken more pictures," he finished quickly.

Molly nodded, collecting her coat. She had a feeling that was not what he'd meant to say at all.

The crowd surged up the aisles toward the exits. Molly held Jill's hand so they wouldn't get separated. The lobby in front of the auditorium was packed with kids and adults moving in all directions.

"The girls said they would meet us here, near the water fountain," Molly told Matthew.

"There's their chorus teacher," Matthew

remarked. "I'd like to have a word with her about Amanda. Do you mind?"

"Go ahead. We'll wait right here."

"Molly! I've been looking all over for you."

Molly felt her heart jump in her chest, and she looked up to find Phil standing right in front of her, as if he'd dropped down from the sky.

Dressed in a dark blue suit and yellow patterned tie, he looked so smart and polished that she barely recognized him. She'd never seen him look this handsome—not even on their wedding day, for goodness' sake. The flowers certainly added to the effect, she thought. Phil carried an armload of bouquets, enough to open a flower stand on the spot.

"What are you doing here?"

"I came to see Lauren. Didn't she tell you?"

"No, she did not." Molly guessed that the small detail had slipped Lauren's adolescent brain. Or maybe Lauren didn't think her father would really come. Molly was certainly having a hard enough time believing he was there.

"Daddy!" Jill ran over to give him a big

hug, then gazed longingly at the flowers. "Are those for Lauren?"

"Hello, honey. Yes, there's one for Lauren. And one for you," he said, handing her a bouquet. "And one for Mommy." He smiled at Molly and held out a bunch of pink roses.

Molly didn't know what to do. She took the flowers without even looking at them.

"How thoughtful. Is this supposed to make up for all those times you forgot our anniversary?"

"Molly . . ." He smiled and shook his head at her.

Lauren suddenly appeared, her face glowing when she spotted her father. Molly stepped aside, feeling invisible.

"Dad! Did you see me?"

"Of course, I did, sweetie. I was sitting front and center. I even got a video." He held up a tiny expensive-looking camera. "You were great. I was so proud of you."

"Thanks, Dad." Lauren looked suddenly shy. "I didn't see you in the audience. I wasn't sure you would come."

"I promised you, didn't I?"

Lauren nodded but didn't reply.

"Here, I brought you some flowers." Phil

handed her the bouquet, and her eyes lit with pleasure.

"They're beautiful, Daddy. Thanks." Finally, she glanced at Molly. "Look what Daddy got me. Aren't they awesome?"

"Absolutely," Molly agreed with a tight smile. She wondered now why she didn't think of flowers. Too distracted getting herself ready to see Matthew, she realized with a guilty twinge.

"You were great, honey. I loved the show." Molly reached out and stroked Lauren's hair.

But she wasn't even sure Lauren heard her. She had turned back to Phil, her attention totally fixed on her father. As was Jill, who stood on his other side, holding his hand.

Molly felt small and mean and overlooked. She sighed, thinking at least her daughters were happy. She had to give Phil a few points for tonight. He was clearly trying, and the girls appreciated his efforts.

"So where should we go for dinner?" Phil asked. "I made reservations at this terrific steak house, but I wasn't sure if that's what you'd all like to do." He looked hopefully at

Molly. "I'd love it if you'd join us, Molly. I'm sure the girls would love it, too."

Molly felt thrown for a loop for the second time in fifteen minutes. This wasn't really happening, was it?

"Thanks, Phil. That's a nice invitation. But we have plans," she said quickly.

Phil's cheerful expression sagged like a sail that had suddenly lost the wind. She could see he had not anticipated this reply. Lauren and Jill clung to him, staring at her with downcast expressions. Molly just glared at them.

"But I want to have dinner with Daddy," Lauren complained. "Why can't we go?"

"You know why, Lauren. We've promised the Hardings. You don't want to disappoint Amanda, do you?"

Molly noticed Phil's gaze shift, and she looked up to see Matthew and Amanda standing beside her. "Sorry to keep you waiting," Matt said. "Mrs. Pickering had quite a lot to say."

Matthew looked at Molly and then around the group, his gaze finally coming to rest on Phil. The two men stared at each other for a minute, as if to say, "Who's *that* guy?"

Molly should have been horrified at the

scene, but it suddenly seemed amusing. She hadn't been on a date with a man she truly liked in ages. Here she was, finally . . . and Phil shows up. If she didn't laugh at this, she would break down crying.

She quickly made introductions, summoning her best garden-party voice. The men briefly shook hands, and Phil shook hands with Amanda, as well, remembering to compliment her solo.

"That was lovely, Amanda," Molly agreed, catching the girl's eye. "I actually started crying," she admitted.

"Oh, Mom, you're such a waterworks sometimes," Lauren teased.

"She always gets like that." Phil laughed knowingly. "Cries at the drop of a hat. Even at TV commercials."

Molly glared at him. Matthew smiled in a tight, polite way.

Will this ever end? Molly thought desperately. She was not the praying kind, but she suddenly heard herself sending up a silent plea. Would somebody up there have pity on her and please get rid of Phil?

"We were just discussing dinner." Phil looked straight at Matthew. "I thought I'd surprise Molly and the girls. . . . But I guess they have plans with you."

Oh, Phil! How could you put Matthew on the spot like that! Molly wanted to shriek at him. He was as slippery as a bar of soap.

"Phil invited us out, but I told him we already had plans with you and Amanda," Molly quickly explained to Matt.

Matthew looked confused, then glanced at Lauren, still standing beside her father, her arm hooked around Phil's waist. "That's all right," he said graciously. "Amanda and I understand if Lauren would like to see her father tonight."

Molly felt a little jolt. Did it really mean so little to him if she went off with Phil, or was he just trying to be nice?

"Don't be silly, Matt. We don't want to change our plans and leave you flat. That wouldn't be polite."

There was a moment of tense silence. Lauren looked disappointed but resigned, and Molly felt sorry for her. Still, this was Phil's fault. He should have checked beforehand and not assumed that they'd be at his beck and call.

Of course she looked like the bad guy again. Not him.

"Maybe we should all go out together?" Matthew suggested.

Molly stared at him. She knew he was just trying to be polite, but did he have to invite her ex-husband out on their first *almost* date? That wasn't a good sign at all, she thought dejectedly.

She looked over at Phil, sure he was going to say yes. He met her gaze and must have seen the silent scream of horror in her eyes.

"Thank you, Matt. That's nice of you to offer. But I don't think I'll crash the party." He hugged Lauren and Jill, one in each arm. "I'll see you two tomorrow. We'll have all day together," he reminded them. "You have a good time tonight and don't get to bed too late. I have a lot of plans."

The girls both nodded and kissed him good night. "Nice to meet you." Phil extended his hand and shook Matt's again. "I'll see you around," he added.

He cast Molly a knowing look, which she pretended not to notice. Phil knew she was interested in Matt. It was embarrassing being so transparent to him. Then again, he did know her well.

"Good night, Molly. See you tomorrow."

Phil gave her a lazy grin. "By the way, you look super in that dress. Blue is definitely your color."

"Good night, Phil." Molly kept her tone light. She secretly felt like flinging her bouquet at him but struggled not to lose her temper in front of Matthew.

The three girls chatted nonstop in the backseat on the way to the restaurant. Which was just as well, Matthew thought, since an awkward silence had fallen between him and Molly.

She stared out the passenger's side window, lost in thought. He couldn't help wondering if she was brooding over her exhusband.

He was just as Matt had imagined—and even more so. Though he couldn't say why, Matt had not expected Phil to be so goodlooking. Maybe he was just protecting his own ego. Molly was certainly lovely enough. She could attract any man she set her sights on, he thought.

Phil was a charming, smooth-talking guy. Whatever failings he may have had as a husband and father in the past, he now had

Lauren and Jill wrapped around his little finger, though Matt could see he clearly loved both of them.

What about Molly? Was Phil hoping to win her back, too? Matt wouldn't be surprised. He glanced over at Molly, realizing he didn't like that idea.

"I'm sorry if Phil put you on the spot." Molly's quiet voice broke into his thoughts. "He's so . . . inconsiderate sometimes. Well, most of the time, actually."

"That's okay. I just didn't know what to say. I wasn't sure if you wanted to go with him. I'm happy you decided not to," he added.

He saw her smile and knew he had said the right thing. Finally.

"It all worked out, I guess." She settled back in her seat and sighed. "I thought he'd never get the hint. He really should have just let it go. He's going to see the girls all day tomorrow," she said. "He spoils them something awful. They're like little wildcats after a day out with him."

Molly shook her head, staring down at the flowers in her lap. "How can they forgive him so easily?"

Matthew looked out at the road. He didn't

reply right away. "Children do have an amazing capacity to forgive and forget, God bless them. Especially a parent. It's a good thing, too. We do make so many mistakes."

Molly didn't answer right away. "Yes, that is a good thing. An amazing thing, really." She sighed. "I didn't mean to rant. He rattled me, showing up like that. I haven't seen him for months and now he's just popping out of the woodwork wherever I go. It's starting to feel like a bad horror movie."

Matthew laughed at the exaggeration. But he could tell that Molly still had some lingering feelings for Phil. Why else would she get so unhinged? She seemed to think it was all residual anger, but Matthew wondered if there was something more going on—something Molly might not even realize.

The rest of the evening went smoothly. The three girls kept the conversation lively. Molly quickly recovered from her distress over Phil and was her usual bright and vivacious self—times ten, Matthew thought. Or maybe it was just the candlelight flickering in her big blue eyes. Matthew knew he must be staring but found he could barely take his eyes off her.

Her emotions flashed across her lovely face like quicksilver, like sunlight sparkling on water. She was witty and irreverent one minute, tender and serious the next. She was warm. She was bold. She was outspoken, brimming with heartfelt emotion, then shy and suddenly self-conscious. She was honest and intelligent, totally without guile.

She was nothing like Sharon, he thought, who always did and said just the right thing. No one would ever accuse Molly Willoughby of that, he thought, smiling to himself.

She was not like anyone he'd ever met before. If he wasn't careful, he would fall for her. Big time. By the end of the night, he felt lightheaded and happy, oddly at peace though he didn't quite know why.

After dessert, the three girls asked if they could take a walk around the restaurant, which had been a house. On a previous trek to the restroom they'd caught sight of the front parlor, which was filled with antiques, a game table, and a player piano. They were now eager to explore it.

"There's a Scrabble game in there with

gold tiles," Jill told her mother in an awe-struck tone.

"Go for it, Jill. Those vocabulary words are going to come in handy now," Matthew teased.

Molly glanced at him and laughed. "You're incorrigible," she said as the three girls ran off.

Matthew sat back, suddenly bashful at being completely alone with Molly. She looked so beautiful tonight. He felt a little dizzy every time he looked at her.

"I'm sorry about before," she said suddenly. "About getting all worked up over running into Phil at the concert." She shook her head; a silky curl fell against her cheek, he noticed. "He sure knows how to push my buttons. I guess he just knows me too well by now."

She glanced up at him with an uneasy smile. He could tell it was hard for her to talk about her ex-husband. Still, he was curious. He wanted to know more about her feelings for Phil. He suddenly wanted to know everything.

"When did you and Phil meet?" he asked quietly.

"I was fifteen years old, if you can believe

that. A freshman in high school. I ended up marrying the first guy who ever asked me out on a date, for goodness' sake. I guess you could say I was a little insecure."

Matthew didn't mean to, but he couldn't help smiling at the way she told her story. "When did you get married?"

"Right after graduation. I was eighteen and Phil was twenty. I didn't want to go to college, and I wouldn't listen to my parents. I thought I knew everything. I was a little wild. Had a bad attitude. I was every parent's nightmare."

"Oh, I'm sure you weren't that bad." Matthew *was* sure, too. He knew by now how Molly loved to exaggerate to make her point. She could never have turned out this wonderful if she was half as bad as she claimed.

"Oh, but I was. You have no idea. My parents should be awarded gold medals for putting up with me. I realize that now as Lauren is hitting that impossible stage." She sighed and took a sip of her coffee, glancing at him over the rim of her cup. "I bet you were a total angel. Honor roll, student government, all that stuff."

He smiled slowly at her. "Actually, I was

pretty bad myself for a while. Had that bad attitude thing you just mentioned."

Molly's eyes widened in shock. "No, you didn't. You're just saying that to make me feel better."

He shook his head. "No, I'm not. I really did have a bad stretch there for a while. See, we have more in common than you thought."

"You're right about that." Molly still looked surprised, and he couldn't help grinning at her.

"I was rebelling against my father, I guess. It was always assumed I'd be a doctor, just like him. I was determined to show everyone I was different. Even if it meant ruining my chances to get into a good college."

Molly cast him a thoughtful look. "I get it. But what happened after that? I mean, here you are. You turned out to be a doctor, after all. What made you change your mind?"

"Well, something happened, something that changed my life, actually." Matthew paused and glanced away. "My best friend crashed his car a few weeks before high-school graduation. He died on the scene, almost instantly. It was a horrific bloody mess. I was in the backseat and somehow hardly got a scratch. I still have nightmares about it."

Matthew saw her draw in a sharp breath. "How awful for you." Her voice was warm with sympathy.

"It was awful, all right . . . but it made me wake up and realize I'd been wasting time. You see, I really did want to be a doctor. I had always wanted to do this, ever since I was a little kid. I would have wanted it even if my father had been a fireman or owned a hardware store. I just wanted everyone to realize that it was my choice. I wasn't just doing it because my parents wanted that for me."

Molly nodded. "I understand what you mean, and I'm glad it turned out okay for you. I'm glad you got what you wanted."

"Thanks," he said quietly. He met her gaze and held it. He felt she did understand. "How about you, Molly? Did you get what you wanted?"

She smiled softly and shook her head. "No, not yet . . . But I'm working on it."

He reached over and covered her hand with his own. "It will come to you. I have a feeling about that."

"I hope so," she said quietly.

Matthew didn't answer her. He didn't know what to say. He sat holding her hand on the linen cloth until Molly quite suddenly sat up and slipped her hand into her lap. He followed her gaze and saw the girls returning to the table. He glanced at Molly and shared a smile.

Well, there would be other times to talk to her alone like this, he thought. He hoped so, anyway.

On the drive home, she didn't say much. But she looked content—much more at ease than she had looked earlier.

Matthew drove down Main Street and parked in front of Molly's building. "I'll walk you to the door," he offered before she could say otherwise.

Amanda waited in the car and waved good night. At the door to their apartment building, Molly looked down at her daughters expectantly. They both responded to the silent prompt, turning to Matthew.

"Thank you for dinner, Dr. Harding," Lauren said politely.

"Yes, thank you," Jill chimed in.

He smiled at them. "You're very welcome.

We must do it again sometime," he teased the girls in a formal tone.

"Indubitably," Jill said, and then she giggled, covering her mouth with her hand.

Lauren poked her with an elbow. "Come on, silly." They turned and ran upstairs.

Molly smiled up at him. "Well, thank you again. We had a great time. It was very, very nice of you."

"My pleasure. Honestly." He stared down into her eyes. "We *should* do it again . . . without the kids, I mean."

Molly's bright eyes widened. "Sure," she said slowly.

Her mouth made a perfect circle of surprise, and he wanted very badly to kiss her. But then remembered Amanda sitting in the car only a few feet away. She was watching them carefully, he was certain.

He leaned forward and quickly kissed her on the cheek instead. "I'll call you, okay?"

"Sure," she said again. He could tell she was wondering if he really would.

He suddenly wondered the same thing. This was hard, much harder than he remembered. Or was it only so difficult for him because of his past? He forced a smile and dug his hands in his pockets, taking a few steps away from her.

"See you," he called out as he got back in the car.

Molly lifted her hand and waved goodbye. Then she turned and went inside.

He started the car, feeling strangely unsettled. He could really care for her. He knew that now. Maybe he already did.

He just didn't want to be another man who let her down.

On Sunday morning Sophie skipped coffee hour and left church with Miranda right after the service. She wanted to get home to Gus, of course. But she also knew that many friends from the congregation would soon be on their way to the orchard to visit.

Her daughters and their families were on hand to help out with the entertaining. As she gave her directions and did the little chores they permitted, she felt the familiar anticipation that came with expecting company tinged with melancholy, like a photo of happier days, browned and frayed at the edges. Their friends would gather in the familiar rooms as they had for years and years. The guests would talk and laugh and enjoy each other's company. Everyone would pretend it was a get-well visit. But everyone knew the truth. Sophie and Gus did, too. They were all really coming to say good-bye.

Gus was fading fast. Right before her very eyes it seemed. Sometimes, when she came upon him resting, drifting in his own thoughts, it seemed so clear that he was not there anymore. His spirit was testing the waters, venturing out beyond her husband's worn body, then drifting back again.

It was like watching the tide go out, each wave that comes in growing almost imperceptibly shorter. At first you can barely tell anything is happening. But over time, as an hour and then another slips by, you can see how the shoreline has pulled away.

That was how it was now, Sophie thought. Gus was moving away from her. Steadily, irreversibly. Like the tide in the sea.

"Should I put out the good china, Grandma?" Miranda called from the dining room.

"Yes, dear. And the silver flatware, too. The good everything. Take it all out," Sophie said with emphasis.

She set a homemade pie on a glass cake stand, sighing to herself. She wondered why she never realized before that life was so short, so precious. Why had she saved all these things? What for? So they could sit dusty and yellowed on a shelf? She should have used the good china every day. She should have dressed in her best clothes and dabbed on her treasured perfume just to go out and pick apples or dig in the garden. Gus's time had just about run out, and it felt as if her time had, too.

"I'll get the door," Miranda announced some time later from the front hallway.

Sophie was in the bedroom with Gus, making him presentable. He'd insisted on wearing a white shirt with a red bow tie and his favorite argyle vest. Gray trousers and his fancy black Sunday shoes completed the outfit. He hadn't been dressed up in real clothes for days. Sophie could see the effort had tired him but also lifted his spirits.

His normally ruddy complexion had taken on a yellowish cast. She knew what that meant. His liver and kidneys were giving out. If he noticed, he didn't say. He eyed himself in the mirror, combing his thin gray hair.

"Do I look okay?"

She stepped behind him and placed her hands on his shoulders. "Best-looking man in the room, as always," she assured him.

He turned his face to kiss her hand. "You're too good to me."

Sophie's reply caught in her throat, so she didn't say anything. He was mistaken. She could never be too good to Gus. It wasn't possible.

She rolled Gus out into the living room, into a circle of smiling faces and cheerful greetings. Jessica and Sam Morgan were there; Grace Hegman and her father, Digger; along with Harry Reilly, who owned the boatyard downtown.

"Gus, good to see you. You look swell," Harry said, shaking Gus's hand. "Better hurry up and get well. I've got myself a new boat. Did Digger tell you?"

"No, he didn't say. Trading up, are you? It's about time," Gus chided him.

"This rich guy had his boat in my yard, brand new. Had it on the water one season. Then he gets transferred out to Arizona, and he can't wait to get it off his hands. He asks me if I can find a buyer. He was almost giving it away. I couldn't resist." Harry laughed.

"It's top of the line. Practically catches the fish for you."

A few times each summer a group of the men from church got together to go fishing. They went out from sunrise to sunset, and the man who caught the biggest fish had to buy the rest dinner. Gus had always enjoyed those outings, Sophie recalled. It gave him a little break from the orchard.

"Remember that striper you hooked last summer, Gus?" Digger said. "Nearly broke my arm trying to help you reel it in."

"That was a beauty," Sam agreed. "I caught one half the size, and we still have plenty in the freezer."

"Oh, dear, tell me about it." Jessica sighed with a rueful smile. "How many ways can you cook bass?"

"I have a few recipes I can give you, dear," Sophie offered.

"He was a monster. Wait, I've got a picture of that guy right up on the mantel." Gus turned his chair and pointed.

Sam jumped up and took the photo down, then handed it to him. "That fish was almost as big as you are."

Gus laughed. "Not quite. Forty-six inches, if I remember right." He stared down at the photo, and Sophie noticed his smile slowly dissolve, like a lump of ice cream left out in the sun.

There would be no more fishing trips. No more mysterious tugs on a line. No more aching arms and a sore back from a battle with a big sea bass. No more unbelievable stories. That's what he's thinking, she realized. Her heart ached.

The doorbell rang, catching everyone's attention. "I'll go," Sophie's daughter Una offered.

Sophie heard the sound of Reverend Ben and his wife Carolyn coming into the foyer. She stepped out to greet them. The reverend's daughter, Rachel, and her husband, Jack Anderson, were also there, and Sophie was pleased to see them.

Carolyn gave Sophie a kiss and hug in greeting. "Mark wanted to come so much," she said, "but he volunteered to stay at Rachel's to watch the baby. He asked me to tell you he'll come by during the week to say hello if that's all right."

"Of course, it's all right. We'd love to see him anytime," Sophie said sincerely. She and Gus had known both Rachel and Mark

Lewis since they were little children. So many friends, she thought.

As the Lewis family took off their coats, Emily Warwick and Dan Forbes arrived, along with Emily's daughter, Sara Franklin, and her boyfriend, Luke McAllister.

Sara handed Sophie a bunch of flowers. "These are for you," she said.

"Thank you, dear. How thoughtful." Sophie hardly had time to admire them before Miranda took the bouquet and went off in search of a vase.

Sophie followed Sara and Luke into the living room, remembering the day last fall that they had come apple picking in the orchard. Sara and Luke hardly knew each other at the time, but Sophie could tell something was simmering there.

I was right, too, she thought with satisfaction.

Luke had seemed such a mysterious figure when he first came to Cape Light. That was about a year ago now, Sophie realized. A former policeman, he had bought a piece of property from Dr. Elliot and decided to build a center for troubled teenagers on it. That had caused quite a stir in town. People were up in arms about it for a time, though she and Gus had always thought it was an admirable idea. When some of the kids came up from Boston to help build the place, there had been a terrible fire on the property. She and Gus had taken the kids in, and they all ended up working in the orchard when help was needed badly. Such a fortunate turn of events. *The Lord has a way of working these things out,* she reminded herself, *of untangling life's little knots when you least expect it.*

The construction at Luke's property was halted by the harsh winter but would start up again soon. Luke had told her it would open sometime in May. More kids from the city would come to stay then, and he'd offered to send more helpers her way. But with Gus sick and all, she hadn't made arrangements with him.

The orchard meant so much to so many people in this town. It held so many memories for the friends and family gathered here today, Sophie reflected. Even for total strangers just passing through Cape Light who stopped for a moment and found themselves in a tucked-away corner of paradise.

It won't be the same without Gus, Sophie

reflected as she took a seat again among her company. She brushed the mournful thoughts aside and tried to focus on her guests. Her daughters, Evelyn and Una, along with Miranda, were taking care of all the kitchen work today so she could simply sit and enjoy herself. Sophie was totally un-accustomed to relaxing at one of her own parties, but she forced herself to stay put, knowing this could be the first and last time she'd have the opportunity.

Gus started telling a funny story about getting lost in the woods with his Boy Scout troop, way back when their children were all in grade school. Reverend Ben had been along, and he'd suggested they stop and pray for divine guidance.

"Oh, Ben, you didn't really?" Carolyn burst into laughter.

"Yes, I did. I didn't know what else to do. I'm not much of a woodsman, as you all know."

They all agreed, laughing loudly and long.

"It worked for Moses," Ben said.

"We did find our way eventually," Gus added. "Some ranger came along and took pity on us."

"You see? Our prayers were answered," Ben insisted.

The rest of the group continued laughing and teasing him. *As it should be. This last get-together should be as happy as we can make it,* Sophie thought with a determined spirit. *We might as well be smiling. There will be time enough for tears.*

A light lunch was served—sandwiches, salads, and cheese—along with Sophie's famous scones with honey from her own bees and peaches and plums she'd canned the past summer. Everyone praised the meal lavishly, as usual, and just as predictably insisted that she didn't need to go to so much trouble. But they didn't leave much on the platters, she noticed with satisfaction.

After the coffee and Sophie's famous pies were served, guests began to bid farewell. First they found Gus, still sitting in the living room. It was hard for Sophie to watch them say good-bye to him, everyone acting as if they'd see him again soon, when they all knew that most of them would never see him again. Watching from the doorway, Sophie's eyes welled up with tears, and she had to turn away. She wandered into the foyer and composed herself, then suddenly found herself facing Emily and Dan.

"It was wonderful of you to have us all here, Sophie," Emily said. "And wonderful to see Gus. We don't want to make him too tired, though."

"Yes, of course. He was happy to see everyone. Thank you for coming. Both of you," Sophie said. Emily hugged her and then so did Dan.

"You take care of yourself," Emily added. "If there's anything you need, anything at all, just call me. Okay?"

Sophie tried to make light of her serious expression. "Well, it's good to know I have friends in important places. But don't worry, dear. We'll be fine. I have my children here now. It will be okay."

Dan met her gaze and forced a smile. They knew it would not be okay. Not entirely. But there was nothing more to say.

They said good-bye again and left. Then others began to drift to the door, and very soon, the guests had gone and only family remained. Evelyn's husband, Robert, took Gus into the bedroom so he could rest, then returned to sit in the living room with Una's husband, Ted. Some of the grandchildren wandered about, but most had settled into the family room to watch TV. Sophie's daughters along with Miranda were still in the kitchen, putting away leftovers and washing dishes.

Sophie felt alone in the crowd, outside of each circle. A sinking feeling had settled on her spirit now that the party was over. Her children had hinted that they wanted to have a family talk today, and she dreaded the inevitable debate over what she would do once Gus was gone.

She wandered back into the kitchen seeking some task to get her mind off her worries. "Need a hand in here?" she asked, her tone far brighter than she felt.

"We're all done, Mom." Una glanced at her. "Are you okay?"

"Just a little tired. That was a nice get-together though."

"Yes, it was very nice. Dad really enjoyed it." Una set a china saucer in a stack on the countertop, then looked at Evelyn.

"Would you like a cup of tea, Grandma?" Miranda asked her.

"Thanks, dear. That would be nice."

"Here, Mom. Sit down. I'll fix it for you." Una came up beside her and guided her to a chair at the table. Then Una and Evelyn sat down, too.

Evelyn was her oldest and the one who most resembled her mother. She wore one of Sophie's favorite aprons, and as Sophie looked across the table at her daughter, she almost felt as if she were looking in a mirror at herself . . . herself twenty-five years ago when everything had been ahead of her, so much life still to live, so much to look forward to.

"Mom, we thought we should have a talk," Evelyn began slowly. "We know it's hard to discuss it, but Dad . . . Dad is near the end. It won't be long now before you're on your own."

"Yes . . . yes I know." Sophie looked down at the table. Miranda brought over the tea and set it before her without a word.

"You'll be alone here. It will be very hard for you," Una said.

"We know how you love this place. We all do," Evelyn added. "We've been trying hard to figure out some way around it . . . but we don't think you can stay here all alone, Mom. Una and I have talked with Bart," she went on. "We'd all be too worried about you."

"We know it's hard to face it. But you can't run the orchard on your own. These last few years, you and Dad could hardly manage it together," Una said.

Sophie didn't answer. She sighed and stirred her tea. "I think I could manage. I could hire some help . . ."

"Oh, Mom. Even if you found good help, it would still be a lot of work for you. A lot of responsibility." Evelyn glanced at her sister. "Poor Dad, he worked so hard on this land all his life. We don't want to see you run yourself down out here, too."

"It's just not practical, Mom. Please be reasonable about this," Una implored her.

"I've lived here since the day I was born. That was a long, long time ago," Sophie said, shaking her head. "It seems very unreasonable to me to pick up and make a change at this late date. Impractical, too, come to think about it."

The two sisters shared a look. Sophie felt her eyes blur with tears, and she blew her nose on a paper napkin. Miranda reached over and patted her hand. She glanced at her aunts. "What about if Grandma leases out the land to someone who will work the orchard and let her live here?"

Una sighed. "That's a thought, dear. But she'll still really be alone in this big house. Anything can happen."

"Besides, bringing someone else into the business would be a big headache," Evelyn pointed out. "How would we even find someone to do it? It's almost spring. We'd have to sort it all out right away."

Sophie glanced at Miranda. "I've thought of that myself, honey. But it gets too complicated. It would be hard for me to see someone out in the trees who wasn't family. I've been here too long. Those trees are like my friends. I might not like the way someone else handled them," she offered with a weak smile.

"The thing to do is sell the place and then you can come live with me. Or Una. Or get a little apartment in town," Evelyn suggested.

"In town? Me?" Sophie scoffed as if Evelyn had suggested she move to Paris. "I'm just not a town-type person, honey. You know that. I need to be out in the open. I don't like houses and buildings blocking my view."

"I know it's hard, Mom," Evelyn persisted. "But try to be a little open-minded about what you might do."

Sophie pushed her empty teacup away and pressed her hands flat to the table. "I know you're only trying to take care of me. I know that, girls," she told her daughters. "And I appreciate it, truly. But I can't leave here. I'm just like . . . like a fish out of water away from this place. It's hard enough losing your father. I can't lose this place, too," she beseeched them.

She was trying not to cry but could feel the teardrops squeezing out from the corners of her eyes. "I really don't think I could survive away from here. Not for too long, anyway. I'd rather live on here for a month or a week or even a day than move away and live another ten years somewhere else. I'd rather the good Lord would just take me now. Can either of you understand that?"

"Oh, Mom . . ." Evelyn rose and stepped beside her mother to give her a hug. Una did the same.

"We didn't mean to make you so upset," Una said.

"Don't cry, Mom, please. We don't have to decide any of this now," Evelyn added.

They stood beside her for a second, comforting her while Miranda held her hand. "I'm sorry, Grandma," Miranda said simply. Sophie squeezed her fingers in reply.

Finally, Sophie sat up in her chair and wiped her eyes. "I'm going to look in on your father."

The bedroom she had always shared with Gus was on the second floor. But this time when he came home from the hospital, she had set him up in a hospital bed in the guest room on the first floor and moved in a twin bed from upstairs so she could be near him when he slept. The room was nearly dark, illuminated by a small night-light on a bed stand and the shine of a half moon.

Gus breathed heavily in his sleep with the aid of oxygen. Sophie sat in a chair near him and leaned over to touch the hand that rested outside the covers. He'd had a good day today, a happy day, with long moments of distraction, of being able to forget that he was so sick, so near death. As if he were ever able to forget that entirely.

She stared out the window at the orchard, the stark bare trees outlined in the moonlight. Such a sight, it nearly made her heart break. She had the urge to wake Gus up, just to show him, then thought that wouldn't be right.

Sophie squeezed her eyes shut, still holding Gus's hand. *Dear Lord, I know this is a lot to ask, but please help me. Please find some way for me to stay on this land. I know my children are loving and that's a blessing. They only want to take care of me. But you know my heart, Lord. You know why I can't leave here. People say that You won't send more our way than we can handle. I don't think I can face losing Gus and my orchard, too. . . .*

When she opened her eyes, Gus's eyes were open, too. "Sophie. How long have you been sitting here?"

"Oh, not long. Do you need anything?"

He shook his head. "I don't know why I woke up. Maybe it's the moonlight." He turned to the window, and she pushed aside the curtain so they could look outside.

"Isn't it beautiful," she said quietly. "I wanted to wake you up to see it with me."

"Maybe the Lord heard your thoughts, and he shook my shoulder, just to please you," Gus suggested with a smile.

Sophie felt her heart catch. "Maybe . . ."

she agreed slowly. "I do hope He was really listening tonight."

She took his hand again, and together they watched out the window the fragile branches of the apple trees, waving against the star-filled sky.

CHAPTER SEVEN

Tucker smoothed his uniform jacket, then knocked sharply on the chief's door. He'd no sooner walked in the station house than he had been told that Sanborn wanted to see him.

"Come in," Sanborn called.

Tucker stepped inside and stood in front of the large wooden desk. The police chief was reading through some papers in a file and didn't look up right away.

"You wanted to see me, sir?"

"Yes, shut the door, will you?" Chief Sanborn sat back. The expression on his face made Tucker nervous. "Have a seat."

Tucker took the chair in front of the desk,

the "hot seat" as his fellow officers called it. He wondered what this was all about. He'd taken a lot of personal time since Carl came to town. He suspected that his boss wasn't happy about that.

"How's it going, Tucker?"

"All right." Tucker shrugged, the chief's forced friendly tone making him even more uncomfortable.

"I know I've been taking a lot of personal time, Chief—" he began.

Sanborn held up a hand, and Tucker stopped talking. "Yes, you have. But that's not what I wanted to talk to you about. Well, not exactly." He shifted in his seat. "I know you have your brother at home now. That's quite a responsibility."

"I suppose. He's not much trouble. Stays in his room, watches TV. I do need to bring him to the doctor for checkups."

His boss nodded. "How is he coming along? Is his health improving?"

"He's making progress. Slowly but steady." Tucker paused, still unsure of the chief's motives for this private meeting. Was it to ask after Carl's health? That didn't make sense.

"So, what are his plans? Will he be staying around here long, do you think?"

Tucker blinked. Now he got it. "I don't think so. He talks about going up to Maine to live with a friend in Portland."

"I see." Chief Sanborn nodded. "I wanted you to know I'll be looking into Carl's records, his release records from prison and his parole, any recent arrests and so forth."

"Carl finished his parole without a problem, Chief. It's been a few years now."

Chief Sanborn didn't say anything at first. The look on his face made Tucker feel like a fool for taking Carl's word so easily.

"Well, I'm sure that's what he told you. What else would he say? But I do need to look into it officially. I know Carl is sick and not much of a danger to anyone except himself. But people get upset when they hear somebody with his history is back in town. I'm sure you've heard some of that already."

Tucker nodded. He'd heard it all right. Right under his own roof, although Fran had calmed down considerably, and she seemed resigned to Carl's presence—for now, anyway. Why did people have to be like that? Didn't they have better things to worry about?

"I understand. Is that all you wanted to tell me?" he asked curtly. "I'm due on patrol in five minutes."

"That's it. I'll let you know what I find out," the chief added, dismissing him.

"Fine." Tucker came to his feet, turned on his heel, and left the office, feeling as if smoke were pouring out of his ears. As he went to the locker room, he could feel his fellow officers staring at him, speculating on his visit with the boss; all of them probably knew about Carl and felt the way the chief did.

I'm just imagining things now, he told himself. He picked up his hat and jacket and headed out the door to his squad car. Walking through the parking lot, Tucker passed two other officers and said hello. He saw them glance at each other, then one nodded, the greeting noticeably chilly.

Tucker tried not to show a reaction. He got in his car and drove out of the lot. An old saying came to him, one he'd never quite understood until now: "Just because you're paranoid, it doesn't mean they're not out to get you."

Were people turning against him now because of Carl? It was sure starting to feel like it. Even his boss seemed to think he was a fool for accepting Carl's story about his record. If Carl was violating parole, he could be sent back to prison. In his condition, that would most likely finish him off, Tucker thought.

Now he would have to wait to find out if Carl had lied to him. As if he needed something else to worry about right now.

"Molly! Where have you been? I left two messages on your voice mail," Betty said in greeting to her.

"Racing around like a maniac, as usual. I had a lot of deliveries to make. It's Monday, remember?"

"Oh, right." Betty nodded. "No wonder you're so cranky."

Molly just grinned at her. Betty stood next to Fran Tulley's desk, peering down at two photos in her hand. It looked as if the women were trying to decide which photo to stick on the "House of the Week" poster that now sat on Fran's desk.

"Which do you like?" Betty asked. "This

charming Cape? A steal at this asking price, believe me. Or this lovely Victorian? Needs a little TLC but could be a show place for a buyer with imagination."

Molly glanced at the photos. Neither of the houses looked very appealing, but Betty was a born salesperson.

"Whichever. You'll sell both in about twenty minutes," Molly predicted.

"Why, thanks. I think they will move quickly." Betty looked back at the photos. "I think we should go with the Cape. We did a Victorian last week." She handed the chosen photo to Fran, then turned to Molly again. "So how did it go on Saturday night? I'm dying to hear everything."

Molly was dying to tell everything, too, but didn't feel comfortable talking about Matthew in front of Fran.

"It was a very nice evening. The girls sang beautifully." She smiled at Fran. "I thought Mary Ellen did a nice job up there, Fran. I didn't get to tell you."

Fran looked up from the poster. "Thanks, Molly. Lauren sounded great, too. But Dr. Harding's daughter, she really brought down the house. I bet he was very proud," she added with a meaningful look.

"Yes, he was." Molly turned to Betty, who now looked about to burst from curiosity. "Amanda Harding sang a solo. She was amazing."

"Really? How nice." Betty clutched Molly's arm. "Come into my office. I want to show you something. Excuse us a minute, will you, Fran?"

Fran smiled knowingly, looking down at her work again. Fran wasn't the gossiping type, but Molly still felt uncomfortable. That was the problem with living in a small town. Everyone seemed to know everything almost before it even happened.

Once inside the office, Betty quickly shut the door. "So? What's the story?"

Molly sighed and flopped into an armchair. "I had a great time. I think he did, too, but who can tell about these things? Men just . . . baffle me. He gave me one of those 'I'll call you sometime' good-byes. That's not a good sign, is it?"

Betty sat on the edge of her desk, her shiny, chin-length blond hair swinging around her face.

"Well, that depends. He doesn't seem like the type who would say that and not call. Maybe he just felt self-conscious around the kids. I think you should sit tight and give him time."

"Good advice. As if I have any choice in the matter," Molly added with a small laugh.

"I heard that his office was opening this week. I'm sure he's feeling stressed and expects to be very busy. Maybe he didn't feel able to make any plans right now."

"Maybe." Betty's explanation gave her a little hope but not much. "Wait, I forgot to tell you the funniest part. While I was waiting for Lauren to come out from backstage, Phil showed up."

"He didn't." Betty's eyes widened with astonishment.

"He did. With enough flowers for the entire Miss America pageant, playing his Devoted Dad act to the hilt. It's starting to drive me crazy." Molly's maddened expression made Betty laugh.

"He does sound a little over-the-top."

"Over-the-top would be an improvement. He just assumed that the girls and I would be free to have dinner with him. So that caused a big to-do with Lauren. Then Matthew felt awkward, I guess, and invited Phil to come along with us."

"Oh, no. You poor thing. A first-date disaster. I'd rather have spinach stuck in my teeth," Betty said decidedly.

"This was definitely worse than spinach. Phil finally took a hint and backed off. I guess I looked like I was about to strangle him. But that's what I mean about Matthew. I don't think inviting my ex-husband out to dinner with us was a good sign."

Betty gazed down at her a moment, then patted her shoulder. "Don't worry. I have a good feeling about this, honestly."

Molly felt cheered by her friend's words. "You were right about the dress, though."

"I told you that dress was perfect for you." Betty smiled in a self-satisfied way. "That proves you have to listen to my advice about these things. Don't get too distracted about Matthew. Just let it unfold." Betty gestured with her hands, the many rings on her fingers sparkling.

"Frankly, I'm so stressed about work right now, I don't have time to worry about him, too. That's what I really wanted to talk to you about, Betty. I'm getting cold feet. I think I made a huge mistake giving up all my cleaning jobs, and now it's too late to get them back."

"It's hard to make such a big change,"

Betty said sympathetically. "You're bound to have some second thoughts."

"I'd describe it more like sheer terror. I woke up at three A.M. in a cold sweat. I can't make a living on the cooking and baking alone. And even if I get more business, I can't handle it all. What was I thinking? It's just not going to work."

Betty rested a steady hand on her shoulder. "Take a deep breath, Molly. You're panicking. I think I need to have you breathe into a paper bag." Her tone was serious, but her eyes held a mirthful light.

"Of course I'm panicking! I'm just not like you, Betty. I just don't have what it takes to run a business."

"Now, now. None of that put-down talk. You're as smart as anybody, smarter than most people I know. So that excuse just doesn't work on me," Betty said sternly. "Let's talk about this logically, point by point. What exactly has thrown you into such a tizzy?"

Molly stared at her friend. As much as she felt like falling apart at the seams, clearly Betty wouldn't let her. She took another deep breath and tried to organize her thoughts.

"First of all, I don't have enough orders to make the amount of money I need."

"Okay, fair enough. But Phil is giving you support checks for the girls now, so that should help. More importantly, there must be loads more possible clients out there for you. Now that you're not wasting your time cleaning, you can go after new business—in that fabulous dress, of course," she added, making Molly smile again. "So, do you have any new prospects lined up?"

"Well, I do have an appointment tomorrow at the country club in Hamilton," Molly had to admit.

"Excellent. That horsie set throws tons of parties. You're bound to get a lot of contacts there."

"If I get the work."

"Of course you'll get it. Think positively," Betty urged her. "The first thing I want you to do after that is sit with the phone book and make a list of all the possible places you can call for work. Then try to set up some appointments. Mention your classy clients, like the Spoon Harbor Inn and the Pequot Inn. They'll be impressed. They won't want to miss out. If you don't have enough new clients after that, then . . . well, then we'll figure out some other strategy. Refrigerator magnets or sky writing, maybe," Betty said, waving her hands in the air.

"Betty, be serious. Besides, even if I get more clients, I can't fill the orders. I can't be cooking and baking night and day. And how about delivering all this stuff? I've been driving around all day as it is."

"Many hands make light work," Betty told her. "It's not just a saying in a fortune cookie. Did you ever check into hiring a helper? I thought we already covered that."

"Oh, right. No, I guess I didn't."

Betty gazed at her and shook her head. "Listen, this is what I'm hearing: The old way was familiar and comforting, even though it wasn't getting you from point A to point B. The new path is scary, unknown. There are problems to solve around every corner, very discouraging. So it seems easier now—smarter even—to turn back and hide in your dark, cozy little hole. But that's not like you, Molly. You're not a quitter," Betty insisted. "I know this is what you really want, and I wouldn't be a real friend if I let you give up now, would I?"

Molly gazed at Betty for a long moment,

then shook her head. "So you won't let me whine and wiggle my way out of this? Is that what you're saying?"

"See, you catch on pretty quickly." Betty smiled again. "Here's an idea for you. I'm going to teach an adult-ed course up at the high school about real-estate sales. Classes begin this week. There's also a course being offered about working in restaurants and catering, and I heard the instructor is great. I'm sure it would give you the nuts-and-bolts information you really need to get going."

"Take a course?" Molly considered the idea. Although she had thought of taking a class in starting a small business, it never seemed to be the right time. *But if not now, when?* she asked herself bluntly. Besides, what did she have to lose? She'd get an idea of the real problems she'd face trying to do this work full-time and possibly some of the solutions as well.

"That's a good suggestion," she said. "I'll go up to the high school today and look into it."

"That's the spirit. Don't delay; you might start getting second thoughts," Betty warned her.

Molly smiled. Sometimes Betty knew her too well.

"And I'll check the student job list while I'm there, too," Molly promised. She knew Betty was bound to mention that next.

When Molly was finally ready to leave, she gave Betty a huge impulsive hug. "Thanks. I guess I came unglued there for a minute."

"Yes, you did. Nothing I couldn't handle, though," Betty admitted with a grin. Then her voice turned serious as she said, "Just remember, 'Whatever you can do, begin it. Boldness has genius, power, and magic in it.' "

Molly blinked. "Don't tell me, Ann Landers?"

Betty shook her head. "Johann Wolfgang von Goethe, a German poet. The point is, I know you can do it, Molly. Trust me on this, okay?"

Molly nodded, suddenly feeling her throat too tight to speak.

She did trust Betty. Implicitly. She only wished she could trust herself as much.

* * *

Fran marched into the family room and stood beside the TV. Tucker glanced at her, then looked back at the set. He was watching some sporting event as usual—basketball tonight—and he had barely said hello when she came in.

At least Carl isn't in here, too, she thought. That would really be the icing on her cake today.

"I'm home," she announced, still wearing her coat.

Tucker gave her a confused look. "I can see that. Can you step to the side, please? I'm trying to watch the game."

Fran turned and clicked off the TV.

Tucker sat up straight in his armchair as if prodded by an electric shock. "What did you do that for? It's a big game, for goodness' sake. It's the Celtics, Fran."

"Sorry, Tucker. We have to talk." She took off her coat and sat down on the sofa.

"This is about Carl again. Isn't it?"

Fran nodded. She could see Tucker's expression change and readied herself for another argument. She just had to make him see this time.

"Did something happen?"

"Yes, something happened. It was awful

for me. You really have no idea. Or maybe you do but you prefer to keep your head stuck in the sand."

Tucker took a breath. She could see that he was trying hard to control his temper. "Let's see, you went down the street to Sylvia North's house for a PTA meeting. Is that right so far?"

Fran nodded. "The Teacher Appreciation Day planning committee. We talked for a while about the event. The luncheon plans, should we buy corsages or give plants, that sort of thing. Then Sylvia brought out the coffee and everyone started chatting about their kids and things going on in the neighborhood—"

"Okay, I get the picture. So, what was so awful that you turned off the Celtics with two minutes left on the clock?"

Tucker's impatient tone upset her all over again. "Sorry to bore you, Tucker. First my feelings aren't as important as your brother's and now I don't even beat out the Celtics."

"I never said that, Fran."

"You didn't have to say it. It's perfectly obvious." Fran sat back and crossed her arms over her chest. She could feel Tucker watching her, but she avoided meeting his gaze.

"Just tell me what happened at the meeting. Somebody said something nasty about Carl living here, is that it?"

"Brilliant deduction. You should be a detective. You're really wasted in uniform." Tucker took a sharp breath, and she knew that she had hurt him. Still, she pressed on, "I don't even want to tell you now. You don't care what I've been through over this situation. I lost a good client this week."

Tucker sighed. "You told me. But you don't know that for sure, Fran. They could have given the listing to someone else for a lot of reasons."

"It was because of Carl," she insisted. "I know you don't like hearing that, Tucker, but it's true. You know what they said at the meeting tonight? All the neighbors are concerned about Carl being here. They're afraid about getting their houses broken into and even their property values going down once the word gets out that the newest resident on our street is an ex-convict. Sylvia wants to put her house on the market soon. Not that I'll get the listing, believe me," Fran said, shaking her head.

"She's the one who cornered me, asking how long he'll be here. 'Aren't you afraid to have him in the house with you like that?' she said. Well, what could I say? I *am* afraid sometimes."

"Oh, come on, Fran. Carl is no threat to anyone around here. That's just ridiculous. You have to just ignore that kind of talk."

"I'm sorry, Tucker. I just can't. It really upsets me." She shrugged. "Maybe I care too much what people think. Or maybe I'm not as good-hearted as you are," she said honestly. "But that's just who I am. I can't help it."

Her husband glanced at her, folding his hands together. He didn't say anything. He didn't have to.

The thing was, Fran knew she could help it if she really wanted to. She could try harder to live her faith. That's what the right attitude would be. But she didn't have patience or the energy for that. Not like Tucker, Lord bless him. Sometimes it seemed he had enough patience and integrity for both of them.

Her husband was special. He had a good heart; she'd always known that about him.

He's never changed but maybe I have, she thought with a pang.

She could have married someone else, someone more ambitious, bound to achieve more material success in life. But she chose Tucker Tulley because of who he was inside. He wanted to do something meaningful with his life, and she had admired that. She'd been idealistic back then, with youthful values. Unrealistic ones, it now seemed.

"What do you want me to do, Fran?" Tucker asked slowly. "Should I take out an advertisement in the *Messenger* and promise people Carl poses no threat to their safety? Do you want me to tell people that it's all my fault, that you have nothing to do with this?"

"Tucker, of course not. But—" Fran hesitated, wondering if she should just let it go. No, she had to be honest. "I want you to find other arrangements," she continued in a halting voice. "You said he'd only be here a few days. Well, it's been more than a few days now, and he seems to be improving. Maybe you can find him another place at that shelter in Beverly."

Tucker didn't say a word, but by the stiff way he was holding himself, she could see how hard she'd pushed him. She felt awful and nearly took back her demand.

"I'm sorry, Tucker. I just hate being talked about. Our own neighbors are mad at us. Maybe you don't mind that so much. Maybe you have thicker skin than I do. But it's hard for me. Don't you understand even a little bit?"

Tucker nodded and moved over onto the couch to sit near her. "Sure, I understand. I'm sorry, too, Fran. I don't mean to fight with you every night about this. We never really fight, do we?"

"No," she said bleakly. "Most of the time we're pretty good about talking things through."

Tucker put his arm around her shoulders, and the familiar gesture of affection made her feel a little better.

"This is a problem, Fran," he admitted. "I don't know what to do about it. I don't want you to think I don't care about your feelings in this matter. I do. But I promised Carl he could stay here until he recuperates, and I meant it. I promised him," he repeated.

Fran didn't know what to say. The same reply from some other man might not mean so much, but Tucker's promises were not empty words spoken lightly then broken on a whim. It would hurt Tucker to go back on his word to his brother. It would cut deep. *It would hurt our marriage, too, if I force him to do that for me.* And that, Fran realized, might be far worse than suffering the dirty looks of neighbors.

She felt Tucker watching her, but she didn't look up at him.

"All right," she said at last. "You promised him. You don't want to go back on your word. I have to respect that, I suppose."

He stared at her and blinked. She could tell he was surprised that she'd backed down, though his expression didn't show much.

"Can we at least figure out a time frame here? Something I can tell people?"

Tucker shrugged. "I guess that's a reasonable request. But it's not as if when the clock runs down, I'm going to throw him out. Carl's making good progress, though. I have to bring him to the doctor on Friday. Let's see what kind of report he gets. I guess it might be two or three weeks more?"

Fran felt deflated. Three weeks? It sounded like such a long time. But there didn't seem to be any help for it. She could manage, she decided. It wasn't as if Tucker was insisting that Carl move in with them.

Not yet, anyway. Thank goodness.

"All right. I just wanted some idea."

Tucker gave her a questioning look. "I suppose he could go sooner if he improves quickly."

"That's all right. I understand," Fran insisted. "I guess I could help you out by taking care of him a bit more. He could eat dinner with us, if he feels up to it. It's not right to keep him cooped up in that little room. He probably gets lonely."

"He must," Tucker agreed. "Even if he'd never admit it."

Tucker had been dutiful about taking care of Carl and spending time with him in the evenings. Fran suspected that Carl often chased him out of the room, always acting as if he didn't need anybody.

"You have a lot of patience with him."

"Thanks. I try." Tucker dipped his head and smiled.

"And with me," she added with a grin. She paused and bit her lip. "I'm sorry I turned off the Celtics."

Tucker laughed and squeezed her shoulder. "That's okay. I'll catch the ending on the late news. Just don't try that again. I might not let you get away with it a second time."

"Fair enough. I wouldn't dare do it if the Red Sox were playing."

"Not if you know what's good for you."

Fran smiled at him. It felt good to laugh with her husband again, as if life were getting back to normal. She only hoped the rest of their time taking care of Carl would pass quickly so things really could get back to normal.

CHAPTER EIGHT

Molly started off the week with a hectic schedule, though not busy enough to keep her from thinking about Matthew and from jumping out of her skin every time the phone rang. He was probably busy with work, this being the first week of his practice, Molly would remind herself. But as the week wore on, the thought became less and less consoling.

She was rolling out pastry dough for pie shells on Wednesday afternoon when the kitchen phone rang. Her hands were sticky and full of flour, and she nearly let the machine pick up. But thinking it might be the school nurse or something having to do with the girls, she scurried to answer it.

"Molly? Hi, it's me, Matthew." Molly was so surprised to hear his voice, she nearly dropped the rolling pin on her foot.

"Matthew . . . hi. How's it going?" Upbeat, casual, and friendly, she reminded herself. The attitude magazine articles about dating advise so you don't scare men off. As if an eligible male was a timid woodland creature. Like a chipmunk, for instance, Molly thought fancifully.

"I'm in a bit of a bind. I was hoping you could help me out."

"Sure, what's the problem?" Her heart plummeted. This wasn't about anything personal, like a date. He just wanted a favor.

"Do you think you could pick up Amanda today after school and keep her at your place for a while? I have an emergency. I have to check a little girl into the hospital. She needs surgery. It's pretty serious. Thankfully her parents brought her to see me in time. But I wanted to stay here with them, see how it turns out."

She could hear the tension in his voice now, even over the static-filled connection. She felt guilty for her snide thoughts. He was dealing with a life-or-death situation, and she was worried about her social life.

"Of course I'll pick up Amanda. Don't give it a second thought."

"Thanks. I knew I could count on you."

Molly didn't know what to say. At least he thought of her as a friend, someone he could turn to when he had a problem. That was something, right?

"Amanda is old enough to stay home alone, of course. But I have no idea when I'll be done here. Not before seven and it could be later."

"It's no problem, really. She'll be fine with us. Take all the time you need. And good luck with your patient. I hope it turns out all right."

"Thanks. Say a prayer for her, will you? The surgeon will need all the help he can get in there." He paused and she could hear him talking to someone else in the background. A moment later he returned. "I have to run. See you later."

Molly said good-bye but suspected he'd already hung up. She wasn't a prayerful person under normal circumstances. Growing up, she went to church every Sunday with her parents, who were still active at

Bible Community Church, as was her brother, Sam. But somehow, somewhere Molly had fallen off the track. She didn't have anything *against* church exactly. She just didn't have much time to go, it seemed. Or if she had the time, she felt too tired to get herself out so early on a Sunday unless it was for a holiday like Easter or Christmas.

She did believe in God . . . or something up there, watching over the whole messy works of the world. But as for prayer, Molly knew she was the type who only remembered God in a dire emergency. Then she prayed like a house on fire. She was sure the Lord found people like her annoying, like friends who only call when they need a favor.

She had even told that to Reverend Ben once. He had found it so amusing, he asked if he could use it in a sermon. The reverend had promised her that God wasn't like that at all. God didn't hold grudges and was interested in hearing her prayers no matter when she offered them. Molly found the words reassuring but had only half-believed him.

It seemed funny to her that Matthew would ask her to pray for his patient. The other night he'd mentioned he'd already joined Bible Community Church. She could tell he was a believer and seemed to assume she was, too.

We're going to need extra help tonight, he had said, recognizing that the fate of his young patient wasn't completely in his hands or even in the hands of the surgeon. It must help him as a doctor to believe in some greater power, she realized. Or maybe that's why he did believe. Because he dealt with life and death so closely.

Molly brushed off her hands on her apron, closed her eyes, and took a long, steadying breath. *Dear God,* she silently began, *please help Matthew's patient. I hope her surgery turns out all right. Please comfort her parents, and help them to stay calm. Please comfort that little girl, too. I'm sure she must be very frightened right now.* She thought for a moment, not knowing what else to say. *By the way,* she added, *I know you don't hear from me much, Lord, but Matthew asked me to call.*

She smiled to herself, realizing that she was being silly now. Yet somehow she had a feeling that the Lord didn't mind a little joke now and then. He had to have a good sense of humor in order to have created humans, she thought.

As Molly had predicted, Amanda and Lauren were thrilled to spend some unexpected time together. By six o'clock there was still no word from Matthew, so Molly served the three girls dinner. Lauren had begged for tacos, not exactly a culinary challenge but appropriate for the setting and the impromptu guest, Molly thought, both of which are important considerations, as she'd learned last week in the first session of her catering course. "Let the food match the mood," her instructor had advised.

The mood seemed to be a free-for-all giggle fest, and it was survival of the fittest once Molly set the taco fixings on the table. Even Amanda forgot her impressive table manners and dove in up to her elbows, Molly noticed, which was probably a good thing. Amanda seemed to be growing accustomed to their chaotic household and though she was still shy and almost too well-behaved, Molly sensed she was opening up a bit.

As the girls chatted about a TV show they

wanted to watch after dinner, Molly's thoughts wandered. She wondered what Amanda's mother had been like. From the little Matthew had mentioned, it sounded as if his late wife had been quite intelligent and accomplished, the well-bred type. You could see it in the way Amanda conducted herself, as if she had gone to an old-fashioned finishing school.

Molly bit into her taco, and it exploded in her hand. *Nothing like me, of course,* she thought, licking her saucy fingers. *No wonder he hasn't asked me out. No mystery there.*

"We're done, Mom. Thanks, that was yummy." Lauren spoke in a rush, wiping her mouth with a paper napkin. "Can we watch TV until Amanda's dad comes?"

"Um, sure. As long as the homework is done."

"Thank you for dinner. The tacos were great," Amanda said, carrying her plate to the sink.

"You're very welcome." Molly smiled at her. Maybe she and Matthew would never be anything more than friends, but she felt genuine affection for his daughter.

"I'm done, too. Can I go with them?" Jill asked, talking around a mouthful of food.

"Sure, honey. Go ahead." Molly finished the last bite on her plate and was tempted to fix another taco. She counted to ten and squelched the urge, chomping down on a carrot stick instead.

She had taken Betty's advice and made some cold calls, coming up with a few new prospects to see next week. She needed to look good in her new dress, and control-top panty hose could only get a person so far. Besides, after an hour or two, wearing control tops always gave her a whopping migraine. *Probably squishing all the blood up to my head,* she thought as she started the dishes, *like squeezing a tube of toothpaste in the middle.*

Molly had just finished cleaning up when the door buzzer sounded. "Who is it?" she called. She was surprised to hear Matthew answer. He was earlier than she expected. She had hoped to have time enough to change her shirt and put on some lipstick, but it was too late now.

What difference does it make? she thought, pulling open the door. *It doesn't seem as if this situation is going to take any romantic turns.*

"Hi, Molly." He glanced at her with a weary grin. "Gee, something smells good in here, as usual."

"We just finished dinner—tacos. There are leftovers, if you want some." Molly closed the front door and led him into the kitchen.

The look on Matt's face suggested that leftover tacos were the most appetizing offer he'd had in years. Then he shook his head and stuck his hands in his jacket pockets.

"No, thanks. I really don't want to trouble you."

"It's no trouble." Molly met his gaze, then pulled back. She didn't want to be pushy. *The man does not want tacos. What part of that sentence don't you understand?* she coached herself.

"How about some coffee? I was just making some."

"That would be great. I could use some caffeine just to get home," he admitted with a laugh.

Molly glanced over her shoulder and smiled. She took out two mugs and served the coffee with a dish of brownies she had on hand for dessert. She didn't feel like calling the girls in yet, though. She was sure Lauren would smell the chocolate and come streaking into the room soon enough.

"It was great of you to have Amanda over like this," Matthew said as she joined him at the table. "I hope I can repay the favor sometime."

"It was no trouble," Molly said honestly. "What happened with your patient? Did the surgery go okay?"

"Yes, as a matter of fact, she came through with flying colors. She's in the ICU tonight, but she won't be there long."

He looked exhausted but when he spoke about his patient, his smile widened and a light seemed to shine from deep within.

"That's good news. Her parents must be extremely relieved."

"Yes, they were. I was relieved to give them a good report, quite frankly. It's so hard when children are involved. My heart really goes out to the parents. You know they'd move heaven and earth to help their child and they feel so helpless. They look to a doctor as if he's a miracle worker. But sometimes, the miracles just don't happen."

"That must be tough. My kids have only had health emergencies once or twice so far, thank goodness. I know what you mean about that desperate, terrified feeling. But I never thought about the pressure on the doctor. It must be awesome."

Matthew glanced at her. " 'Awesome' is a real good word for it." He picked up a brownie, looking lost in thought. Molly watched as he took a bite and chewed, his eyes slowly widening.

"Speaking of the word, these brownies are awesome, as Amanda might say. Just what I needed."

Molly laughed, feeling a chill when he suddenly winked at her. "Black coffee and brownies aren't exactly a balanced meal."

"Yes, I know. But it's been one of those days when you have to go straight for dessert, if you know what I mean."

"Do I ever," Molly commiserated with a laugh. She sipped her coffee, and their eyes met over the rim of her mug. A slow smile tilted up the corners of his mouth. She wanted to look away but couldn't. She felt sure he wasn't thinking about the brownies anymore. He was thinking about her and that was why he was smiling. She had promised herself she would be friendly to him and nothing more. This was starting to feel like something more . . . but she couldn't quite stop herself.

"That was fun last week, when we went out after the concert," he said suddenly.

Molly nearly choked on her coffee and set the mug down. "Yes . . . yes it was," she agreed. Then she stopped herself. She didn't want to start blabbing away and ruin it. Was he going to ask her out? Finally?

She held her breath, waiting to see what he would say next.

"I wanted to call you this week, but I got so busy with the office opening up—"

"Oh, sure. I understand. How is that going? You didn't even mention it."

"I've been swamped with patients. Ezra was right. People around here really have been waiting for a local doctor to move in."

The door buzzer suddenly sounded, and Molly jolted as if some invisible hand had reached down and shook her shoulder.

"Would you excuse me a minute? I'll just see who that is."

She rose and walked to the door, wondering who it could be. Her neighbor, maybe, needing to borrow something or dropping by to chat?

She pulled open the door and found Phil standing there. He smiled widely, not seeming the least bit embarrassed by or apologetic for the unexpected visit.

"Hey, Molly. How you doing? I was at my mother's house tonight, and on my way home, I saw your lights on. I just wanted to say hello to the kids for a few minutes."

"Phil." She stood in the doorway, blocking his entrance. "Don't you ever think of calling first?"

Phil peeked over her shoulder into the kitchen. She saw his expression change and was sure he had caught sight of Matthew sitting at the table. "Oh . . . sorry. I didn't know you were entertaining. I just want to see the girls for a minute. I won't be in your way at all," he promised, giving her a look.

Molly felt instantly infuriated. "You really need to call first, Phil. You can't just drop in here any time you're in the neighborhood."

He stared at her a moment, then dipped his head. "Sure. Sure thing. I know what you mean. I won't do it again, really."

Molly could see that despite his apology, he wasn't leaving. She sighed, not knowing what to do. She noticed Phil's gaze shift and looked up to find Matthew standing beside her.

"Hello, Phil," Matthew said cordially. "We met the other night at the chorus concert."

"Sure, I remember. Matt, right? Good to see you again." Phil leaned across Molly and shook Matthew's hand. "Sorry to interrupt your evening. I just wanted to say hello to the girls."

"That's all right. We really need to get going." Matt glanced down at Molly. She thought she saw a flash of regret in his eyes but then wondered if she had imagined it. "I'll just go pry Amanda away from the TV." Before Molly could protest, he turned and walked back toward the living room.

Molly glared at Phil, then turned her back on him and went inside. She didn't invite him in, but he followed her anyway.

"What? What did I do?" he asked innocently. "I didn't mean to chase the guy out." His tone was nearly a whisper, but Molly felt sure Matthew could hear. She felt doubly mad at Phil for the smirk on his handsome face. He seemed to be finding the entire situation highly amusing.

She crossed her arms over her chest, ignoring him. He stood beside her quietly for a moment, then leaned toward the table.

"Hmm. Brownies. May I?" he asked politely.

"Help yourself," Molly said tightly.

Matthew appeared with Amanda, who looked reluctant to go. Lauren followed, also wearing a long face.

"Hi, sweetie," Phil greeted her brightly. She barely glanced at him. Was the novelty wearing off? Molly wondered.

"Hi, Dad," Lauren replied. She quickly turned to Molly, grabbing onto her arm. "Can Amanda sleep over on Friday night? Pul-eassse?"

It was Matthew who answered. "I'm sorry, honey. Amanda and I are going into Boston for the day on Saturday. We need to leave very early so it wouldn't work out."

"Another time, I guess," Molly promised Lauren. "We'll figure it out."

Lauren refused to give up. "Maybe next weekend?"

"We'll see," Molly said almost automatically.

Molly followed Matthew and Amanda to the door. "Well, good night. Thanks again." Their eyes met briefly.

Molly felt odd. She yearned for some sign that Matthew intended on calling and finishing the conversation Phil had interrupted. But what could she say? Everything that came to mind seemed far too obvious.

"Have a nice time in Boston," she finally offered.

Wow, did that sound original and witty or what?

She watched briefly as they walked down the hallway, then closed the door.

Phil was sitting at the kitchen table with Lauren and Jill. Jill was showing him a report she had written on ancient Egypt. She had gotten an A on it and was very proud.

Phil was making all the right responses. "Wow, what a great cover. Did you draw that yourself?"

Jill nodded. "Look at this one." She flipped some pages to show a drawing of a mummy. "That's my favorite."

"It's beautiful," Phil said thoughtfully. He turned to his older daughter. "How about you, Lauren? Anything interesting going on in school this week?"

Lauren shrugged. "The usual. We had a big math test."

"How did you do?" Phil asked.

"Not too bad. B plus," Lauren reported.

"Can I see it?" Phil asked.

Lauren seemed surprised at the request, Molly noticed, but got up from her seat. "Okay. It's in my backpack." She left the room, and Phil looked up at Molly.

"Just trying to keep up with what they're doing in school. It's important, right?"

"No argument there," Molly said tightly. Had he been taking dad lessons in his spare time lately?

She was steaming mad at him but wasn't sure what to do about it. She didn't want to blast him right in front of the girls and look like the bully again.

But she still had to have a talk with him, a serious talk. Yes, she was angry because his surprise visit had interrupted her conversation with Matthew just as it seemed he was about to ask her out. But it was more than that. Much more. Phil couldn't just walk in here anytime he liked. He didn't live here anymore. He seemed to have suddenly forgotten that small important detail.

Molly decided to retreat and regroup. "I

think I'll take a little walk while you guys visit. I could use some fresh air."

Phil and the girls looked at her curiously. "It's really cold out there," he warned her.

"That's all right," Molly said, heading for the door. "I really need to cool off. I'll be back in about twenty minutes and then you can go, Phil. Right?"

He met her gaze. "Uh, sure. That sounds fine."

Molly pulled on her jacket and stalked out of the apartment. She headed down Main Street at a brisk pace but felt a stinging cold wind as she neared the harbor. At the end of the street, the steamy windows and warm yellow lights inside the Beanery looked inviting. No, Molly thought. If she went in, she would surely run into one of the owners, Jonathan or Felicity Bean, or someone else she knew, and she was in no mood for small talk.

She turned and walked back up the other side of the street, the wind against her back. She was still so angry at Phil, she could hardly see straight. Walking seemed to help clear her head and slow her racing heartbeat. It didn't, though, change her determination to confront him.

When Molly came in she heard the girls and Phil in the bedroom. She slammed the door theatrically.

"I'm back," she announced, shrugging out of her jacket.

To his credit, Phil began saying good night and soon came out to the kitchen. He picked up his coat and pulled it on. "How was your walk? Your cheeks are sure red."

"My cheeks were red when I left, Phil. Probably because I'm so mad at you I could just scream."

He stared at her with a blank expression. "For interrupting your date, right? I'm sorry about that Molly. He really didn't have to go—"

"It wasn't a *date*. It's not about that at all. You are so dense sometimes, it's just amazing."

She glanced in the direction of the girls' bedroom, deciding that they needed some privacy.

"Come out in the hallway. I need to talk to you." Without waiting for his reply, she walked ahead and opened the door. He followed, looking curiously at her.

"Okay. What's on your mind?" he asked politely.

"Plenty. For starters, you can't just drop in here anytime you like. You don't live here anymore."

"I know." He raised his hands in a gesture of surrender. "I should have called. I won't forget next time."

His mild, nonchalant attitude annoyed her even more.

"You can't just drop out of the sky and decide you want to be a father again. You can't make up for all the time you missed in just a week or with a few trips to the mall."

Phil's mild expression hardened, like molten sugar cooling on a plate. "That's not what I'm trying to do and you know it, Molly. I think you're just peeved because I broke up your little coffee klatch with the doctor. Why are you hanging around in the kitchen? Why doesn't he take you someplace nice?"

Molly was so angry, she felt her head spin. "How dare you say that to me! I know what you're doing. You're just trying to distract me and it's not going to work. And that is not why I'm so angry." Molly took a long, ragged breath, her hands balled into fists at her side.

"What is it then? I just dropped in for five

minutes to say hello to the girls. Now I'm leaving, just like you asked. I don't get it."

"Of course you don't get it. You have no idea, not the foggiest notion, of what it is to be a parent. A real parent. I've been taking care of your daughters on my own for a long time and doing a pretty good job of it. I don't need you to sweep in here, playing Santa Claus in July, and spoiling them rotten and screwing everything up. Maybe you can make them forget how you've ignored them all these years. But you can't make me forget, Phil. I'm a grown-up. I'm not fooled that easily."

Phil's eyes narrowed. He flinched for a moment, as if he had been slapped across the face. "Of course you won't forget, Molly, or forgive me. Not if we live to be a hundred and three. I'll tell you what I think. I think you're just jealous."

Molly gasped. "Jealous? That's insane! What would I be jealous of?"

"Jealous of me. Jealous because the girls do love me and want to give me another chance. You can't stand it. It's driving you up the wall. Go ahead, admit it. Be honest at least."

"You are crazy." Molly shook her head,

feeling incredulous. "Where do you come up with this stuff?"

"You're an open book to me, Molly. You always were and always will be. You've had those girls to yourself for years, and you don't like sharing them. It's as simple as that. You don't like them looking up to somebody else now or seeing that they can love somebody else as much as they love you. Even if it's their own father."

His tone was low and grating, like an annoying appliance grinding away at her nerves. She felt raw and ragged, ready to lash out at him. Yet for some reason, she could hardly speak.

"That's a horrible thing to say to me. It's totally hateful. All the years that you ignored them, I've felt so awful that the girls never had a real father."

He didn't reply. His cold blue stare stated flatly that he stood by his accusation.

He's wrong, she told herself, yet deep inside, his words had struck home. She did feel jealous sometimes when she watched the girls with Phil. Pushed aside and displaced after all the years she had devoted to their needs and care.

She could be rational about it, of course.

All this fuss over Phil didn't mean that they didn't love her anymore. Phil had appeared in a puff of smoke: Santa Claus, the Good Humor Man, and Dream Dad all rolled into one. How could they resist?

But in her heart it had all been very jarring. His reappearance had rocked her world. The deck was still rolling, and Molly felt as if she might be swept overboard.

"I'm here now, Molly. I'm here to stay, and you just have to accept it." Phil's tone was hard edged and maddeningly confident.

"Not so fast, pal. You want to be their dad again? Yippee. But that doesn't mean you can drop in here anytime the mood strikes. From now on, I'm in charge of the visiting schedule. One night a week. You can pick them up after school and have them home by seven—"

"That's impossible with my job!" Phil cut in. "You know that, Molly."

"As for the weekends, every other Saturday from noon to six P.M.," she continued, talking over his objections.

Phil's face turned an angry, mottled shade of red. "I'm their father. I have some rights."

"You gave up those rights when you

walked out on us, Phil. If you don't like my schedule, take me to court. Let a judge hear what a model dad you've been all these years. Let him decide about your *rights.*"

Would she really go to court over this? Probably not, but she could see her threat was working. Phil knew if they ever did go head-to-head in front of a family court judge, his track record would look awful. He had a better chance working things out with her—and that wasn't saying much.

Phil let out a long breath and stepped back, his hands on his hips. Molly watched him, feeling exhausted, as if she'd just run a marathon. She waited to see what he would say, sensing she had won this round.

"I know what you said is true. I know it better than anybody, believe me," he stated slowly. "I've been a washout as a father so far. Which is probably why I'm overdoing it a little now."

"A *little*? Try a lot, Phil. You're overdoing it a lot. . . ."

His sharp look silenced her. "I'm ashamed of myself. Is that what you need to hear? Okay. There, I said it." He leaned back against the wall, looking sad and angry and suddenly as drained as she felt.

"I'm trying to do better. I'm trying to be a better man. Can't you see that? Can't you cut me a little slack here?"

To her surprise his honest admission of failure touched her. She would never have guessed he was capable of that kind of soul-baring confession. Still, she kept her arms crossed over her chest, not wanting him to sense her softening.

"Give me a chance. That's all I'm asking for. And how about I see the girls every weekend? Every other is a little harsh, don't you think?"

His persuasive salesman tone was back, a quick recovery, like one of those toy figures with the round bottoms. You push them down and they spring right up again.

"All right, every weekend," she consented, knowing that the girls would object to the limited schedule as well. "So, the ground rules are understood? Do you have any questions?"

Phil looked as if he were about to reply with some cutting remark, but he pursed his lips closed and shook his head. "No questions. I'll be back on Saturday, I guess."

"Yes, I guess so. Good night."

She turned and went back inside her

apartment, shutting the door and leaning back against it for a moment. She wondered if the girls had been standing in this same spot, eavesdropping, moments before. She was sure that they must have been curious about what was going on out in the hallway between her and Phil. They wouldn't be happy to hear they'd be seeing Phil less. But she would deal with that problem when the time came, Molly decided. They couldn't go out with him so many nights of the week and get home late. It just wasn't practical. They were both falling behind in their schoolwork, and Lauren had barely touched the piano since Phil appeared on the scene. She would have to explain it to them and hope they understood. But of course, once again, she would be the one playing the villain in this domestic soap opera.

Might as well get myself a stovepipe hat and fake mustache, Molly thought wearily as she finally locked the door and turned off the lights.

CHAPTER NINE

Carl left the house and closed the door, then realized he didn't have a key to lock up. He looked under the mat, ran his hand on the ledge above the door, and even checked around the hedges for one of those fake rocks that people think are so clever for hiding spare keys. He was about to give up when his gaze happened upon a white flowerpot filled with yellow straw flowers on the top step. He picked it up and shook it. Just as he had suspected, the loose key in the bottom rattled noisily.

He tipped the pot, locked the door, and replaced the key, chuckling to himself. A flower pot, for pity's sake. A policeman ought to think of a better spot than that. Originality was never Tucker's strong suit, that was for sure.

He wondered what Tucker or Fran would think if one of them stopped home today for lunch and found the house empty. Fran would probably assume he was gone for good and start cleaning his room, as if he'd had bubonic plague. Then she would celebrate. He wasn't so sure about Tucker, though, and brushed the question from his mind.

It would be a while before he could leave for good. Though the swelling was down on his leg, he still needed something to help him walk. He hated using the crutches. It made him feel like a broken old man, but he knew he wouldn't make it too far without them. And he needed to get out. He was going stir-crazy in that flowered little tissue box of a room.

Hobbling along at a fairly quick pace, Carl reached the end of Tucker's street and turned onto Emerson. He paused and caught his breath. It was a fairly mild day, the sky clear and the air cool but humid with a hint of the spring weather soon to come. He wasn't having as much trouble breathing as he had expected, but he wondered if it was wiser to just take himself around the block a time or two and call it a day.

Then looking down to the end of the street, he decided what the heck, might as well try to make it all the way to town. It wasn't so far. Worse comes to worst, he would collapse on the sidewalk and someone would call Tucker.

He hadn't gotten a good look at the village that first night he landed here. Wasn't in much shape for sightseeing, he recalled. Now he was curious to see what the place had turned into. Tucker claimed it was almost the same as when he left years ago, but Carl had his doubts. Nothing stays the same. He didn't know much, but he sure knew that well enough by now.

He limped along, resting every few minutes to catch his breath. He had borrowed one of Tucker's jackets and a baseball cap and thought he looked fairly respectable, though he hadn't shaved for a few days.

He rounded the corner and found himself on Main Street. He stopped and stared down the street, feeling as if he had just walked onto a movie set. Everything looked so nice here, so pretty and clean. Like a picture postcard. The kind of town he could never afford to live in. He had never noticed that as a kid or even a young man. He'd just taken it all for granted.

He limped past a Victorian that held an antique shop. The Bramble, the sign read. He remembered that place. It was called something else in his time. An old man sat in a rocker on the porch, whittling a piece of wood. A yellow Labrador lay at his feet, as calm as a statue.

The old man stopped carving for a moment and met his eye, peering out from under the edge of his cap. Carl paused, leaning on his crutches. Digger Hegman, that was his name. An old fisherman, famous for clamming and predicting the weather. Carl was surprised to see the old geezer still alive.

"Hey, there," Digger called out to him. "Do I know you?"

Carl hesitated, not knowing how to reply. "I doubt it, mister. I'm a stranger here. Just visiting."

Digger kept staring at him, appearing unsatisfied with the reply. Finally, though, he returned to his carving.

Carl turned away and continued down the street. A short time later he spotted the Clam Box. He stopped, his body rigid as he recalled so many memories. After all these years, just looking at that sign still brought a sour feeling to the pit of his stomach. He remembered when old Otto Bates accused him of robbing the place. Though he certainly hadn't been any choirboy, he hadn't stolen so much as a teaspoon from that place. Didn't matter to Otto though. His mind had been made up, and he managed to convince half the town that he was right, too, no matter that the police said differently. Carl took a deep breath. Otto had barred him from going in there for years, as if Carl were carrying some contagious disease.

Some small voice still told him not to cross the street. But something else goaded him on. *Old Otto is dead and buried, and besides that, nobody would even recognize me now. Except maybe Charlie.* Charlie had never liked Carl, and the feeling had been mutual. Tucker and Charlie were still friends, Carl gathered from his brother's conversations. Though from

Tucker's tone, it sounded like the magic was gone from that romance.

Carl wasn't sure what was pushing him to go in there; it certainly wasn't fond memories. But he was tired and wanted some coffee before he headed back to Tucker's. He pushed off on his crutches and hobbled across the street. He hadn't come this far to be scared off by the memory of old Otto Bates. *No sir,* he thought with a small smile, as he slowly opened the door. *Going in here after all this time, all things considered, might even be fun.*

It was midmorning and the place looked almost empty. A bell above the door jangled when he opened it, but no one paid him any mind. There were only two or three customers.

A waitress glanced up from behind the counter and smiled. "Take a seat anywhere. I'll be right with you."

He made his way to a booth by the window, slipped into the seat, and set the crutches on the seat opposite. There was a mimeographed menu in a plastic holder propped up between the salt and pepper shakers. It looked just the same as it always had. The same typos, too. "Fred Chicken in a Basket" was his favorite. *Poor old Fred,* he thought. *We're in the same boat now, pal.*

"So, what can I get you?" The waitress's voice interrupted his thoughts. He glanced at her under the brim of his hat, afraid she was someone he used to know.

"Just coffee, thanks," he mumbled. She jotted down the order, and he watched her walk back to the counter.

He did know her. Lucy Dooley. She had been a pretty one. Still had her looks, too. She would be Lucy Bates now, he suddenly remembered. She could have done better, that was for sure. Some women didn't have much sense when it came to picking men. A few had even latched onto him when he was younger.

A few minutes later Lucy returned with the coffee. He turned away, acting suddenly interested in the view out the window.

"Here you are, sir." She set down the coffee mug, a teaspoon, and a pitcher of milk with practiced efficiency. "Anything else?"

"Uh . . . no, thanks. That's okay for now." He coughed into his hand, and he sensed her looking at him. He looked away again, but couldn't help coughing.

She leaned over and gently touched his shoulder. "How about some water?" Not waiting for his reply, she went off to get it.

She soon returned and set the glass down in front of him. He thought she would leave again, but she stood there waiting for him to drink. He picked it up, his hand shaking a bit, and took a long swallow.

She was still there when he was done. There was a soft look in her eyes. He knew that look. She pitied him. He felt sure now that she recognized him but was too nice to say so.

"Thank you for the water, Lucy," he said slowly. Her eyes widened with surprise, but he smiled a little and pointed to the tag on her uniform. "That's your name, right?"

She smiled back. "Sure, that's me. Let me know if you need anything else, sir."

She walked away, and he breathed a sigh of relief. He had thought he was ready to face these people. Well, it appeared he wasn't up to it. Not today anyway, he realized.

A few minutes later, almost done with his coffee, Carl glanced around to ask for the check. The bell above the door jangled, and

Charlie Bates stalked in, carrying a carton that appeared to be filled with cans.

He walked to the counter and dropped his load, then he turned and glanced at Carl. His gaze didn't linger, Carl noticed with relief. But then Charlie turned his head again and pinned Carl with a stare. Carl looked down at his coffee cup, burrowing into his coat and tugging the brim of his hat over his eyes.

Too late. Charlie started toward him with determined steps.

He stood at Carl's table, fists on his hips. "You have a lot of nerve showing up here. Didn't your brother warn you not to come in here?"

All heads turned in their direction. The other customers stopped talking and eating. Carl slowly lifted his head and met Charlie's angry stare.

"Tucker never said a word to me about you. What are you talking about?"

"He didn't, huh? Well, how about I don't believe you? I told him I didn't want to see you in here. Now I'm telling you."

Charlie leaned over, his angry face filling Carl's field of vision. "You know why, too," he added bitterly. "Don't play dumb with me, Carl. I'm not like Tucker. I see right through you. Now get out."

Carl didn't move a muscle. He didn't even breathe. He felt a surge of anger simmering up inside. Then he sat back and laughed like a crazy man until tears came into his eyes.

"You getting tough with me, Bates? That's a laugh. Places I've been, you couldn't scare a cockroach back into his hole." He shook his head, wheezing harshly between words.

"Why you—get up!" Charlie pushed Carl's shoulder.

Staring back defiantly, Carl barely budged.

Lucy rushed over and tugged on her husband's arm. "He's a customer, Charlie. Have you lost your mind?"

"Get away, Lucy. I know what I'm doing," Charlie snapped.

Carl came slowly to his feet, his stance shaky. "You want a fight? Go on, take the first swing. I dare you."

Carl felt his heart pound, the blood rushing into his head. He was a little dizzy and wasn't sure what he'd do if Charlie actually took a swing at him. Fight back as best he could, he guessed. He didn't care if he was half dead. He wasn't going to back down from this puffed up, bug-eyed bully.

Charlie stood staring at him, considering his next move.

He'll probably grab me by the collar and drag me out of here, Carl thought. *Not without a struggle though.*

The bell above the door jangled and the door opened. Reverend Ben Lewis stepped inside and stared around. He spotted the two men and paused for a moment, then slowly walked over. "Hello, Charlie. Hello, Carl," he spoke in a normal tone, seemingly unaware of the tense standoff he had interrupted. "Glad to see you up and around, Carl. How are you feeling?"

"I walked into town to get some air," Carl answered awkwardly.

"That was ambitious. You must be hungry. Did you eat lunch yet?"

"He was just leaving," Charlie said flatly.

"Really? I hate to eat alone. Maybe you can sit awhile and keep me company," Reverend Ben persisted.

Carl glanced at Charlie's warning glare, then back at the reverend. Finally, he nodded. "Have a seat, Reverend. I've got all the

time in the world." He swallowed a lump in
his throat and sat down again, avoiding
Charlie's scowl. "I guess I am hungry, after
all."

Lucy stepped deftly around her husband
and slipped the crutches off the seat opposite Carl, clearing the space for the reverend.

"I'll just put this aside for now," she said.
"Your menus are on the table, gentlemen.
Specials are on the board."

She glanced at Charlie's frozen expression, then went to get the reverend a glass
of water and to refill Carl's glass. Charlie
glanced at Carl a moment, then back at the
reverend. Carl could see he knew he'd been
beat.

"I'd better get back in the kitchen. See
you later," he mumbled as he walked away.

Carl peered at the reverend from under
the brim of his hat. Reverend Ben had
pulled his fat from the fire just now, that was
for sure. But he didn't know how to thank
him. He pretended to read his menu, then
stared out the window.

Lucy came by and took their orders, a
grilled cheese and tomato sandwich for
Reverend Ben and a burger for Carl.

Finally Reverend Ben slipped his menu back between the salt and pepper shakers. "I don't know why I spend so much time reading that thing. I could recite it by heart by now."

"I know it up and down, and I haven't stepped foot in this place for twenty years."

Reverend Ben grinned. "So, what do you think of the town, Carl? Does it look different to you?"

Carl shrugged. "Not as much as I expected. That was always the good thing about this place as well as the bad. It doesn't change much." He glanced over his shoulder at Charlie, who was working behind the counter. "The people around here don't either."

The reverend nodded. He removed his wire-rimmed glasses and polished them with a hanky. "Do you think people can change? Or that God just makes a person a certain way and that's it?"

Carl laughed nervously. How did God get mixed up in it all of a sudden? Leave it to a preacher to pull a fast move like that on you.

"I don't know. What do I know about God?" Carl shrugged but the reverend kept looking at him, as if he didn't accept that as a fair answer. "I guess people can change, sure. Why not?"

"Exactly. Why not." The reverend put his glasses back on and stared straight at Carl, a mild smile on his bearded face.

Carl felt the silence between them pressing him to speak.

"The question is, what's a guy going to get out of all the effort it takes to change. If there's no payoff, why bother?"

"That's one way of looking at it." The reverend nodded. "Of course, in my line of work, I see it from a different perspective. I see people struggling to change and sometimes failing at it, wondering, like you say, what's the payoff? Meanwhile they don't see that they already have the payoff in hand. Before they even try. And even if they never try at all."

Carl cast the reverend a puzzled look. He gave a nervous laugh and leaned back in his seat. "I'm sorry, Reverend. You lost me now. This kind of talk is getting a little heavy for me."

"It's simple, Carl. God loves us just the way we are. He loves us and forgives us, no matter what we do. That's the payoff I'm talking about."

Carl felt uneasy. He shifted in his seat, not knowing what to say.

"Sure . . . I get you," he finally replied.

Lucy brought their food, and the two men began to eat. Carl's thoughts wandered back to the days when his stepmother would bring him and Tucker to church on Sunday mornings. She would hold his hand when they walked across the village green, maybe just the way good mothers do. Or maybe because she was afraid he was going to take off on her.

He did remember some of this stuff. Of course in prison the ministers were always coming by, hoping you were so bored staring at four walls, you would try reading the Bible and talking with them, but they had never gotten far with him.

Carl set his hamburger down and wiped his hands on a napkin. "I never thanked you for taking me to the hospital. And visiting me there."

"That's okay. I'm glad I could help you." The reverend sat back. "I've been meaning to ask, Carl, why did you come back here?"

"I just wanted to see the place again. I'm not really sure why."

"Because it was home?"

"Yeah, maybe. For better or worse. I have more unhappy memories than good ones, I guess. But they're all mine."

The reverend took a sip of coffee. "I'm glad you came back," he said suddenly. "I think it's good for you and Tucker to see each other again."

Carl laughed. "Then you're the only one with that opinion. Tucker doesn't want me here. Neither does his wife. I don't even think the dog likes me."

"No, Carl. I think you're wrong. It might take time, but I think that eventually you'll see what I'm saying is true."

"Yeah, well, that's the thing. I won't be here for long. Not that long, anyway."

The reverend didn't reply, looking at Carl as if he knew something Carl didn't know. The look made Carl uneasy. *These preachers get ideas in their heads sometimes. Doesn't mean I have to listen,* Carl told himself. He wasn't going to stay around much longer. He'd been here too long already.

* * *

On Thursday night, Molly drove home from her second class feeling hopeful and energized. The instructor, a woman named Pauline Turner, spiced up her lessons with strange but true catering and restaurant adventures that were funny and instructive. She had started her own business in circumstances much like Molly's and was very successful, despite some struggles along the way. Her story gave Molly heart, and the practical how-to instruction—on everything from renting equipment to hiring helpers to timing each course—helped Molly feel that at some point, she too could manage her own catering business.

Still, she didn't feel ready to disclose her plan to the world-at-large. That would add too much pressure. What if she decided *not* to go through with it? Then she'd feel like a failure for not even trying.

She did have to ask Sam and even Phil to help her out by watching the girls while she was in class, but she had told them she was taking a first-aid course in CPR. She already knew CPR, but fortunately neither of them remembered.

Tonight at the last minute Sam got held

up, so Jessica had come over to stay with Lauren and Jill.

"I'm home," Molly announced. She found Jessica in the living room, reading a book in the armchair. "How did it go?"

"Just fine. Your daughters are perfect angels."

"Right, tell me about it." Molly sat down on the couch and found a bunched-up sock wedged between the cushions. She plucked it out and tossed it on the floor. "They're so neat with their belongings, too. What are you reading?"

"Nothing special." Jessica held up her book so Molly could see the jacket. "Some historical for my book group. It's a little boring, actually . . . but I was also reading this, which looked very interesting."

Jessica leaned over and picked up a book from the side table. Molly recognized one of her textbooks from the class, the one she had forgotten to bring with her tonight.

"Food with Flair: A Complete Guide to the Catering Business." Jessica looked up at Molly, then opened the book and pulled out Molly's registration card. "You're not studying CPR at the high school, are you?" she asked with a small smile.

Molly sighed and shook her head. "The canapé is out of the bag, I guess."

"I guess," Jessica agreed with a short laugh. "Why the big secret? Why didn't you tell anybody?"

"I don't know. . . . I'm thinking about starting up a little business. A shop, maybe, where I can sell stuff I cook and then use it as a home base for catering."

Jessica sat up with an excited expression. "That's a great idea! You'd be perfect for that."

"Not so fast, please. I'm just taking the course for now to see what's really involved. I didn't want to tell anyone because . . . well, if I don't do it, then everyone will be bugging me and asking why and making me feel dumb or something."

Jessica didn't say anything for a moment. She closed the textbook and put it back on the table. "I see what you mean. Sometimes it's better to plan something like this privately. What are you going to do for capital?"

Leave it to a banker to go straight to the bottom line, Molly thought. "Well, that's the problem right there. I have zero assets.

Who's going to loan me enough money to get this thing off the ground?"

"A bank can make you a loan, even if you don't own a house or have a lot of assets. There are still ways to finance a start-up business. I can help you," Jessica offered. "I'd love to help you, really. That's what I do. You know that."

Molly was moved by the offer. She didn't have the best relationship with her sister-in-law; she never expected Jessica to believe that she could make a go of this catering idea. Molly had never felt that Jessica thought that well of her.

"A loan like that is a big commitment," Molly finally answered. "That part worries me, too. What if I screw up and the business fails? Then I'd be stuck with this huge debt." She looked up at Jessica. "I don't think I'm ready for that yet."

Jessica gazed at her a moment and then gave her small smile. "I understand." She looked back at the book. "I noticed the course doesn't cover the finance chapter until later. Maybe after you go over it at school, you'll feel more comfortable talking about it with me."

"Maybe," Molly agreed. She took a

breath. It actually felt good to talk to someone besides Betty about this instead of
keeping it all inside her head. She was
still surprised, though, that her confidante
turned out to be Jessica.

"You've met a lot of people who try to
start a business. Tell me the truth, do you
really think I can do this? My feelings won't
be hurt if you say no," Molly added hastily,
even if it wasn't entirely true.

"Absolutely," Jessica replied. "I'm sure
you can. But you have to believe you can
do it, even if other people don't. I guess
that's the common denominator in the people who come to me and really make a go
of it."

"Yeah, the confidence thing. I have trouble with that," Molly admitted. "I did find a
great dress for meeting new clients. That's
helped a lot," she joked.

"Hey, don't knock the clothes factor.
There's nothing like a good hair day to
make you feel you can take on the world.
But everyone feels shaky from time to time,
Molly. Nobody has it all together all the
time."

"Sure, I know that. Not even Oprah," she
said, making Jessica smile. "But sometimes

I feel like other people have it together a lot more than I do. It's like, they know some trick that I don't know."

"You mean like in a self-help book?" Jessica glanced around and found one in a stack of books on the table. "I used to read these all the time, too. Some of them aren't so bad. Then I realized something that helps when I feel down about life and everything seems to be going wrong."

"Really? What's the secret?" Molly asked with a grin.

"That I don't have to do it all myself."

Molly knew Jessica was talking about God and felt distinctly uncomfortable. But she also knew that Jessica had not always been so spiritually minded. *When she came back to Cape Light last year to help take care of her mother, before she met Sam, she was like me,* Molly recalled. But Jessica had seemed much happier since then. Molly always thought the change was because of Sam. But maybe it was more.

"You mean thinking about God helps you have more confidence? Is that what you're saying?"

"Something like that. Let God into your life. Tell Him your problems, your worries about the future. Let Him help you. He created the whole world in six days. A little catering business shouldn't be so tough."

Molly laughed. "That's pretty odd advice from a banker."

"Maybe, maybe not." Jessica smiled and came to her feet. "You wouldn't think it was strange if I recommended some new self-help book, right? Well, think of the Scriptures as a really good self-help book."

Molly didn't know what to say. She knew she had a Bible in the house somewhere, but she'd probably get an allergy attack from the dust if she ever dug it out.

"I hope your plan does succeed, Molly. I really do," Jessica added sincerely.

Molly felt embarrassed. "Thanks . . . so do I."

All in all, Tucker thought, the talk with Fran had helped. She wasn't walking around the house with that tight, angry look anymore. That didn't mean she'd changed her mind about Carl. The other night Michael asked Carl if he wanted to play a video game with him. Fran hadn't said anything, but she kept making excuses for Tucker to go into the den and check on them. Carl, it turned out, was good at video games.

On Saturday Tucker had the perfect excuse to escape the house for a while. He had promised Reverend Ben he would stop by the church and do some small repairs around the building. Gus Potter used to take care of those things. Since he got sick, there had been talk of hiring a regular groundskeeper, but so far nothing had been done and all of the deacons took turns. Today was Tucker's.

Reverend Ben was not very handy, but he liked to watch an ongoing repair. He seemed fascinated, always studying just how it was done. So Tucker wasn't really surprised when he heard the reverend's footsteps approach. The timing could have been better, though. Tucker was on his back, his head stuck under a sink as he attempted to repair a leaky pipe.

"How is it going, Tucker? At home, I mean." That question wasn't a surprise, either. "Is Fran getting used to the idea of having Carl around?" the reverend asked, handing Tucker a wrench.

"Things are better with Fran. We talked it

out and she's resigned herself to the idea of him being there, at least for a while."

Tucker fitted the wrench to the pipe joint and gave it a yank. It didn't budge at first. He took a deep breath and pushed with all his might. It moved a fraction of an inch.

"I see. So Carl is accepted but not exactly welcome?"

"Pretty much." Tucker grunted, pushing hard on the wrench and finally unfastening the pipe section. "Fran's doing the best she can, but it's hard for her. She's like a lot of other people in this town. She thinks he's trouble." Tucker came out from under the sink and shook his head. "I feel for Fran. But I also feel bad for Carl. He knows she doesn't really want him there."

"That's not the best situation for either one," Reverend Ben agreed. "What do *you* want?"

"Search me," Tucker said ruefully. "All I know is Carl's got no other place to go, and I promised him he could stay with us until he's strong enough to be on his own."

The reverend reached out and patted Tucker's shoulder. "You're doing the right thing, Tucker. Don't forget that."

"Thanks, Reverend. I know you're in my

corner. The problem is, I worry that maybe Fran, and even Charlie, might be right. Maybe Carl hasn't changed and never will. I could be the one making a big mistake here."

"If Carl hasn't changed, you'll find out and have to deal with it. But you can never make a mistake by sticking to your principles and showing compassion for your brother. Especially under such pressure."

"I'm feeling the pressure all right," Tucker admitted.

The reverend didn't reply. He watched as Tucker checked the threaded edges of the pipe, then eased himself back under the sink.

"I'm not that great a plumber, Reverend. I think it's fixed for now. But keep your eye on it."

"I will."

"Hand me that wrench again, will you?" Tucker called to him. The wrench appeared, and Tucker took hold of it.

"I think you've just given me an idea." The reverend stuck his head under the sink, looking surprised and happy. "If Carl feels good enough to walk into town, he's probably able to take a job. The church needs a handyman, and I have the authority to hire anyone I choose."

"You'd hire Carl to work here?" Tucker began to sit up and hit his head on the bottom of the sink. He came out again, rubbing the sore spot.

"Exactly. Carl needs a real job, a sense of purpose—somewhere to go every day and money in his pocket. I think this is a good solution all around, don't you?"

"It could be if Carl wants to stay here," Tucker said cautiously. "He is feeling much better. And he had a good report from the doctor yesterday." Tucker rubbed his head again. "He's handy, too. Much better than me. I'll talk to him about it, see what he thinks."

"Tell him he can drop by anytime to see me. The job is his for the asking."

"Thanks, Reverend. I appreciate your help," Tucker said sincerely.

"No thanks necessary. You know that, Tucker." The reverend smiled. "Now about this sink . . . I don't know much about this stuff but what about this piece? Doesn't it go somewhere?"

He held up a thin metal washer, and Tucker groaned. "I forgot to put it back on.

Now I'm going to have to take apart the whole thing and start over."

Reverend Ben looked contrite. "I'm sorry. I distracted you with all my questions."

"My fault," Tucker said. "I should have known it was missing. Carl would have. He would have had this fixed by now."

The reverend smiled. "Then let's hope he agrees to take the job."

CHAPTER TEN

On Sunday, after the service, Reverend Ben went to his office where Carolyn waited. A fresh, cool breeze filtered through the open window, ruffling his papers and nearly blowing them away. It was the first truly mild day the town had seen in many months, but for once the promise of spring did nothing to lift his spirits. Wordlessly, Carolyn helped him remove his vestments, then they walked out together to their car and headed for the orchard.

They drove out of town and along the Beach Road, the radio tuned to the classical station. Neither spoke for a long time.

"I might have to stay awhile. Sophie sounded as if he was very bad."

"I understand. I'll have Mark come pick me up later. I'll leave you the car."

"All right. I guess that would be best."

Carolyn sat with her gloved hands clutching her purse on her lap. It was good of her to come today, he thought. She knew that this visit was hard for him. Visits like this always were, but this one especially. He was sure that when she married him, she had no idea of what it would be like to be a minister's wife: the tedious hours of bake sales and the Christmas Fair committee spliced between life's most intense moments. Yet Carolyn seemed to sail through it all so smoothly. She kept him balanced and sane. She'd never know how much.

The Potter house was filled with people, food, and flowers, all the trappings of one of their famous parties, framed within a mournful, somber atmosphere. The living room was crowded with relatives. Ben recognized some of the grandchildren and Sophie's brother, Fred, who lived down in Florida.

Sophie's daughter Una came to greet them and take their coats. Ben and Carolyn embraced her, and he could see that her eyes were puffy from crying. Una led them to Gus, who lay in a hospital bed in the guest room on the first floor. Sophie sat by his side and held his hand. With her back to the door, she didn't even notice that Ben and Carolyn were there.

The smell of sickness filled the room. For a moment Ben felt as if he couldn't breathe. He stepped closer to the bed. Gus's eyes were closed. Ben wondered if Gus had already lost consciousness.

Sophie's daughter Evelyn and her son, Bart, stood on the other side of the bed. Evelyn walked up to him and took his hand. "Thank you for coming, Reverend."

"Evelyn, how are you holding up?"

"I'm managing. The waiting is so hard. It's very hard on Mom," she said, glancing at Sophie.

"Yes, of course. This is the most difficult time of all." It was true. Ben remembered when his own mother was dying, watching her cling to the last threads of life. He had been torn between desperate hopes that she would live just a little longer and equally desperate prayers for her painless release into the Lord's loving embrace.

"He goes in and out," Evelyn said. "The

doctor said it would be like this. He's not in any pain, though, thank God."

"That is a blessing," Carolyn agreed.

Sophie turned her head, finally noticing Ben and Carolyn. Wordlessly, she held out her hand, and Ben stepped forward. He clasped her hand and then bent to kiss her cheek. Her skin was dry and papery, her stare, glassy.

"He can hear you if you talk to him," she said quietly. "I'm sure he can. He opens his eyes from time to time."

Ben nodded. There was nothing to say. He swallowed hard and glanced at Gus. His skin, which once glowed with health and vitality, was yellow and sickly, his face and limbs bloated.

He took Gus's swollen hand and sat at the edge of the bed. "Gus, it's Reverend Ben. Can you hear me?"

He didn't think Gus had heard at first. Then he saw the sick man's head move against the pillow. Gus's eyes fluttered open for a moment, and he stared up at Ben. "Reverend . . . good. I think I'm ready. . . . Will you send me off?"

"He wants to receive the sacrament," Evelyn said. "Can you do that for him?"

"Of course. I've brought everything." Ben swallowed hard.

He stroked Gus's hand. Gus had already closed his eyes, but Ben could see a peaceful expression on his face, and he knew Gus had heard him.

A short time later, Ben completed celebrating the sacrament at Gus's bedside. Sophie, her children, and a few of her grandchildren circled the bed, and Una led the group in a prayer. With their heads bowed and hands clasped, it seemed to Ben for a moment that they composed a circle of living, vibrating love, their final gift to Gus, a parting embrace as he journeyed on.

Ben felt witness to something awesome and powerful. *This is what life is all about,* he thought. *What love is all about. Forget the hearts and flowers. It's a mighty force, frightening in its power.*

Of all Gus had experienced in his long life, above all, he was loved, Ben thought. And that was saying a great deal.

Carolyn left a short time later. Ben sat with Sophie in the room while others came in and out over the long hours. The afternoon faded black into night, and the night then crept along slowly.

Ben found himself dozing in a chair. Someone had tossed an afghan over him, Sophie probably. He sat up, feeling cramped and sore. He checked his watch. A little past five in the morning. The room was shadowy, the day's first light mingled with the glow of a small lamp by Gus's bed. Sophie still sat in her chair, holding Gus's hand, as focused and alert as when Ben had arrived that afternoon.

"Any change?" he asked, resting his hand on her shoulder.

"Yes . . . I think he's really going now." She rose and sat on the edge of the bed, then leaned toward Gus and placed her arm around his shoulders. "I'm here, Gus. I'm right here with you. Don't be afraid. Just let go now, darling," she whispered.

Gus didn't respond. Ben felt his breath catch. Was he already gone?

Then he saw Gus's hand stir, reaching to touch Sophie. She bowed her head to his chest, and his fingers found her hair. She was crying now, silent tears that fell from her eyes and dropped onto Gus.

Seconds later, Gus's hand fell limp and

lifeless on his chest. Ben saw it and realized what had happened. No matter how many sickrooms he attended, no matter how many times he witnessed a person's passing, it was always so startling to him, the way the spirit of life leaves the body. When it finally happens, it's in the blink of an eye, as if someone had simply blown out a match.

Sophie seemed to stop breathing, too. For a minute everything in the room seemed to freeze. Then she released a long, keening wail that echoed through the house to the silent trees outside the window, to the very corners of the world beyond.

She collapsed in a heap on her husband as her children rushed to her side. She clung to his body for a moment, then with resignation, bowed her head and kissed his cheek before allowing her daughters and son to help her to her feet.

"It's over, Mother. Dad is gone." Una sobbed, embracing Sophie.

"Yes, he's gone from us," Sophie managed between tears. "But I know he's at peace. He's with the angels now."

* * *

The weekend passed, and Tucker never quite got around to telling Carl about the handyman job at the church. He wondered if he should tell Fran about it first, but he knew what her reaction would be: Why make it so easy for Carl to settle in? Wasn't the plan for him to go?

The truth was, Tucker felt the same way. He hadn't quite realized it when he was talking to Reverend Ben. But in the days since, he hadn't told Carl about the job because he wasn't sure he wanted Carl to stay. Carl had gotten a good report from the doctor on Friday. In a week or two, he would be well enough to travel. Considering all the upset he'd caused so far, did it really make sense for him to stay?

On Monday morning, Tucker dressed and went off to work, the guilty secret heavy inside him. He went on patrol, cruising around the village and mulling over the problem all morning. When it was time for his lunch break, he decided to stop at home. Maybe with no one else in the house, he'd find the courage to talk to Carl. There was always the chance Carl didn't even want the job, that he was set on moving on. Tucker tried to focus on that possibility. He felt bound by his talk with the reverend to say something though. It just didn't seem right not to let Carl know.

He let himself in through the side door and heard Carl in the kitchen. His brother looked startled to see him. Guilty even, though when Tucker checked to see what Carl was up to, he was only making sandwiches on the countertop.

A great many sandwiches, actually. It looked like half the contents of the refrigerator had been emptied out—packages of lunch meats, cheese, pickles, and other condiments. About twenty slices of bread were lined up. Some were covered with cold cuts, others with peanut butter, while another stack of bread slices stood waiting on the side.

Tucker was just grateful Fran never came home at this time. "What's going on?" he asked, keeping his voice casual. "Are you opening up a restaurant in here or something?"

Carl forced a smile but didn't look up from his task. "Nope. These are all for me. I'm going on sort of a picnic."

Tucker got it now. Carl was getting ready to leave. Right away, too. He felt a funny shock ripple through his body, as if he'd just been cut free from a tangled line.

Carl was leaving by his own choice. There wouldn't be any angry scenes or confrontations. No drawn-out stay. No more arguments with Fran. It looked as though he wasn't even going to say good-bye. To his surprise, Tucker realized he was hurt by that.

"You're leaving?" Tucker asked bluntly.

"That's right." Carl began slapping bread slices on the open-faced sandwiches, as if working on an assembly line.

"Weren't you even going to say good-bye?"

Carl glanced at him. "I was going to leave a note."

Right, about three or four words long, Tucker guessed. Carl never was a big one for letter writing.

He picked up the corner of a piece of bread and peeked underneath. "Can I have one of these?"

"Help yourself; they're your cold cuts." Carl gave a short laugh and shook his head.

Tucker took the sandwich and put it on a plate, then sat down at the table. "Why are you leaving? Because of what happened in the diner with Charlie Bates? I don't know how I stayed friends with him for so long. He's a troublemaker and a fool."

"I won't argue with that. But that's not why. I told you from the start I wasn't going to stay long."

"The doctor says you need more time to recover. At least a week more. I was right there when he told you."

"What does he know? I've been in worse shape than this and gotten along just fine, believe me."

Tucker did believe him. That was half the problem. He chewed on his sandwich, suddenly feeling reluctant to see Carl go.

"There's a lot of mustard on this," he muttered. "What do you use, half a bottle per sandwich?"

"Mustard's the best thing. Soaks into the bread. Ketchup and relish, too. Keeps it from getting too stale. You can't use mayonnaise. It can kill you, sitting there a day or two."

Tucker's stomach recoiled at the thought. Carl was planning on carrying this food around for a long time, he realized, a frighteningly long time.

"You can't go yet," he told Carl. "Fran is

finally getting used to having you around. She told me this morning she was going to make meatloaf tonight, and she knows how I hate it. 'Your brother likes my meatloaf,' she said to me."

"She didn't say that. You're making it up." Carl pulled off a piece of plastic wrap and folded it around a sandwich.

"She did, too. My right hand to God." Tucker sat up, raising his hand.

"You're swearing now, see? My bad influence is rubbing off on you. I've got to go."

"Look," Tucker said, "I understand if you're tired of sitting around this place. You can get out a little now. Get a change of scenery."

"Right. And have some guy like Charlie try to push me around just to prove what an upstanding citizen he is? No, thanks. People in this town have short tempers and long memories, Tucker. Too many of them can't forget my past. I don't even know why I came back in the first place. And not to see you, if that's what you're thinking," he added gruffly over his shoulder.

"I wasn't thinking that." But now Tucker wondered about it. *Carl is such a twisted soul. Maybe he did come back to see me.*

"People like to gossip in this town," Tucker reminded him. "Before you know it, you'll be old news. They'll be on to something else."

Carl didn't look at him. He didn't even seem to be listening as he sorted the wrapped sandwiches, packing them into large plastic bags.

"Why give in to jerks like Charlie Bates? Why let him win? That's not the Carl I know," Tucker goaded him.

Carl turned to face him. "You hit the nail on the head right there, Tucker. We haven't seen each other in over twenty years. You don't know me anymore and I don't know you."

"Of course we know each other," Tucker protested. "Neither one of us has changed that much—except maybe we've both gotten more stubborn."

"For pity's sake . . . what difference does it make?" Carl's hands trembled as he jammed the last of the sandwiches into a bag. "Why do you want me here? What's in it for you? Your wife isn't happy about it. Neither are your neighbors. I just don't get it, Tucker. You ought to be offering me a ride to the bus station, not dredging up reasons for me to stay."

"I'll take you to the bus station, if that's what you really want," Tucker said slowly. "I just don't want to see you forced out. That's not right. It's not fair."

"Oh, no. Here we go again." Carl looked up at the ceiling and shook his head. "I'll tell you something, sonny. The word 'fair' isn't in my dictionary. I don't worry about fair and not fair. I'd go a little crazy if I did."

Tucker sat back and crossed his arms over his chest. He felt the heavy knot of his secret lodged at the bottom of his throat.

"Would you stay if you had a job?"

"A job?" Carl laughed and rubbed the back of his neck. "Who would hire me?"

"There's a job at the church. A grounds-keeper/handyman kind of thing. Reverend Ben says it's yours for the asking."

Carl stared at him, then turned slowly back to the counter where he started to clean up the mess he had made.

"When were you going to tell me about this? After I left?"

Tucker felt his face get hot. Carl was sharp, sharper than he liked to let on. "I'm telling you now, aren't I? This might work out for you. You were always good with your hands."

"I've had jobs like that. Plenty of them," Carl said gruffly. "No question I can do it."

Tucker wondered if he had insulted Carl. His brother used to have such grandiose ideas about himself. This job probably sounded too lowly to him. Well, it was, Tucker thought sadly. It was also as good an offer as he might get.

"It's kind of hard to imagine me going off to church every day," Carl said wryly. "But I wouldn't mind working for the reverend. He's not so bad—when he lays off the God talk."

Tucker was about to reply but held his tongue, waiting to see what Carl would decide.

"I don't know. People might not like it. They might cause more trouble for you," Carl added.

"I'm not afraid of that." Suddenly, Tucker really wasn't afraid. He recalled what the reverend had told him, and he felt himself on solid ground. "I wouldn't have told you about the job if I didn't want you to take it."

That was true, too, he realized. He had been waffling about this for days, but now that he finally put it on the table for Carl, he knew he had done the right thing. This job could change Carl's life. He would have steady work and be near family. He would be far less likely to slip back into the life of a homeless drifter.

Carl turned from the sink and looked at him. "I guess I could talk to the reverend about it, see what he says. If it doesn't pan out, I'll leave tomorrow. Or the next day."

"Sure, you go talk to him. You know the reverend. He's a good guy."

"Yeah, he's all right." Carl dried his hands on a paper towel, then tossed it in the trash. "You're not so bad, either, come to think of it. I give you a hard time, but you turned out all right, Tucker. You're a stand-up guy."

CHAPTER ELEVEN

On Tuesday morning the church was packed with mourners. Everyone in town seemed to have put their jobs and other responsibilities on hold in order to pay their last respects to Gus Potter.

Surrounded by her family, Sophie sat in the first pew, looking exhausted and bereft. Ben's heart went out to her. He had discussed the service with the Potters over the weekend, and they had chosen the hymns and Scriptures and designated readers from their circle of friends and relations. Gus had requested a favorite hymn, "I've Got Peace like a River," and Ben found his eyes filling with tears as the choir sang the familiar verses.

Finally, it was time to give the eulogy. Ben slowly approached the pulpit. The congregation sat in silent, sad attention. The task before him—to capture some sense of Gus's long virtuous life and somehow ease their sorrow—felt suddenly insurmountable. He glanced down at his notes and took a sip of water, then began.

"Dear friends, we are gathered this morning to celebrate the passing of Gus Potter. Yes, I said 'celebrate,' not 'mourn.' " He paused and held Sophie's gaze for a long moment. "For those of you who believe the promise of almighty Jesus, our Lord and Savior, for those who have taken Him into your hearts as I know Gus Potter did, there really is no death. For true Christians, our earthly end is an illusion. It is a time to rejoice, not to weep, because at that moment that seems like defeat, an ebbing away of life, we are really victorious, delivered into life everlasting and God's abundant love and care.

"Death remains a fearful moment, a tragedy to us, a mystery that confounds our limited understanding. 'Poor Gus,' we say. But when we look at this mystery through the lens of faith, we see it differently. We see that we must put our limited, flawed logic aside and hold fast to our faith. Like a hand in the darkness, the Lord's hand will lead us forward into the everlasting light. Through the power of that guiding touch, that faith, we can believe and rest easy in our hearts, knowing Gus Potter is saved and waits for us at the hand of our Lord. . . ."

Sophie nodded and began weeping. Her daughters, Evelyn and Una, one on each side, put their arms around her shoulders.

Ben swallowed hard, fearful that he, too, might start crying and not be able to finish.

"As many of you know, I have stood up here and delivered many eulogies for beloved members of this congregation. But Gus Potter was special.

"By some standards, Gus was an ordinary man. He never ran for election or had his picture in the paper or made any startling discoveries. He worked hard all his life, finding great joy in caring for his family and tending the orchard. He was an honest man, a steadfast and loyal friend. A scout leader when our boys were young, a loyal Red Sox fan. Never a great fisherman, but sometimes a lucky one," Ben added with a small, sad smile.

"An ordinary man, some would say, but by the standards that really count, he was truly extraordinary. Gus was a man who lived his faith every day. He was a model of kindness and goodness to us all. Now he will live in our hearts and in our prayers. Let us give thanks today for having known him, for having been blessed by his grace and humanity. Let us also pray for the salvation of his eternal soul and his deliverance into the hands of our almighty Father. We ask this in the name of our Lord, Jesus Christ."

Ben paused but could not bring himself to look out at the congregation or even at Sophie and her family. He didn't know if they had found any solace in his words, but surely he had tried his best to comfort them and honor Gus's memory.

Gus was buried in the village cemetery outside town, on a sloping green hill studded with headstones that protruded from the ground like rows of crooked teeth. Some were so old that the names and dates carved in the stone were completely worn away.

After the burial, the mourners gathered at

Sophie's house. Friends from the church brought food and cakes and helped to serve the Potters' guests. It was a somber gathering, as such events always are, Ben noticed. Yet, here and there, in a small child's laughter or when a happy memory about Gus was shared, Ben sensed the irresistible forward motion of life, pushing on, out of the shadow of death and loss.

As the house began to empty out, he looked around for Carolyn and found her in the kitchen, helping to clean up along with Jessica Morgan; her sister, Emily Warwick; and Grace Hegman.

He walked up to his wife and touched her on the shoulder. "I'm just going to speak to Sophie for a moment, and then we'll go."

Carolyn nodded. "All right, Ben. I'll be here. You come and find me when you're ready."

A few minutes later Bart Potter found him. "She's gone upstairs to rest, but I know she wanted to speak to you."

Sophie's son led the way upstairs to the master bedroom, the room Sophie and Gus had shared all their married life. Bart was a big man, dignified and elegantly dressed in a dark suit that looked custom-made. Ben knew he was a successful corporate attorney, a partner in a large Boston firm, but he could still remember Bart knee-high to a grasshopper, a mischievous boy with strawberry-blond hair like his mother's and a perpetually dirty face.

"I don't want to disturb her if she's sleeping," Ben said quietly, as they came to the half-opened door. "I can come back later, tonight perhaps, if she'd like to talk."

"Is that you, Reverend? I'm not sleeping," Sophie called out from the room.

Bart offered the minister a small smile. "She always had wonderful hearing. We could never get away with a thing." He touched Ben's arm briefly, then turned to go back down.

Ben entered the room slowly. Sophie sat in an armchair by the window. Sunbeams filtered through lace curtains, casting her in a golden light.

"I just needed to be by myself for a while."

"Understandably." Ben sat on the edge of the bed, facing her.

"Quite a crowd at the funeral. Everyone came to say good-bye. That was nice. Gus would have liked that."

"He was loved. We'll all miss him very much."

"I liked what you said at church, Reverend. It reminded me not to be so mournful. I'm mournful for myself, of course. But not for Gus. He's with the angels now, smiling down on me. I can feel it."

Her quiet voice was calm and confident and oddly reassuring. How ironic, Ben thought, that she should be the one comforting him now.

"Good. I feel it, too," he said honestly. He paused, wondering if it was too soon to ask her the question on his mind. On everyone's mind today, actually. He decided to go ahead with it. "What will you do now, Sophie? Do you know yet?"

She sighed and shook her head, looking more downhearted now than when she'd spoken of Gus moments before.

"My children think it's best if I leave and put the place up for sale. It's not what I want, of course. Everyone knows that. But they've got me in a corner. They're worried about me . . . and I am old. I feel about a hundred and one with Gus gone." She paused, her eyes moist with tears. "Maybe they're right. Maybe I'm not up to keeping this place going on my own anymore. They don't want to find out, anyway. That path is too dangerous, they say."

"I see. . . . That's too bad. But perhaps they're right."

Ben covered her hand with his own. It was hard to think of Sophie gone from here and the orchard gone, too, even though he knew it was probably the best and safest solution for everyone.

Sophie didn't look at him. She dabbed her eyes with a flowered hanky then stared out the window at the rows of bare apple trees.

"I'm going to live with Evelyn in a few weeks. Miranda is going to stay and help me pack up a few things. I'm not going to take much to Evelyn's, but I don't want to leave my good things around with the house empty."

"Yes, I understand." Though the situation was what he had expected, Ben felt a wave of sadness at hearing Sophie outline her plans so plainly.

"The place will go up for sale eventually. And that will be that."

The reverend didn't answer at first. Finally, he forced himself to say what seemed to be the right thing. "This is very hard for you. I'm sorry, Sophie. But your children want to take care of you now. They want what's best for you."

"I know. I know . . . I just wish it wasn't so."

They sat together for a few minutes more, and then Ben embraced her as they said good-bye. "You'll keep me up-to-date with what's happening here, right?"

"Yes, I will, Reverend." She sighed and glanced in the mirror, adjusting a few pins that had come loose from her upswept hair. "I suppose I should go down now and say good-bye to everyone. This is the last gathering we'll have in this house, I guess. It's funny but somehow I always thought we would go out on a happier note."

So did I, Ben thought sadly. Without making any reply, he took her arm and escorted her from the room.

The good news was that Molly's parents were finally coming home from Florida tonight. A lot seemed to have happened to her since they'd left in mid-February. Though her mother could be intrusive at times—with the best of intentions, of course—Molly had really missed them.

The task of picking them up at Logan Airport in Boston had somehow fallen to her, which wasn't such good news. Molly didn't drive into Boston often, and the Big Dig project had made navigating the city a near nightmare. Add to that Friday night traffic. It wasn't going to be pretty.

But Sam had gone out of town for a few days to take a construction job in Vermont, and Jessica, who offered to go to the airport, wound up stuck with a business obligation. It was just as well, Molly thought. She was their daughter; it was her responsibility. The problem was, that didn't leave anyone to watch the girls. And with her parents and all their luggage, there wasn't room in the hatchback for two extra passengers.

Molly had not spoken to Matthew in over a week, but he did come to mind as someone who owed her a baby-sitting favor. Well, he came to mind a lot, she had to admit. But this seemed like a good excuse to call him.

When she explained her problem, he was more than happy to help her out. He'd even sounded happy to hear from her, she thought. Or maybe she had just been imagining that part? The question lingered as she took a bit of extra care on Friday night with her outfit and makeup.

The girls were waiting in the kitchen with their jackets on as Molly checked her purse one last time, making sure she had all the essentials: cell phone, flight information, change for tolls, a bottle of water, something to read in case the flight was delayed.

"You're just going to Boston, not the moon, Mom," Lauren groaned.

"Shush, you just made me forget something."

The phone rang and Molly stared at it. They really did need to leave. She didn't want to be hung up on a phone call with some client or chatty friend. Then she wouldn't have any extra time to see Matthew.

"Let's just see who it is," she told the girls. A moment later the machine picked up, and she heard Phil's voice on the line.

"Hi everybody. It's me. I wondered if I could take the girls out tonight instead of tomorrow. This guy at work gave me some tickets for the In-Tranzit concert in Southport. We can still make it in time. Give me a call on my cell phone right away, okay?"

Lauren jumped to pick up the phone, but Molly blocked her way. "Come on, let's go," she said curtly.

Lauren and Jill stared at her, not moving a muscle.

"What about Daddy? We have to call him back," Jill said.

"We'll call him later," Molly promised, "from the car."

"But what about the concert? I want to go." Lauren stared at her as if this had to be the most obvious thing in the world.

"You can't go. It doesn't work out."

"What do you mean? Why can't we go out with Dad while you're at the airport? What's the difference?"

Molly managed to keep her voice calm as she said, "The difference is we've already made plans. First of all, Lauren, Dr. Harding and Amanda are expecting you to visit them tonight. Second, it wasn't right of your father to call and invite you out at the last minute."

"But he just got those tickets, and everybody wants to see In-Tranzit," Lauren objected.

"I want to go to the concert, too," Jill chimed in. "This isn't fair. We'll never get a chance like this again. We have to go!"

Molly put her hands to the sides of her head, trying to clear her thoughts. Was this the right call? Was she being too tough on Phil about this scheduling thing? He had toed the line since their confrontation two weeks ago. But this maneuver was just like him; he was back to his old tricks. Even if he got the tickets on the spur of the moment, he should have never left a message like that. He was hoping the kids would hear it and wear her down. It was his usual game, and she wasn't going to let him win, Molly decided. The girls would be angry with her but what else was new?

"I'm sorry. I know you don't understand, but your father knows when he is supposed to see you. Tonight is not one of his nights." Molly spoke in a firm voice, glancing at each of the girls in turn, trying to give the look that said she wasn't going to change her mind. "We've made our plans and that phone call doesn't change them. Let's go."

With her head bowed, Jill sighed and shuffled toward the door. But Lauren didn't budge. She crossed her arms over her chest and met Molly's stare.

"You're so mean! You never want us to see Daddy. If it was up to you, he'd never be allowed to take us anywhere."

Molly stood openmouthed, feeling as if she'd been slapped. Somehow Lauren's defection made her even angrier at Phil. She struggled to hold her temper and not overreact.

"Lauren, that is not true and you know it. Any more backtalk like that and you're going to be in real trouble." Molly paused and took a deep breath. The girls stared at her. "Go ahead. I need to lock up."

Lauren made a sour face, pursing her lips in a frown, then stormed past Molly and out the door. Jill quietly followed.

As Molly had promised, she called Phil from the car. She was glad when his voice mail picked up so she didn't have to speak to him. The girls didn't say a word to her during the drive to Hawthorne Street. Their silent treatment worked. Though she was convinced she was in the right, Molly somehow felt awful.

As soon as they got to Matthew's house, Lauren and Jill ran upstairs to join Amanda in her room. Matthew and Molly watched them from the foyer, then Matthew gave her a quizzical look.

"Are you okay?" he asked quietly.

Molly wondered if she should tell him what was really going on. Men didn't like women who whined about their ex-husbands. Everyone knew that. But right now she felt like whining her head off, and the look of concern in Matt's warm brown eyes melted her reserve.

"No, I'm not okay," she admitted. "I just had this thing with the girls over Phil right before we left the house. It really rattled me. Lauren said I was mean and horrible and I never want them to see their father."

"Wow, that does sound bad. Here, come inside and we can talk." He put his arm lightly around her shoulders and led her into the living room.

Despite feeling so upset, Molly liked the feeling of Matthew's caring embrace and felt a little pang of loss when he stepped away.

She sat on the edge of the sofa. "We were just about to leave for your house when the phone rang. I let the machine pick up. It was Phil. He left a message that he had some free tickets and wanted to take the girls to a rock concert in Southport. But I didn't want them to go."

"Because you had planned to bring them here, you mean?"

"Well, partly. But also because I've told Phil that he can't just call up like that or drop in any time he wants and think the girls will always be at his beck and call. We've worked out a schedule, and I want him to stick with it."

She let out a long breath, realizing that she'd been talking a blue streak.

Matthew sat in an armchair across from her, his brow set in a look of concern. He didn't seem bored with her venting, but his expression wasn't one of complete sympathy, either.

"So, what do you think? Am I a mean mother? I just want Phil to hold it together for five minutes and act responsibly. He shouldn't have left a message like that. He knew he would just be causing problems for me."

"Well, you're right. It was careless of him. Maybe he was so excited to get the free tickets, he didn't stop to think it through. He does seem . . . impulsive."

Molly glanced at Matthew, not sure he really understood why she was so upset and angry.

"I know it's hard when your kids get mad at you like that," he added. "It hurts a lot because you feel like you've been tying yourself in knots to do what's best for them."

"Yes, exactly." Molly nodded, feeling a bit calmer.

"Phil should be more mindful of his schedule and more considerate of you that way. You might need to talk to him again about it."

"Looks like I will. I'm not sure if he'll ever get it, though."

Matthew didn't reply. He sat looking at her, then glanced down at the floor.

Molly felt uncomfortable. "You look like you want to say something to me, but you're not sure you should."

He gave a short laugh. "You're right. I'm not."

"Go ahead. I'm interested in your opinion. Just say what's on your mind. I won't get upset," she promised, though she had the distinct feeling that she would.

"You've only told me a little about Phil,

but from what I can see, there seems to be more going on here between the two of you."

Molly sat up straighter, suddenly feeling self-conscious. "What are you talking about? I don't have feelings for him any-more—romantic feelings, I mean."

"But you're still angry at him. Not just about what he did tonight. About the past. And that's not good."

Molly felt stunned and embarrassed by his quiet words. It felt as if he could see right through her.

"Phil was a bad husband and a bad fa-ther," she said. "You don't forget that so easily."

"No, of course not. It sounds as if you had every right to be angry at him." Matt's tone was compassionate and understand-ing. "But you've been divorced now, what, seven years?"

Molly nodded. She met his gaze and looked away. It did sound like a long time when Matthew said it.

"I'm not trying to criticize you, honestly. But he's trying hard now. Anybody can see that. Give the guy some credit. Don't make it even harder for him."

Molly felt herself flushing with anger and disbelief. How could Matthew take Phil's side in this? What was going on here, some man club thing?

"I don't think you get it at all," Molly said curtly. "Phil can't just knock on the door one day and wave a magic wand and expect me to forget everything. He's done this before. Sooner or later he always gets tired of playing Dad and disappears again."

"Gets tired of it? Or are you trying to make it so hard for him that he gives up?" Matthew asked quietly.

Molly didn't know what to say. She had been wrong to confide in him. She suddenly felt wrong about a lot of things and didn't even understand why she was still sitting there.

"I'm sorry," Matt said, and she could tell from his expression that he knew he had hurt her. "I should never have said that, Molly."

"That's okay. I asked you what you thought. And you told me." She took a deep breath, not wanting him to see how upset she truly was. "Well, I've got to go. It's getting late."

She jumped to her feet and picked up her bag. "Thanks again for having the girls. It shouldn't take too long if the flight is on time."

Matthew followed her to the door. "Molly . . . please. Don't go like this. I'm sorry I said that to you. This subject pushes some buttons for me, I guess."

He paused and ran his hand through his hair. He was very handsome, and it annoyed her that now, after everything, she still felt so attracted to him.

"Do you have to go right now?" he asked. "I wish we could sit and talk more about this. I'm not sure you understand what I was trying to say."

Molly zipped up her jacket and opened the front door.

"I understand. But I need to go. Thanks for the advice." Then she turned and called up the stairs to her daughters, "Lauren, Jill . . . I'm leaving. See you later."

Nobody answered. "They probably can't hear you over the music. I'll go up and get them."

Molly shook her head. "That's okay. Nobody seems to hear me lately." She tried for a joking tone, but it didn't quite come out that way.

Then she pulled open the door and left.

Matthew felt terrible watching Molly go. But there was nothing he could do to stop her. He watched her get into her car and drive away, then he closed the door and walked back into the living room. He had planned to catch up on some reading tonight—his medical journals were piling up to the ceiling—but he knew he wouldn't be able to concentrate now. He stretched out on the couch and stared at the ceiling, his arms folded under his head.

He cared for Molly. He had never meant to hurt her. He knew that under her tough, wisecracking act she was sensitive. It had cost her something to confide in him, and he had blown it. But he had to be honest with her. She clearly wasn't being honest with herself. She clung to her anger at Phil like a badge of honor. She was so worried about how Phil's behavior might hurt her daughters, she couldn't see how her behavior already was hurting them. And hurting herself.

But she wasn't ready to hear that, Matthew realized. *Not from me, anyway. Little did she know that I'm a specialist with that particular affliction. If only she had stayed, maybe I could have explained that to her, showed her that I now know that anger like that is quicksand. You can get stuck. You can go under.*

His marriage had been an emotional tug-of-war, too, the kind that nobody ever won. When he and his wife hit rough patches, he hadn't faced up to them. He clung to his grievances, just as Molly was doing, feeling totally justified and totally unwilling to step beyond that square on the game board. He retreated even deeper into his work, which was exactly what Sharon always accused him of doing. He stuck with the marriage for Amanda's sake while ignoring his wife's unhappiness . . . and his own.

But when he was finally ready to look beyond his anger and try to work things out, they learned that Sharon had cancer—the swift and vicious variety. Her illness became the focus of their life together, her futile struggle to survive, his even more futile one to help her. He did everything he could, and he realized that he still loved her. But it was too late. They never grew truly close again, not even at the very end.

Now he was left with regrets, a heart and soul full of them. He should have given up his resentment and anger and tried to simply be happy. Happy and grateful for so much that was right in their life together, the blessings they did enjoy. It seemed so simple now. Why had it seemed so difficult then? So obscured?

Almost three years had passed since Sharon's death. He thought by now he would have worked this all out. Everyone told him he had to forgive himself; he had to let go. But he couldn't forgive himself. He couldn't forget. He felt stuck, unable to change the past and undeserving of a future where he could be happy and feel love again.

He did what he could to get out of his rut. He moved from Worcester, changed his job, cut back his working hours. But they were all changes to the surface of his life. It was like getting a haircut to cure a headache, Matt thought cynically. And of course, what he really needed was some sort of spiritual healing.

He put his hand over his eyes to block

the light from the reading lamp. With his eyes shut, his thoughts turned toward praying. He hadn't done too much of that lately. Maybe that was part of his problem right there.

God, I'm sort of confused right now, he began. *I didn't mean to hurt Molly tonight. Please give me the chance to make it up to her somehow. Please let her be ready to listen when I talk to her, too. She's such a wonderful person. I do care about her, more than I even want to sometimes. I hate to see her eaten up by her anger. Show her how to find forgiveness for Phil and freedom for herself. I know that's what I need, too. But I can't seem to get there either. Please help me. Show me what to do.*

CHAPTER TWELVE

Whenever Molly saw Emily Warwick around town, she would say hello but would rarely stop to chat. Molly didn't have much time for small talk, for one thing, and Emily was . . . well, Emily. She was the mayor of Cape Light, and Molly had always found her intimidating. Emily had manners, poise, and a certain way of speaking that made Molly feel like she was back in school, forced to talk with one of her teachers. Emily had, in fact, been a high-school English teacher before entering politics. Even having her brother Sam married to Emily's sister hadn't done much to dispel Molly's apprehension.

But when they came face to face outside

the Beanery on Monday afternoon, it just didn't seem right to pass by without acknowledging the news of Emily's engagement to Dan Forbes.

"Emily, congratulations! I saw Jessica over the weekend. She told me your good news."

Molly wasn't just trying to say the right thing. She did feel genuinely happy for Emily. It was hard not to once you saw her smile. "So, where's the ring?" she added in a teasing tone.

Emily held out her hand, looking as if she felt silly but also proud.

It was stunning, Molly thought, a square-cut blue sapphire flanked by two small diamonds. Impressive yet tasteful, just like Emily. "It's beautiful. I wish you the best."

"Thank you, Molly. I appreciate your good wishes." Emily smiled at her, then looked down at the ring. "I didn't even think I wanted an engagement ring, but Dan practically dragged me to a jeweler and insisted I pick something out."

Molly shook her head in mock sympathy. "I know what you mean. I hate when that happens." Emily just laughed. "Have you and Dan set a wedding date?"

"Not yet. Sometime this summer, probably. Dan wants a honeymoon trip on his sailboat, so it can't be too long off. I'm not much of a sailor, though," she admitted. "But 'in sickness and in health' covers seasickness, too, I suppose."

Now it was Molly's turn to laugh. "Are you going in for lunch? I'm meeting Betty here. Want to join us?"

Now, how did that happen? Molly wondered. *I guess I'm not as intimidated by Emily as I thought. Or maybe she's nicer than I realized, once she relaxes a little.*

"Oh, thanks, Molly. I can't today. I have to get back to the office. But you just reminded me of something I want to ask you."

What would Emily Warwick want to ask her? A recommendation on the best brand of silver polish?

"Betty told me you were starting a catering business, and I wondered if you would do an engagement party for me and Dan. It wouldn't be anything huge. We were thinking of about fifty people. Well, maybe more like seventy-five. We both know so many people in town, it's hard to keep control of the guest list."

Molly felt her eyes widen in shock but forced herself to keep a lid on her reaction. Which was, in fact, sheer panic. She couldn't cater a party for seventy-five people. Especially the seventy-five people that Emily and Dan would invite, the cream of Cape Light society . . . if there was such a thing.

It was flattering, though, that Emily had even thought to ask her.

"It's nice of you to think of me, Emily, but I really haven't started the business yet. I'm just in the planning stages. I probably won't be ready in time to do it for you."

"Oh, that's too bad. Are you sure? You did such a great job with Jessica's shower. The food, the flowers, everything was so beautiful. Are you sure you couldn't manage it?"

Emily's tone was so flattering and hopeful, Molly was tempted to reconsider. But Jessica's bridal shower had only been a small gathering of women in Emily's living room. Not a full-blown formal affair for seventy-five, which would probably grow to a guest list of over a hundred before Emily and Dan were through with it.

Molly glanced up at Emily, searching for

the right words to politely decline. But before she could speak, Emily continued, "We're flexible about the date. Maybe we could figure out something that works with your schedule. What if I call you during the week?"

"All right. That's a good idea." Molly nodded, not sure what she was getting herself into. Part of her wanted to jump for joy. If she could pull this off, it would be a quantum leap forward for her. But the other part of her, the larger part, shrank back in pure terror.

"Great. I'll talk to you soon." Emily gave her another cheery smile and headed up Main Street to the Village Hall.

Molly was just about to go in the Beanery when she saw Betty's white Volvo pull up and park nearby.

"Sorry I'm late," Betty said. "Waiting long? I tried to call you, but your phone isn't on—"

"Just answer one question. Have you been telling everyone that I've started a catering business?"

Betty shrugged. "I may have mentioned it to a few people."

"Like Emily Warwick?"

Betty looked so pleased with herself, Molly knew for sure it had been one of her little schemes. "Did she call you already? She's so efficient. No wonder she's mayor."

"Look, I know you're just trying to help me, but I can't do a big party like that. I'm nowhere near ready for it."

"Now, now. Just calm down. You need some lunch. Let's go inside and talk about this." Betty took her arm and led her through the door. Molly felt like a small child being coaxed out of a tantrum. She had a feeling that once Betty was through with her, she would be eating all her vegetables. Or rather figuring out the roasted vegetable platter for Emily's party.

They were soon seated at a small table in the back of the café, and they quickly gave their orders.

Plenty of privacy, Molly thought gratefully. She hated to argue in public, and the look in Betty's eye told her she wasn't going to give up that easily on this.

"Did you see Emily's ring?" Betty started off in a chatty tone. "It's a beauty."

"Absolutely," Molly agreed flatly.

"She looks very happy. Dan does, too. For Dan, I mean."

"And I'd hate to be the one to ruin it for them with an awful party. Why am I even discussing this at all? I couldn't even attempt to do that party, Betty. You know that."

"Of course you could. You just have to think big, Molly. You can't live your life on a small-screen TV, you know. It's a great opportunity for you. Everyone in town will be there."

"That's exactly what I'm thinking. If I screw up, it will definitely be on a big screen. That's not exactly a great way to launch a business."

"Okay, I understand." Betty reached over and patted her hand. For a moment, Molly thought she might relent. "This is a big risk for you. But you have to leave your comfort zone if you want to succeed. You have to put yourself out there and risk being a big flop."

"All right, point taken . . . but can't I be a big flop a few months from now? And in some other town, where they don't know me as well? This all seems just a little too rushed for me."

"That's the way life is. Opportunities like this don't always come around at your convenience, Molly. I really think you're ready for this. I wouldn't have recommended you to Emily otherwise. Stop thinking about being a failure and focus on the payoff if you do a good job. It could launch your whole business plan like that." Betty snapped her fingers, which sounded like a tiny firecracker exploding at the table.

"I don't have a business plan," Molly reminded her.

"Well, then you need one. I'm sure it's covered in your textbooks somewhere. You'll need it to get financing, you know."

"What financing?"

"Well, you need some capital to get started. Emily will give you a deposit, of course. But there's going to be some outlay of funds for your supplies and wages and all. You'll have to hire help and rent tables and chairs, that sort of thing."

Molly sighed as the waitress set their orders down. She knew if she let Betty proceed on this track much longer, they would wind up their lunch with a walk down to the bank.

"Why don't you talk to your sister-in-law about it? She does small-business loans, right?"

"I just knew you were going to say that." Molly forked up a bite of salad, tempted to confess she and Jessica had already sort of started talking about this, but Molly knew that would only encourage Betty more.

"You definitely ought to talk to Jessica," Betty was saying. "She might have some ideas for you. And just promise me that you'll talk to Emily and see what kind of party she wants before you flat-out refuse? Will you do that one thing for me?"

Molly sighed, unable to avoid Betty's pleading gaze. "All right. I'll talk to both of them. Happy now?"

"Perfectly. You're going to thank me for this someday. I guarantee it."

Betty began eating her salad with a pleased expression on her face. Molly didn't answer. She hoped Betty was right. Her friend's unflinching confidence in her boosted her spirits. But she still struggled with a voice in her head that insisted she couldn't do it and was a fool to even try.

It was hard to change. It was hard to leave her comfort zone, as Betty had said. That was the bottom line here. It was easier to stay in one place and complain and remind herself of all the reasons she couldn't get ahead.

And maybe that was also true for the way she dealt with Phil, she thought, remembering what Matthew had said.

But that was another matter entirely. *One crisis at a time,* she decided. *Your other worry goblins will have to take a number.*

Now a real chance to get her business started had been thrown in her path, and Betty wouldn't let her ignore it. But Molly still wasn't sure she had the courage to pick up the prize and run with it.

"Good morning, Carl. Up and at it already, I see." The reverend shielded his eyes from the sun with his hand.

Carl stood high upon a ladder, working on a gutter pipe that ran down from the church's roof. Patching a leak with some tar, it looked like to Ben. His nose wrinkled at the smell of it.

"I heard it might rain again on Thursday," Carl said. "I wanted to fix this pipe while we had some dry weather."

"Good idea. That's been bad for a while.

Well, when you're done come into my office, will you? I wanted to have a word."

Carl looked down at him. Even from the distance between them Ben could see a look of alarm on his face. "I'm just about finished if you want to wait a minute," Carl said.

Ben nodded. "All right. Don't rush."

He hadn't meant to make Carl worry. Ben wondered if the poor man thought he might be getting fired. Of course, it was nothing like that. He had started at the church last Tuesday, exactly a week ago, and so far his work had been exemplary.

"There's no problem, Carl," Ben called up to him. "It's nothing urgent."

Carl began the descent down the ladder. He still favored one leg but never complained. He actually looked somewhat healthier, Ben thought, since he had started working. Maybe the fresh air and exercise had done him good.

"I wanted to talk to you anyway, Reverend. I'm just about done with this list you gave me last week." Carl fished in his shirt pocket and pulled out a grubby piece of paper, the list of repairs that needed to be done around the building and grounds.

"Done already? That was fast." Ben took the list in hand and reviewed it, noticing Carl's scrawled notes and check marks, as well as the careful accounting he had kept of the costs of supplies. The reverend had given him two hundred dollars in petty cash. The church had an account at the hardware store in town, but he thought that it would do Carl good to see that he was trusted with the money. People tend to live up to the expectations others have of them, Ben had always noticed.

"What's this note here about the window?" Ben squinted through his glasses, unable to read Carl's writing.

"Oh, that . . . that was the window I busted when I broke in that night. I thought you ought to take the cost of fixing it out of my pay." Carl shrugged, as if it were unimportant.

The reverend looked at him a moment, then back at the list. He wanted to keep this as a reminder, to show the naysayers in the congregation—a small but vocal contingent who had come to him after service on Sunday, unhappy to learn that Carl had been hired. Ben had stood his ground, reminding them of their Christian duty, exhorting them to take a more compassionate attitude toward their unfortunate brother. They had backed down, but Ben knew they were watching from a distance, waiting for the slightest excuse to make Carl go.

The list gave Ben heart. It renewed his faith in the capacity of people to grow, to turn over a new leaf. Not only had Carl completed the tasks in record time, he had chipped in money from his own pay to make amends for his mistake.

"All right, Carl. Thanks. I'll put that on the record." Ben looked up at him. "You're doing a fine job here so far. I'm pleased with your work."

"Um, thanks. Is that what you wanted to say to me?"

"Actually, I wanted to talk to you about Easter. It's coming up about three weeks from now."

Carl laughed. "I remember Easter, Reverend. I'm not that far gone."

"Good to hear it. My prayers are working then. The thing is, the church should really look picture-perfect on Easter Sunday. I mean, as close as you can get it. I know we've let things go around here. But I've seen what you can do in just a week. I have

a feeling you'll pull it all together beautifully."

Carl looked pleased by his praise, Ben
thought, but also as if he now felt a bit of
pressure.

"Well, I'll do what I can, I guess. It depends on what you have in mind. This is a
pretty old building, Reverend."

"That it is. There's always something in
need of repair. The first church was built
here, oh, around 1660. Right after the town
was founded. It was just clapboard, and at
some point, it burned down. This church
was built to replace it in the early 1800s.
They say right after it was finished a huge
blizzard hit, and the minister was trapped
inside for a week with only a bag of clams.
He came out promising he'd never eat a
clam again."

"I can believe that." Carl grinned and
looked up at the church steeple. "The place
sure could use a coat of paint. But I don't
know how my leg will hold up on a ladder all
that time."

"Painting wasn't even on the list. It's a
good suggestion, though. Maybe during the
summer we can get to that, when your leg
is feeling better. I guess I'm talking more

about a general sprucing up—waxing the floors, some new varnish on the pews, cleaning the windows, that sort of thing. You could paint just the front doors, I suppose."

"Sure, I can do that. You just write it all down, and I'll get to work on it."

"All right, I will. I'll see you later then." Ben nodded at Carl and continued walking down the path that ran along the side of the church.

When he reached the side door, he turned and looked back. Carl stood by the ladder, carefully stirring the unctuous black mixture in the can. Dressed in his painter's cap, coveralls, and sweatshirt, he looked like any workman, starting off his day, focusing on the task he'd been set, putting interest and heart into the work of his hands.

That was good, Ben thought. Carl had come to this place a rootless wanderer with no purpose or direction. Now he was evolving into something else altogether.

Molly had not spoken to Matthew in a week, not since the night she'd gone out to the airport to pick up her parents. He had left a message on her machine on Wednesday, but she didn't call him back. That was amazing to her, when she stopped to think about it. She figured he was calling to apologize, and she hadn't been ready at the time to talk to him about their confrontation.

But now it was Friday night. Amanda was coming for a sleepover, and Molly knew she had to face him.

Amanda walked in, toting her duffel bag and looking as relaxed as if she lived there. "Hi, Molly. Sorry I'm late. Dad got stuck at the office."

"That's okay, honey. Lauren's waiting for you. She's in her room."

Amanda sauntered off, and Molly was left alone with Matthew. He stood in the doorway, looking hesitant. He looked handsome, too, she couldn't help noticing, dressed in a gray suit and blue shirt with an expensive-looking silk tie that hung loose around his neck.

"Would you like to come in for some coffee or something?" Molly asked politely.

"Uh, no thanks." He smiled, looking uneasy. "I have to get over to the hospital and check on a patient."

"Oh, sure." Molly nodded. She felt nervous seeing him again but glad at the same time. It was strange. She had expected to still be mad at him, yet she wasn't.

"I need to pick up Amanda on the early side tomorrow. We have to drive out to Worcester for a family party. My dad's going to be seventy."

"How nice. That's a big event."

"My mother seems to think so," he noted with a laugh.

"What time would you like to pick her up?"

"About nine? I promised we would be there in time to help set up. Oh, she has a special outfit to wear in that hanging bag. I'm sure she'll remember. But just in case."

"I'll do my best." Molly had to smile. "You know how they are. I can barely get them to go to sleep before sunrise."

"Sure, I understand. Let her have a good time. She can sleep more in the car."

"I'll set a few alarm clocks," she promised. "That usually works."

"Oh, sure. Good idea."

He smiled back at her, looking as if he wanted to say something more, something important.

She didn't know what to do. He didn't

seem to be leaving, but he didn't seem to be staying, either.

"It's good to see you," he said finally.

"Um . . . thanks. It's nice to see you."

Another long awkward pause. Now he was staring at the carpet in the hallway. He was driving her crazy. She wanted to just shake him, but she didn't have the nerve, of course.

Finally, he looked up at her again. "Listen, Molly . . . I tried to call you this week. Maybe you didn't get the message or something."

"Oh, right." She felt instantly embarrassed. "I'm sorry. I was in such a rush this week, I guess I forgot to get back to you."

"That's okay. I just wanted to apologize again for the other night. What I said to you about Phil—I should have never spoken to you like that. I'm truly sorry if I hurt your feelings. I know you're just trying to do what's best for the girls."

She didn't know how to reply. She didn't want to start imagining things again, but it really seemed as if he'd been thinking about this a lot. Thinking about her.

"It's okay, Matt. I have to admit I was a little miffed at you. Well, a lot miffed. I nearly broke the sound barrier driving down to Logan," she admitted with a small smile. "But a funny thing happened this week. Phil did it again. He called on Wednesday, which isn't his night, and asked to take the girls to his mother's house for dinner. I nearly said no, just on principle. Then I looked at the way Lauren and Jill were staring at me, and I said okay."

"You did?" Matthew looked surprised.

It had taken a few days of licking her wounds, but she realized there was some truth to what Matthew told her. When she took a good look at Lauren and Jill's sullen faces, she knew that she had to lighten up on their father.

"Even if Phil hasn't really changed, I have to give him the benefit of the doubt for now. At least, I have to try. And you were right. I have to stop reacting to him the way I did seven years ago." She shook her head and grinned at him. "For one thing, it's not very attractive to get hysterical all the time."

"Oh, I don't know," he joked. "I like to be around women who can really express their emotions."

"That was diplomatic," Molly said with a laugh.

"Well, it's true. . . . I like to be around you, right?"

She met his warm gaze, then looked away, a firm grip on the doorknob. She hoped he couldn't tell that she suddenly needed the solid support.

"Mom, did you order the pizza yet? We're totally starving." Feeling dazed, Molly turned around to find Lauren, Amanda, and Jill staring at her.

"In a minute. I'll be right there," she promised. She turned back to Matthew, feeling three sets of eyes boring into her back.

"I guess I'd better order the pizza."

"Looks like you might have a mutiny on your hands otherwise. Well, good night. See you tomorrow," he said lightly. "Good night, Amanda," he called to his daughter.

"Good night, Dad. What are you still doing here anyway?"

"Just talking to Molly." Molly glanced at him, noticing the color suddenly rise in his cheeks. She was totally charmed.

Matthew disappeared down the hallway, and Molly shut the door with a sigh. She wished she had time to sit and analyze his behavior, word by word, look by look, hitting the mental replay button freely. But that would have to wait. Right now, she had to order a pizza and referee a sleepover.

Molly woke to the annoying buzz of her alarm clock. She peered at it with one eye and slapped the off button. It was Saturday. She didn't need to get up. She closed her eyes, instantly falling back to sleep again. Until a second alarm clock went off on the other side of the bed. She scrambled toward it like a crab, scuttling under the sheets, then realized Jill was sleeping in her bed, hidden under the blankets. She must have wandered in during the middle of the night, probably to escape the teenage talk fest in the other bedroom.

Molly reached over her and grabbed the second alarm clock, amazed that Jill didn't budge an inch. This one made a nature sound, like waves lapping on a shoreline. Sometimes it sounded more like water sloshing around the washing machine, but what do you expect for seven ninety-nine at the discount store?

She sat up and sighed, finally silencing the sound.

Then she remembered why she had set

two alarm clocks. Matt was coming in less than an hour to pick up Amanda. She had to wake her up and get her ready.

Molly got out of bed and grabbed her robe. Her eyes felt scratchy. She had managed to stay up until about midnight reading a book, then finally drifted off to sleep.

The girls were still awake when she fell asleep. She was sure that they had stayed up into the single digit hours. Well, it was only once in a while, she thought, as she quietly entered Lauren's dark room. It was nice to see that they were such close friends. These are the memories you treasure and look back on—staying up all night with your best friend, trying on each other's clothes, and talking about teachers and boys or whatever.

She lifted a shade to let in a little light, then turned to Jill's bed, where Amanda was curled up in her sleeping bag. "Amanda, honey. It's time to get up. Your dad will be here soon."

Amanda rolled over and stretched, her eyes still closed.

Molly's eyes widened as she stared at Amanda's hair. What in heaven's name?

She ran to the bed, silently praying that she didn't really see what she thought she saw.

No, it was true. Amanda's beautiful auburn hair was chopped into a ragged chin-length bob and colored a hideous, iridescent shade of red. Or maybe it was really more of a purple, Molly thought, feeling her stomach knot with nerves.

She quickly turned to look at Lauren. Just as she feared, an almost identical makeover.

"Amanda. Lauren! Wake up this instant! What in the world have you two done to your hair?"

The two girls sat up and stared at her groggily. Amanda focused on Molly and a look of sheer panic took hold of her.

"It's henna, Mom," Lauren said reassuringly. "It's not like dye or anything."

"Does it wash out?" Molly asked.

"Um, well it's supposed to. But I'm not really sure."

"We really thought it did, Molly. Lauren read the box, and it sounded like you could wash it right out."

Oh, dear. They must have tried already. That isn't a good sign.

"Where's the box?" Molly asked desperately.

"It's in the bathroom somewhere, I guess." Lauren shrugged her thin shoulders under her T-shirt.

Molly ran into the bathroom. It was strewn with wet towels that had purple streaks. She found the box on the floor and snatched it up, searching for the instructions. Yes, it did say it washed out—in four to six weeks.

"Four to six weeks!" She screamed the words out loud.

She ran back into the bedroom and glared at the girls, waving the box in the air. "Four to six weeks. It says so right on the package. How could you do this to yourselves? And what about those haircuts? What did you use, Lauren, a grapefruit spoon? What in the world possessed you?"

"I'm sorry, Molly. We just wanted to do something fun. My dad's going to have a fit," Amanda said.

Yes, he was. Molly felt like crying herself just thinking about facing him. Amanda's eyes were brimming with tears, and Molly knew she couldn't be too hard on her. Besides, she was sure this whole thing was Lauren's idea.

She spun around to face her daughter, who was scrunched in the corner of her bed, her back against the wall, as if she wanted to melt right through it.

"Lauren Marie, how could you? Look at Amanda's hair. Her father is going to be furious!"

"But I did it, too," Lauren pointed out.

"That is not the point! You know you shouldn't have done something like this without my permission. And you know I never would have let you dye your hair."

"It's not dye, Mom. It's henna. It's all natural, no chemicals. They used it all the time in ancient Egypt," Lauren informed her, sounding like a TV infomercial.

Molly felt her head pounding, as if the top were going to blow right off. She took a deep breath and closed her eyes.

God, give me patience, she silently prayed.

When she opened her eyes, they were both staring at her, looking suitably terrified.

"Into the bathroom, both of you. I'm going to see if I can get that stuff out."

Lauren and Amanda glanced at each

other. They slowly slipped out of their beds and headed toward the bathroom. Lauren glanced over her shoulder at Molly. "You can try if you want," she said in a small voice. "But I don't think this is going to work."

Molly had a feeling Lauren was right. Still, she had to try. She wondered if Matthew would notice if she sent Amanda home in a big, floppy hat. . . .

Matthew arrived promptly at nine. The girls spotted his car driving up and parking in front of Molly's building. Amanda was ready and waiting in the special outfit she had brought for her grandfather's party. She looked lovely, Molly thought.

Except, of course, for her hair.

"Oh, no. My dad's here." Amanda turned to Molly, looking stricken. "Would you just tell him what happened before he sees me, Molly, please? Like sort of break the news to him?"

Molly swallowed hard. The old story about the messenger who brings bad news came to mind. Especially the ending.

Last night she had once again imagined

she had some chance of dating Matt. But this unexpected calamity would put them back to square one, she expected. Or even further, into a negative zone, if there was one.

The door buzzer sounded. Molly gulped. "Okay, you two stay in here," she said to the girls. "I'll go talk to him first."

"Thanks, Molly." The look of gratitude on Amanda's face bolstered Molly's courage.

"That's okay, Amanda. Don't worry. I have on my bulletproof vest."

She heard them giggle nervously as she headed for the front door. She took a deep breath and pulled the door open.

"Good morning. Sorry to make everyone get up so early on Saturday." Matt smiled at her, but she could hardly smile back. "Is Amanda ready?"

"She's all dressed and packed," Molly reported. "Come on in a minute."

"Sure." Matthew stepped inside. He, too, had dressed up for the occasion in a navy blue blazer, khaki pants, a white shirt, and a red-patterned tie. He looked like one of those ads for men's clothes where the guys are always hopping off sailboats. His dark hair was still wet from the shower, slicked back on his head.

Of course, they'd have to be going to a major family party today on top of it all. Just my luck.

"So, where is she? Does she know I'm here?" He rubbed his hands together and looked down at Molly.

"Yes, she saw you drive up. She's in the living room with Lauren. . . . It's just that I need to talk to you a minute."

He stared at her. She could tell he suspected this was something personal, about their relationship—or about the relationship they didn't actually have, Molly corrected herself.

"It's about Amanda," she said quickly. "She and Lauren were up very late last night. I must have fallen asleep. I didn't hear a thing—"

"She's not hurt or anything?" he broke in.

"Oh, no, nothing like that. But they decided to give themselves new hairdos." She swallowed hard. "With henna, actually."

"Henna? What in the world is that?"

"It's all natural, a plant extract. The ancient Egyptians used it."

His expression changed from mild alarm

to what Molly would describe as Code Red. Sirens screamed and red whirling lights flashed in his eyes.

"Let me see her, will you?" he said curtly. He nearly pushed Molly aside as he made tracks for the living room.

Amanda sat in the corner of the sofa, her hands pressed between her knees. She peered up at her father.

"Hi, Dad," she said weakly.

Matthew's face turned pale as paper. "Amanda . . . *what* in the world did you do to yourself?"

"It's only my hair. It will grow back, you know." Her voice trailed off, and tears squeezed out of the corners of her eyes.

"Your beautiful hair! For goodness' sake, we have to go to Grandpa's party! Doesn't this stuff wash out?"

"Well, it did wash out a little," Molly put in.

"You mean it looked worse than this?"

"A little brighter, I guess. The box said four to six weeks. But if you work at it with strong shampoo, I think you can get it out quicker than that. Or you could have Amanda's hair dyed her regular color so you wouldn't notice it so much."

"Great!" Matthew took a deep breath. He looked down at his daughter again, then back up at Molly.

She braced herself for what was coming next.

"How could you let this happen? I send her over here, trusting you to take care of her. This is totally irresponsible!"

Molly nodded, realizing she did deserve to take some of the heat for this episode.

"I'm sorry, Matthew. Really. But I had no idea that they were still even up—"

"You should have had some idea. What would it take? Maybe if they'd shaved their heads bald, you would have heard the electric razor?"

"Now, please. Try to calm down. Lauren did the same exact thing to herself," Molly pointed out. "I was furious at first, too. But really, it's just hair. It will grow out."

"Sure, maybe by the time she's in college," he railed.

Molly was shocked at his temper. Matthew was normally so easygoing. She knew the hair thing was bad, but he was overreacting just a bit, wasn't he?

"Matthew, girls do things like this to

themselves from time to time. It's really just part of the territory."

"Not my territory! This wouldn't have happened if they had been at my house, I'll tell you that much."

"Oh, really?" Now Molly felt angry, too. He wasn't such a perfect parent. If anything, he didn't give Amanda enough breathing room. "You know, after a certain age, parents really don't have all that much control. But I don't think you've really faced that. Maybe Amanda just needed to experiment, to express herself."

Amanda and Lauren glanced at each other, shocked to hear Molly defending their case.

Matthew's face turned red, either with embarrassment because he knew what she said was true or because he was now even madder at her.

"Thanks for the insight. I didn't know you were a psychologist now, too. I guess the advice comes with the new hairstyle—a package deal?"

"No charge," she snapped back.

"Come on, Amanda. Where are your things?"

"By the door," she squeaked.

"Okay, let's go." He glanced at Molly. "I'd thank you for having her over, but—"

"Skip it. I won't tell Miss Manners on you."

Molly stood with her arms crossed over her chest. She didn't even look at him as he walked past.

Matt picked up Amanda's duffel and sleeping bag. "Say good-bye, Amanda. I'll be waiting in the car." With that he swept out the door.

Amanda glanced back at Lauren, who now trailed behind her.

"Bye, Lauren. See you in school Monday . . . if my father doesn't ground me for the rest of my life."

"He won't." Despite her mood, Molly had to smile.

"Don't worry," Lauren reminded her in a whisper. "You know how they get. He'll get over it in a day or two."

"I hope so." Amanda stopped in front of Molly. "I'm sorry he yelled at you. But thanks for telling him for me."

"That's okay, honey." Molly reached out and touched her hair. "It doesn't look so bad. I'm kind of getting used to it."

Amanda smiled, her braces glittering. "Thanks. I am, too."

A few moments later Molly and Lauren stood by the window and watched the Land Rover disappear down Main Street.

She wasn't sure if she should laugh or cry. *Well, another relationship goes down the drain,* Molly thought. *If only the henna had disappeared so easily.*

CHAPTER THIRTEEN

Fran decided to wear her new suit to church. It was linen and had a long jacket in a tasteful toast color that went well with her reddish-brown hair. She buttoned the jacket, smoothing the edge of her silk blouse underneath. It would do, she thought. She had to run an open house today in the estate section near Lilac Hall, the old Warwick mansion. She still had a million things to do: set up the signs, check to make sure the house was in order, set up the flowers, and study the specs one more time. Wealthier buyers asked more questions, she noticed.

Betty had asked her to handle the property at the last minute. Not that Fran was complaining. Although Betty had brought in the listing, she promised Fran a full percentage if she sold it. Betty was good that way.

Besides, Betty had other worries right now. She had to drive down to Connecticut this weekend to visit her son. Fran felt badly for her. Betty rarely let on, but Fran knew that it had been difficult for her ever since her son asked to live with his father. She didn't know what she would do if she and Tucker ever split and the kids had to live away from her, even on weekends.

She slipped on her rings and her watch and a gold bracelet, then checked her appearance in the mirror. All she needed was her diamond stickpin, the perfect touch for this outfit. She found the velvet box in the top drawer of her dresser but opened it to find the box empty. She checked the other boxes carefully, one by one, but didn't find the pin. She didn't keep much jewelry in the house. Most of it was at the bank in a safe-deposit box. There weren't too many boxes to look through.

Fran removed the boxes and searched the drawer, thinking it could have fallen out somehow. She shook out a few scarves and a pair of gloves. But then the drawer was empty and, still, no pin.

Her best piece of jewelry. She felt panicked. Tucker had it specially made and gave it to her for their anniversary two years ago. Tucker would be so upset if she had lost it somewhere.

"Fran, what's taking you so long? We're going to be late."

Tucker stood in the doorway, an impatient look on his face. He wore a sports jacket and gray pants; a tie hung loosely around his neck. "The kids are already outside. Mike's going to start shooting baskets, and he'll look like a mess in no time."

"Come in a second . . . and shut the door," she said quietly.

He looked puzzled but did as she asked. "What is it? What's the matter?"

She picked up the empty case and showed it to him. "I wanted to wear my stickpin today. But look, it's gone."

Tucker glanced at the box for a moment. "Well, maybe you just put it someplace else. Did you check?"

"I looked through everything. I took everything out of the drawer. It's not here. I'm positive."

Tucker's mouth tightened to a thin line. "Maybe you took it off someplace. You could have left it at work. Or it might be stuck on some other dress in your closet."

"I'd never take it off and just leave it somewhere. Don't be silly." She was very careful with her belongings, especially jewelry. "It was right in that box. I'm sure of it."

"What are you trying to say, Fran? It didn't disappear into thin air."

"It's perfectly obvious," she said. "Carl took it. He must have. Nobody else has been here."

Tucker's reply was immediate. "You don't know that. Maybe you just put it someplace else. Or brought it down to the bank."

"I'd remember going to the bank with it, Tucker. The pin was right in my dresser drawer." Fran paused, trying to calm her rising frustration. What would it take to get through to Tucker? He was completely blind where his half brother was concerned. "It's got to be Carl. I can't see any other explanation for it."

Tucker looked angry now, his jaw set in a tight line. "You're just mad because Carl is staying here longer. That pin could be anywhere. Maybe you lost it."

"I didn't lose it."

"Well, I'm not going to accuse Carl of something like that without a shred of proof. So maybe you ought to look harder."

Tucker marched out of the bedroom, not knowing what to think. The trouble was, he could imagine Carl taking the stickpin. Yet he drew back from that image. He wanted to believe his brother had changed. But Fran sounded so sure that she had left the pin in the box. What else could have happened to it? There weren't too many explanations left.

He felt his gut clench as he saw Carl standing at the bottom of the stairs. He must have heard every word, despite the closed door. It was a small house with thin walls; voices carried.

Carl stepped aside to let him pass. "I'll go. You don't have to say anything."

Tucker turned to him. "Did you take that pin, yes or no?"

The second he asked the question he knew he had made a mistake.

Carl's head jerked back at a sharp angle.

"Why even ask? Sounds like you already know."

"What's that supposed to mean?"

"I didn't take your wife's jewelry. But you think I did. Same difference to me."

Tucker was instantly sorry. But it was too late. The damage was done. "I didn't mean it like that. Fran is upset up there. I was only asking you."

"Sure, who else would you ask? Tell her I'm leaving. That should cheer her up again."

Carl started walking back toward his room. Tucker wanted to tell him to wait. But he didn't. He would talk to him later, after church. When they had all calmed down.

Ben walked into his office, picked up a letter he wanted to answer, and slipped it into his jacket pocket. He didn't notice Carl sitting in the straight-backed chair by the door until he turned to go, and when he did, he jumped back in surprise.

"Carl . . . in heaven's name. You startled me."

"Sorry. The door was open, so I came in

here to wait. You took a long time out there."

"There was a meeting of the youth group after coffee hour. What are you doing here? Is something wrong?"

"Well, yes and no. See, the thing is I need to go. Leave town, I mean. I thought you might give me some of my pay if you have any cash on hand, Reverend."

"Oh. I see." Ben suspected it was something like that. He had noticed the tattered pack leaning against the chair. But why so suddenly? Just yesterday he had seen Carl and everything seemed fine.

"Of course. I don't mind giving you your pay. But first, will you tell me why you're leaving so suddenly? You didn't mention a word about this yesterday."

"Oh, I don't know. It just seems time. The weather is warmer and all. I feel better, too."

Ben caught his eye. "The weather has been warmer for a while now, Carl. Did something happen today? Did someone say something to you?"

Carl looked down at the floor for a long moment and rubbed his chin. "Fran thinks I stole a piece of jewelry out of her dresser drawer. I didn't. . . . But that's what she thinks."

Ben felt the words like a blow. No wonder he was leaving. Ben could hardly blame him.

"What about Tucker? What did he say?"

"He asked me if I did it. Not exactly saying I did. But what's the difference? He wouldn't ask you."

Ben knew that was true. He paused, wondering what he should say. It seemed so wrong for Carl to leave this way.

Help me, Lord. I need some words here. He's doing so well. I need to persuade him to stay.

Ben sat down in a chair next to Carl. "Listen, Carl. I know you're angry. You have every right to be. But if you go now, Fran will only think she was right to accuse you. Don't run away as if you were guilty."

Carl considered his words, then shook his head. "What's the difference? There's only going to be more of this."

"There is a difference, a real difference. You said before Tucker wouldn't ask me if I stole the jewelry. That's true. What would I do if he did? I wouldn't run away, right?"

Ben watched Carl think about the question, then he slowly nodded. "No, I guess not."

"Well, it's the same for you, Carl. You have nothing to be ashamed of, nothing to run away from. But you do have a reason to stay. You've got a job here, and you're good at it. I don't want you to quit on me now. We were just getting started. What about Easter?"

Carl frowned. "What about it?"

"You were fixing up the church for Easter. You still have a long list."

"Oh, yeah, the list."

"You like the job, right?"

"Sure, I like working here. It's quiet. Nobody's breathing down my neck every minute, getting on my case."

Ben's hopes sparked. "You do have your autonomy. That's hard to find."

"Tell me about it." Carl shifted in his chair. "The thing is, I can't go back to Tucker's house anymore."

Ben understood, but he felt bad for Tucker. He had tried hard. It just hadn't worked out.

"Maybe it's time to find your own place. You can stay here tonight if you want. There's a cot in the infirmary, over near the classrooms. You can make yourself something to eat in the pantry. I'm sure there's plenty of food. Tomorrow I'll help you find a room to rent in town. I know a place or two we can try."

Carl glanced up at him, looking pleased with the suggestion. "All right. That might work out."

"I'm sure it will. I know you're angry, Carl. But it's better not to run. You'll just take all of this with you. If you stay, you have some chance of moving beyond it someday."

Carl nodded. "I know what you mean. I'm not surprised at Fran. But Tucker . . ." He shook his head.

"I know. But think of all he's done for you since you got here. That should count for more than a few words spoken in anger. Everyone loses his patience once in a while."

Carl chose to ignore that. "I guess you need to get home, Reverend. Just show me where the cot is. I'll be okay."

Feeling relieved, Ben silently thanked the Lord for his help. It was disheartening to see that after all Tucker had done, Carl was now mad at him. But at least Carl was staying. There was still a chance they would make amends. Ben would pray for it.

After church on Sunday, Matthew drove out to the beach with Amanda. It seemed the perfect day to walk to the lighthouse on Durham Point Beach. The warm sunshine beat down from a clear sky, and the breeze from the water was soft and mild. Amanda was so elated, she immediately kicked off her sneakers and ran down to the shoreline. Then she pulled off her heavy sweatshirt and tossed it on the sand.

"Look at the water, Dad. Isn't it great?" she called back to him.

"Yes, it's beautiful here today," he agreed.

Worcester was so far inland, they hardly ever got to an ocean beach. There were lakes, of course, but nothing compared to this.

Amanda seemed to think so, too. He saw her lean over to roll up the legs of her jeans and suspected she was going to get her feet wet. He started to call out to her, then stopped himself. She could get her feet wet if she wanted to. She wasn't going to catch

pneumonia. He was too protective sometimes.

Watching her from this distance, it was
startling to him to see that she was quickly
evolving into a young woman. Some traces
of the little girl remained but fewer and
fewer every day. With her hair cut short like
that, she resembled her mother, especially
from far away.

He wondered how Sharon would have re-
acted to the new hairdo. Probably better
than he had, he thought. A chest-beating
father gorilla would have handled it with
more sensitivity. He sat on a driftwood log
that had washed up above the shoreline
and watched Amanda amble along, squeal-
ing at the cold water every time her feet
touched the foam.

He had tried to have a father-daughter
talk with Amanda on the way to Worcester,
but it ended up as a screaming match—
their first. He had been nearly as shocked
by her temper and rebellious attitude as
he had been by the new hair color. For
heaven's sake, what was in that stuff? he
wondered.

By the time they had reached his parents'
house, Amanda wasn't speaking to him,

and he was almost too exhausted to explain her appearance.

But then his sister Erica reminded him of the time she had actually burned off chunks of her hair with an iron, trying to make it straight. Remembering that event did give him some perspective.

He expected his parents to be appalled, especially since they loved to show off their granddaughter to all their family and friends. But they seemed to find Amanda's outrageous behavior absolutely charming. His mother made a great fuss, saying Amanda looked very exotic, like a cover girl on a magazine.

"Don't worry, dear. She's just acting her age. It's good to see her misbehaving a little. I think it shows she's getting past her grief a little. I do worry sometimes that she's too perfect," his mother had confided to him.

Interesting . . . Molly had said just about the same thing. He hadn't given her any credit for the insight, though. Just the opposite in fact. *Maybe I should have thanked her instead of blaming her,* he thought, feeling badly.

Now he realized it was one of the first

times Amanda had ever gotten into real trouble and acted like a regular kid, not some robot child, shy and uptight and too worried about the rules to have any fun. Wasn't that one of the reasons he had moved to Cape Light, so that Amanda could make a new start and open up a little?

He saw her coming back, chasing some birds down at the water's edge. Her beautiful long hair didn't trail behind anymore, like little girls in picture books. She looked more like a rock singer on the cover of a CD.

But maybe that was okay. More than okay, it was the way it should be right now. He couldn't keep Amanda from growing up, from moving away from him. They both had to move forward, to embrace the new— even if it meant strange hairdos. At least she'd found the courage to try, he realized.

Amanda ran up to him and flopped on the sand at his feet. She looked breathless but happy. "What are you doing up here, Dad?"

"Oh, I don't know. Just thinking."

"About Mom?" she asked quietly.

"A little," he admitted. "I was thinking that she'd probably like your new hair."

"I don't know," Amanda said. "It's not ex-actly . . . perfect."

"Maybe not," he allowed, "but your mother knew that thing that all women seem to know: It's only hair. It grows back. It's not the end of the world if you have fun with it." He smiled at her. "So, I was won-dering what I would look like in a pink Mo-hawk and maybe an earring or two?"

Amanda stared at him a moment, then shook her head, her face deadpan. "Uh, no. I don't *think* so."

Her tone was so purely teenage sound-ing, he just had to laugh.

Sophie woke early, well before her usual time. She wasn't sure why. It was almost as if a hand had jostled her shoulder, which was an uncanny feeling. What day was it? Tuesday, she realized. A week since Gus's funeral. She bowed her head and said a silent prayer.

Then she climbed out of bed, scuffing to the kitchen in her slippers as her hands au-tomatically pulled some pins from her robe pocket and pinned up her hair.

She heard people needed less sleep

when they got older, but that had rarely been her experience. *Maybe it's getting to me now,* she thought. She set up the coffeepot and peered out the window. It was not quite light out. A heavy mist settled among the trees, making the orchard look dreamlike.

Sophie poured a cup of coffee and took a sip, her gaze still fixed on the trees. Then she turned and walked to the mud room. She pulled Gus's old green barn jacket from a peg and put it on over her robe and nightgown. She sat on the bench and stuck her bare feet into a pair of work boots. She found some gloves in the pocket and put those on, too, then covered her head with a wool cap. She opened the side door, the cool moist air shocking her fully awake. She paused for just a moment, then stepped outside, breathing in the rich, misty air.

It was chilly now, but it would warm up nicely today, she predicted. Sunlight glowed on the far horizon, dabbing the gray pre-dawn sky with a rosy hue. The sun would burn off this mist in a few hours. It would be a clear, sunny day. A spring day, she realized, walking toward the apple trees.

There was so much to do out here. The

trees needed attention, a knowing hand. There was pruning to take care of and the ground to clear. Fertilizer was needed. She should do a check for cocoons and insects.

Sophie reached up to touch a branch as if she were reaching for the hand of an old friend. It didn't make much sense to do any of that now. Not with the land going up for sale soon, and someone coming along and knocking all these trees down to build houses, most likely. There was slim chance of finding a buyer who would keep the orchard running. Her son, Bart, had told her she had a better chance of getting hit by lightning.

Sophie sighed. That was probably true, though he didn't have to put it so bluntly. She noticed a rake on the ground and bent to pick it up. Had it been out here all winter? She and Gus had grown careless last fall with Gus's health failing. They never would have forgotten a good tool like this otherwise.

She picked it up and began raking the ground around the tree roots, gathering the dried leaves and winter's debris into a small pile. Without thinking, she moved on down the row, raking another area. She lost herself in the rhythm of the work, not noticing the sun rising or the time passing. She lost herself in thoughts of the past and found herself humming a familiar song as she worked along.

"Grandma! What are you doing out here?"

Sophie looked up to find Miranda staring at her. Her tall, long-limbed body looked hastily dressed in sweats. Her long thick hair was a mess, making her appear as if she had just tumbled out of bed.

"Oh dear, you startled me." Sophie stood back, leaning on the rake. She pressed her hand to her chest and laughed.

"Are you okay, Gram?" Miranda's concerned look made her want to laugh even harder.

"Of course, I'm okay. I just woke up early for some reason and felt like getting some air. I saw this rake on the ground and thought I would make myself useful." She sighed and looked around at the apple trees. "There's so much work to be done out here—spring work. I know nobody is going to buy this place and keep the trees, but I hate to neglect them."

Miranda gently took the rake from her

grandmother's hands. "Let's forget about the packing. We can work out here today, if you like. You never know. Someone might want the orchard. You don't want the trees to look shabby. It would bring down the price."

"I'll say it would." They both knew Sophie didn't care much about the price. But she did take great pride in her trees.

"Just tell me what to do. I always used to come and help you and Granddad when I was in high school."

"I remember." Sophie glanced at Miranda, then back at the row of trees. "It would be nice if we could just prune back some of these stray branches and maybe clear up the ground a bit. So the roots can get the fertilizer."

"All right. I'll go get a wheelbarrow and some tools from the shed."

"Get some for me, too, honey. I'm not a bit tired."

Miranda smiled at her over her shoulder. "You don't look tired, Grandma. You look raring to go." Then she stopped and turned to face her. "I do think you ought to go back inside and put some clothes on, though.

Just in case somebody stops by to say hello."

Sophie glanced down at herself and laughed. "I'm out here in my nightgown, for goodness' sake. I almost forgot." She looked up at Miranda and shook her head. "Guess I got carried away."

"I guess so," Miranda agreed. She looked up at the sky which had turned a deep shade of blue. "It's going to be a great day. We can get a lot done."

"Yes. We'll get a lot done out here today," Sophie agreed happily. She turned and headed for the house, eager to change into her clothes and get back to work.

"Here are some sample menus I've put together for you. This one is mainly seafood," Molly pointed out. "This one is a little more gourmet—more exotic ingredients, different sauces. This one is pretty standard, a lot of all-time crowd pleasers. But you can switch things around if you like. Or if there's something special you have in mind, we can figure that in, too."

Emily glanced at the menus with interest, her reading glasses perched on the tip of her nose. "Hmmm, these look good," she said.

Molly took a breath. She had been talking nonstop since she arrived and hoped she didn't sound as if she were babbling. They sat in Emily's living room, with Molly's papers and photos of table settings spread out on the couch and coffee table. Molly had arrived at five. Her mother was at her place, visiting with the girls. It was now after six, but they weren't quite done. Emily had some idea of what she wanted the event to be like; so far, though, she seemed to be an easygoing client.

Which was a good thing, Molly knew, since she wasn't sure how she would handle anyone tougher. She was barely out of Catering 101. Preparing for this appointment had been a do-it-yourself crash course. Thank goodness her teacher had given her lots of advice about what to bring along and key points to discuss. She even loaned her a book with photos of table settings and told her where she could find samples of table linen and flatware to show. Lauren had helped her type out menus on the computer. Her teacher had also encouraged Molly's classmates to help out to gain some practical experience, so there was her staff . . . if she needed one.

"Just try to play the part," Betty had advised in a last-minute pep talk. "I know you feel like you're faking it, but you're really not. It's just a new side of your personality, one you're going to see a lot more of."

Molly did feel a little as if she were acting. So far Emily hadn't asked any questions she couldn't answer, but she kept waiting for Emily to see through her act. It was funny how now she wanted this job so much when last week the entire idea seemed horrifying.

Finally Emily looked up, holding the menus out in front of her. "I like the idea of doing something a little different, not the same old buffet you see everywhere. I think most of this will be wonderful," she said, pointing to the gourmet choices. "And maybe you can add the ubiquitous ham or turkey, tucked away in the corner for the less adventurous eaters."

Molly laughed at her analysis, surprised to realize she even knew what *ubiquitous* meant, thanks to Jill's vocabulary list.

"I think we can do that. No problem." She

jotted a note on a pad: *Add boring roast entrée.* Wow, this was really happening.

They went on to talk about the decor. Molly had a lot of ideas for creating an atmosphere that was both sophisticated and festive and even had suggestions for making the invitations match the party ambience. Emily seemed to love her ideas.

"I could have it here if we keep the guest list down. But the party seems to be growing by the hour." Emily gazed around. "It might be more comfortable at my mother's. The rooms are so much larger, especially if we're going to set up small tables at dinner time."

Molly gulped. Lillian Warwick's house? Now there was an unexpected speed bump. She didn't get along with Lillian Warwick. Last summer, after Lillian's stroke, she was hired to clean for her and bring over meals. The job came to an abrupt end when Lillian insulted her brother Sam, and Molly stomped out in a fury. Molly was sure Emily would remember and tried to keep her own expression blank. She couldn't risk making any waves. She was lucky to get this job at all.

"You know my mother's place. But

maybe you'll need to look the house over again sometime. Just let me know," Emily suggested.

"Uh, sure. Once we get closer to the date." *If the old dragon will even let me in.*

Emily glanced at her, and Molly could tell she had guessed her thoughts. "Don't worry about my mother. I'll handle her."

"I'm not worried," Molly fibbed. She *was* worried about dealing with Lillian Warwick, but she was also worried about so many other issues that Lillian seemed just one hurdle among many.

Emily had some questions about the flowers, which distracted Molly from her worries about Lillian. The meeting wound up a few minutes later. Emily sat back on the couch and slipped off her glasses, looking pleased.

"Well, it takes a lot to put together a big party, doesn't it? I wouldn't really know where to begin on my own."

"You just have to show up and be the hostess—with your fiancé, of course."

"Oh, Dan hates parties. I'm surprised he even agreed to this one. But he's a lot more social than he lets on once you get him out of the house."

Emily smiled at her, and Molly could see that she was really in love; her expression took on a glow just talking about her husband-to-be.

The two women parted with Molly agreeing to send Emily an estimate of the cost by the end of the week. As she walked down the path from Emily's house to her car, she felt like jumping in the air and shouting, "Yes!"

But she was afraid that someone would see, so she just smiled and said it softly to herself.

Ten minutes later Molly arrived home and was met at the door by her mother. "How did it go?"

"Pretty good. Thank goodness, I can finally take off these shoes." She kicked off her dressy pumps and sighed with relief. Her poor feet were used to spending the day in cushy old sneakers. They were totally in shock.

"All we did was talk. I don't know why I'm so exhausted." She dumped her portfolio on the kitchen table and dropped down into a chair.

"Don't worry, dear. I know you can do it. Think of all the cooking you've done for our family parties. It's not so different."

Molly's father was a professional cook, and her mother was quite impressive in the kitchen as well. With her five siblings, there had always been something to celebrate. Or maybe her family just liked having big parties. Like her sisters and brothers, Molly had learned to cook from her dad. He always made it look easy and fun. It was true in a way; preparing for a party wasn't a big deal. It shouldn't be with her experience, anyway.

But there seemed to be so much riding on this. Molly almost felt as if she couldn't breathe if she thought about it too long.

"This is different, Mom. It's not just our family. I'm trying to start a real business here."

"Yes, dear. I know. Just don't let yourself get too stressed about it. That's not going to help you." Marie Morgan picked up a pot and dried it with a dish towel. "Emily's a nice lady. I've always liked her."

"Yes, she is nice," Molly agreed. "I was pretty surprised to hear she was getting married, though. She always seemed the forever-single type to me."

"Every pot has a lid." Her mother gave her a meaningful glance. "Even—"

"—yes, even the bent one," Molly finished for her. How many times had she heard that one? Clearly, she belonged in the bent-pot category, though her lid had yet to proclaim himself.

Her mother kept looking at her, making Molly feel distinctly uncomfortable. "What's the matter, Mom? Why are you looking at me like that?"

"You must be tired. You didn't even notice the flowers."

Molly followed her mother's gaze and suddenly saw a huge bouquet sitting on the counter by the phone. She got up to take a closer look.

It had to be Phil, always going for the grand gesture. What he was trying to trick her into now? Or was he apologizing for some slipup she didn't even know about yet?

"Where's the card?" she asked, looking around.

"I left it there by the phone book." Molly

could feel her mother watching as she pulled the card from the tiny envelope.

Dear Molly,
So sorry I lost it on Saturday. You were right. It's a girl thing, and it's only hair. (I'm actually starting to like it . . . but don't tell Amanda.)
Thinking of you, Matthew

Molly laughed a little at his message, and her mother gave her a curious stare. "Who was it? I'm dying to know," she admitted.

"Oh, just this guy, the father of one of Lauren's friends." *Keep it vague,* she advised herself. *You'll have fewer questions to deal with later.*

"That new doctor?" Marie's eyes were bright with interest. "I've heard he's quite nice. People seem to like him already. Why did he send you flowers? Did you go out with him or something?"

"Mom, slow down." Molly gave her mother an exasperated look. "He got a little upset when Lauren and Amanda dyed their hair, and he just wanted to apologize."

"Oh. Well, that was considerate." Her

mother looked a little disappointed, Molly thought, but not without hope.

Molly gazed at the flowers. It was a thoughtful gesture. That "thinking of you" part had given her hope again, too, though she hated to admit it.

Molly knew she had to call him now. The idea made her nervous. She would just thank him and see if he had anything more to say. *Like finally inviting me out on a date, for instance.*

"Dinner's almost ready," her mother said. "Why don't you call the girls? They're doing their homework."

"All right. What did you make for us?" Molly peeked under a pot as she passed the stove.

"Spaghetti and meatballs. Jill wanted it."

"Looks yummy. I'm starved." Molly touched her mother's shoulder as she left to get the girls. As much as she liked to cook, it was a sweet break when someone else did it so she could just relax and sit down at the table.

After the girls were in bed and her mother had gone, Molly made herself a cup of tea and took the phone into the living room. She had promised Betty she would call after seeing Emily. But first, she thought, she ought to call Matthew.

She felt silly, noticing how her hand shook as she pressed the numbers. She hoped her voice wouldn't betray the butterflies in her stomach.

When was the last time she had called a man she really liked? She wasn't sure. Boring Micky didn't count. *When was the last time I even* met *a man I really liked, come to think of it?*

"Hello." Matthew's voice came on the other end of the line, and she coughed to clear her throat.

"Hi . . . it's me, Molly. Thank you for the flowers. They're really beautiful. You didn't have to go to all that trouble."

"Yes, I did. I was totally over the top. Amanda told me she was mortified. She had to have a long talk with me in the car about my behavior."

Molly laughed. At least he was starting to see the humor in the situation. "Sorry to hear it. I hope she wasn't too hard on you."

"Not so bad. She did let me watch TV tonight."

He sounded really happy to hear from her—and relieved. He must have thought

she was angry at him. She had been so distracted getting ready to see Emily, she
hadn't really had the time to dwell on it.
Well, not as much as she had expected to.

"How was your father's party?"

"It was fine. It was good to see everybody. But I don't miss Worcester much. I
guess Cape Light is starting to grow on me.
Amanda and I went to the beach on Sunday
and walked to the lighthouse. It was a
beautiful day."

"Yes, it was almost like summer," she
agreed.

He was prolonging the conversation. That
seemed a good sign. For some reason, she
didn't want to tell him about her appointment with Emily. It was all too new and ten-
tative.

They talked about some events going on
at school, safe topics, Molly thought. Then
the conversation seemed to dwindle. Molly
felt awkward, wondering if she should be
the first to say she had to go.

"I noticed that there's some good music
in Newburyport this weekend. On Saturday
night at Bay Street Café," Matthew said
suddenly. "It's jazz, a pianist who's really

great. I know this is short notice, but I wondered if you would like to go with me?"

Molly couldn't answer. Had he actually asked her out on a real date, no children involved?

"Um, sure. I'd love to. That sounds like fun." She actually hated jazz but knew she couldn't say that. She also didn't think she would notice the music too much. She'd be too distracted by Matthew.

"Great. I think the first set starts at nine, but we can grab dinner first. How about we say around seven?"

"Seven sounds fine."

Molly hung up the phone, totally elated. Now she did jump up from the couch and pump her fist in the air. "Yes!" she said out loud.

She sank back onto the couch, quickly dialing Betty. She had a lot to report.

Chapter Fourteen

"So, you've finally got a Saturday off. What are you going to do today, honey?" Tucker bit into a slice of toast, looking interested in her answer.

Fran shrugged. "Just some spring cleaning. I guess I'll start in our bedroom. The curtains need to be washed. And maybe this afternoon we can give Scout a bath together. He's been looking a little scruffy lately."

"Poor Scout. I didn't realize he was on the list, too. I just don't have the heart to tell him. You'd better." Tucker's glum expression made her laugh.

"Come on, Tucker. It's almost halfway

through April. You know I always do heavy cleaning in the spring."

"I remember. It's serious. Guess I'd better take the dog and clear out for the day."

"Good idea," she agreed with another laugh. She didn't often have a Saturday off from the office, and even though she knew it sounded terribly boring, she was secretly looking forward to a cleaning spree and having the house to herself for the day.

Fran cleared up the breakfast dishes, then headed for the master bedroom. She took the curtains down and washed the windows. The closet was next. There was a rummage sale coming up at the church, and she was sure her closet was stocked with donations.

She sorted out her clothes quickly, making piles on the bed for the cleaners and the rummage sale. Then she used the step stool to get at the handbags on the top shelf. There were so many dusty old bags up there, most of them totally out of style. She had to be careful with what she wore to work. She had to make a good impression on her clients.

She pulled down an old straw bag with a broken handle and tossed it on the floor. A suede fringed number followed; Mary Ellen might like that one, Fran thought. There was a leather bag behind that one, a shoulder bag she used to like a lot. She smoothed her hand over the leather flap. It still might do after a polish, she thought. She lifted the flap, noticing some loose change on the bottom, along with a pen that read Bowman Realty.

Then something else caught her eye. A small white box, the kind that jewelry comes in. She took it out and opened it.

Her diamond stickpin. She was so happy to see it. Then she felt a clutch in her chest, remembering how she had accused Carl. She was so sure he had stolen the pin. But here it was, sitting in her bag all along. How had it gotten in here? She stepped down from the stool, her legs feeling shaky.

She suddenly remembered. Months ago they'd had the bedrooms painted, and she had to leave the painters alone in the house all day. She brought most of her jewelry to the bank, but at the last minute realized that the stickpin was still in her dresser drawer, so she rushed around looking for a place to hide it.

And then she forgot all about it, obviously. She hadn't had a reason to look for it until that open house.

She sighed, looking down at the pin in her hand. Carl had moved out because she accused him of stealing it. *I panicked,* she realized. She sat on the edge of the bed, not knowing what to do. *Should I go see him at the church and apologize?*

She really didn't want to do that. She and Carl hardly spoke, even when he lived there. It would just be so awkward for both of them. She had to admit that she was afraid of what he might say, especially if she went on her own.

Maybe Tucker could speak to him and apologize for her. She would tell him later, when he came back to wash the dog. Then they could decide what to do.

She put the pin back in its box and tucked it away in her dresser drawer. She did feel guilty about accusing Carl. But she was still relieved that he had moved out.

"Do you want to pack these teapots, Grandma?"

The teapot collection. Sophie had nearly forgotten about it. It had been there for so long, she almost stopped seeing it. Late afternoon sunlight slanted through the kitchen windows, falling on the row of china. The teapots were all shapes, sizes, and colors. Two had glazes that were quite unique: a shiny, obsidian with white peonies; and an iridescent gray-blue with a spray of plum blossoms.

Although Sophie had rarely set foot beyond Cape Light, her teapots had come to her from all corners. Her brother Fred and others would buy them for her in far-off places, souvenirs of their travels. She did love them all. Looking at them was like a trip around the world.

But what would she do with them now? They wouldn't fit in at Evelyn's house. Her oldest daughter was particular about her decor. Maybe Una would like them or even Miranda. Still, Sophie didn't feel quite ready to give them away.

"I'm not sure, dear," she finally answered Miranda. "We don't have to pack up everything right now. There'll be time later."

After the house was sold, Sophie meant. It was still too hard to say the words aloud. The poor house. Sophie wondered if it would be knocked down to make way for something more modern.

Oh, she couldn't worry about that now on top of everything. Not with all three of her children coming tomorrow—coming to settle things before she moved to Evelyn's house.

She suddenly felt so overwhelmed, so distraught. She felt light-headed and clammy, too. She held onto the back of a kitchen chair and abruptly sat down.

"Grandma, are you all right?" Miranda hopped off the step stool and ran to her side.

"I'm fine. Just a little winded. All this packing. It gets on my nerves," Sophie confessed.

Miranda brought her a glass of cold water, and Sophie drank it thirstily. "The dust bothers me, too," she added with a small smile. "I guess I let things go a bit once Granddad got sick."

"What's the difference? Don't worry about that now." Miranda touched her shoulder.

Truly, what was the difference now? She never heard anyone at her stage in life say, "Gee, I don't think I dusted enough." With

Gus gone, the simple things that had once ordered and organized her life, like keeping up with the housework and deciding what to cook for dinner, seemed to have slipped away.

This was just a phase, people told her, part of the grieving process. "You'll get through it," they said. "Things will get back to normal, little by little."

But she knew they were wrong. She was leaving the orchard. Her life would never get back to normal or anything like it.

"Grandma, do you feel okay? Maybe I should take you over to the doctor. There's a new one in town. He might have office hours on a Saturday."

"No. I don't need a doctor." Sophie forced a smile and patted Miranda's hand. "I need a time machine."

One that could take me back ten or twenty years, so I could live my life all over-again, Sophie thought. *I don't think I would be bored one bit.*

Miranda sat watching her for a long time. "Why are you leaving here?" she asked finally. "I know you don't want to."

"What a question! Everyone seems to know why I have to go. Ask your father, he'll tell you." She didn't mean to snap at Miranda, but her nerves were raw; she couldn't help herself.

"It just seems so wrong."

Miranda's gentle tone nearly made Sophie cry, but she wouldn't let herself break down that way.

"It feels wrong to me, too, I have to admit. But there doesn't seem to be any other way. Your father and your aunts won't allow me to stay here alone. That's what happens when you reach a certain age—everything goes in reverse, and you get ordered around by your children. Next thing you know, they'll be setting my bedtime and telling me I've had enough TV."

"I know how they're pressuring you, Gram. But there must be a way you can stay. You can't give up so easily."

"Oh, but there isn't, dear. We've been over and over this. It just pains me now to keep talking about it. Honestly."

Sophie knew Miranda meant well, but she wished she would just give up. Still, she had only herself to blame for the Potter stubborn streak. She was the one who taught her children and grandchildren to be persistent, to fight to the very end. "A diamond is just a lump of coal that stuck to its job," she would tell them, quoting one of her favorite sayings. Still, she didn't see how persistence or even sheer stubbornness would help her now. Miranda was so young. She didn't understand.

"Listen, I've been thinking about this," Miranda said. "What if I stayed here with you? Moved in permanently, I mean. You could tell me what to do, and I could run the orchard for you."

Sophie felt her heart catch. *If only,* she answered silently.

"Oh, my. That's a lovely offer, Miranda, and I appreciate it. But what about your career, your acting? You can't give that up and come live out here in the middle of nowhere."

"I don't think I'm cut out to be an actress, Gram. The auditions are like cattle calls, and I never get called back. Well, not enough to make it feel worthwhile. I've been plugging away at it for a while now, and I'm tired of it. I guess I didn't even realize that until I came up here to see you and Granddad. Even if I go back to New York, I'm going to give up acting."

She sounded so definite. Sophie had a lot

of respect for that. It was good to see that despite the stubborn streak, her granddaughter was flexible and wouldn't stay stuck in a rut.

"Well, it sounds as if you've thought about it and made up your mind," Sophie said. "But I don't see why you would want to stay up here. It's so isolated and you're so young."

"I'm twenty-five, Grandma. The same age you were when you took over."

"Yes, that's true. But things were different then. There was a war going on. We got old fast back then."

"Oh, Grandma. Come on, you know that's not true."

Sophie laughed. "I can't help it, honey. You do seem so young to me. And it's such hard work to run this place. I'm not sure you really know what you would be getting into."

"I'm not afraid of hard work. I worked here every summer when I was in high school. And I've loved working in the orchard with you these last weeks. We got a lot done out there. Don't you think?"

Sophie bit down on her lip. So many times she had seen her granddaughter out there and thought she was seeing an old movie of herself. Only Miranda was so tall and fit, she hardly needed a ladder to reach the branches.

"Yes, we did get a lot accomplished," Sophie admitted. "You're a good worker, too. You've got a real feel for the trees. I always said that to your grandfather, even when you were in high school."

"Grandma, please. Just think about it, okay?" Miranda leaned closer and squeezed her hand. "I don't want to see you leave here. Not yet. I know we could do this together. I really do."

Sophie couldn't help it. The touch of Miranda's hand and the light in her young eyes sparked hope in her heart.

"Well, you've given me a lot to consider, young lady. I'll be up half the night probably . . . but it might work out. If we can persuade my children."

"We will. We won't take no for an answer," Miranda promised.

Sophie just smiled. In her heart, she quietly spoke to Gus, for she suddenly felt sure he was nearby, listening.

Did you hear that, Gus? Didn't I tell you that if the Lord wanted me to stay he'd send a way? Well, here it is. Our own Miranda. My prayers have been answered. Then she decided to say a few words to God, too.

Thank you, Lord. She was right under my nose, and I didn't even see. But we're going to need your help tomorrow. It's not over yet . . .

"Well, here they are. Thanks again for having them over." Molly led Lauren and Jill into Sam and Jessica's house.

Jessica stood in the front hall, taking the girls' backpacks. "Gosh, you look gorgeous. I love that outfit."

"Thanks. I bought it in sort of a rush at one of the outlet stores. I need some more good clothes for appointments."

Jessica's remark made Molly feel self-conscious. They both knew she had run out the day after Matt had called to get something new to wear. She had found a peach-colored sweater set with a matching paisley skirt in a sheer layered material. It floated to a graceful length that was flattering to her figure.

The high-heeled sandals, though painful, helped a lot in that department, too. Luckily,

Matthew was tall, and she could get away with such tricks without towering over him.

Sam appeared on the stairway. "I thought I heard you come in." He stepped over and gave her a quick kiss on the cheek. "Looking good, Molly. So, what's going on?"

"I told you, she's going out with Dr. Harding." Something in Jessica's tone made Molly blush.

"Oh, the doctor. Yeah, I heard all about it." Sam stuck his hands in the pockets of his jeans. "Where are you guys going?"

"Dinner and then to hear some jazz at Bay Street Café."

Sam looked amused. "You hate jazz. You always say it gives you a headache."

"I do not say that. I like jazz. I like all kinds of music." Molly knew she sounded huffy, but she was a little nervous tonight. She didn't need Sam's teasing.

He probably didn't think Matthew was a good match for her—not like his couch-potato friend, Micky.

"I like it a lot better than watching sports on TV, I'll tell you that much," she said brightly.

Sam didn't answer, but she could tell by his expression that he caught her meaning.

"Oh, don't pay any attention to him. You never took me on such interesting dates, pal, come to think about it," Jessica reminded her husband.

Sam turned to his wife and flashed his notoriously charming smile. "I must have done something right. You married me, honey."

Jessica looked as if she didn't want to smile back at him but finally couldn't help herself. "Yeah, I did, didn't I?"

"Have a good time, Moll," Sam said.

"Thanks, I will."

"Yes, have a great time. And don't rush," Jessica added. "The girls can sleep in the guest room if they get tired."

Molly thanked Jessica and said good-bye. Then she stepped carefully in her high-heeled sandals down the gravel driveway to her car. She slowly eased herself in so she wouldn't wrinkle her skirt on the way to Matthew's house.

Her hands were sweating on the steering wheel. *It's ridiculous to be so nervous,* she told herself. It wasn't as if they had never spent time together. By now she felt she knew Matt pretty well. But they had never really spent time alone together. She wondered if it would be hard to keep up a conversation without the girls constantly distracting them.

Was he too good for her? Too smart, too sophisticated?

She was feeling a lot better about herself lately and about her life . . . but this was different.

"Don't turn this into some kind of test," Betty had wisely advised. "You're not going to an audition, for goodness' sake. Try to figure out if he's good enough for you."

He's good enough, she thought. *He's just right.*

Molly turned off the Beach Road into the village. Just as she passed the harbor on her way to Hawthorne Street, her cell phone rang. She dug in her bag with one hand and answered it. Was it a call from Lauren or Jill already? She hoped they weren't going to haunt her all night.

"Molly? It's Matthew. I'm glad I caught you. Where are you?"

"In the village. On the way to your house."

"I'm not at home. A patient needs to be admitted to the hospital. I'm on my way to Southport now to meet her."

"Oh . . . that's too bad." She meant it was bad for his patient, but she also felt bad for herself.

"I know. I'm so sorry. It's a really rotten break. But listen, the table is still reserved. Why don't you take a friend or something?"

A friend? She didn't want to take a friend. She wanted to go with him. Molly swallowed hard, fighting back tears.

"Um, thanks. Good idea. I'm not sure who I could ask on such short notice, though."

"Well if you can find someone, it should be a great show. I'll try to . . ." The connection began to break up, and Molly couldn't hear what Matthew said next.

"Matt? I can't hear you." She listened to the static for a moment, then shut her phone. The car seemed to drive itself down Main Street. Molly saw an empty space in front of the movie theater and pulled over.

She had a few single friends she could call, but she knew that most of them wouldn't be able to run out at a minute's notice, anyway. She didn't really feel like calling anyone; she had told Matthew she would just to be polite. And to save face, too. She didn't want him to know how disappointed she felt. He said he was, too, but he didn't really sound it.

She sighed and looked out the window. Wrong place to park, she realized, watching couples walk hand in hand into the movie theater. She felt her eyes fill up with tears again. This time she pulled out a pack of tissues and let herself cry.

She permitted herself a few moments of abject misery, then blew her nose and rallied. This wouldn't do. It was just a canceled date, not the end of the world. He did have a good reason, not some lame excuse—and she had heard enough of those to know the difference.

She fixed her runny eye makeup with a tissue, then took a deep breath. She didn't really relish the idea of going back to Sam and Jessica's and explaining what happened. Hiding out at a movie for a while was an option. But that was silly. Matt was a doctor. He had emergencies. She had nothing to feel ashamed of.

She started her car and headed back to Sam's house. The ride on the Beach Road, with its lush greenery and sea breeze, calmed her a bit more. When she reached the house, she gritted her teeth and climbed up the gravel driveway again, nearly tipping over in her heels. Jessica answered the door, looking surpised.

"Molly, are you okay? Did you have car trouble?" she asked with concern.

"I'm fine. Matthew had an emergency. He had to admit a patient to the hospital and had to cancel on me."

Though she tried to sound matter-of-fact about it, she knew she really sounded glum.

"Gee, that's too bad." Jessica's sympathetic look nearly made her come unglued again. Molly smiled wanly, struggling not to start crying again.

"I'll survive. I don't really like jazz anyway. I guess I'll take the girls home."

"Sure. We were just about to have dinner. Would you like to stay?"

Molly considered the invitation. On one hand, it would give her something to do; on the other, it would be too depressing.

"That's nice of you to offer, Jessica, but I think I'll just take them out somewhere."

Just as Molly was about to call the girls, Sam walked into the living room. "Hey, Moll. What are you doing back here?"

"Matt had to go to the hospital on an emergency," Jessica explained.

"Oh, that's a tough break."

Molly glanced at him, daring him to say she'd been stood up. Sam just crossed his arms over his chest and gazed at her with a sympathetic expression that made her feel even worse somehow.

"Oh well. He couldn't help it, I guess," Sam said finally.

"Of course, he couldn't help it," Jessica replied.

Sam was caught off balance by his wife's defensive tone. "Well, that's too bad. The hazards of dating a doctor, I guess. Want to hang out with us tonight? We rented a movie."

"Thanks, but I think I'll just take the girls and go. You've been helping me out so much with the kids lately. You guys deserve a Saturday night alone," Molly said sincerely.

Jessica smiled at her. "You know I never mind having them here but thanks."

A few minutes later, Molly had Jill and Lauren back in the car, and they headed toward the village.

"Are we going home already?" Jill asked.

"What happened to your date with Matthew?" Lauren asked bluntly.

Molly didn't answer right away. "I guess you guys didn't have dinner yet, right?"

"No, and I'm starving I might add," Lauren answered.

"I might add that, too," Jill said in a serious tone.

"I might add that three," Molly replied, starting to smile again. "Tell me what you think. The barbeque chicken place on the turnpike and then we try out that new tropical mini-golf with the waterfalls?"

"Yes!" Jill answered.

"I'm getting a little *old* for mini-golf, Mom, in case you haven't noticed."

Molly met her gaze in the rearview mirror. "I hear you, honey. It's not my first choice, either, to be perfectly honest. But the palm trees and waterfalls sound like fun."

Lauren sighed, sparing a small smile. "Okay, if you guys really want to."

"I want to," Jill said.

"I do, too." Molly summoned up a burst of enthusiasm she didn't know was in her. It was the old "making lemonade from life's lemons" trick. *I've had a lot of practice at that one,* she realized.

"Let's go," she said. She turned the car around and headed for the turnpike, trying not to think of how her feet would feel in her fancy shoes at the end of a night of mini-golf. Or how her new outfit would look after the barbeque. At least Lauren and Jill thought she was a great Saturday night date.

As for Matthew's opinion, it didn't look like she was ever going to find out.

The next morning, Molly woke to the sound of rain spattering against the windows. The change in the weather seemed to mirror her dark mood. She rose and made the girls' breakfast, then got them ready for a day out with Phil.

It was a relief to have the apartment to herself. Still, facing a full day's worth of baking left her feeling depleted and depressed. A new helper, whom she had found through the high school, was due to start today but had left a message last night canceling on her. *It seems to be my weekend to be stood up,* Molly thought, as she put on her apron.

She worked through the morning, focusing on her orders and trying not to think about Matthew. He *would* call, right? It was hard to guess. Maybe he would wait a day or two. Maybe he didn't want to ask her out again and wouldn't call at all.

After pushing herself through several hours of baking, Molly needed a break. She was exhausted. She hadn't slept well and even an entire pot of coffee hadn't burned through the dense fog in her head.

She went inside and allowed herself to lie down on her unmade bed. *I never do this,* she told herself as her head hit the pillow. *What's wrong with me today? Maybe I'm coming down with something.*

Right, that little bug women get when they've been rejected by a man.

The steady patter of rain quieted her scattered thoughts as she drifted off to sleep.

Bart Potter sat at the end of the worn kitchen table. He had his father's build, tall and broad shouldered, though he was carrying some extra weight around the middle as he moved into middle age. In his fancy sport clothes, her son still looked every inch a corporate lawyer, Sophie thought, as if he were sitting at the head of a boardroom table instead of in her old homey kitchen. He frowned at his daughter.

"I'm surprised at you, Miranda. If you're disappointed with your career, that's one thing. But you can't hide out here. Your grandmother has to move. You have no right to talk her into staying."

"She didn't talk me into anything. You sound like I was hypnotized or something," Sophie grumbled.

"What I said was that I'm done with acting and I like it here and I'll stay if Grandma wants us to run the orchard together," Miranda explained.

"But you can't stay. Neither of you can. That's just my point," Bart said firmly.

Evelyn and Una sat together on one long side of the table, opposite Miranda. The two sisters glanced at each other and then at their brother.

"Calm down, Bart. Let's not lose our tempers," Evelyn said. "Miranda's been here with Mother through the worst of it. I'm sure she's feeling some strain after the last few weeks, too. We all know how distressed Mom is about leaving."

"I'm sure Miranda feels badly for her grandmother and just wants to help," Una added. She gave Miranda a sad smile. "We all feel badly about Grandma having to leave here, honey."

"We grew up here. We have so many memories. It's hard for everyone in the family to give up this place," Evelyn agreed.

Bart shook his head and exhaled noisily. Snorting like a horse, Sophie thought. Normally, she was proud of the way he had turned out. But this was one argument he wasn't going to win.

"All right. She just wanted to help. It was a nice gesture. And we all feel badly about giving up the orchard. But these matters have been discussed and decided," Bart pointed out. "I don't see any purpose in backtracking again. It's been hard enough to get Mom this far." He stared around the table. Una and Evelyn avoided his gaze, Sophie noticed, but she met it head on, unflinchingly. He finally looked away.

He sat back and cleared his throat. "I thought we were going to talk about how and when we'll put this place up for sale."

Sophie sat up straight and folded her hands in front of her on the table. She took a breath and was surprised to feel a small smile forming on her lips. "I'm not selling."

"Oh, Mom . . ." Una shook her head and glanced at Evelyn.

"Mother, please. Be reasonable now." Evelyn's tone was coaxing.

"Of course you are," Bart said flatly. He frowned at Sophie, a cold blue-eyed stare. "This has already been decided."

She remembered that look from when he was a little boy and didn't want to clean up his room or finish his homework before he could go outside and play.

It was suddenly very quiet while Sophie met Bart's gaze and held it. Outside, the wind picked up, spattering raindrops against the kitchen windowpane. Finally, Sophie answered her son. "No, I'm not. And you can't make me."

Sophie noticed Miranda smile and duck her head. *Yes, Grandma sounds like a rebellious child,* she thought, enjoying the irony. She kept a straight face, though, and went on in a measured tone, "This property is still in my name. While I'm still alive and sane, I decide when and if it goes on the market. Not you three."

Una tilted her head in Sophie's direction. "But, Mom, you know that we're just concerned for you—"

"It seems to me that if you're that worried about me, you would see that I can't leave. Not yet. It would break my heart, even worse than it's already been broken by losing your father."

Sophie reached over to pat her granddaughter's hand. "There's only one person who understood that—and who offered real help to me. Why, we've been taking care of the place together for the past few weeks now and doing just fine. She wants to stay, and I'm glad to hear it. I'm taking this girl up on her offer no matter what the rest of you think about it."

Her children looked at each other nervously, feeling shamed perhaps by her words. She could see that they were giving up on changing her mind, even Bart. She could tell by the way he sat back from the table and took a deep breath.

"Frankly, I don't see how you're going to make this work." He fixed his daughter with a stern glare. "I told you the same thing when you said you wanted to go to New York and be an actress. Maybe you always need to find out the hard way."

"Maybe we do," Miranda shot back. "If

we fail, it won't be for lack of trying, right Grandma?"

"That's right." Sophie nodded emphatically. " 'Whatsoever thy hand findeth to do, do with thy might. . . .' I'm not afraid of this not working out. All things are possible with God's help."

Bart laughed nervously. "Oh, dear. She's starting to quote the Bible at me. I guess it's time to give up."

"You ought to try it in court sometime, son. It will definitely get people's attention," Sophie advised.

"Well, Mom, looks like you got your way." Evelyn smiled ruefully and shook her head. "You know we're nearby if you need anything," she said to Miranda.

"Me, too, dear," Una said to her niece. "I can't say that I'm entirely in favor of this plan, Mom, but I am glad you're not leaving here yet." She glanced at her older sister and brother. "I suppose we'll just have to wait and see."

"Thank you, Una. Thank you, Evelyn and Bart. I know you all have my best interest at heart. But this is best for me. Miranda and I will make it work. I know it in my heart."

Sophie sat back in her chair, smiling with

satisfaction. She felt as if she'd just come home after a long exhausting trip. She was back where she belonged, finally, and didn't plan to leave any time soon.

The sound of the door buzzer woke Molly from a deep, dreamless sleep. She opened her eyes to find the room steeped in shadows. She turned and picked up the clock. Half past four? How could that be?

She sat up and rubbed her forehead, then launched herself toward the front door. "Be right there," she shouted.

Phil and the girls, back early. She hated for anyone to see her looking such a mess, rumpled and wrinkled, as if she had just rolled out of bed, which, come to think of it, she had. It was only Phil, though. It didn't matter.

But Molly pulled opened the door to find Matthew instead. Dressed in a yellow slicker, he stood with his face and hair wet from the rain. He held a bunch of daffodils wrapped in paper in his hand, their droopy yellow heads looking half-drowned.

"Matthew . . . hi." She tucked a thick lock of hair behind her ear, wondering now why she hadn't even bothered to stop and splash her face.

"I hope I'm not bothering you. I knew you were probably home working today. . . . I just wanted to say hello."

Molly was sure her shock at his unexpected appearance showed all over her face. She ducked her head and stepped aside to let him in.

"Come on in. I was just taking a break." *Sleeping away the afternoon, if the truth be told,* she silently added.

He handed her the bouquet. "These are for you. A little soggy though, sorry."

"Thanks, they're very pretty. I love daffodils. They always look so optimistic."

"Yes, they do seem that way, now that you mention it."

He hung his slicker on a row of hooks near the door and followed her into the kitchen. He stood in the doorway, watching her place the flowers in a vase. The expression on his face made her uneasy. It was a sad, thoughtful look that didn't bode well.

"Can I make you some coffee or tea?" She carried the small vase to the table. "I have loads of muffins and stuff," she added, pointing to the trays she had already baked.

"Um, no, thank you. I'm fine."

"I think I'd better have some coffee to wake up again," she said honestly. "I don't know why I'm so sleepy today."

"It must be the rain."

"I suppose." *More likely feeling blue over you,* she wanted to add. She poured out a cup of coffee from what was still in the carafe from that morning and stuck it in the microwave.

"Did you get over to Newburyport to hear the music last night?"

"Um, no, I didn't after all." The microwave beeped, saving her from facing him. She carefully took out the hot cup and blew on it. She was about to tell him what she did end up doing, but she caught herself. Tropical paradise mini-golf with her kids sounded so pathetic.

Matthew nodded politely. "Well, it's too bad you couldn't go. I'm sorry again I had to cancel on you like that."

"That's okay. I understand, honestly." Molly pulled out a chair and sat down at the table with him. "How is your patient doing?"

"Oh, not too bad. It was an older woman, lives alone, not taking care of herself properly. She came in complaining of stomach pains. It turned out to be her gall bladder. She needed surgery right away. I went down to the hospital today to look in on her. She seems to be feeling a little better."

"Well, that's some good news," Molly said sympathetically.

She knew that he hadn't been lying to her last night. She'd never suspected that. Yet, something about his mood right now made her uneasy. She couldn't quite put her finger on it.

Maybe he's just tired, she thought. He handled an emergency last night and drove to Southport and back today. But that didn't seem to be it, either. She felt herself sitting there, sensing she wasn't going to like whatever he had to say next.

Matthew cleared his throat and rubbed his hands together. *Here it comes,* Molly thought. She tried but couldn't stop herself from filling in the heavy silence, just to change the subject and forestall the inevitable.

"Where's Amanda today?"

Matthew looked up suddenly. She could tell his thoughts had been wandering. "She's visiting her grandparents, Sharon's folks, in Amherst. I was supposed to drive out there today actually, but I decided not to."

"To pick her up, you mean?"

"Yes. And to visit Sharon's grave. It's three years this week since she passed away."

Molly felt a sudden jolt. She suddenly had some clue to his strange withdrawn mood. She didn't quite know what to say to him, though. "I'm sorry. It must be a hard day for you."

"It is. I feel sad, of course, thinking about the past. But it stirs up a lot of questions for me." He paused and met her gaze. "About starting a relationship again, for one thing."

Molly swallowed hard.

He sat silently again, but Molly couldn't stand the suspense.

"Like . . . with me for instance, you mean?"

He nodded and forced a small smile. "Yes, exactly. Who else would I be talking about?" He reached across the table and took her hand.

"Oh." That was all she could manage to say. She felt the warm pressure of his hand on hers and squeezed back.

"The problem is, it's hard for me, Molly.

Thinking about the past makes me remember that I wasn't very good at being in a relationship."

Molly waited, but he didn't say more. She felt uneasy about pushing him, but she couldn't help herself.

"When you say you weren't good at it, what do you mean?" she asked gently.

He glanced at her and then looked away. "I mean I didn't have a happy marriage. My wife felt neglected. She felt I worked too hard and gave my best to my patients. I tried to work things out with her, but I don't think I ever really pleased her." He shrugged. Molly could see it was hard for him to continue, and she willed herself not to interrupt him.

"I don't know," he said finally. "Maybe Sharon was right. Maybe I'm not really cut out for marriage, for giving another person all they need. Maybe I do give my all to my work. In all this time, I haven't been able to figure that out. To get past it, I guess you'd say."

"Oh. I see." Molly continued to hold onto his hand, but suddenly his touch meant something else entirely to her, not a hint of things to come but a bittersweet ending to something that had never quite begun.

Matthew shook his head, looking frustrated with himself. "I'm saying this all wrong. The thing is, I wasn't lying last night when I had to break our date—"

"I know that," Molly cut in.

"Well, okay then. But afterward and today, I've had a lot of time to think about this . . . you and me dating, I mean. It's hard to say this to you, but I know I'm just not ready to start seeing someone again. Not even you. Especially you, in some way. There's so much that's good between us now, just the way it is. I don't want to lose that."

"Being friends, you mean," she said abruptly. *Oh, so this is the "let's just be friends" speech,* she realized. She felt she might cry and slipped her hand from his grasp.

He stared at her a moment. "Sure, I think of you as a friend. But I really care for you, Molly. I think you're amazing. Absolutely great in every possible way. The problem is, I've been through a lot the last few years. Moving has been another big upheaval. I need to focus now on the new practice and on Amanda, making a home for her here. I don't want to start something with you and end up disappointing you or leading you on. When I look into the future, I really don't see myself getting married again."

He'd been staring down at the table, delivering his words slowly and carefully. Molly took them in, one by one, feeling her heart drop by degrees. She felt too sad and stunned to speak.

Finally Matthew looked up at her, his dark eyes shining with emotion. Molly realized she didn't feel mad at him. She felt embarrassed. Had she been so obvious? It made her cringe now to see herself that way.

"Matthew, it's okay." She forced her voice to sound even and light. "It was just a date. I wasn't expecting a marriage proposal. Maybe on the third date or so. But not on the first one."

He looked at her, trying to smile, but not quite managing it. He ran his hand nervously over his damp hair, pushing it back from his forehead. "I guess I really meant you're not the kind of woman *I* could take lightly. If we ever did get involved, I know it would be serious for *me.*"

His honesty was startling. It gave her

hope and at the same time, made her feel even sadder and more frustrated.

"Well, that's nice of you to say."

"I'm not just saying it. It's true." His voice was quiet but emphatic.

But the other part—the more important part—was also true. He didn't have to repeat those words again. They still hung in the air between them, changing everything.

She stared at the vase of daffodils, their green stems looped over the edge, their golden heads sagging. Disappointed and dispirited, exactly the way she now felt.

But she knew she had to rally, at least for the few minutes he would remain here. *I can put the pillow over my face and cry my heart out later.*

"I understand what you're trying to say. Thanks for being up front with me."

His dark gaze sought hers out, but she avoided looking at him. "I know it doesn't sound like much," he said, "but I wish this could have worked out differently."

"It's all right. Maybe it's better this way. At least everything's out in the open now, right?" Her voice sounded a bit sharper than she intended, but she couldn't help it.

"Yes, I guess it is." He sighed and looked

down at the table, then pushed himself up from his chair. "All right then. I guess I'd better go."

"Matt . . . please. We'll still be friends. It's okay."

She didn't know why she found herself suddenly trying to reassure him, to make him feel better, when she was clearly the injured party here. But he looked so forlorn as he rose from the table, almost as if he might be having second thoughts about what he'd just done.

She stopped herself. More wishful thinking. That was her problem—what had gotten her into this spot in the first place.

He walked over to the door and grabbed his rain jacket. She followed from a safe distance.

"Don't work too hard. I'll see you around, I guess," he said gently.

"It's a small town. You won't be able to avoid me."

Her tart reply reminded them both of the time they'd met. He gave her a brief smile, one that didn't quite touch his eyes.

"I wouldn't want to. You should know that by now."

Molly watched him walk down the hall,

then closed the door. She immediately felt tears welling up in her eyes and then streaming down her face. She tried to hold them back but couldn't. She covered her face with her hands a moment, briefly considered running back into the bedroom and flinging herself on the bed, then shook her head.

No, she'd lost too much time over this already. She had to work. She wasn't half through on her orders. Lauren and Jill would be home in an hour, she realized. She couldn't let them find her looking so upset.

"I'm sorry, Betty. I just don't want to talk about this anymore. Can we change the subject, please?"

Molly sat at a table in the Beanery with Betty on Tuesday afternoon. Betty had been quite sympathetic as Molly related the story of Matthew's broken date and his heart-to-heart chat on Sunday. But despite Betty's sympathy and sound advice, she just didn't want to pick it apart anymore. The whole topic was still too painful.

"How did it go in Connecticut? How's Brian doing?" Molly asked suddenly.

"Oh, well now. There's a fresh topic for you."

Betty pursed her lips and stared down at her salad. Molly could tell that Betty didn't like the attention deflected to her own problems.

A few months ago, Betty's sixteen-year-old son, Brian, had more or less demanded to leave Betty's custody and live with his father. Betty's ex-husband had recently remarried and moved to New Canaan, Connecticut. At first Betty had refused to let Brian go, but finally she decided she had to give in.

"Brian is doing fine. He seems happy to be with his father," she reported. "I have to admit, I miss him a lot and feel badly that he didn't want to stay here with me. I'd be lying if I said differently. But it's good to be getting along with him again. We actually had fun together. So that's some benefit, I suppose."

Molly felt a wave of sympathy for her. She knew Betty had gone through a lot lately over Brian. She had also handled the news that her ex-husband was now the proud father of another baby with his second wife.

"How does Brian feel about the baby?" Molly asked.

"He's wild about the baby apparently. But I'm not surprised. The baby was part of the draw. I think Brian was afraid Ted was going to forget about him once he had another child. Ted, of course, is not quite *that* bad," Betty added with a short laugh. "But Brian didn't want to get shut out. He wanted to stake his claim in the new family."

"That's probably true," Molly agreed. Meanwhile, she could see that Betty was the one who felt shut out. Not that Betty held any grudges against her ex-husband; she seemed genuinely happy that he had started over. But Molly could see that Ted having a baby made her feel older, and now she felt rejected by her son, who seemed to prefer Ted's new family circle. The music had stopped, and Betty had found herself without a chair.

"How's it going with Richard?" Molly asked, hoping to steer the conversation in a more positive direction.

"Oh, Richard. That fizzled out." Betty sighed and put her napkin on the table. "We get along well enough, I suppose. We have the same interests and all that. He's a really nice guy, very thoughtful. But there wasn't much chemistry." She shrugged. "It was a mutual decision. We'll still be friends."

"Sounds like you feel okay about it."

"I do," Betty assured her. She glanced up at Molly.

"You can't expect every relationship to work out. Few do, actually."

Molly took a long sip of her diet soda, remembering the way Matthew had looked at her, saying he wished it could work out differently for them. She wanted to believe that he meant it, even though it didn't change anything.

No, she didn't want to think about that anymore. It didn't help one bit.

"What's going on with Emily's party? Did you give her your estimate yet?" Betty asked suddenly.

"Oh, I've been working on that. I'm not sure I'm going to do the party, though." Molly braced herself for Betty's reaction, sure of what would come.

"Molly, what do you mean? I thought it was all settled."

"It was never settled, Betty. I had a good meeting with Emily. But I never agreed to do it. We didn't even talk about a date."

"But I'm sure she's counting on you. You can't back out now."

"I'm not backing out, for heaven's sake. I didn't get far enough to be backing out. The more I looked into what was really involved in pulling this off, the more I could see that right now it's beyond me. I need to be more realistic. I can't do it."

"More realistic. Okay." Betty paused, nodding to herself. "I know what's going on here. You can't fool me."

Molly felt her mouth go dry. She never could fool Betty. But she could try.

"Okay, I'm game. What's going on? I don't have a clue."

"You do, too. Or maybe you're just so deeply in denial, you can't see it."

"See what Betty?" she asked a bit impatiently.

"It's because of Matthew. That's what made you suddenly 'realistic.' That's what made you think you don't want to do Emily's party."

"Oh, Betty, that's not true. I've just thought about the work involved, and I changed my mind."

"You can't do this to yourself. I won't let you."

"You won't let me do what?"

"Use this rejection—from some guy who doesn't appreciate you or is just in a bad place emotionally right now—as an excuse to throw away everything you've been working for. Forget about Matthew. You have a really great chance to get your business going, and you can't lose confidence in yourself and toss it away because this romance didn't work out. One thing has nothing to do with the other."

"I know that," Molly answered.

She stared down at her plate and pushed a bit of lettuce around with her fork. All last week she had felt wary but excited about the opportunity. It was Sunday night and Monday when doubts started moving in like storm clouds—just after her talk with Matthew, she realized. She couldn't help it. Nothing seemed right since then.

"What have you done so far? Did you figure out your costs and overhead and that sort of thing?"

Molly nodded. "I called up Pauline," she said, referring to her instructor. "We went over everything on the phone."

"That's great. Then you must be ready to give Emily an estimate."

Molly didn't answer for a moment. "I could be."

"Look, I'm sorry to be so hard on you about this." Molly noticed her smiling a little. "Think of it as a tough love kind of thing."

Molly smiled, too. "If you say so."

"I do. I know you had your hopes up about Matthew. I'm sure you feel like your heart has just been tossed in a food processor or something."

She did. With the setting on puree.

"But working hard is the best revenge, Molly. It's the best way to get over anything—a failed romance, a bad haircut. Even your ex-husband having a new baby," she added with a wry smile. "I've been through this a million times. Believe me."

Molly looked up and met her friend's sympathetic gaze. Betty was a fighter, that was for sure. She didn't let anything hold her back.

"You've already done all the groundwork, Molly. It would be a shame to just let this go."

It would be a shame. Betty was right. One thing didn't have anything to do with the other, though somehow in her mind, they had gotten all tangled up. She had to hold fast to some idea of herself, of what she could do. She couldn't let herself be so affected by other people's opinions—even Matthew's.

"All right, I'll meet with Emily again. I'll give her the estimate," Molly agreed with a long sigh. "Are you happy now?"

Betty sat back, quietly beaming. "Yes, very. Just for that, lunch is on me. And let's get dessert. Not one of yours, though. We need to check out the competition. And don't worry about your diet. This is market research."

"Right. The calories don't count then, I guess."

Betty nodded. "Exactly. Like writing it off on your income tax."

Molly laughed and shook her head. "Betty, you're too much."

Betty raised her hand, waving the waitress over. "Thanks. I'll take that as a compliment."

Bolstered by her lunch with Betty, Molly called Emily later that afternoon. Emily sounded happy to hear from her and eager to see her estimate for the party.

"When do you think you'll have it ready?"

"I guess I can drop it off at your house sometime tomorrow."

"Great, but don't bring it there. I won't be home tomorrow until very late. Come by my office. I'm eager to see it and talk it over with Dan."

"Um, sure. No problem. I'll drop it off at your office sometime tomorrow," Molly agreed.

They said good-bye, and Molly had a sudden moment of panic. She gulped it back, thinking of Betty's advice. The best cure was just to get at it.

By working late at night after the girls had gone to sleep and calling her course teacher with a few more questions, Molly managed to pull together a professional-looking estimate. She arranged it in an attractive glossy folder—a discard from one of Jill's many school reports—then packed it in a manila envelope. She even whipped up some attractive letterhead on the computer, though she still didn't have an official name for her business.

As promised, she drove over to Village

Hall the next day and walked back to the mayor's office. Emily's secretary was out, and Molly wondered where she should leave her package. Then she heard Emily call to her through the half-open door of her office.

"Molly, come in. I'm glad I spotted you out there."

Molly went into Emily's office and handed her the envelope. "Here it is. If you have any questions, or if I misunderstood anything we talked about, just give me a call."

"Yes, I will." Emily opened the envelope and then drew out the sheaf of papers from the folder. Molly felt a little twist in her stomach. She didn't want Emily to read it right in front of her.

Emily must have sensed her dismay. She glanced at Molly and smiled, then stuck the papers back in the folder.

"I've come up with a date." Emily picked up a calendar from her desk and flipped the page. "Dan and I thought May seventeenth could work out well. What do you think?"

"May seventeenth?" Molly looked down at the calendar to the little square where Emily now pointed. She suddenly felt so nervous, she practically couldn't see straight. It seemed as if Emily had glanced at the price quote on the top page and was going to agree to it.

Molly felt terrified. This was really happening. The party would be a month from now. Plenty of time to get ready, and yet it felt too soon. Way too soon.

"It's a Sunday. Do you have anything else scheduled that day, do you think?"

"Um, no. I don't think so." Molly took a breath. Her calendar was clear. Completely clear. Emily was her first and only client. Didn't she know that?

"I'll check to make sure, though." Molly forced her voice to sound more professional.

"Great. You check and see if that date works out. I'll look over the estimate and get back to you promptly." Emily smiled at her. "Thanks for coming by. I appreciate it."

"That's okay. I guess we'll talk later in the week then."

Molly said good-bye and left Emily's office. She had the strangest feeling that Emily and Betty were in this together somehow, a conspiracy to help her out, whether she liked it or not. Jessica might even be in on it, too, she thought vaguely.

No, that's just plain silly. I'm being paranoid about people being too nice to me and
treating me so respectfully. I always have to
think there's some catch. That's just like me,
isn't it?

CHAPTER FIFTEEN

A week of solid rain finally abated, and on Easter Sunday a brilliant sun rose against a spring blue sky. The air smelled of moist earth, green buds, and new grass. The cleansing breeze flowed through the open windows and wide open doors at the rear of the sanctuary.

As the choir sang the first hymn, Ben gazed out at the congregation. The church was full today. The men were dressed in their best suits and ties, the women in bright colors and flower patterns, and the children looked scrubbed and fancied up to within an inch of their lives.

The church was decked out in its own

Easter finery, the altar covered in an abundance of white lilies and baskets of blue hyacinths, filling Ben's head with their heavy scent. More than that, the pews and floors were polished and the windows bright. Carl had completed the list and more, and Ben was sure the Lord was pleased with his efforts. He told Carl as much yesterday afternoon. Carl accepted the praise in his typical taciturn manner, but Ben could see that he was touched by the words.

Ben saw Carl sitting in a pew with Tucker and his family. His dark jacket and white shirt had been borrowed from Tucker, no doubt. But he was there, gazing down at the hymnal and mouthing the words along with everyone else. Tucker sat beside him, staring straight ahead, as did Fran and their children. Ben was sure they had weathered some curious stares that morning. He knew it took courage on Carl's part to brave this crowd. He was so reclusive. Maybe that was slowly changing, too.

Ben had asked Carl if he had plans for Easter Sunday. If Carl was going to spend the day alone, Ben intended to invite him to his own home for Sunday dinner, but he had been pleased to hear that Carl was going to Tucker's house. Considering the hasty way he had left the Tulleys, this seemed a step back in the right direction. Ben asked God to bless them all for their efforts.

Soon it was time for the sermon, and Ben took the pulpit, his notes in hand. "Welcome, everyone. My heart is full with the good news. Like the angel said, 'He is risen.' Let us rejoice and give thanks for this message and the mystery that redeems us.

"And let us pray that this miracle lives in our hearts, not just today, on Easter Sunday, but every day. Let us be mindful of this fantastic event, which not only promises us forgiveness and salvation for all eternity but new life in this life here on earth, as we struggle with our human frailty and imperfections.

"Each time we feel discouraged and wish for a second chance, let us look back on this day and remember the story of Easter morning, the good news that comes to us in the Scriptures. Yes, we do have another chance. Let us put our faith in the Lord and the power of prayer and we can experience the miracle of change and rebirth, just as surely as spring stirs life in the earth again after the long, deadening winter."

As the service continued, Molly shifted in her seat, willing herself not to glance to the side where Matthew sat with Amanda farther down the pew.

She usually didn't attend church but Easter was special, like Christmas. You just had to go. Now that she was here, she wasn't sorry. The short sermon, powerfully spoken, really struck a chord. She could see herself in the reverend's words, despairing as she struggled to start a new life and chase after her dreams, losing her energy and faith. But maybe she could do this. She squeezed her eyes shut and sent up a quick prayer. *Please Lord, help me get things moving in the right direction. Help me with my plans and all I'm trying to do.*

Down the pew, Matthew thought about the sermon, too, and how he had come here, to Cape Light, hoping for a new life, for renewal that hadn't yet come to him. Maybe he just needed more time here. Maybe the spring would help, though in some strange way the new season only made him sadder.

Part of it was Molly. She was so much like

spring—so full of life—it hurt to see her here. More than he ever expected.

He missed her and thought about her and almost called her up to say hello a dozen times. Of course they had run into each other a few times during the past weeks because of the girls. But it wasn't the same between them anymore, and Matthew regretted that. He missed the easy banter and warmth.

Like the reverend said, he was discouraged. He felt stuck. But he knew in his heart that he had never really called upon the Lord to help him. He was still too scared, afraid of failing Molly, disappointing her the same way he had disappointed Sharon—and of disappointing himself. He had missed his chance with Molly, the chance of a lifetime. Mainly because he just couldn't get out of his own way.

Sophie Potter listened attentively as Reverend Ben concluded the service with the benediction and response. The choir sang the final hymn, and Miranda smiled at her. "Ready to go, Grandma?"

Sophie nodded. "That was lovely. I do love church on Easter morning. All the flowers and the sunlight. It's my favorite holiday."

"I know what you mean. It doesn't feel like it's really spring until Easter, does it?"

Sophie followed the others down the aisle. She held Miranda's arm but thought of Gus, missing his presence beside her even though she felt sure he was up in heaven, celebrating with the angels. She thought of Reverend Ben's words and thanked the Lord again for answering her prayers and granting her a new life at the orchard. *I know this isn't a permanent thing. I'll keep working hard, Lord, and try to live your Word. I won't squander the time I have left here, believe me.*

The Morgans gathered at Molly's parents' house after church. It was a small house in the section of town that had once been a community of summer cottages. The Morgans had expanded it over the years, but the cozy little Cape was never ideal for raising so many children or feeding so many at a sit-down dinner. Somehow, though, they all managed to squeeze together every holiday around the dining-room table.

Sam and Jessica were there along with Molly's younger brother Glen and his family, who lived in Burlington. Molly's younger sister Laurie and her oldest brother Jim were at their in-laws' houses, but Molly's mother couldn't abide a holiday gathering with fewer than twenty, so she had invited other relatives to fill the gaps—Molly's Aunt Mary and Uncle Lou along with Molly's cousin Beth and her husband and children.

Molly was so busy catching up with her siblings that she nearly forgot about Phil. She had agreed he could stop by and take Lauren and Jill to visit with his parents today.

They were all finishing the main course when Molly suddenly noticed the time and sent the girls upstairs to wash their faces and brush their hair. Playing with their cousins had left both girls looking rumpled. Not that Phil would mind; she knew he would show them off as proudly as if displaying two princesses.

Moments later the doorbell rang. "I'll get it. It's just Phil," she announced as she left the table.

"Phil? Phil Willoughby is here?" Her father sounded dismayed. Then she heard her mother shushing him.

"He's coming to get the girls, Joe. I told you that."

Molly knew that while she left the room her mother would be filling in her aunts and other interested guests on the news that Phil was trying to clean up his act and be a real dad again. She wasn't sure how her family would react. They hadn't seen Phil for a long time, and she knew that her father, at least, was still angry with his ex-son-in-law for the way he had treated Molly.

"Come on in," Molly greeted Phil. "The girls are upstairs, cleaning up. I'll try to hurry them along."

"No hurry. That's okay." She could tell from his voice that he was apprehensive about facing her family. Well, he should be.

Molly walked into the dining room while Phil hung back in the doorway. "Hello everyone. Happy Easter," he said politely.

Her father continued to chew his food, glancing at Molly's mother.

"Happy Easter, Phil," Marie replied. "It's beautiful out there, isn't it? I thought the rain would never stop."

"Yes, it's a beautiful day," Phil agreed

heartily, seeming relieved to have something so mundane to talk about.

"Phil, how are you doing?" Sam walked in from the kitchen and shook Phil's hand.

"Sam, good to see you." Phil smiled widely at his old friend. "I heard you got married. Where's the lucky girl?"

"She's right here." Sam proudly rested his hand on Jessica's shoulder. "Jessica, this is Phil. Do you remember him from school, honey? We were in the same year."

"Nice to see you again, Phil." Jessica's tone was diplomatic. Molly couldn't tell if she remembered Phil or not.

Molly heard Lauren and Jill come down the stairs. Phil turned to greet them, holding out his arms. "There they are, my two beauties. How lucky can a guy get?" Phil asked, kissing them each on the cheek.

Molly saw her mother and father exchange a look as the girls both hugged Phil, obviously thrilled to see him. "I have some Easter surprises in the car for you," Phil confided in a whisper.

Jill's smile widened, her eyes alight with greed. "Bye, Mom, see you later."

"I'll walk you all to the door," Molly told

her. "Say good-bye to everyone, girls. Show some nice manners."

Her daughters politely bid the group good-bye, running to the head of the table to kiss their grandparents, then back to Phil. Molly followed Phil and the girls out to the foyer.

"We won't be too late," Phil told her. "What about next week—don't they have off from school?"

"Spring break," Molly groaned. "I have so much work right now. I need this school vacation like a root canal from the Easter Bunny."

Phil laughed. He always did like her stupid jokes. "Don't worry. I can take some time off. I'll take them off your hands for a few days. It will be fun now that the weather is warmer."

"Would you? That would be great." Molly smiled at him with relief.

"As long you don't mind if I change my schedule," he added. "Maybe you have some stone-carving tools handy?"

"Okay," she said, returning his smile. "I'll see what kind of stone-carving tools I can find. Just call ahead and give us fair warning?"

"Sure. I can do that." He smiled widely and touched her shoulder. "Happy Easter, Molly. You look good in that color, sort of a peaches-and-cream thing going on there."

"Right. Thanks, Phil." Molly nodded and stepped back into the door. "I'll see you. Have fun with your family."

"Sure, see you." He smiled again and walked down to his car where Lauren and Jill were already waiting. Phil was a character, Molly thought, watching them pull away. At least he did show up here today, as promised. It scared her to even think it, but he was *practically* getting reliable.

When Molly returned to the dining room, dinner had ended. The guests had dispersed, waiting to be called back for dessert and coffee. Jessica and Sam were among the helping hands clearing the table.

"Funny to see Phil after all this time." Sam stacked some dinner dishes, putting the silverware on top. "He looks like he's doing well. It's good to see him pulling himself together and doing right by you and the girls."

Molly picked up some glasses. She felt an impulse to make some disparaging remark about Phil but caught herself. She didn't want to be like that anymore.

"So far, so good," she said. "We've hit a few bumps, but we're managing to work things out."

"That's great. Maybe you guys will get back together again."

Molly turned her head to look at him, thinking he had to be joking. "Are you crazy? I'd never get back together with Phil. Not in a million years."

Sam stood with his stack of plates. "What's so crazy about it? It happens to people all the time. The kids would be happy. Maybe Phil's finally grown up. He's always been a good-hearted guy, even though he messed up with you. You could do a lot worse than him, Molly."

Molly stood there, stunned. The entire idea was so unthinkable to her that she couldn't reply.

Yes, I could do a lot worse than Phil Willoughby. He's not the most awful man in the world. But I could do a lot better, she thought, turning toward the kitchen. *Though I seem to be the only one who thinks so.*

When it was time to serve dessert and

coffee, Molly was still helping out in the kitchen. She had made a number of desserts for the party, including a cheesecake, a lemon meringue pie, and for the younger members of the group, a rabbit-shaped cake covered with coconut icing. She finished decorating the platter, adding a few jelly beans for color around the edge. Jessica swept by and popped one into her mouth.

"Wow, that looks beautiful. What's inside?"

"Chocolate cake. Well, more of a fudge cake, actually."

"I'm not sure I could tell the difference. But I'm willing to try." Jessica smiled and took another jelly bean. "I hear you're going to do my sister's party. You must be excited."

"More like terrified," Molly confided. She shook some powdered sugar on the cheesecake then took another critical look at it. "The woman who teaches my course is giving me a lot of help, but I'm still sort of nervous."

"How about your financing? How's that going?"

Molly laughed. "So far I'm working off my

Visa card. . . . That's not the way you're really supposed to do this, right?"

"Well, it's one way, I suppose. I can give you a few more ideas if you come down to the bank sometime." Jessica smiled at her, then stole another bean. "You're in business now, Molly. You can get a line of credit or a loan."

Molly didn't answer right away. She concentrated on arranging a cluster of strawberries on top of the cheesecake. "I don't know. Do you really think the bank would loan someone like me money?"

"You're not so bad. I'll put in a good word for you, promise," Jessica gently teased. "Just call me next week, okay?"

Molly met Jessica's gaze. Her smile was so sincere, it was hard to refuse. *She really does want to help me,* Molly realized. *I really haven't been fair to her.*

Jessica brushed off her hands. "Can I help you put these cakes on the table?"

Molly nodded. "Sure. The bunny cake is ready to go."

Jessica picked up the platter and gazed down at it. "That's one thing I dislike about Easter," she said, walking slowly into the dining room. "Decapitating these poor, defenseless chocolate rabbits."

Molly had to laugh. When she stopped to think about it, that part always made her squeamish, too.

Matthew had spent the day at his sister's house. He and Amanda had come home in the early evening. Amanda quickly changed into her jeans and now sat glued in front of the TV. He sat in the living room, trying to read a book but not quite focusing on the story.

His parents had been at Erica's house, too. Erica was divorced and didn't have children so it had been a quiet afternoon but a pleasant visit with his family. Erica was a good cook.

Not as good as Molly, of course. He had been thinking of her a lot today. She hadn't been far from his thoughts ever since he saw her in church that morning. The truth was, she was never far from his thoughts. He missed talking to her. He missed the way she smiled, the way she moved, the way she just lit up a room. He missed her smart aleck sense of humor. His life seemed dull lately without Molly.

He had been tempted to talk to Erica today when he helped her in the kitchen. But just as he worked himself up to asking for her advice, his father had come into the room.

What could Erica tell him anyway? He had to figure this out himself. It didn't take a rocket scientist. He was stuck on Molly Willoughby.

But what to do about it? He had backed himself into a safe, comfortable little corner with that "let's just be friends" speech. He could kick himself now, just thinking about it. *She must hate me now. Or at least think I'm a jerk.*

Which I have been. Totally, as Amanda would say.

He glanced at the phone and took a deep breath. What if he called her right now? He could say something like, "I saw you in church today, and I didn't get to say much. I just wanted to wish you a happy Easter. . . ."

He shook his head. That wouldn't work. She was mad at him. She had a perfect right to be. He had hurt her feelings. She might not even talk to him. He had to do better than that.

Not tonight, he told himself. He was too tired. It wouldn't come out right. He needed to go to bed and get some sleep. He had a big day tomorrow, booked solid with appointments and a patient going in for bypass surgery.

Matt closed his book and put it aside. *Molly, Molly, Molly. What did you do to me? Even thinking about work can't make me forget you entirely.*

He sighed and rubbed his eyes with his hands. He thought of Molly again, how lovely she looked in church today. What had she been thinking, sitting there so close to him? She had said hello, then barely glanced his way, her attention fixed on Reverend Ben.

The sermon had touched him, and the message came back to him now, along with his fears. Matthew swallowed and whispered a prayer. "Dear Lord, I'm sort of a mess tonight. I think I've finally found someone I could truly love. But I'm afraid to move forward, afraid to disappoint her and fail her, like I failed Sharon. Please help me change. Give me a second chance to do better."

He took a deep breath, then opened his eyes. He didn't know what else to say. He hoped the Lord had heard his words, but he also knew that praying wasn't like waving a magic wand. For his prayers to work, he would have to do his share.

Tucker was out on patrol Monday afternoon when the call came in, a break-in on North Creek Road. Kevin Degan, the homeowner, had called to report it. Since Tucker was the nearest car, the dispatcher directed him to the property.

Tucker pulled into the driveway, parking behind an SUV. The open hatch revealed a jumble of suitcases, pillows, and golf clubs—the usual paraphernalia from a family car trip.

The Degans were waiting for him at the front door. "Officer, we've been robbed," Mr. Degan began. "We just pulled in from a few days in Vermont, visiting relatives. We opened the door and found this." He gestured to the living room behind him, where an end table had been knocked over and sofa cushions lay scattered on the rug.

"I'm going to take a full report," Tucker assured him. "Let's just go step by step. What time do you think you got in?"

"It was half past two. I know because I checked my watch."

"Kevin always checks to see if we've made good time," Mrs. Degan added. Her face was tear streaked as she pointed to the back of the house. "They came in through the glass door in back. It's broken in a million pieces."

"It must have happened last night. The rain got in and wet the carpeting," her husband said.

Though it was clear and sunny now, it had poured the night before. "That's a good guess, sir," Tucker said. "But just to be on the safe side, I'm going to have a look around and make sure the intruder is really gone."

Mrs. Degan gasped, and her husband put his arm around her shoulder. "That's fine. My boys are back in the kitchen, having a snack. Nothing stops teenagers from eating, right?" He shook his head. "Should I call them in here, too?"

"That's all right. They're okay. I'll start up-stairs."

Tucker checked the house, jotting some notes on a pad. It was a messy job, ama-teurs. It looked as if they'd been in a rush but hadn't taken anything too big—no com-puter monitors or TV sets. They had torn the bedroom apart, especially the woman's closet and dresser. Looking for jewelry, he figured. He felt a twinge, remembering Fran's stickpin. She still hadn't found it.

He checked the house room by room, then returned to the Degans and took down their story. He called the station from his car radio and made a quick report. Mr. Degan had some pull in town, and the chief was sending another car over with a team that would dust for prints, question the couple more closely, and talk to the neighbors about anything they might have heard or seen.

Tucker continued his part of the process, finishing up the standard questions he needed for his report. When his colleagues arrived, he was free to go.

He got back in his car and radioed the station, then resumed his usual route around familiar village neighborhoods. The

Degans' break-in nagged at him. He couldn't remember the last time he heard of a robbery like this in Cape Light. It was unlikely the thieves would be caught, he knew. That was just the way these things usually went. The family would collect on their homeowner's insurance and probably install an alarm system.

Back at the station, he began to type up his report. The other officers at the Degan house had come back earlier; he had seen them leaving Chief Sanborn's office.

He was nearly done with his paperwork when the chief stopped at his desk.

"I'm almost done with the report on that break-in on North Creek, Chief. Is that what you're looking for?"

"Yes, I'd like to see that as soon as you're done. Bring it into my office, will you?"

Something in the chief's tone and expression set off silent alarm bells, but Tucker showed no reaction. He checked through the document quickly, fixed a messy spot with white out, then carried the papers back to the chief's office.

Sanborn beckoned him in. "Shut the door, will you, Tucker?"

Tucker closed the door and gave the

chief his copy of the crime report, then took his usual seat. "The Degans were pretty upset. There wasn't much to go on out there, though. Looks as if it happened last night."

"Yes, so I've heard. Myers and Paretsky talked to some neighbors. One of them says he saw someone in the Degans' backyard. Claims he got a good look at him, too."

"Really? In the rain and all? He must have good eyesight."

"It didn't start raining until about midnight. This was around ten. The neighbor took out his newspapers for recycling, says he saw some guy running through the Degans' backyard."

"Well, that's something I guess." Tucker wondered what this was all adding up to.

"I like to think I'm a fair man," Sanborn said. "I checked Carl's record. You were right. He served his time, had no parole violations. But this neighbor's description fits your brother, fits him to a tee."

Tucker didn't say anything at first. It couldn't be Carl. This was just Sanborn needing to make a quick arrest.

"That's interesting," Tucker said finally.

"Did this neighbor see the guy breaking into the house?"

"No, just running out of the yard." The chief leaned back in his chair. "He claims he got a good look at his face, though. The guy taking off nearly ran right into him."

"Did the neighbor hear anything, the glass door breaking, for instance?"

The chief shook his head. "He couldn't say. It appears that whoever broke the door may have cut his hand on the glass. There were also some fingerprints around the place. Myers sent them to the county, so they can run them through the computer."

Sounded as if he was talking about laundry being sent out to the dry cleaners, Tucker thought. Not something as weighty as Carl's guilt or innocence.

Tucker's heart felt like a brick in his chest. He was not really surprised that Sanborn would suspect Carl, but a cold dread filled him as he wondered if Carl really did it. They had just had Carl over Sunday night for Easter dinner. Could he possibly have robbed the Degans' house that same night? Tucker still didn't have a high opinion of Carl, but he truly doubted he would do something like that. Carl had been doing so well, working at the church and living on his own, not causing any problems for anyone.

"I'm going to bring him in for questioning," Sanborn went on. "I've sent out a car to pick him up. They should be back any minute. I wanted you to know that."

Tucker held his tongue, not trusting himself to speak. Chief Sanborn almost seemed to be enjoying this. He couldn't wait to prove that he was right about Carl and that Tucker was wrong.

"What's your plan here, to see if the neighbor can I.D. him?"

"Something like that."

"That doesn't mean much, Chief." Tucker swallowed back a hard ball of anger in his throat, struggling to keep his voice even. "Witnesses like that make ridiculous mistakes all the time. You know that. Just because some neighbor identifies Carl doesn't mean he did it."

The chief let out a long slow breath, rubbing his chin with his hand. "I knew you were going to say something like that. Your loyalty is admirable, Tucker. But I think it's been sadly misplaced."

Tucker stood up from his chair, though he hadn't been dismissed. He was so angry, he could feel himself shaking with it. "I guess we'll have to wait and see, Chief."

The chief glanced up at him. He had already begun reading the report. "Yes, we'll see. You ought to go now. I'll let you know what's happening."

"Fine. But I'm going to stick around until Carl is done here tonight."

They both knew Tucker meant to see if he needed a lawyer.

"We're just going to talk to him."

"Yeah, I know. I know the drill by now." Tucker knew his tone was a shade disrespectful and wondered if his boss would call him on it.

Chief Sanborn didn't look up again. "Suit yourself."

Tucker was sitting at his desk when Carl was brought in. He felt the other cops looking at him as he went over to the desk Sergeant, who was checking Carl in.

"They just want to talk to you, Carl. There's nothing to worry about," Tucker promised. "Just answer their questions and they'll let you go."

Carl, flanked by his two police escorts,

gave a short, bitter laugh. "Sure, that's what they always say."

Tucker suddenly noticed a large bandage on Carl's left hand. "What happened to your hand?"

"I cut myself fixing something at the church. What's the problem? Didn't you ever see a bandage before?"

Tucker swallowed hard, still unwilling to think the worst.

"You don't have to say anything without a lawyer present. I'll call one for you."

"I don't need no lawyer. I can speak for myself. I'm not afraid."

Carl needed to have an attorney present, Tucker thought with alarm. There was no telling what he might say once he got angry. Tucker had questioned his share of suspects. He knew the tricks. Carl might incriminate himself without even realizing it.

"Hold up here awhile. I'm going to get him a lawyer," Tucker told Tom Schmidt, one of the officers with Carl.

"We're just delivering him to the questioning room, Tucker. They'll read him his rights, like always. He's got to ask for the lawyer. Not you."

"The man is right," Carl said. "I been

through this before. I remember how it goes." He turned to Schmidt. "All right, let's get this over with. I don't have all night to hang around here. I'm a busy man."

Tucker waited at his desk, pretending to be working while Carl was questioned. He called home and left a message for Fran, warning her that he was held up at work and would be late. He didn't explain what was going on with Carl. He wanted to wait to see what happened before he told her anything.

Two hours passed. Tucker walked back to the interview room and asked what was going on. An officer standing near the closed door told him a detective from the county was still questioning his brother and taking his statement. They were waiting for the Degans' neighbor to arrive to see if he could identify Carl.

Tucker nodded and headed for the locker room, where he got a soda from the machine. Frank Myers, who was on the team sent to the Degans' house after him, was in there, pulling on his jacket.

"Tough break, Tucker. I heard they brought in your brother."

"Yeah, some county detective is talking

to him now. I just hope they don't get him talking, make him say something stupid."

Myers stared at him, and Tucker suddenly felt a cold distance between them. "Like what? A confession, you mean?"

"There's no proof Carl did this, Myers. Not a shred. Just some neighbor who *might* have seen some guy who *might* look like my brother on a pitch-black rainy night."

"It wasn't raining yet. But I get your point. I'd feel the same if one of my relatives was brought in." Myers touched Tucker's arm in a gesture of camaraderie, but Tucker shrank back.

"See you around," Myers said softly.

"Right, see you." Tucker turned away and headed back into the station. As he passed the front desk, he saw a man walking in and gazing around, looking confused. He guessed it was the Degans' neighbor, coming to view Carl through the one-way window.

Well, at least this would be over soon. He sat at his desk again, forcing himself to look busy and unconcerned. The truth was, he felt torn apart, seesawing between believing Carl was innocent and feeling as if he'd been played for a fool.

Carl was once picked up for breaking and entering, back when he was a teenager. It had to be thirty-five years ago by now. But Sanborn would find that on his record, if he hadn't already, and jump on it like a dog on a bone.

Tucker wondered what Carl's alibi would be. He remembered the bandage on Carl's hand. The burglar had cut his hand on the glass door, Sanborn said. They would probably match the blood type, though that didn't mean much unless they used DNA testing, which Tucker knew was so expensive it would never be used on a case where there was only property damage. Carl could have cut his hand at work, like he said. But it didn't look good.

He thought of the missing stickpin again and felt as if its needle point had jabbed right into his heart. Maybe he should have known back then. Maybe Fran was right.

Still, Tucker found himself wanting to believe Carl was innocent. It seemed as if he had really changed these last few weeks. Was that all just an act?

Tom Schmidt stopped by Tucker's desk and spoke in a confidential tone. "I wanted to tell you. I was just back there. They're going to let him go."

"The neighbor couldn't I.D. him?" Tucker asked hopefully.

"It was shaky. The guy got rattled, kept wiping his glasses. That doesn't look so good in court. Sanborn got annoyed. The blood on the door was a match—O positive. But everybody's got O positive, even Sanborn's mother."

Tucker forced a smile. "How about the fingerprints? Did they hear back yet on that?"

"No, the prints they had weren't clear. Sanborn's sending someone back to the house tomorrow to see if they can find more."

That was unlikely, Tucker thought. By the next day, with the family walking around carrying on with their lives, they wouldn't find anything matchable. He felt relieved—until he realized that feeling this way must mean he thought Carl was guilty.

Tucker rubbed the side of his cheek and looked up at Schmidt, thinking, *He thinks Carl is guilty, but he feels badly for me and is trying to help me out.*

"Will he be out soon?"

"Sounds like it." Schmidt glanced over his shoulder, then moved closer to Tucker and lowered his voice. "They were trying to get a warrant to search Carl's place for stolen goods, but the judge wouldn't sign off. Not enough cause."

Tucker hadn't even thought of that. A search through Carl's belongings might explain everything—or not. He could have hidden small items anywhere, not just in his room. He could have hidden things at the church, for instance, Tucker thought. He pulled back from the idea; it seemed too sad and cynical.

"Thanks, Schmidt. I owe you one," Tucker said quietly.

"That's okay." Schmidt rested a heavy hand on his shoulder. "See you tomorrow. I'm checking out."

Nearly an hour later, Carl emerged. He looked even more worn and haggard than usual, with deep, dark rings under his eyes and a glassy angry stare as he approached Tucker.

"Well, I'm out of here. I told you I didn't need no lawyer."

Tucker felt every eye in the station house

watching them. "Come on, I'll give you a lift home."

Carl nodded and followed him, seeming oblivious to the attention. "A police station has a certain smell. Ever notice? I sure hate that smell."

Tucker didn't answer. The truth was, he was starting to dislike it, too.

They got in Tucker's car and started toward the house where Carl now rented a room. It was an old-fashioned building outside the village, three stories high and squarely built. At the turn of the century it had been a boardinghouse for summer visitors. The present owner, an elderly lady, rented furnished rooms at cheap rates. Tucker knew what it looked like inside, though he'd never been to see Carl there. The rooms were small and dark, hot in the summer and cold in the winter. But the place was clean overall, not a complete dump.

He pulled up outside and parked. "So, I heard the neighbor couldn't really identify you. Were you even there?" He tried to sound mildly curious, no pressure.

Carl's back went up at once. "I just sat

through umpteen hours of questions. Now you're starting in on me, too?"

"I'm just curious, Carl. You might have been there. It doesn't mean anything."

"It seemed to mean a lot to that county detective."

Tucker felt his gut clench. "You told him you were there? Did you put that in a statement or something?"

Carl shook his head. "Oh, man. Let me out of here. I got nothing else to say to you, Tucker. Maybe I *do* need a lawyer."

He started to open the car door. Tucker touched his arm. "Look, Carl, this is serious. They tried to get a warrant to search your room tonight, but the judge wouldn't give it to them. Tomorrow, though, they might find one who will."

"You know what they say, if at first you don't succeed." Carl laughed bitterly at the expression on Tucker's face. "What do you think they're going to find up there anyway, Tucker? Besides a bunch of dirty laundry and soup cans, I mean. Why do you look so nervous, man?"

"I'm concerned for you. Can't you see that? I don't want you put away for something you didn't do."

"Neither do I, when you put it like that." Carl stared straight ahead. "You act as if you think I did do it. That's what is sounds like to me."

Tucker felt as if his head might just explode. "Stop talking in circles for a minute, will you, please? Did you do it? Is that what you're trying to tell me?"

Carl leaned back, laughing quietly. "You're the cop, what do you think? Some neighbor says I was running through the backyard but face-to-face doesn't recognize me. I cut my hand, see?" He raised his bandaged hand. "And I did time for killing a man and have a record of breaking and entering—"

"Did you give a statement? Did you sign anything?" Tucker interrupted him.

"Sure I did. They wouldn't let me out otherwise."

"They can use that in court against you. Don't you know that?"

Carl turned and looked at him. "Who says I'm going to court? They've got nothing on me."

Tucker sighed in frustration, not knowing what to believe.

"You're the one who's in hot water," Carl

taunted him. "I saw the way you were moping around the station house, Tucker. You had a bad day at work. You ought to get home."

"Right, I need to go home." Tucker felt totally frustrated with Carl. Not that he ever expected a thank you. He'd had enough of talking in circles for one night.

"Good night, Carl. I'll speak to you tomorrow."

Carl slipped out of the car and closed the door. He leaned in through the half-open window. "So long, Tucker. Take it easy." Then he turned and walked toward the boardinghouse, looking like a man who didn't have a care in the world.

Tucker walked out to his squad car the next morning, eager to leave the station house and get out on duty. He unlocked the door and looked up to see Reverend Ben crossing the parking lot.

"Reverend, good morning," Tucker said as Ben approached him.

"Sorry to bother you at work, Tucker. I hoped to catch you before you left the station. I need to talk with you."

"This is about Carl, right?"

The reverend nodded. "I went down to the church this morning and found this note." He reached into his jacket pocket and pulled out a folded sheet of paper. He handed it to Tucker, but Tucker didn't even bother to open it. He had a feeling he already knew what it said. "He's gone, right?"

"Yes. He left for Maine to see that friend of his. He says he'll call when he has an address so I can send some back pay. But I don't understand what he's talking about in the note. What robbery? When did the police question him?"

Tucker felt his body sag. Whether it was with sadness or relief, he couldn't tell. He took a deep breath before he answered the reverend's question.

"Two nights ago there was a break-in on North Creek Road. A neighbor claimed he saw a man who fit Carl's description. So they brought Carl in for questioning."

"I see . . . and you were there, too, I gather?"

Tucker nodded. "I wasn't allowed in the interview. But I waited for him. I drove him home last night."

"Do the police think he's guilty?"

"Well, he's the only suspect so far. It's all circumstantial evidence—not even a fingerprint to go on. But Carl did admit to being in the neighborhood that night. His alibi isn't strong."

He had finally heard Carl's story this morning from another officer on the case. The story made Tucker cringe with embarrassment. It seemed so trumped up and transparent.

"What was it?" the reverend asked with interest.

"Carl says he was walking a dog down North Creek Road. Says he takes out the trash and walks the landlady's dog some nights as part of the deal on his rent."

"Yes, I know. I helped him find that room. That was the arrangement," the reverend confirmed.

Tucker paused. So Carl hadn't been lying about that part.

"Well, he said the dog spotted a cat or a raccoon or something and ran away from him. So he chased the dog through some backyards and wound up coming back out to the street through the Degans' yard. That's why the neighbor saw him, he said."

The reverend nodded. "That makes

sense to me. But you don't sound as if you believe him."

"I don't know what to believe, Reverend. I tried to believe he's changed . . . but yesterday I felt like a fool, trying to defend him. Now he's taken off, run away from this whole mess, which definitely makes it look like he's guilty. If they get some solid proof, they'll go looking for him."

"Carl's leaving town doesn't prove anything. And even if he is guilty, you have nothing to be ashamed of, Tucker. You tried to help him. You went out of your way to give your brother a new start here. You acted with kindness and courage."

"Thanks, Reverend," Tucker said, feeling better about sticking up for Carl and looking out for his rights. He'd probably do it again, given the chance.

It didn't look like there would be another chance, Tucker realized. Carl was gone. He'd probably never see him or even hear from him again. Tucker had a strange feeling and swallowed back a lump in his throat. When he looked up, he realized the reverend was still standing there, watching him.

"I better get to work. Appreciate you stopping by, Reverend."

"That's all right, Tucker. If you want to talk about this some more, you know where to find me."

"Yes, I do." Tucker nodded and jammed the unread note into his pocket. He doubted he would want to discuss Carl anymore with anyone. Just thinking about Carl made him confused and depressed. He wished he could forget his brother ever existed.

CHAPTER SIXTEEN

"Are you sure it's safe? I mean, the water isn't very deep, is it?" Molly stood in the middle of her kitchen, clutching a knapsack of extra clothes she had packed for Lauren and Jill in case they got wet. They were going kayaking today with Phil down in Essex, but now Molly felt reluctant to let them go, even though they were on spring break and she needed to work. "How do you know there won't be any rapids or currents or things?"

Phil and Lauren stood staring at her. Lauren rolled her eyes, then glanced at her father.

"Really, Molly. It's very safe," Phil said.

"Really? Then why do you need all these extra clothes? Don't those boats tip over a lot?"

"It will be fine, honestly. They're going to love it."

"It's not too cold out for this?"

"Perfect weather. You don't want it too hot." Phil took the knapsack from her grasp and hooked it over his broad shoulder. "Listen, if you're so worried, why don't you come with us? You need a day off, Molly. You've been working too hard."

She had been working hard. She had a lot of new clients and had started training her helpers from the high school. She was also preparing for Emily's party and had just seen Jessica at the bank yesterday, where she had applied for a small-business loan.

She was worn out from work and all the excitement. But she still didn't feel right just goofing off.

"I can't. I have too much to do. It does sound like fun, though." She picked up her apron from the back of a chair.

Phil reached over and snatched it out of her hands. "You won't be needing that today. They do make you wear something called an apron, but it's a part of the boat that keeps you dry."

"Mom's going with us? Great!" Jill walked into the room, beaming at Molly.

"Mom in a kayak?" Lauren rolled her eyes again. "This I've got to see."

"Why, don't you think I could do it?" Molly challenged her. "I would probably be great with a paddle. All this baking builds up arm muscles, you know." Molly flexed her biceps, and the girls started laughing.

"Not bad," Phil nodded, looking impressed. "I think you ought to have Lauren in your boat. She's the heavier freight."

"Thanks a lot, Dad!" Lauren gave her father a playful nudge.

"Oops. Guess I said something wrong."

"Yeah, I guess," Molly said dryly. She sighed and glanced around the kitchen, her work pulling her in one direction and Jill tugging her arm in the other.

"Come on, you're going with us," her younger daughter insisted. "You need some fresh air and exercise."

"Besides, our vacation is almost over and you haven't done anything fun with us all week, Mom," Lauren added.

Molly glanced at Lauren, then back at

Phil. The girls were right. She needed to take a break and be with them. Even if it meant spending the day with her ex-husband.

Although Molly was apprehensive at first, she found the hardest part was getting herself into the boat. Once they were out on the water, a smooth quiet inlet near the Essex River, Molly felt an extraordinary sense of peace. They paddled out across the smooth blue surface that showed barely a ripple in the morning light. Except for the slap of water against the hull and the dip of the paddle, it was silent. Birds balanced gracefully on long stalks of marsh grass, and fish wriggled past under the boat, their slick silver bodies darting through the clear water. The two kayaks glided across the calm inlet, and Molly fell into a smooth rhythm both with her own breath and heartbeat and with Jill, who sat in front of her, also paddling.

At one point they got their signals crossed and the boat started to tip to one side. "Jill, watch out!" Molly cried. She tried to reach forward to her daughter, which only made it worse. Then somehow she managed to get them righted despite Jill's screeching. Phil paddled over to check out the fuss, and the two boats bumped together, making the girls laugh out loud.

"Aren't there any brakes on this thing?" Molly called out as her boat collided with Phil's.

"Dad, for goodness' sake. You're such a bad driver. You need to let me steer on the way back," Lauren told her father.

"Great. I'll just rest. My arms are getting tired already," Phil complained in a good-natured tone.

Molly glanced at him. His muscular arms were bared by a T-shirt under his life vest, and he didn't look the least bit tired. Attractive, yes. Tired, no. She looked away, surprised that she had even noticed him that way. Well, he always was a handsome guy. There was never any question about that.

Finally, they paddled up to a beach that appeared to be a sandbar. The sand was nearly white, covered with shells, and Molly felt as if she were paddling up to a deserted island. They pushed their boats up to the shoreline and hopped out.

It wasn't really warm enough to swim, but

the girls were so hot from paddling in the strong sun, they jumped into the water with their shorts and T-shirts on and splashed around wildly.

"Now you see why you need all the extra clothes," Phil said.

Molly stood on the edge of the water, watching with a smile. "They have the right idea. It gets pretty hot out there." She tipped her head back and took a long drink from a water bottle.

Phil thoughtfully waited until she was done, then gave her a hard shove, pushing her in with her daughters. "I was hoping you'd say something like that."

"Phil . . . you're horrible." Molly couldn't help laughing at him. She climbed out of the water, soaked to the skin. She came after him, but he was too quick and dashed away, laughing.

"Get him, Mom! You can't let him get away with that," Lauren called out. Then Lauren and Jill joined in the chase, and Phil let himself be caught. With each girl tugging an arm, they pulled him into the water.

"Oh, man, that is cold!" He jumped out like a pop-up toy. "I can't believe you guys did that to me. Three against one, no fair.

Just for that, I'm going to hide your pad-
dles. You'll be stranded out here."

"No way!" Jill shouted at him.

"Yes, way. Just try me," he warned her.
But the girls pounced on him as he hurried
to get out of the water and pulled him down
again.

Molly was laughing so hard, she couldn't
speak. She couldn't remember the last time
she had this much fun. For an instant, she
felt as if they were a real family again. Sam's
words suddenly echoed in her mind. *Maybe
you guys will get back together again.* She
pulled out a towel from the pack and dried
off. Was it even remotely possible?

They ended up at the Woodsman, an Essex landmark that offered no-frills seafood
and a rustic ambiance. Everyone wanted
the same lunch, a cup of chowder and a
lobster roll. They carried their trays of food
outside to the wooden tables set up under
long awnings. Molly felt tired, and she
ached in places she didn't even know she
had. But she was hungry, and the tasty food
and view of the open meadow behind the
restaurant took her mind off her pains.

The girls finished quickly and went for a
walk in the meadow. "I can't believe they

have any energy left after all the paddling. I can barely chew," Phil confessed.

"Me, either, but it was fun. Thanks for making me go with you. It's been a great day."

Phil smiled at her. "It would have been fun with Lauren and Jill. Having you with us made it really special. I'd forgotten how much fun you are, Molly."

"So did I," Molly said with a small smile. "Sorry you got dunked by my assistants."

"That's okay. I deserved it. I did it to you first."

"So you did. I almost forgot about that."

Phil was quiet for a moment. "I almost forgot how pretty you look when you're smiling like that."

Molly glanced up at him quickly, then looked out at the meadow. What was going on here? She didn't like that look in his eyes.

"I've been thinking about you, Molly. I've missed you."

"Oh? Really?" Molly coughed. She didn't know what else to say. She picked up her soda and sipped from the straw.

Phil's blue-eyed gaze became intent. "I

know this probably sounds crazy, but I think we should get back together."

Molly put the cup down abruptly. She started to speak, but he interrupted her before she could get any words out.

"I know we had some bad times. But we're older now. We're calmer. Well, I am," he added. "We were happy together sometimes, Molly, really happy, like today. It wasn't all bad times—"

"No, it wasn't, Phil," she cut in. "I would never say that. But that doesn't mean we should get back together again."

"The girls would love it. I've never seen them as happy as they were today. Well, not recently anyway."

She couldn't argue with that. Still, getting back together for the sake of the girls wasn't a good reason, was it?

"Just think it over. I have a good job now. We could buy a house. You wouldn't have to work so hard. A lot of our fights were about money. It wouldn't be like that anymore."

He met her eyes, trying to persuade her to see the reason in his unexpected proposal. Molly stared at him, stunned. *He's a born salesman,* she reminded herself. *A few minutes more of this and I'll start to agree with him.*

Well, almost.

She saw Lauren and Jill walking back toward them and breathed a little easier. He wouldn't keep this up in front of the girls. He had better sense than that. She hoped so, anyway.

"Hi, guys. Ready to go?" Molly's voice was bright.

Phil rubbed his chin, looking as if he realized he hadn't gotten very far but wasn't going to give up quite so easily. The look in his eyes made her nervous. She couldn't quite believe this was happening.

Molly was relieved when spring break ended and the girls went back to school. As of tomorrow, she had two weeks left to prepare for Emily's party, which wasn't long at all. And she had cold feet again about applying for the small-business loan. Jessica was calling regularly, gently pressuring her for the paperwork. It just seemed like an awful lot to bite off, Molly thought, especially since Emily was her first and only client and could be her last if it didn't go well.

Of course, if she didn't get the loan, she might not have the means to do this right, so there was another dilemma.

She had also been putting off the visit to Lillian Warwick's house to check the rooms and plan the setup. But on Friday she realized she had to face the inevitable. She called Emily, and they made a plan to meet there at two.

Molly was apprehensive enough about facing Lillian with Emily by her side, but just as Molly was about to leave the house her cell phone rang.

"Molly, it's Emily. I'm stuck in a meeting. I'm not sure when this will be over. My mother is expecting us. Why don't you go on over, and I'll try to catch up?"

"Um, sure. I was just leaving to go there," Molly told her. "See you later then."

She hung up the phone, feeling her stomach twist into a knot. *You're a businesswoman now,* she told herself. *You have to be polite to the client's mother. Even if it is Lillian Warwick.*

Molly arrived at Lillian's grand old house on Providence Street a few minutes later.

She rang the doorbell and glanced around. The place looked deserted. Then again, it always looked like that. The curtain in the front window stirred. Still, no one came to the door.

Molly rang the bell again, then knocked. Finally, she turned around to go, and as she did, she heard the door open behind her.

She whirled around to see Lillian peering outside, her mouth set in a frown. "I thought my daughter was coming with you."

"Emily got held up in a meeting. She told me to come ahead since you were expecting us."

"I was expecting my daughter . . . but never mind, come in."

Lillian pulled open the door and stood back, taking in Molly with an appraising glance. Molly felt as if she didn't quite pass muster, even though she had pulled her wild, curly hair back into a neat upswept hairstyle and wore a dress and heels. She also carried a professional-looking black portfolio, hugging it in front of her now like a shield.

"Let's see, where should we start?" Molly tried for a light yet professional tone.

"How should I know? I really don't want

this party here in the first placc—strangers tramping through my house, breaking things. I wish they would have it in a restaurant or an inn. I'm not running a catering hall here, you know."

"Of course not." Molly struggled for a pleasant tone. "But house parties are so much more personal and comfortable than something in a restaurant."

"How preposterous. Emily has no nostalgic feelings for this house, believe me. She was never happy one minute under this roof. It's just for convenience's sake. Her convenience . . . and my inconvenience."

It was a wasted effort trying to be pleasant to Lillian Warwick, that was for sure. Molly decided it was best to just do what she'd come to do and get it over with.

"May I see the dining room?" Molly asked.

"You know where it is. You don't need a tour guide."

Molly thought Lillian would stay out of her way after that, but she followed her, walking carefully with the use of her cane. Lillian stood in the doorway while Molly surveyed the room. The heavy drapes were drawn, and the room was so dark Molly could hardly get a good idea of the size.

A long banquet-sized table took up most of the space. It was really too large for the room and must have been brought from Lilac Hall, the old family estate.

"Can this table be closed to a smaller size?" Molly tried to check to see if it could, but the table was covered by a lace cloth.

"Why ask me? I thought you were the expert. Though I don't see how one can make such a leap, from cleaning girl to party planner or whatever it is you call yourself now."

Molly felt stung. She held her breath, not permitting herself to react to Lillian's barbs. She had done more for Lillian than clean house. She had also made meals for her, though Lillian never thought much of her cooking.

"I'm starting a catering business, Lillian. It's not brain surgery."

"I'll say it's not." Lillian tugged on the edges of her cardigan sweater. "That's my daughter for you, always doing people favors, even at her own expense. This party will humiliate her, mark my words. She hires a cleaning girl to stage an engagement party for a hundred guests. At her stage in life, mind you. I must say, I'm aghast."

Molly had rarely heard that word used but didn't need a dictionary to gather its meaning. She felt her face turn beet red, and she swallowed back an angry response.

The problem was, Lillian's cruel taunts had hit a nerve. She was a cleaning girl trying to stage a formal party for the town's mayor. She wasn't fooling anybody in her stylish new clothes and upswept hairdo, least of all, Lillian.

She couldn't let Lillian see that she had rattled her. Determined, Molly strode into the living room and started a quick sketch, noting the arrangement of the heavy old pieces of furniture. Later she would figure out how they might be rearranged to make more room for the guests and extra tables.

Lillian peered at her sketch. "Don't tell me you're going to redecorate in here as well. Or is that another sideline for you?"

The place could use a little freshening up, Molly thought. It looked as if Lillian had hired Teddy Roosevelt to do her decorating.

The doorbell rang, and Lillian glanced at Molly. "That must be Emily, late as usual.

She'll be late for her own funeral," she complained as she started toward the foyer.

Molly sighed with relief. She never imagined she would be so happy to see Emily Warwick enter a room. She had been a heartbeat away from losing it and congratulated herself now for keeping her temper.

"Hi, Molly, sorry I'm late." Emily walked into the room and bent to kiss Lillian's cheek. "Hello, Mother."

"Since you're finally here, I'll let you handle things," Lillian said with a last disparaging glance at Molly. "I'm going upstairs. I find this all very tiresome, Emily."

Emily ignored that and turned back to Molly. "So, what are you up to? Any questions so far?"

Just one. How have you survived with such a mother? Molly wanted to ask her. Of course, she didn't.

"I was just doing a sketch of this room to figure out how we'll set up the tables. Isn't there a patio outside?"

"Yes, the patio is right off the kitchen. Would you like to see it?"

"Let's take a look. If the warm weather keeps up, we can set up cocktails and hors d'oeuvres out there."

"That's a great idea." Emily led the way through the kitchen to a back door. Molly followed, grateful that Lillian had retreated for now. Still, Molly couldn't help feeling a little battered by Lillian's cutting words, in part because of her own doubts. What if she couldn't pull this off? What if Lillian was right?

Molly left Lillian's house feeling weary and stressed but also encouraged. Emily had seemed pleased with her ideas for the setup and decorating.

Checking her watch, Molly realized she needed to rush over to the middle school to pick up Lauren, who had stayed late for lacrosse practice. Her mother had already picked up Jill and brought her to her own house.

Molly pulled into the parking lot by the athletic fields and soon spotted her daughter, standing in a cluster of other girls. Amanda Harding was there as well. Lauren ran over to the car and bent down to talk to Molly.

"Can Amanda come home with us? She's not feeling well."

"Um, sure. Of course she can. Where's her dad?"

"We don't know. She tried to reach him on his cell phone, but he hasn't gotten back to her yet."

"No problem. Go get her." Molly wondered about Matthew. It wasn't like him not to answer his cell phone. She knew he'd been working long hours the last few weeks. She had seen a lot of Amanda lately. During the vacation, Amanda had hardly been home at all, shuttling between Molly's and her aunt's in Newburyport.

She hadn't seen much of Matthew since their talk. She told him they would still be friends, but it was too hard for her. She still had feelings for him—deep feelings that wouldn't go away that easily.

The two girls jumped into the back seat. Molly stopped at her mother's house and picked up Jill, then took everyone home.

Amanda seemed subdued during the car ride. When Molly asked if she was all right, she just nodded.

There seemed to be something else going on; Molly knew that look on Lauren's face by now. She would get to the bottom of this sooner or later.

Once they got home, Molly suggested that Amanda call her father again. Amanda got a machine this time and left a message that she was at Molly's house. Jill ran off to watch TV in the living room, pleased to have the remote all to herself. The two older girls started toward Lauren's room, but Molly stopped them.

"Dinner will be awhile. How about a snack—some popcorn?"

Lauren and Amanda glanced at each other. "Okay," Lauren said.

Molly slipped a bag of popcorn in the microwave and took out a big bowl. "Eat in here, okay? I don't want a lot of crumbs in your room."

"I'll get something to drink," Lauren said, going into the refrigerator. Amanda sat at the table, and Molly joined her.

"So, how was school today? Anything interesting going on?"

Molly waited. She wasn't sure this would work. Sometimes the direct approach was best, though, catching them off guard.

Amanda swallowed and shook her head no. Molly could tell that really meant yes, and whatever had happened wasn't all that easy to talk about.

Lauren came to the table with a carton of orange juice and a funny look on her face.

"Amanda had this . . . thing happen to her today." She rested her hand on her friend's shoulder. Amanda sat staring down at the table, and Molly saw her eyes glistening with unshed tears.

"Was she hurt at practice or something?" Molly asked with concern. "Amanda, can you tell me? You don't have to if you don't feel like it," she added.

Amanda lifted her head and rubbed the back of her hand across her eyes. "N-n-no . . . it's okay." She winced, hearing herself stutter.

Molly hadn't heard the speech defect in a while, and though it wasn't terribly obvious, she could tell it upset Amanda.

"Amanda had to give a book report today in English, and she had trouble talking," Lauren explained. "And when the teacher left the room for a minute, this dumb guy in our class, Ricky Hanratty, started imitating Amanda, and she got really upset."

"Oh, Amanda, honey. That's just awful." Molly rose and went over to Amanda. She put her arm around Amanda's shoulder and gave her a hug. For a long moment Amanda sat stiffly; then the tears came, and she seemed to melt. She turned and pressed her face against Molly's hip.

Molly leaned over and stroked her hair. "That was such a cruel thing to do. What a creep," she stated flatly. "You just can't pay attention to dumb kids like that."

She hugged Amanda. After a moment, Amanda pulled away, collecting herself. Molly got the popcorn from the microwave, poured it into a bowl, and brought it to the table. Amanda was drying her eyes with a tissue, but she still looked shaken. *Maybe I helped a little,* Molly thought, *but what she really needs is her father.*

"I'm so sorry, dear. You had a really bad day. But soon everyone will forget all about it. You'll see."

"I hope so," Amanda managed to say.

Lauren glanced at her mother. "Can't we take this stuff in the bedroom? I don't see what the difference is. I eat in there every minute of my life."

"That's just the problem. Okay, take it in if you have to. Just try to pick up the crumbs later so they don't get smashed into the carpeting."

As if Lauren would remember to do that, Molly thought, shaking her head.

Molly started to fix dinner. She was rinsing some lettuce in the sink when the door buzzer sounded. Wiping her hands on a towel, she went to answer it. Phil was coming tonight to visit the girls. She had felt a little uneasy about seeing him ever since he had made his wild proposal to get back together again.

She took a breath and pulled open the door—and found Matthew on the other side.

"Molly, hi. I'm sorry I didn't call first. I picked up Amanda's message, and I came right over."

Molly stepped aside to let him in. "That's all right. You didn't have to rush. She just wasn't sure where you were today. She couldn't reach your cell phone."

"I was having some trouble with the phone today. I've been running around, as usual. A patient had to be taken by helicopter to Mass General this afternoon for emergency heart surgery."

He sat at the kitchen table, looking beat, his handsome looks marred by dark circles beneath his eyes.

Molly felt sorry for him, yet she could also see now what had been going on between him and Amanda. She sat down at the table across from him, determined to have a talk.

"Amanda had a problem at school today. That's why she came home with us."

"What happened? Is she okay?"

"She's fine . . . or she will be. A boy in their English class made fun of her speech problem after she gave a report. She's very upset. It must have been quite painful for her."

Matthew looked alarmed and angry. "Why do kids act like that? Don't they know any better? You would think they were old enough by now to understand and have some consideration." He shook his head. "I'm going to call the school. No kid should get away with behavior like that."

Molly reached over and lightly touched his arm. "Matthew, I know you're upset, but making a big deal about this might upset Amanda even more."

He glanced at her, then nodded. "Good point. I didn't think about that."

Molly withdrew her hand. He seemed very conscious of her touch and of her taking it away from him. "You told me once you came here to make a new start, so you would be able to give Amanda more time and attention."

Matthew looked puzzled. "Yes, that's true. But what does that have to do with it?"

Molly sat back. "You haven't been around much these last few weeks. Not that I don't love having Amanda here. I do. But I feel as if she's here more than at your house lately."

He frowned at her. "I've been busy with work. I can't help my difficult hours."

"Maybe not," Molly agreed mildly. "Or maybe you just can't help falling back into old habits again."

"You're saying I'm doing the same thing I did when I was with Sharon?" he asked sharply.

She shrugged. "I don't know. You're the one who told me that you have a way of disappearing into your work. And I watched you disappear on me." She saw that he was about to interrupt her, and she silenced him with a look. "That's okay. I'm fine," she said calmly. "But it's not okay for Amanda. She needs you, and you're not there for her lately. You ought to think about it. That's all I'm saying."

Matthew looked blindsided. "I guess we ought to go now." His voice was quiet.

Molly stood up. "Okay, I'll go tell Amanda you're here."

Matthew watched as Molly disappeared down the hallway that led to the bedrooms. He let out a long breath. She had all but accused him of running away from her. Had he? He had thought he was doing the honorable thing, trying to protect her feelings, to keep himself from disappointing her. Apparently it added up to the same thing.

As for Amanda, Molly was right on that score. He had fallen into his old workaholic habits again. Even his sister had noticed it on Easter Sunday and said something to him. He had to break out of these tired patterns. It felt as if he was coping, but it caused more damage in the long run.

He could get back on track with Amanda. He was sure of that. But he didn't think he could ever fix things now with Molly.

Tucker was alone in the locker room, getting ready to go home, when Chief Sanborn walked in. "Tucker, glad I caught you. I wanted to have a word."

Tucker closed his locker door. "What's up, Chief?"

"It's about North Creek Road. The Degan house."

Tucker had already guessed that would be the topic. "Did you find more evidence?"

"Not really." The chief's tone was vague. The crime had been reported nearly two weeks ago, but Tucker knew from gossip around the station house that no real progress had been made since then.

"We're still looking at Carl. The neighbor wants another chance to identify him. If we do get a clear I.D., I think Carl will give us a confession."

Tucker laughed; he couldn't help himself. "If he did it, that is, and if you can find him. He could be anywhere by now."

"That's why I'm talking to you, Tucker. Any idea of where he went?"

Tucker considered his boss's question for a moment. "I have some idea," he admitted. "But I don't have an address, if that's what you're asking for. You can't have him picked up without any hard evidence, Chief."

"I know that, Tucker." Sanborn's tone was harsh and impatient. Tucker realized he'd gone too far, but somehow he didn't really care anymore. He respected Chief Sanborn a lot more, he realized, before this whole business with Carl.

The chief stared at him a moment. "When the time comes, I expect you will be more forthcoming."

Tucker leaned back and squared his shoulders. "*If* the time comes, you mean," he corrected, and he left the station without waiting to be dismissed.

Tucker arrived home to find Fran cooking dinner. He brushed by her without a greeting, took some headache medicine from the cupboard, and poured himself a glass of water.

"You don't look well," Fran said sympathetically. "Did you have a hard day?"

"They all feel hard lately." Tucker swallowed the pills and drank some water. "The chief stopped me on the way out. He wants me to tell him where Carl is. He has absolutely no hard evidence, but he wants to make that arrest." Tucker's tone was bitter as he sat down in a kitchen chair.

"Tucker, calm down. You're taking this so hard." Fran rested her hand on his shoulder.

"How am I supposed to take it? First Carl is accused of robbing a house, then he disappears and Sanborn is after me as if I'm some kind of accomplice because I won't tell him where Carl is. I don't even know where Carl is." Tucker shook his head. "I still can't believe he robbed that house."

Fran sighed. "I think it's fairly likely he did. A neighbor saw him running from the yard. He even had that cut on his hand from breaking the glass."

"You sound just like Sanborn now, Fran. Whatever happened to innocent until proven guilty?"

Fran sat down near him. He could tell she felt sorry for him, but that seemed to make it even worse, as if she felt he were a naive fool to believe Carl could be innocent.

"I have a feeling no one will ever know for sure, Tucker. He did run away though," she reminded him. "That should tell you something."

Tucker didn't know what to think anymore. One minute he believed Carl was unjustly accused, the next he believed he was the guilty culprit who had played him for a fool.

"There was your diamond stickpin."

Tucker's tone was reluctant. "Maybe I should have known after that."

Fran got up from the table and checked a pot on the stove. "I finally found that. It was the funniest thing. I hid it in an old handbag and totally forgot about it. I thought I had told you."

Tucker turned to look at her. "No, you didn't tell me that. I would have remembered. I *definitely* would have remembered."

Fran stirred the food in the pot with a wooden spoon. "I'm sorry. It just slipped my mind. But honestly, Tucker, one thing has nothing to do with the other. So, he didn't steal the stickpin. That doesn't mean he didn't rob that house."

"It means a lot to me, Fran," Tucker practically shouted at her. He was so angry, he could barely see straight. "You should have told me you found the pin, Fran. How could you *not* tell me such a thing? Why, we practically chased Carl out of the house over that. Doesn't that mean anything to you?"

Fran stepped away from the stove. "You're right. I should have told you, Tucker. I don't know why I forgot. I was embarrassed, I guess, for making such a fuss about it at the time. I even thought one of us should apologize to Carl for the things I said." She sighed and looked down at the floor.

"Well, we can't now. Nobody can apologize to him," Tucker said. "It would have made a big difference to me, Fran, knowing you found that pin. I would have treated him differently that night he was at the station house. I wouldn't have doubted him the way I did. Maybe he wouldn't have run away. It wasn't just about you being embarrassed. Don't you understand that?"

"I-I guess I didn't think of it that way." Fran looked up at him, her expression remorseful. "I'm sorry, Tucker. I wasn't thinking."

"I'll say you weren't."

Tucker came to his feet. He was stunned and furious and sick at heart. He had more to say to Fran—a lot more—but he felt himself choking on his anger. He strode past her and into the mud room, then pulled open the side door and left the house. He heard Fran calling after him, but he didn't turn around. His mind was whirling. Carl hadn't stolen that stickpin, after all. It seemed to change everything.

CHAPTER SEVENTEEN

~

"Molly . . . wait!" Molly heard the sound of Matthew's voice calling out to her from down the street. She turned slowly, her arms filled with the sample books of linen swatches she'd borrowed from her teacher.

Matthew walked up to her, looking breathless and happy. She hadn't seen him for over a week, since he'd come to pick up Amanda and they'd had words about his long hours.

"What are you up to? Did you just rob the library?"

"I'm meeting with Emily Warwick here." She tilted her head toward the door of the Beanery, which was a few feet away. "I'm catering her engagement party."

"Wow, that's great. It sounds pretty involved."

"You have no idea." Molly rolled her eyes. "Neither did I, or I probably wouldn't have gone through with it."

"When is the party?"

"A week from Saturday." She paused, unsure of how much she wanted to tell him. "I'm trying to start a new business. Emily is my first client."

"I'm impressed—the town's most prominent personality. That's quite a start." Matthew smiled at her. "Here, let me help you with that stuff."

She let him take some of the heavy books, feeling as if they were suddenly in high school.

"I'm a little early for my meeting. Would you like to have some coffee?" She felt nervous asking him, wondering if he was mad at her for the unsolicited advice she had given him.

"I would love to," he replied. "I don't want to interrupt your business meeting, though." So, she was a businesswoman now, having meetings that shouldn't be interrupted. She rather liked that idea.

"It's really fine. She's not due here until

four, and Emily's always late," Molly added with a grin.

Matthew opened the door for her, and they went inside and found a table. They both ordered espressos. Matthew glanced at the desserts in the glass display case. "Those chocolate chip cookies look good— and familiar. Did you bake those?"

Molly nodded. "A standing order."

He smiled. "You're going to be famous someday, Molly. I just have a feeling."

"You can say you knew me when." Her tone was light, but her heartbeat suddenly raced, set off by the look in his eyes.

"I'm hoping I'll *still* know you then, to be perfectly honest."

He caught her gaze, and Molly again found herself at a loss for words. She was relieved when the coffee arrived, and she stirred her cup with the pretty stick of crystalized sugar that came with it. *A nice touch,* she thought. *I'll have to remember that.*

"So, how is your practice going?" She meant it as a neutral topic of conversation, then realized he might think she was checking up on him after their talk about Amanda.

"It's fine. I've figured out a way to cut

back on my hours a bit. I guess I was over-whelmed at first. The town hasn't had a local doctor in so long, people ran in with everything from a hangnail to acute appendicitis. And I tried to accommodate them all—even the hangnail." Matthew gave her a wry smile. "But I've found a doctor in Essex who will see my patients on my off hours."

Molly nodded. "That sounds like a good arrangement."

"Yes, it should work. I probably would have done something like this sooner or later, but I have to admit talking to you gave me the push I needed to look for someone right away."

Molly took a sip of coffee, still unsure of what to say.

"You were right. I was letting the practice take over my life. That's not why I came here. It's not fair to Amanda."

"I didn't mean to be hard on you, Matt. I just felt badly for her. She was so upset."

"Yes, she was. She's better now, and she's getting some speech therapy again, too. I know she loves living here. It was a good move for her."

How about for you? Molly wanted to ask, but she didn't have the courage.

"So, this business of yours . . . have you come up with a name yet?"

Molly shook her head. "Lauren suggested Awesome Food. No, I got that wrong, *Totally* Awesome Food," Molly corrected herself in a serious tone that made Matthew laugh. "Jill came up with a good one, Incredible Edibles."

"I vote for Totally Awesome Food. Maybe you should have a contest. It could be good publicity."

"Good idea. I'll make a note of it."

Molly enjoyed talking and laughing with him like this more than she wanted to admit. She had missed him. Matthew was special to her, different from all the men she had met after her divorce. He had somehow won a place in her heart. She couldn't say how that had happened, only that mysteriously it had.

"You're going to be a big success, Molly. I just know it." His tone was quiet but sincere, and Molly felt her spirits lift with his praise.

"Thanks. I'm trying," she said with a small smile.

He reached over suddenly and took her hand. Molly's heart skipped a beat. He sat staring at her hand in his, seeming lost in thought. When he looked up at her, his gaze wandered over her face, resting on her mouth. She felt as if he wanted to kiss her. He wouldn't do that here, in the middle of the Beanery, would he?

Not that she didn't want him to, she suddenly realized.

"Mayor Warwick, good to see you." She turned to see that Emily had just walked in, and Felicity Bean was talking with her. Felicity and Jonathan Bean had given Molly's baking business—and her confidence—a big boost that Molly would always be grateful for.

Matthew eased his hand away and sat back in his chair. "I guess your four o'clock is here, Ms. Willoughby."

She laughed at his secretary impersonation. "The mayor again. Guess I have to take a meeting." Her blasé tone made him smile.

Then she paused before speaking again in her own voice, which emerged sounding a bit shaky and shy, she noticed with dismay. "It was good to run into you, Matt."

He stood up and sighed. "Good to see you, too. Don't work too hard, okay?" Then he did lean over and kiss her, a quick hard kiss on her lips that stole her breath away. As he pulled back, the look in his eyes was challenging, as if to say, "I really wanted to do that. So I did."

Molly took a deep breath. "See you," she said quietly. He nodded and walked away.

Molly felt stunned. What ever happened to his "let's be friends" agenda? That kiss—which was definitely more than friendly—seemed to cancel out that plan, though Molly wasn't sure what was left in its place. He had her guessing, as usual. But she had hope again, hope that something more would come of the connection between them.

Maybe it's not just me, she realized. *Maybe Matt couldn't just let it go, either.*

Reverend Ben sat up on the examining table, the sleeve on his left arm rolled up to his elbow. A bloody, makeshift bandage covered a deep, jagged gash on his forearm.

Matthew leaned over him, carefully cutting off the bandage. "You've got quite a cut here."

"I thought you might say that."

"How did this happen, Reverend?"

"I was just working around the church, trimming back some bushes on the side of the building. I lost my balance and scraped my arm on the edge of the shears."

"That's a bit more than a scrape." Matthew surveyed the cut once it was exposed.

"I shouldn't have been out there. The deacons usually take care of those things. We had a good handyman for a few weeks, Carl Tulley. But he had to leave the job rather suddenly."

"Yes, I heard about that." Matthew had heard all about Carl Tulley, though he didn't believe half of it.

He turned to the cabinet behind him and took out some gauze and tape. "You're going to need some stitches. When was your last tetanus shot?"

The reverend shrugged. "I don't remember."

"You'll need one today. Just to be on the safe side."

Matthew assembled the materials he needed and started to work on Reverend

Ben. "Ever had stitches before?" he asked as he quickly pulled the needle through.

The reverend glanced briefly at his arm and then away again. "Once or twice, years ago."

"These are the melt-away kind. You won't have to come back to get them out. I do want you to watch for any signs of infection, though."

The reverend nodded. "So, how do you like it here so far, Matthew? Are you and Amanda settling in okay?"

Matthew smiled. "I'm the one who's supposed to start in on the small talk—to distract you."

The reverend smiled. "You forgot to ask me what I do for a living. Isn't that the standard question?"

"More or less," Matthew admitted with a short laugh. He applied a strip of adhesive on the gauze, then turned to cut another. "We're doing okay, I guess. This office is extremely busy. Sometimes I think I could stay open twenty-four hours a day."

The reverend gazed at him. "I think you mentioned that you came here to work less, not more."

"That was part of the reason." Matthew

had finished with the bandage and turned to put the materials away in the cabinet.

When the reverend didn't say anything, he added, "My wife died about three years ago."

"Yes, I know that. I'm sorry for your loss."

"I've never quite gotten over it. I guess I moved here for a change. To see if it would help."

The reverend leaned forward, folding his bandaged arm across his chest. "Has it helped you, Matt?"

Matt looked at him, then shook his head. "Not completely. Not as much as I had hoped. But that's my own fault, too."

"How so?"

Matthew shrugged. "It's just hard. Even moving to the moon might not really help me."

"What part is hard, Matt? You still grieve for your wife—is that what you mean?"

Matt didn't know how to explain it. He wondered now how he'd even gotten so deeply into this subject. There was something about Reverend Ben that made him want to talk, to unburden himself.

"We had an unhappy marriage. My wife felt neglected. She said I worked too hard."

Matt paused and shook his head. "Maybe I did. I know I could have been a better husband to her. But when I finally tried, it was too late. Sharon was sick. We didn't have much chance to make it better. I never got the chance to make it up to her."

"And you feel sad about that."

Matt nodded. "Yes, and guilty, too. I feel sort of stuck, to tell you the truth. Like I can't fix the past and can't do any better in the future, so I'm afraid to even try."

"But you would like to try, I gather. Or else you wouldn't even be thinking of it."

Matt thought of Molly. Yes, he would like to try. If she would give him another chance. If it worked out between them, it would be like a new life, he thought.

"I have tried, in a way. But I keep slipping back. Until I resolve my feelings about my wife, I can't seem to move forward, and I just don't know how to do that."

"I see." The reverend nodded. He met Matt's gaze. "You believe in God, right?"

"Yes, of course I do."

"Do you believe that God alone has the right to judge us? That we don't have the right to judge each other—or even to judge ourselves?"

Matthew considered his words. He didn't answer at first. "It's hard not to judge myself, Reverend. Very hard."

The reverend nodded in agreement. "Yes, I know. I feel the same way myself at times. What about your wife? Would she have wanted you to feel this way, so burdened and stuck, so unhappy?"

"No, not at all. She wasn't like that."

"She would have forgiven you then?"

Matthew glanced at him, unsure of what to say. "I guess so."

The reverend didn't say anything for a moment; he just looked over his bandage again and started rolling down his sleeve.

"You know the Lord's Prayer, of course. I bet you say it often, maybe even every day. Some people say that prayer alone summarizes the entire Gospel."

"I never heard that," Matthew replied.

" 'Forgive us our debts, as we forgive our debtors.' The key, you see, is forgiveness. There's so much of Christianity in that single word." The reverend looked up at him. "God forgives you, Matthew. That's a given. He asks that you reflect that forgiveness to those around you—even to yourself. Forgiveness is a virtue, no doubt. But it's also medicine to a troubled soul. It can heal and bring resolution and tranquility."

Tranquility. There was a sweet-sounding word. Matthew swallowed hard. Could he forgive himself? he wondered now. He'd never really tried, he realized.

"You've given me something to think about, Reverend."

Reverend Ben smiled and hopped down off the table. "Not the usual distracting small talk?"

Matt shook his head. "No, not in the least, sir."

The reverend didn't say anything. But Matthew could tell by his small smile that he felt quite satisfied with that reply.

"Lillian? I know you're in there. You really need to just open the door now and let us in." Molly's tone wavered between a sugary, coaxing voice and one edged with the anger and frustration she truly felt.

She listened again at the thick wooden front door, wanting to stamp her feet in sheer outrage. But she controlled the impulse, well aware of the eyes on her of the group of helpers she had hired for the day.

They were watching her from the sidewalk, where they stood by a rented van loaded with party supplies, waiting for her instructions.

Molly knew Lillian was in there. She just wouldn't answer the door. Oh blast! What else would go wrong? It was hard enough to do this party, the event that was supposed to launch her new business. Now she had Lillian to contend with. How could she have everything set up in time if she couldn't even get inside?

Molly sat down on the top porch step and put her head in her hands, feeling as if she were about to cry. One of her helpers, a girl named Christine whom Molly had hired from the high school, walked up to her. "Isn't anybody home?"

"She's home. She doesn't want us to *think* she's home. But she's in there, believe me. She just won't let us in."

"Oh." Christine gazed up at the house. "What about a back door?"

"I tried. The house is locked tight as a drum."

"Is there someone you can call? How about Mayor Warwick?" Christine persisted. Molly sighed. As if she hadn't already thought of these things. Still, the kid was only trying to be helpful. "I left a message on her cell phone. I think she's off at a day spa in Newburyport or something."

And Jessica went with her, Molly added silently. She had left a message at Jessica's house, too. Now there was no one left to call and, short of breaking and entering, no way to get in the house and set up for this party. Every minute spent melting out here in the hot sun was time wasted. It had taken all morning to pick up the tables, chairs, linens, and tableware and to assemble her crew. It was already one o'clock, and Molly knew she was an hour behind schedule.

Christine walked up the steps and stared at the front door. "Gee, too bad you don't know where she keeps a spare key. There must be one around."

Molly blinked and suddenly sat up straight. She did know where Lillian left her spare key. She had used it when she used to come here to clean. Working for Lillian had been so miserable, she'd blocked the entire episode out of her mind.

She jumped up, hoping the key was still in the same place, inside a cushion on a wicker rocking chair out on the porch. As

Christine watched, Molly grabbed the cushion and unzipped it.

She pulled out the key and held it in front of her like a prize.

"Yes!"

"Is that the key?" Christine asked.

"Yes, for the front door." The question was, did she have the courage to use it? Molly took a breath. What was the worst that could happen?

Lillian could call the police and have her carted away for breaking in.

Knowing Lillian, it was definitely a possibility. Molly glanced over at Christine. "You go down and tell the others to start emptying the truck. I'll leave the door open. Just start coming in with the stuff."

Christine nodded and skipped down the steps. Molly took a deep breath and approached the door. Lillian would put up a fuss, she was sure. But maybe if the crew started marching in with all the equipment, she would feel outnumbered.

Molly hoped so. She slipped the key into the lock and slowly turned it, then pushed the door open. The house was silent and dark. The foyer felt cool, despite the heat outside.

"How did you get in here!" Molly looked up at the top of the stairs to see her nemesis dressed in a long robe and leaning on her cane.

"I used the spare key. I guess you didn't hear me knocking," Molly said diplomatically.

"I heard you." Lillian shifted on her cane. "I'm not feeling well. I can't have all this hubbub in the house today."

"I'm sorry, Lillian. We have to start setting up. I need a few hours to get everything ready."

Lillian peered down at her, then slowly began to come down the steps. "But you can't start working in here. Don't you understand me?"

Lillian's tone was sharp, her voice piercing. Molly felt intimidated but forced herself to keep her own voice steady and calm. "But Emily must have told you I was coming—"

"This is my house, not Emily's." Lillian stood at the bottom of the steps now. "I've already told you. Your presence here is most inconvenient and unwelcome. I won't have it!"

Lillian's eyes widened in astonishment as

Molly's helpers began to troop into the house, carrying stacks of rented chairs and folding tables.

"Who are these people? Where do you think you're going? Get out! All of you!" She turned to Molly and glared at her. "Stop them. Stop them immediately!"

Molly's crew paused, looking from Molly to Lillian, their faces growing red and strained as they held their heavy loads.

Molly quietly nodded and waved her hand. "Go on in. It's okay. I'll work this out."

At Molly's last remark Lillian's face grew pale. Her mouth opened to speak, then closed again. Molly suddenly worried that the old woman might make herself sick over this.

She didn't know what to do. Should she stay out and keep trying to get in touch with Emily? But that might take all day. She wouldn't be ready in time, and this party would be the disaster Lillian had predicted.

"Mother, what in the world is going on here?"

Molly suddenly turned to see Jessica in the doorway. She had never been so happy to see her sister-in-law. "Jessica . . ."

Jessica glanced quickly at Molly. "Sam

picked up your message and found me. Thank goodness." She looked back at her mother. "What's the problem here, Mother? You knew Molly was coming today."

Lillian swallowed and sniffed but looked her daughter straight in the eye. "Yes, your sister talked me into having this debacle of a party at my home. But I never agreed to having it torn apart by this band of riffraff." Lillian stood up straight. "I'm not at all well. I need my rest. I can't have these people milling about, tearing the place apart."

Jessica moved toward her mother. "Mother, you knew what was going to happen here today. Molly needs to set everything up."

"A professional party expert could manage in far less time with far less fuss, if you ask me. Not to mention her employees. Why, there's a girl in there with an earring in her nose!"

She referred to Christine's unfortunate nose piercing. Christine had promised to take the nose ring out this evening for the event; it never occurred to Molly that it would be a problem during the setup. She was such a good kid, Molly hardly noticed it anymore.

Jessica ignored the comment. She took Lillian's arm and began to lead her back upstairs. "You need to have your hair done, Mother. You're practically the hostess tonight, you know."

"The hostess? I'll probably be up in my room with a horrid migraine."

"Of course, you won't. You don't want to embarrass Emily and Dan like that. I have an appointment for you at the beauty shop in town. Now, what are you going to wear? Is the blue dress back from the cleaners?"

Molly heaved a huge sigh of relief as she watched Jessica and Lillian disappear down the upstairs hallway. The coast was clear for now. Molly turned her attention back to the business of getting this party together. She had a little over four hours to set up. She just hoped she could do it all in time.

Molly was out on the patio, checking a flower arrangement, when she spotted Emily and Dan inside. She could tell immediately from the look on Emily's face that the preparations had been a success. More

than a success. Emily looked absolutely astounded.

"Molly, the house looks beautiful! The
flowers, the tables—everything looks great."
Emily beamed at her. "How long have you
been here?"

"Oh, a few hours." Molly wondered if Jessica had told Emily about Lillian's behavior.
It seemed almost beside the point now. The
setup phase was over. All she had to do
was serve the food.

"Molly, can you come in the kitchen a
second?" Nick, one of her helpers, stood in
the doorway to the kitchen, his eyes wide
with alarm. *This is not good,* Molly thought.

"I can see you have a lot going on. I won't
keep you," Emily said to her. "I'll see you
later."

"Absolutely." Molly smiled mechanically
at Emily, then did a speed walk back to the
kitchen to find a minor crisis. The crab
spread had not completely jelled. Instead of
artful swirls, it had turned into ugly mis-
shapen globs as her helpers squeezed it
out of the pastry tube and onto the rounds
of garlic toast.

"It looks awful. Should we skip it?" Christine asked.

Molly took a breath and stared down at the crab spread. She had never had so many people looking to her for directions—and expecting the right answers. She had raised two children. But that was different. Her kids didn't listen to half of what she said and argued with the rest of it.

This crew was listening and really expected her to know what she was doing.

"Is there any extra cream cheese from that spinach thing?"

"A bar or two," Christine reported.

"Okay. Get the cream cheese, and mix some into the crab spread, about half a bar to start. It should start molding. Test it with a spoon before you put in the bag again. And add a little dill if it starts to taste too watered down."

Christine's expression brightened. "Extra dill. Got it." She raced off to find the cream cheese, and Molly felt quietly pleased to have solved the problem.

She turned and surveyed the kitchen. The rest of the crew was hard at work, some preparing the hors d'oeuvres, others working on the entrées and side dishes. She walked around with her list in hand, making sure everything was on track.

The hands of the kitchen clock approached six. Molly called her group around the table. "You're all doing a great job. Emily is very pleased with the setup, and the food looks terrific. All we have to do now is serve it," she added, making them laugh.

"Don't worry. It will all be fine," Molly promised them. She was in charge now, like a general going into battle. Even if she had her private doubts, she had to give her crew confidence. "We can do it, no problem."

They smiled and nodded at her. Nick poked Christine in the ribs with his elbow. The clock struck six, and Molly took a deep breath. "Okay, guys. Back to your stations. It's show time."

The rest of the night flew by as one course led to the next. Molly's inexperienced crew made a few slip ups—a tray of glasses crashed to the floor, a batch of canapés caught fire, setting off the kitchen smoke detector. Molly leaped up on a chair and yanked the batteries out of the alarm. Luckily the jazz trio in the backyard was playing a loud number that covered the noise. And as the entrées began to come out of the kitchen a short time later, a roast fish flew off its platter when one of her helpers tripped. Molly miraculously caught it midair. She quickly set it back on its platter, artfully covering the damage with some creative garnish. She never realized how much you had to think on your feet in this business—or how resourceful she could be.

After the dessert had been served, Betty snuck into the kitchen. She walked straight up to Molly and gave her a huge hug. "Everything is fabulous! I knew you could do it!"

"Thanks, Betty. I couldn't have done it without you."

"Without my nagging and pushing, you mean?" Betty gave her a knowing grin.

"Well . . . that, too," Molly admitted.

"You didn't need me. You did this all on your own and don't forget it." Betty patted her on the shoulder. "I did find the blue dress for you, though. I'll take credit for that."

"Okay," Molly readily agreed. "You get credit for the dress—and a whole lot more."

A short time later, the guests had departed and her crew was busily breaking down the tables and chairs and putting the house back in order. Emily and Dan found

Molly in the dining room, packing up the rented dishes and flatware.

"Molly, we just want to thank you again," Emily said. "And I'm sorry my mother gave you a hard time earlier. But you know, when she finally came down for the party, she actually *almost* looked like she was enjoying herself."

"That's a lot for Lillian," Dan assured her. "I'm not big on parties, Molly, but this was a great one."

Molly felt pleased by their compliments—pleased and proud.

"Thanks for hiring me. You knew this was my first real job and well . . . you didn't have to take a chance."

"Oh, I knew you could do it." Emily smiled at her, her blue eyes warm with affection.

Molly smiled back, feeling suddenly shy. It seemed everyone in town—except Lillian, of course—believed she could do it. She was the only one who had doubted herself.

Molly arrived at her mother's house on Sunday afternoon, feeling exhausted but victorious. It was Lauren's birthday, and her mother had invited them over for cake. Molly had taken the girls out to dinner beforehand, letting Lauren choose the restaurant.

She usually did something even more elaborate for a birthday, hosting a party or taking a group of kids on an outing. But Lauren was going to have another party with her friends next weekend; Phil had offered to take a group to a water park.

Molly knew Phil was coming later. Lauren had invited him. It was only right, Molly thought, now that he'd become such a big part of their lives again. Still, she felt apprehensive about seeing him. They hadn't really talked since the kayaking trip almost three weeks ago, but something in the way he looked at her lately suggested he hadn't forgotten his question.

"Where's Lauren's friend, Amanda?" Marie carried out a pitcher of lemonade and set it on the picnic table alongside a platter of appetizers. "Isn't she here, yet?"

Molly didn't realize Amanda had been invited. But she'd been so busy with Emily's party, she had let her mother take care of all the preparations for this small one.

"I just spoke to her yesterday. She's definitely coming," Lauren said, pouring herself a glass of lemonade.

"I just spoke to her father on Friday," Marie added. "I'm sure I told him the right time. Well, no problem really. The cake won't be out for a while. I'm sure they'll be here by then."

Molly's ears perked up at the plural noun. It sounded as if Matt had been invited as well. A cherry tomato lodged in her throat. She coughed before she was able to speak again.

"Did you invite Matt Harding, too?" She tried to sound casual, but her mother glanced at her sharply.

"Of course I invited him. . . . Did you not want me to?"

"Uh, no, that's okay. I just didn't realize." Molly turned to Lauren, hoping to quickly change the subject. "Go help Grandma carry out the rest of the snacks, will you, honey?"

While I duck behind the garage and scream, she thought.

Lauren complied and followed her grandmother back into the house. Molly had barely checked her lipstick when Matthew and Amanda appeared at the back gate.

Molly walked up to them and met Matt's gaze. His dark eyes studied her and his smile widened. Slightly unnerved, Molly took the gift Amanda was holding. "Here, let me add this to Lauren's pile of loot. She's in the house with Jill. Go right in."

"Thanks. See you." Amanda ran off, leaving Molly with Matt.

"So, you had your big debut last night. How did it go?"

"Fine. Great actually. There were a few speed bumps, but overall it was a success."

"Glad to hear it, but I'm not surprised. Sounds like you're on your way."

"I hope so. I did get some interest from other guests. I'll have to see how it goes, I guess."

"Did you decide on a name yet? Or are you going to stick with Totally Awesome Foods?"

Molly laughed, surprised he'd remembered. "Still working on it." She looked up at him and smiled. He looked different somehow, more relaxed and happy. He was tan, as if he'd been out in the sun. His warm brown eyes were brighter, too, framed by crinkly lines at the corners when he smiled.

"Sorry we're late. Amanda really wanted to try sailing. We rented a boat and were out on the water all day."

"That sounds like fun. I didn't know you sail."

Matthew grinned. "I don't really. I only know enough to get us in and back and not capsize. But it's a wonderful break. I can see how people really get into it. Amanda is already trying to talk me into buying a boat."

"You ought to try Reilly's boatyard. He's always got a few bargains lying around," Molly advised him.

"Maybe I will. Do you like to sail?" he asked.

"I love it. I haven't been out on a sailboat in years, though. I'm not sure I'd remember what to do."

"Maybe we could go out sometime and figure out the ropes together."

Molly laughed. "That sounds like fun. And by the way, they're called lines."

"Right, the lines, I mean. See, you're ahead of me already."

Molly's father had just returned with a tray of cold drinks, and she could tell he had overheard a bit of their conversation.

She saw her father look at her, and she felt her cheeks get warm, matching her pink sweater top.

"Have a soda, Matt." Her father politely handed his guest a tall plastic cup. Then he turned to Molly. "Phil is inside, with your mother. He's asking for you."

Molly felt her stomach drop. She glanced up at Matthew and could have sworn he paled a bit under his bronze complexion.

"Lauren wanted her dad here for her birthday."

"That's nice. It's good of him to come." Matt's tone sounded bright, but his expression didn't match it.

"Excuse me, I'd better go say hello." She turned away from Matt, feeling flustered. For goodness' sake, she had thought she could just kick back and relax today. Now she had to play dueling single dads. This was a twist. Not uncommon for some women, maybe, but she had never had this much attention from men, at the same party no less.

Inside, Phil greeted her happily. "Wow, you look great. Pink is your color, Molly."

"Thanks, Phil." It occurred to her that no

matter what she wore, Phil told her it was her color.

Lauren rushed into the kitchen with Amanda and Jill. "Hi Dad." She jumped up and gave Phil a big hug.

"How's the birthday girl?" He held her at arm's length and took her in, then slowly shook his head. "Fifteen. I can't believe it. It feels like yesterday me and your mom were just waiting for you to be born. . . . Remember, Molly?"

"I remember. The car was out of gas. We had to call Sam."

"Oh, boy. She'll never let me live that down, will she?" Phil shook his head, laughing with Lauren. "I was so excited to be having a baby, I just couldn't see straight. It was a good thing I didn't have to drive, after all."

Everyone in the kitchen laughed at Phil's story—even Molly. It used to be that whenever she thought about that bit of their history, she felt a spurt of residual anger at Phil's thoughtlessness. Now, she saw it differently. They had been so young. He had been nervous and excited. His forgetfulness seemed touching to her now.

"The car we had back then was such a

wreck. It probably wouldn't have made it in time anyway," Molly remembered.

"Probably not," Phil agreed. He glanced at her and caught her eye. Molly smiled briefly and looked away. She could tell he was thinking about them getting back together again.

She suddenly noticed Matt standing in the doorway and wondered how long he'd been there. Long enough to hear her and Phil reminiscing?

Phil seemed surprised to see him. "Hello, Matt. Good to see you." His voice held a questioning note, as if he doubted his own words.

"Nice to see you, Phil." The two men briefly shook hands.

Squaring off before a duel, Molly thought. Now what was she supposed to do? *I'm not exactly Scarlett O'Hara, able to entertain a circle of gentleman callers with my wit and charm.* She just didn't feel up to it after yesterday.

She quickly turned to her mother, who looked delighted at what was going on right in her very kitchen. Annoyingly so, Molly thought. In fact, she realized her innocent-looking mother had cooked up this whole thing by inviting Matt here and not telling her.

"Can I help you with anything, Mom?" Molly asked.

"No, dear. I'm fine. You go entertain the guests."

"No, Mom, I really want to help you. You've done *enough* already, honestly."

Molly gave her mother a look, and Marie finally seemed to get the message. "Well . . . if you insist. Why don't you bring those dishes and things outside and set everything up?"

Molly grabbed the tray of tableware and stalked outside again. She stacked the dishes and paper cups, then looked around to see what Phil and Matt were up to.

Phil suddenly appeared beside her, slipping his arm around her shoulder in a proprietary manner. "How are you doing, Molly? Need any help?"

"It's just a stack of paper plates, Phil. I think I can handle it."

Phil laughed and squeezed her shoulder. Molly felt Matthew watching from a distance as he chatted with her father. She tried to wiggle away, but Phil's arm felt glued to her shoulder.

"I wanted to tell you what I got Lauren—" He leaned closer, attempting to whisper in her ear.

Molly quickly slipped out from under his arm. "That's all right. Surprise me."

Phil was unconscionable at times. He knew she liked Matthew but obviously thought he could scare him off. She wasn't sure what she was going to do to stop him, but she definitely was not going to let Phil get away with it.

Five minutes later, while clearing the way for the birthday cake, Molly spotted Phil and Matt off in a corner and had a sudden awful thought: Phil was telling Matt how they were going to get back together.

He wouldn't do that, would he? Molly realized with horror that he would.

She ran across the lawn to where they stood. "What are you guys talking about?" she asked breathlessly.

Phil glanced at Matt and back to Molly. "I was just telling Matthew about that time Lauren got out of her crib and left the apartment all on her own. She went downstairs in the elevator. We didn't even think she was tall enough to reach the buttons. Luckily, a neighbor found her in the lobby and brought her back."

"Luckily," Molly agreed. A walk down memory lane. How charming for Matthew.

Matthew smiled politely. "It's amazing that kids survive to be teenagers considering some of the stunts they pull."

"Yeah, I know what you mean." Phil nodded sagely. "That probably wouldn't happen now, though. I mean, if Molly and I were still married and say, had another baby or something. First of all, we'd be a lot more careful, childproofing everything. And we'd probably live in a house and all. It will be a lot safer."

Molly stared at him, wide eyed with shock. "*Would* be a lot safer you mean, not *will* be."

Phil smiled slowly and shrugged. "Sure, would be. What did I say?"

Molly was about to explain it to him when she caught Matthew staring at her. She decided it was best to just let it go.

"Forget it, Phil." She took a step back and shook her head. "The birthday cake is coming out in a minute."

She turned and walked back to the

house, feeling two sets of eyes boring into her back.

Later, as Molly sat with her mother, sipping coffee and watching Lauren open her gifts, Matthew came over to them.

"Marie, thank you so much for having us. I had a great time and so did Amanda."

"Oh, thank you for coming, Matt. It was so nice to finally meet you."

Molly could tell her mother was totally charmed. She was practically batting her eyelashes at him. Molly cringed with embarrassment.

"I hope you'll come again soon," Marie added.

"I hope so, too." Matt turned to Molly, and she met his smile. *Now it's my turn to feel watery knees,* she realized as she looked up at him.

"Good to see you, Molly. Sorry we didn't talk more. Don't forget our sailing idea, okay?"

She hadn't forgotten but was surprised to hear him mention it again. Maybe Phil's tactics hadn't scared him off.

"No, I won't forget."

"Maybe we can go out next weekend—if you're not catering any celebrity parties."

She smiled at him. "I'll check my book."

Before she could say anything more, Phil suddenly appeared.

"Leaving, Matt?" Phil stuck out his hand. "Good to see you again. Good night, now."

Molly shrunk into her folding chair. *Why don't you just push him through the gate, Phil?* she wanted to ask.

Matt glared around, looking as if he was ready to give up for the night. "Good night, everyone. Thanks again."

He glanced one more time at Molly, but she couldn't quite interpret his look.

Molly stayed on to help her parents clean up. And so did Phil. As Molly gathered a stack of paper plates and tossed them in a bag, Phil walked up beside her.

"Your parents always did know how to throw a nice party."

"Lauren seems to have enjoyed it." She glanced at him. "She liked having you here, Phil. It's been a while since you've been to any of their birthday parties."

"Yeah, I know." He rubbed a hand through his thick blond hair. "We had some cute ones when they were little. Remember when I got dressed up as Barney? 'Hi, kids!' " He waved, doing a voice that made her laugh.

"Stop . . . I remember." She collected the plastic forks, shaking her head. "That was fun."

"Except the suit was so hot, I nearly fainted." He sighed. "Sometimes I think about having another kid. I know I would be a better father. I'd appreciate it more, you know?"

"Yes, I do. We had our kids so young. We didn't realize what we had."

She thought about having another child sometimes, too. But she never pictured Phil as the father.

He didn't speak for a minute, and Molly guessed what was coming next.

"Did you think anymore about us getting back together?"

No beating around the bush with Phil. She had to say that for him.

"Yes. I did think about it." He stared at her intently, looking uncharacteristically nervous. This really mattered to him; she hadn't realized how much.

"And what did you decide?"

"I'm flattered, honestly. I know the girls would be in favor of it, too. . . . But I don't think it would be the right thing for us to do. For either of us."

"Speak for yourself, Molly. I know what I want."

"Do you really?" she asked him gently. "I know you want to make amends, Phil. The girls forgive you. And I do, too. You've shown a lot of character coming back here, trying to face up to your mistakes. When you first told me you had changed, I didn't believe you."

"Tell me about it."

"But you did change. Even I can see that now."

He nodded, his expression serious. "But not enough to win you back, I guess."

"That's not it, Phil. We can't turn back the clock and rewrite history. We shouldn't try. I don't think it would work out in the long run. We were young when we got married and we made some mistakes. That's okay. Let's just turn the page and try to do better now."

Phil let out a long slow sigh. Then he put his arms around her and gave her a big hug. A friendly hug, she thought. Well, mostly friendly.

He stepped back and smiled. "Okay. I understand. I thought that's what you would say, but I couldn't help giving it a try. And listen, I want to wish you luck on your new business."

"Thanks, Phil. That's good of you to say."

"I know you'll do well at it. You're such a hard worker. I can't see how you'll miss. I want to help you. If I had given you more support for the girls all these years, maybe you wouldn't have waited so long to start this."

That was true, Molly thought, though she didn't openly agree with him.

"I have some money saved for the girls' college fund. I want you to have it."

Molly was stunned by his generous gesture, which seemed even more poignant considering that she had just turned him down.

"Phil . . . you never fail to surprise me."

He seemed pleased with the comment, taking it as a compliment.

"The girls have turned out great, just like you, no thanks to me. I owe you for that alone."

"I've done what I could for them because I love them, Phil. You never have to repay me for that." She smiled at him. "I appreciate your offer, honestly. But I really don't need the money. I have my own banker, and I've made arrangements to get things up and running. Save the money for college, the way you planned. That would mean a lot to me."

Phil nodded. "All right, if that's what you want. Consider it done." His expression turned mischievous. "A banker, huh? Gee, you are going places."

"It's my sister-in-law," she admitted with a grin.

He shrugged. "That still counts."

Yes, it did, Molly thought, feeling pleased with herself. Maybe she really was on her way.

CHAPTER EIGHTEEN

Tucker had just finished his patrol when, driving up Emerson Street, he spotted another police cruiser coming in the opposite direction. The officer signaled with his lights for Tucker to pull up and talk. It was Tom Schmidt.

Schmidt walked over to him after they'd both parked. "I've got some news for you, Tucker. I just heard from this friend of mine on the job in Hamilton. He collared some kids breaking and entering at about two A.M. last night. The silent alarm went off, and they were caught red-handed. My buddy says they found a load of stolen goods back at the ranch, including some trinkets from the Degan house. How do you like that?"

Tucker's mouth went dry. He had mixed emotions about the news, that was for sure: happy to hear Carl wasn't the guilty one after all but feeling even guiltier now for having doubted his brother.

"Thanks for letting me in on this, Schmidt. I appreciate it."

"Some of the guys have been hard on you. I don't think that's right. Sanborn, too. He owes you an apology in my book."

My book, too, Tucker thought, though he doubted he'd ever hear it. The two police officers parted, and Tucker drove on, with a lot to think about.

Once he went off duty, he called a friend at the Hamilton police department and got the full story. The thieves were two teenage boys with a history of truancy, shoplifting, vandalism, and a general all-around bad attitude. Future Carls. After their cache of stolen property was found, they confessed to the North Creek Road burglary, which was just one among many.

Fran was up in the bedroom, putting laundry away, when Tucker got home that evening. Things had been strained between them ever since her revelation about the stickpin. He knew she was sorry. He kept reminding himself that he loved her—he knew he did—but he just felt hollow and sad inside. Something between them was injured and neither one knew how to heal it.

Now she looked at him, and he could tell from her reaction that he had a strange expression on his face.

"What is it, Tucker? Are you all right?"

"I had some news today." He took his shield off his shirt and dropped it on his dresser. "They caught some kids in Hamilton who have been robbing houses. They did the Degan house on North Creek Road. Confessed to it and everything."

"Oh." Fran looked surprised. She sat down suddenly on the bed, a bundle of towels in her lap. "That is news."

"I'll say." Tucker turned to her, feeling angry all over again. "Everybody around here had Carl made out for guilty, and he was telling the truth all along. We weren't fair to him."

Fran sighed and shrugged. "Well, we tried, Tucker."

Tucker glared at her. He felt suddenly as if he were about to explode. "That's supposed to be okay? That's a good enough excuse for you? That we tried?" He laughed harshly and shook his head. "We didn't try hard enough. We were ready to believe the worst of him the first chance we got. Both of us."

Fran lifted her head, looking indignant at his accusation. "I know I was wrong to think he took my pin. But honestly, Tucker, given his history . . . even you suspected him."

"You see, that's it exactly." Tucker heard his voice rising on a note of anger, but he felt so frustrated with Fran all of a sudden, he couldn't control it. "It's not fair to have suspected Carl of taking your pin or of the robbery. It's not right. We didn't treat him like other people—like a decent human being ought to be treated. We never gave him the benefit of the doubt. And he's my brother, besides. Don't you see? It makes me sick to think about it. And I'm as guilty of it as you are."

He stared at her, breathless from his outburst. She shivered, looking suddenly fragile. Then she met his eyes.

"You're right," she said. "We were terribly unfair to Carl."

Just hearing her say that eased something in Tucker's heart.

"It's a shame Carl isn't around to hear about those kids in Hamilton," she went on.

Tucker turned suddenly and yanked his blue shirt out of his pants. "I'm going to take a few days off and go look for him. He should know his name has been cleared around here, and I'm going to tell him."

"Where will you look?"

"Up in Portland, Maine. Reverend Ben gave me an address where Carl asked him to send a paycheck. I can start there, I guess. I'll take some personal time and leave tomorrow."

"How long will you be gone?"

Tucker shrugged and pulled on a sweatshirt. "I don't know. As long as it takes. I hope he hasn't gone too far by now."

Fran was quiet for a moment. "I hope so, too." She touched Tucker's arm as she walked by him. "I'll get the small blue suitcase. It's in the hall closet somewhere."

Tucker was packed and ready early the next morning, dressed in his sports clothes. After Michael and Mary Ellen left for school, he put his coffee cup in the sink and kissed Fran good-bye.

"Okay, I'm going. I'll call you from the road."

"Yes, don't forget. I like to know where you are." Fran gave him a small smile. "Take care of yourself. Drive safely. Don't eat a lot of junk food on the highway."

Tucker didn't answer. He could see that she didn't know what to say.

"I love you, Tucker," she said quietly.

"I love you, too. You know that."

She nodded, looking suddenly as if she were about to cry. Then she kissed his cheek again, her hand lingering on his chest. "Good luck. I really hope you find him."

"I do, too," he answered.

Tucker reached Portland about two hours later. He hadn't been up this way in years and was surprised to see how much the city had changed, especially down on the waterfront. The rundown wharf areas were filled with restaurants, condos, and hotels. The old warehouses across the way held slick-looking office space, fancy shops, and designer coffeehouses for the tourists who roamed the winding cobblestone streets, toting their shopping bags.

He didn't know the city very well, but with the aid of a map, he located Carl's mailing address. He was not surprised to find himself in a rundown neighborhood, one that had been bypassed by the development boom. Here the houses looked old and badly in need of repair. Some were squat single-family homes on tiny patches of property, others were semidetached two-family homes of post–World War II vintage. It was the kind of neighborhood Tucker more or less expected.

He finally found the address at the end of the street, a larger three-story building that looked as if it was once an old apartment house. Judging from the sign in front, it appeared to be a shelter now, run by some charitable organization.

So, maybe Carl really didn't have a friend up here after all, Tucker realized. Or maybe Carl hadn't been able to find his friend. Whatever the reason, the bottom line was Carl had been reduced again to shelter life, which upset Tucker even more.

He got out of his car and went inside. The place was dark and depressing. He walked into a common room furnished with broken-down armchairs and a slip-covered couch that sagged in the middle. A group of men sat watching a big TV, most of them smoking. A window fan circulated warm air and cigarette ashes.

Tucker scanned the circle of faces but didn't see Carl. They each stared back at him suspiciously. Even out of uniform, Tucker guessed many could still tell he was a cop. Carl once said he could just smell it on him.

Tucker walked farther down a main hall. The scent of pine disinfectant was nearly overpowering. He found an office and, in it, a paunchy middle-aged man with a long, stringy ponytail sitting behind a desk. The name tag on his T-shirt read, "House Manager, Ralph Newman." The guy had a look about him, Tucker thought, as if he'd been through it all and had come out the other side, calmer, wiser, looking to help men like himself find their way back.

"I'm trying to find my brother," Tucker explained. "He gave this place as a mailing address. Can you tell me if he's still here? Maybe you have some log book or records I can look at."

"We don't ask the men to sign anything. It seems easier for most of them that way. Do you have a picture? Maybe I'll remember him."

"No, I don't." Tucker felt bad that he didn't even have a single photo of Carl. He had tried to include him in one on Easter Sunday, but Carl was terribly camera shy.

He ended up describing Carl's physical appearance as best as he could. The man gave him a thoughtful look.

"I think I remember that guy. He looks something like you, now that you mention it."

Tucker felt his face flush. He never thought of himself as resembling Carl, but he supposed it was true.

"Right, Carl Tulley. He was waiting for a letter, and once it came, he left. That was about two weeks ago. I haven't seen him since."

Tucker didn't answer. That must have been the letter from Reverend Ben with Carl's back pay. By now Carl could be any-where.

"Sorry I couldn't help you more." Tucker could tell from the man's expression that he must look awfully disappointed.

"That's all right. Do you have any suggestions about where else I can go? Some other shelters in the city, maybe?"

"Sure. I have a list somewhere around here. I'll get it for you. It's the cold weather that drives them indoors, though," he added while riffling through a desk drawer. "Once it warms up, he really could be anywhere. You should check the parks, especially along the waterfront. The hospitals and police stations, too. But I guess you already know that."

Tucker knew he would find Carl quickly if his brother had either gotten sick again or arrested. But he hoped that wasn't the case.

Ralph handed Tucker the list. Tucker thanked him and said good-bye. Then he remembered to leave his name and cell-phone number just in case Carl returned.

"I haven't found a motel yet. But I'll call you later today with a number where you can reach me in case the cell phone doesn't work. I'd sure appreciate a call if you see him around again."

"Sure, I'll do that. Should I let him know that you're trying to get in touch?" The man's look was curious.

"Uh, no. I'd rather you didn't. It's hard to explain."

"Okay. I understand." Tucker thanked him again and left the shelter. He stood on the sidewalk a long time, clearing his head with the fresh air. On a scale of one to ten, the shelter was about a negative five kind of place to live in, Tucker thought. But right now, Carl might have it even worse.

Tucker grabbed a quick bite at a drive-through window, gobbling the food in his car with one hand while he navigated more of Portland's back streets. He spent the rest of the day checking the shelters on the list and the parks he noticed along the way.

At six o'clock he wasn't close to finished, but he decided to find a motel room. He let himself in and dropped his bag near the door, not even bothering to put on the lights. The day had been exhausting. Despite his best intentions to call Fran, he dropped down on the big bed and closed his eyes to rest.

His determination of last night had been boiled down during the day to a layer of gritty resolve. The faces of the homeless men he'd seen today loomed up before him, their expressions blank, their dark stares accusing.

The task seemed hopeless, but he wasn't going to give up. He would call the police stations and hospitals tonight and try the other shelters tomorrow. Eventually he had to get some lead on Carl. Somebody somewhere had to remember him.

Tucker closed his eyes. *Dear Lord, wherever Carl is tonight, please give him comfort and shelter. Please let me find him and try to make things right.*

Molly's father always said, "If something seems too good to be true, it probably is." A cynical point of view, perhaps, and she'd been making a conscious effort to be more positive lately, but on Saturday morning, she couldn't get that bit of wisdom out of her mind.

Matthew called the day after Lauren's birthday party and invited her to go sailing with him, just as he promised. That was the "too good to be true" part.

On Saturday morning at about six o'clock, Jill shook Molly's shoulder, waking her from a sweet dream.

"Mom, I feel sick. I think I'm going to throw up."

Molly sat up in alarm and felt Jill's forehead. She was burning with a fever. She needed a cool bath and some medicine. The look on Jill's face told Molly that she needed to take immediate action. "Okay, let's get into the bathroom, honey."

It was soon clear that Jill was quite sick. Too sick for Molly to leave—even for a date with Matthew.

Lauren and Amanda were going with Phil to a water park for Lauren's belated birthday celebration. Jill was supposed to go along, too. The poor kid was so miserable that Molly couldn't even feel sorry for herself.

Molly sighed and picked up the phone to call Matthew. So much for the long-awaited date. The fact that she was the one canceling this time did little to help her feel better. *It feels as if this relationship just wasn't meant to be,* she thought dismally as she punched in his number.

Matthew picked up on the second ring. "Molly, hi. I was just going to call you. The weather looks perfect. You'd better bring a hat and wear a lot of sunblock. But don't worry about lunch; I've already taken care of that."

He sounded so excited, as if he was really looking forward to this. Molly hadn't even thought that he might be disappointed, too.

"I'm sorry, Matt, but Jill's come down with some bug or something. She has a high fever and all the classic symptoms. I can't leave her like this. I really have to stay home."

"Oh, I'm sorry to hear that. There's something going around the elementary school. I had a lot of calls this week."

"There's *always* something going around the elementary school." Molly suddenly felt so blue looking ahead to the long day she would spend alone with Jill.

"I'm sure you know what to do. But why don't I take a quick look at her later when I bring Amanda? I can hang out and keep you company awhile."

Molly thought he was just trying to be polite. "It's okay, Matt. You don't have to do that. I'm sure you would rather get outside today."

"Really, I want to. I can stay with Jill awhile if you need to go out anywhere."

If you're here, why would I want to go out? Molly nearly answered.

Finally, she said yes, then raced around trying to quickly ready the apartment and herself and at the same time take care of Jill and get Lauren ready for her outing.

A short time later she opened the door to find Matt and Amanda. Amanda was ready for the water park, wearing her bathing suit under her clothes and carrying a knapsack. Matt still looked as if he were going sailing, wearing a T-shirt, baseball cap, khaki shorts, and boat shoes. He stumbled into her house carrying a large blue cooler.

"What's in there, your medical kit?" Molly couldn't help teasing him.

"Lunch. I packed some food for our trip. I thought we could have a picnic in your living room or something."

"Oh, that sounds fun. No bugs to worry about." Molly stepped aside to let him pass. "Well . . . not too many."

Matt laughed, carrying the cooler into the kitchen. "There's a lot of ice in here, but I'll put the food in the refrigerator anyway."

"Go right ahead." It looked like he planned on staying awhile. This was getting interesting.

She was just about to close the door when she saw Phil coming up the hallway.

"Hi, Molly. Are the girls ready?"

"Lauren and Amanda are. But Jill is sick. She came down with something this morning."

"Gee, that's too bad. Can I see her?" Phil stepped inside, and Molly closed the door.

"Sure, she's in bed, but I know she's not sleeping." Molly followed him to the kitchen. "It's just a little bug. I'm sure she'll be all right in a day or two."

"But you called the doctor anyway, I see." Phil smiled at Matt, who stood at the kitchen counter emptying containers from his cooler into the refrigerator. "I didn't know doctors still made house calls—and stocked refrigerators, no less."

"This one does. Only for special patients, of course." Matt turned and looked at Phil. He smiled, but in his eyes Molly noticed a challenging light, one that suggested he didn't realize that Phil wasn't his competition, after all.

"We had a date to go sailing today. Matt offered to come here and visit for a while instead."

"Oh. I see." Phil nodded. "I'll just run in

and say hello to Jill for a minute. Then we'll get going."

A few minutes later Phil left with Lauren and Amanda. *Amazing,* Molly thought. Phil seemed to be accepting Matthew's presence with far more grace than she expected.

Matthew waited in the kitchen. He stood leaning against the counter as she entered, making her feel self-conscious.

"I was just going in to check on Jill. Have you taken her temperature lately?"

"About an hour ago. It was a little over one hundred and two."

"That's not too bad. I brought her some ice pops. They're a good way to get fluids in her if she can keep them down."

He had thought of everything, hadn't he? Molly watched him retrieve an ice pop from the freezer and pick up a napkin from the counter.

Molly led the way to Jill's room, where Jill looked up from her pillows, her small pale face surrounded by dark hair.

"How do you feel, honey?" Matt asked.

"Terrible." Jill crossed her arms over her chest and looked away. Matt glanced at Molly, suppressing a smile.

"What's wrong, Jill? Does your stomach still bother you?" Molly sat down on the edge of her bed and felt Jill's forehead.

Jill shook her head no, nearly shaking Molly's hand away. "Everybody went to the water park without me. That's not fair." She was about two seconds away from bursting into tears.

"That was a tough break." Matt nodded in agreement. "It really stinks to be left behind like that. Is that park fun? I've never been there."

Jill looked at him in disbelief. "Yeah, I'd say it's fun."

"Jill, don't be fresh." Molly gave her a warning look.

Matt touched her arm. "Well, your mom and I didn't get to go, either. Maybe we could take you and a few of your friends sometime."

Molly turned and stared at him. She had heard he had a nice bedside manner, but he really didn't need to go that far.

"Could we, Mom?" Jill's expression brightened so dramatically, she hardly looked sick anymore.

"We'll see. You just get better for now, okay?"

"Yes, let's get you better. Let me take a look down your throat, Jill. Say 'ah' for me. Nice and wide now."

Matt gave Jill a quick examination then took her temperature. He diagnosed the problem as a virus, hopefully the twenty-four-hour kind and recommended bed rest and lots of fluids. He offered Jill the ice pop, and she ate it eagerly.

Molly rose from the bed, preparing to leave the room. "Would you like to read a book or watch a video?"

"Would you play a game with me, Mom?" Jill asked hopefully. "Can we play Bamboo-zle?"

Normally Molly would. What else was there to do with a sick kid? But now she had Matthew to consider. She didn't think it was fair to subject him to board-game torture.

"What in the world is Bamboozle? I've never heard of that one." Matthew smiled at Jill, and Molly waited for her explanation.

"It's really cool. It's like a trivia game where you have to answer these hard questions about stuff . . . you know, geography and history and stuff. But if you don't know, you can make up an answer, and if you trick everyone you get points. But if you don't trick them and they know the answer instead, they get points. Or if you don't want to try to trick people, then you have do something stupid. Like balance stuff on your head or something. Or you lose points."

Matthew frowned at Jill. Molly could tell she had lost him early in the explanation and nearly laughed out loud at his polite, perplexed expression.

"I see," he said slowly. "Sounds like fun." He glanced at Molly. She could tell what he was thinking.

"No, really. You don't have to play. It's okay. She can watch TV."

He shrugged. "Why not? Just for a little while."

"Please, Mom? Dr. Harding says he wants to." Before Molly could stop her, Jill hopped out of bed to get the game.

"I'm great at trivia games. You guys don't stand a chance," Matthew bragged.

"Really?" Jill returned to the bed with the game and began to set up the board. "Mom says people who know a lot of trivia have their brains stuffed with useless information."

Matthew laughed and glanced at Molly.

She could feel her cheeks turning red. "I never said that."

"Yes, you did," Jill insisted.

Matt grinned. "She might be right. Your mother usually is."

Molly smiled back at him. "How true. You get extra points for that." *In my book, anyway,* she thought.

They gave Matthew a few more instructions and began to play. Jill won the first round, and Molly won the next two. Matt seemed dumbfounded. He clearly wasn't used to losing.

"Okay, I guess that's enough for now." Molly tried to end the game, giving Matt an easy way out.

"Just one more?" Jill pleaded.

"I'll play again." Matt looked determined to win.

"Okay, one more." Molly shrugged and set up the board again. For a while it seemed as if Matt would finally win, but then Molly impressed them all by not only seeing through Jill's bluff but also knowing the name of President Harding's dog.

"Laddie," Molly announced.

Jill suddenly looked sleepy and decided she wanted a nap. "We'll play Monopoly later, okay?" she asked as her eyes began to close.

"Sure. I'm even better at Monopoly," Matt promised.

"That wouldn't take much," Molly teased him. She kissed Jill's forehead, then followed Matt out of the room.

Once they were alone, the glow of her board-game victories faded, and Molly felt nervous. "How about some lunch?" When in doubt eat something. That was her motto.

"Sounds good. I'll take care of it. There's all that food I brought over in the fridge. I have a cloth for the floor, too."

"A cloth for the floor?" Molly didn't have the slightest idea what he was talking about.

"We're having a picnic in the living room, right?"

She had thought he was joking about that this morning. It seemed he was perfectly serious.

A few minutes later she and Matt had set up a picnic lunch on her living-room floor. Molly sat back, leaning against the couch. Sunshine streamed in the window, warming her face, and she closed her eyes, pretending she was outside in a sunny meadow.

"Take a nap if you like." Matt walked in with cans of soda and sat down nearby. "You must have gotten up early."

Molly opened her eyes. "I was just pretending I was outside."

"That reminds me. I forgot my recording of nature sounds." She could see from the look in his eyes that he was joking.

"I have an alarm clock that's supposed to sound like ocean waves . . . but it's more like the washing machine on rinse cycle."

Matthew smiled, handing her a plate and a sandwich. Molly took it from him, feeling a little thrill. She wasn't accustomed to being served, especially by a man.

"Maybe we can go sailing next weekend. Or out to the beach or something."

She liked the way he said that *or something* part. As if it was a definite idea in his mind that they'd see each other, one way or another. Still, maybe he was just trying to make up for another fouled-up date.

"It's nice of you to stay today like this, Matt. You probably have lots of things to do."

She was trying to give him an out in case he didn't want to hang around after lunch.

He stretched out on his side, eating his sandwich. "I'm in no rush. There'll be other sunny days around here. Besides I wanted to spend time with you today. The sailing didn't matter to me, really." He glanced up at her and smiled. Molly felt her breath catch at his words.

He speared an olive with his fork and popped it into his mouth. "So . . . how's it going with Phil these days?"

Molly was surprised at his sudden change of subject. "About the visiting you mean? We've worked it out. He's trying not to be so last minute about calling and coming over here, and I'm trying to be more flexible."

Matt nodded. "That sounds like a good compromise. He looked pretty comfortable at Lauren's party."

Comfortable? Now what did that mean? Molly felt herself flush. Did Matt think there was something going on between her and Phil?

"He always got along well with my family. They were mad at him for the way he acted after the divorce. But they can see he's trying hard to make it up to the girls."

"And make it up to you," Matt added.

Molly paused, not sure how to answer him. "Yes, to me, too. He even offered to help finance my business."

"He did?" Matthew suddenly sat up. He looked upset or as if he had bit into something that didn't agree with him. "That was big of him."

"I thought it was good of him to offer. But I didn't accept. I just didn't think it was right. And I didn't want to give him the wrong impression," she added.

Matthew didn't answer at first. He sat back against the couch and stretched out his legs on the checkered cloth. "What impression was that?"

Molly turned to face him, suddenly distracted by his nearness. "Oh, I don't know. I think Phil had some expectations or something, some fantasy that we might get back together again. I know he really wanted to help me start the business. But I also think he thought it would get us more involved with each other, more tangled up beyond the girls."

"And that's not what you want?" Matthew's dark eyes held a serious light.

"No, not at all. I mean, I'm glad he came back and that we've worked things out. I think we can be good parents together for the girls now and even good friends. But nothing beyond that."

"Well, I'm glad to hear you worked that out with him. I couldn't really tell what was going on at Lauren's party. I thought maybe you two were getting back together. Or at least, you were thinking about it."

Molly felt her heart skip a beat. "Maybe Phil was thinking about it. But I never gave it a thought. Not really."

"Good. I was hoping that's what you'd say." His tone was even and nonchalant, but the corners of his mouth turned up in a smile. Then he reached over and wiped his thumb across her cheek. Molly felt mesmerized by his touch.

"Just a dab of mayonnaise. You're perfect now." He met her gaze with an intense stare, and Molly's mouth went dry.

He was going to kiss her again. She just knew it. She held her breath, unable to move.

"Mom! Can I get up and watch TV now?"

Jill's voice broke the spell, and Molly jumped back, as if waking from a dream. She glanced at Matthew, and he shook his head, nearly laughing. She could see a faint hint of color high on his cheeks, and she knew she had guessed his intentions.

"I'll be right there, honey. Just a minute."

Molly got up and left the room, hoping Matt didn't notice how her knees were shaking.

Well, I guess he's definitely had a change of heart from the "let's be friends" conversation, she thought. Though at this rate it might take years to figure out what—if anything—was going on between them. But it was encouraging to realize that, even though he saw Phil as competition last weekend, he was still eager to keep this date with her.

Very encouraging, Molly thought.

Jill came in to watch TV, wondering about the picnic cloth and the food on the floor in the middle of the living room. She flicked on her favorite kids' channel, and the sound of the kids' show totally dispelled the last trace of romantic ambience. Molly and Matt picked up their mess and carried everything back into the kitchen.

"That was fun. Thanks," Molly said quietly.

He glanced over at her. "It was just practice. We'll have the real thing next time. Promise."

Molly met his gaze and smiled back at him. She warned herself not to get her hopes up again. But she couldn't help it now.

She heard the sound of Matthew's beeper and watched him fish into his pocket for it and check the number.

"My service. I'd better call in." Using Molly's phone, he called his answering service. Molly could only hear half of the conversation, but it sounded as if Reverend Ben Lewis needed Matthew's attention.

Matthew hung up from the service and then called Reverend Ben. They spoke for a few minutes, with Matthew asking a few questions. "I think you ought to have me take a look, Reverend. Can you meet me at my office in, say, half an hour?"

They ended the conversation, and Matthew turned to her. "Sorry, Molly. I have to run. Reverend Ben has some stitches on his arm. It sounds as if they might be infected. I have to see him right away."

Molly felt a pang of disappointment but said, "That's all right. I understand."

"I'll talk to you soon." He stared down at her, looking like he was unwilling to go. He moved toward her and cupped her cheek with his hand. Molly held her breath, bracing herself for another of his quick exciting kisses.

"Mom? Can I have something to drink?" Jill's voice, calling from the living room, broke the heavy silence between them. "And can we play Monopoly now? There's nothing on TV."

Molly sighed and shook her head. "Sure, honey. Just a minute." She looked up at Matthew. "I've been summoned."

"So I noticed." Matt smiled and stepped back. He picked up his cooler and headed for the door. "By the way, you can't lose if you build a hotel on Park Place. That's the whole trick."

Molly walked him to the door and opened it. "Thanks for the tip. I'll try to remember that."

She smiled to herself, watching him walk down the hallway, tilted sideways to balance the cooler.

It had *almost* been like a real date. Good

practice at any rate, she thought, remembering his words.

By Monday, Tucker felt no closer to finding Carl than when he had arrived in Portland five days ago. He had visited every shelter and soup kitchen in the city; he'd checked with the police, the hospitals, and all types of offices for destitute men and women. He'd done all he could think of and then some but still had no clue to Carl's whereabouts.

On a tip from a social worker in one of the city offices, Tucker went to an empty lot on the east side of the city where men who were looking for day work gathered early in the mornings. Many were immigrants without working papers and many looked like Carl, lost souls hanging on by their fingernails, desperate for a day's wages. Trucks would drive by, and foremen would pick out a lucky few.

Tucker stood in the lot, sipping from a cup of coffee, trying to blend in, though he knew very well that he didn't. He waited for several hours, searching the faces that moved through the gates, looking for Carl but not finding him. The place felt to him like a phantom world, a depressing scene that made him feel both more discouraged about finding his brother and, at the same time, even more determined.

He returned to his motel room that night, feeling exhausted. The desk clerk passed him two pink message slips. As Tucker expected, the first was a call from Fran. The second, though, was from Ralph Newman, the man who ran that first shelter, Tucker recalled. Hoping for good news he returned to his room and quickly dialed the number.

"I saw your brother," Ralph Newman told Tucker. "He stopped by late this afternoon to see if there were any more letters for him. Then he gave me a forwarding address. Have a pen handy? I'll give it to you."

Tucker quickly scribbled down the address, wondering who Carl expected to hear from. *Was he expecting another letter from Reverend Ben? Or did he think the reverend passed along the address and perhaps I would write?* Tucker felt a pang of guilt. He'd had the address for almost two weeks and had never gotten around to contacting Carl, though he meant to. *This would have been so much easier if I had,* he realized.

Tucker thanked Ralph and hung up the phone. He grabbed his car keys and headed out again, stopping to ask directions from the desk clerk.

He drove for about fifteen minutes, heading into a neighborhood of brick and brownstone row houses. Most looked rundown, some were abandoned with boarded-up windows, and a few showed signs of hopeful renovation.

Tucker wondered if the address Carl had given was another shelter, but he soon found himself in front of a three-story brick building with a long flight of steps leading up to the front door. He climbed the stairs and peered through the glass on the outer door. Checking the names on the mailboxes, he finally spotted a strip of tape with the name "C. Tulley" and realized Carl was living down in the basement.

His heart hammering, Tucker went down the front steps again to the sidewalk. Under the staircase he saw a battered black metal door. He rang the buzzer and sent up a silent prayer. *Please let Carl be all right.* A few moments later, the door swung open, and Carl stared out at him.

"Tucker? What are you doing here?"

"I missed you, too," Tucker replied. "Can I come in?"

Carl hesitated, and Tucker wondered if, after all the time and trouble he'd gone through, Carl was now going to slam the door in his face. *Not that I don't deserve it,* Tucker thought.

Carl stepped back and let him in. Tucker followed his brother into a small room where high basement windows let in a little of the day's dwindling light. The room was sparsely furnished with a table, two chairs, and a cot covered with army-issue blankets. A sink and an old refrigerator with duct tape on its handle took up most of the opposite wall. A counter held a hot plate and a small portable TV tuned to a baseball game.

Carl stared at him, his arms crossed over his wide chest. He was clean shaven with a recent hair cut. He looked healthy, too. Tucker felt almost weak with relief to see him looking so well and sent up silent thanks to God.

"Who's winning?" Tucker nodded at the TV.

Carl ignored the question. "How did you find me?"

"It wasn't easy." Tucker glanced around. "When did you move in here?"

"A few weeks ago. I'm the janitor for this building and the one next door. The room is part of the deal."

"You got a job pretty quickly. That's good."

The haunting faces of the indigent men and women he had seen that week rose up to taunt him. Again Tucker sent up thanks that Carl hadn't been living in the shelters or out in the open all these weeks. This room was hardly a palace, but it was safer and cleaner than the places he'd visited the last few days.

"The reverend sent me a letter to show around saying what a good worker I was and so on. That helped some." Carl sat down in one of the two kitchen chairs but didn't offer a seat to Tucker. "So, you found me. What now?"

"I came to tell you something, Carl. They caught the kids who broke into the house on North Creek Road. They confessed to it and everything. Your name is cleared. You can come back to Cape Light. No one will bother you."

Carl squinted up at him, then shook his head. "Did you come all the way up here just to tell me that? I know I didn't do it. I don't need you to tell me I'm innocent."

Tucker felt his jaw go tight. He deserved that. He sighed and sat down at the table across from Carl. "I'm sorry I doubted your word that night, Carl. That wasn't right. I believed you mostly. But there was a lot of pressure in the station, and I didn't know what to believe there for a while. That was wrong. I should have taken your word and not let it sway me."

Carl stared at him, his expression unreadable. "All right. You said your piece. I got the news."

Tucker wasn't sure what to say. Carl didn't seem to get his point. "The reverend is saving your job. You can come back. You can stay with us again until you find another place of your own."

Carl gave a short, bitter laugh. "Why would I ever go back there, Tucker? Use your head, for pity's sakes. Those people will never accept me. They'll always be whispering behind my back, suspecting me of everything. You're dreaming, Tucker. I can't go back there. I don't know how I ever ended up in that town again in the first place."

Tucker took a breath. Carl's expression looked determined, his mind made up. "You came back because Cape Light was your home and still is. You didn't do anything wrong, Carl. There's no reason to run away. You have a job there and a place in the world there. You have connections—a family."

Carl frowned at him, shaking his head, but Tucker sensed that he was making some headway.

"I want you to come back, Carl. I don't want you to live out the rest of your days alone, down in some cellar room. I'm your brother. I want to help you. I know I messed up, but I am trying my best. I really am."

Carl didn't speak for a long time. He just got up and fiddled with the TV dials, finally turning the set off. When he faced Tucker again, Tucker thought he saw his brother's chin tremble.

"You did okay by me, Tucker. I know I never thanked you, either. You didn't have to come up here and look for me and all that, just to tell me about those kids."

Carl nodded, looking almost as if he were talking to himself. "I can't go back, though. But it's good of you to ask me. Maybe this place doesn't look like much, but I'm okay here. It's all right for me. And say I get in a jam sometime down the road, I know I can call you. So that's something, right?"

Tucker looked up at him. The room was darker now, and he could barely see Carl's face, only his dark eyes that looked like bright bits of glass.

"Yes, that's something. Don't forget it, either." Tucker stood up and coughed to clear his throat, which felt suddenly thick. "I'm going to try to stay in touch. I know you're not much for that, but just a card or a call from time to time would be enough, Carl. If you move from here, you let me know."

"I will." Carl nodded. He suddenly stuck out his hand, taking Tucker by surprise. Tucker stared at his brother's hand a moment, then took it in his own and shook it hard.

"So long, Tucker. We'll hook up again someday, I guess."

"Sure. I'll see you, Carl. You take care."

Tucker finally let go of Carl's hand, wondering when and if he'd ever see him again. It seemed a sad irony that, after all these years, he finally felt reconciled with his brother, and they were parting with no real hope of ever seeing each other again.

CHAPTER NINETEEN

Tucker packed up and drove back to Cape Light that same night, stopping once on the road for fuel and a bite to eat. He had called Fran from the car as he left Portland, telling her he found Carl and was on his way home again. He also told her not to wait up for him, but when he drove up to the house, he saw that the lights were still on in the family room.

Tucker entered the house quietly. Scout, who had been sleeping at the top of the stairs, ran down to greet him, wildly wagging his tail and jumping up to lick Tucker's face. Tucker patted the dog, then went back to the family room. Fran sat in her bathrobe, watching TV. She looked half asleep and blinked when she saw him.

"Tucker. I didn't even hear you come in." She got up and kissed him hello. "I thought you would be later."

"I made good time. Not much traffic at this hour." Tucker nodded, forcing a small smile.

"Do you want anything? A sandwich or something? There are some leftovers from dinner I can heat for you."

Tucker shook his head and sat down on the couch. "No, thanks. I'm fine." Scout sat at Tucker's side and leaned against his leg. Tucker patted his silky head. "Looks like Scout missed me."

"We all missed you, Tucker." Fran gave him a small smile and sat down in the armchair. "So you found him. I'm surprised."

"It was a lucky break, I guess. Carl went back to some shelter he'd been in to see if he had any mail. He left a forwarding address and this guy who ran the place called me."

Fran didn't say anything for a moment. She picked a thread off the edge of her robe. "Where is he living now? Is it . . . decent?"

Tucker shrugged. "He got a job as a janitor at an apartment house. He gets a room in the basement for free. It isn't much, but it's better than a shelter by a long shot. And it's good to see that he's settled down and working." Tucker paused and leaned back against the couch. "I asked him to come back here again. But he doesn't want to."

"Oh." Fran took a breath. "Why not? Did he say?"

"He's had enough of this place. He says no one here will ever accept him. I don't know. Maybe he's right. I just hated to leave him there, all alone like that. I'm afraid he might get sick again or get into trouble and not let us know."

Fran looked at him a long time. "Maybe if you keep in touch with him, in time, he might move down here again."

Tucker had secretly hoped for the same thing but was surprised to hear Fran say it. She sounded as if she wouldn't mind.

"I don't know if he'll stay in touch. But I'm going to try."

"Tucker, I did a lot of thinking while you were away. I need to apologize to you and not just about the stickpin. I was wrong to give you such a hard time about Carl, about letting him stay here. You were right to help him. I can see that now."

Tucker sighed. He felt so drained. Her words helped, but only a little.

"Thanks, Fran. Thanks for saying that."

"No, I really mean it. I'm truly sorry for the way I acted. It wasn't right. You're a good man. You have a good heart. You've gone the limit for Carl—anyone can see that. It counts for something, even if he doesn't come back. You've been a good brother to him and a wonderful example to our children."

Tucker felt his throat go tight, almost as if he might break down crying. "Thanks," he managed. "It means a lot to me that you would say that."

"Are you okay?"

"I'm spent," he said honestly. "And I'm disappointed in this town, Fran, in the way people acted. They were just too hard on him. That's why Carl's gone." He paused for a moment, collecting his thoughts, ideas he'd been mulling over on the long drive home.

"I don't like the way they acted down at the station house. The way they treated

Carl and treated me, too. Especially the chief. It wasn't right."

"I know what you're saying. I'm one of the guilty ones. I know I was too quick to judge him," Fran said, an embarrassed expression on her face.

Tucker reached over and patted her hand. "At least you figured it out, finally. I knew you would. I was thinking more about Charlie and some guys at the station. I'm not even sure I want to be a cop anymore. Isn't that something? After all these years. It's all I ever wanted to do with my life, since I was a little kid. But after that night with Carl, it just doesn't seem the same to me. I've been thinking about an early retirement. I can do that, you know. I'm coming up to twenty years."

Fran got up from her chair, sat beside him, and put her arm around his shoulders. "You're tired now, Tucker. And you feel badly about Carl. Give it some time, then if you still want to quit, fine. Whatever you decide is okay with me."

Tucker sighed and put his arms around his wife. They sat together without talking. Fran was right. He was tired. He wasn't thinking straight. He would let all of this settle and see how it felt once he was back on the job. He would take it one step at a time. But it was good to know Fran was with him again, understanding his problems, trusting his judgment. That was one good thing to come of this, he thought.

Betty was talking so quickly, Molly could barely keep up with her. She did manage to scribble down the address, 53 Mariner's Way, as Betty rattled on.

"... and I got the key as a special favor from the landlord. You'll be the first one to see it. We can put a binder on it tonight and sign a lease by the end of the week. Oh, I nearly forgot, there's even a brick oven in the basement. Can you beat that? You'll need to get permits and such. But I can work out good terms on a lease, and the zoning is right, too, if you want to put in some little tables eventually. But you really need to get over there right away, Molly. This one will go fast. It's a prime location. The other brokers in town are already breathing down my neck."

"Okay, I'm going. I'm leaving right now. Right this minute." Molly held the phone to her ear with her shoulder and raced around the apartment, grabbing things with both hands as she located her purse and car keys.

She wondered if she looked all right. She didn't want to run into the landlord and make a poor impression. The black capri pants seemed fine, and the sleeveless striped T-shirt was still clean. She switched her sneakers for black slides, swiped on some lip gloss, and yanked a brush through her hair with one hand.

"Call me right away once you see it. I have this walk-through on another property I can't postpone—the closing is tomorrow. It could take a while."

Molly could tell Betty really wanted to see the vacant shop with her rather than keep her appointment. Maybe it's just as well, Molly thought. As much she valued Betty's opinion, Molly wanted to see the place for the first time on her own.

"That's all right, Betty. I understand to-tally. I'll call you first thing."

"Okay, dear. Good luck. Oh, rats, I'm breaking up. . . ."

Betty's voice dissolved into a blur of

static, and Molly sighed with relief, finally able to hang up.

Ten minutes later, after picking up the key from Betty's office, Molly parked on Mariner's Way. Although not a main street, there were quite a few stores here as well as the post office, so everyone passed this way sooner or later.

Molly jumped out of her car and gazed at the storefront of the vacant shop. It was a medium-sized shop, not too narrow and not too wide. There were plate-glass windows in front with window boxes at the bottom that now stood empty. A sign above the door read Shoe Stop, and just below that a canvas awning, dark green with white stripes, stretched out, half open and sagging in the middle.

Molly pictured the storefront painted a cream color with a new sign, a burgundy background with gold lettering: Willoughby's Fine Foods & Catering. That was the name she finally decided on. It sounded solid to her, established, as if she'd been in business a long time and would continue even longer.

Her fantasy renovations continued as she added a matching awning and some interesting swoops of fabric across the windows inside. The window boxes would be full of flowers—bright, eye-catching colors and long trailing vines.

Though she hadn't seen the inside yet, the place already felt good, as if it might work out just right.

Her hand trembled with excitement as she opened the door with her key. The place smelled musty but was full of light. She walked around slowly, picturing where she would put a counter and glass display cabinets. She pulled up a corner of the worn blue carpeting and saw a beautiful wooden floor that only needed some light refinishing. She saw a door in back and entered what appeared to have been a stockroom.

Betty said there was a sink and gas hookup for a stove back there someplace, Molly recalled, as she investigated further. According to Betty, the place had quite a history. It had once been a bakery and before that a tearoom back in the nineteenth century. Molly wondered if she could find some old photographs of how it looked back then and hang them on the walls.

She saw another window and a door to

the back of the store. She knew she could make a good working kitchen in this space.

It was perfect, she thought, just as Betty had promised.

Molly walked out of the dark back room into the front again, her eyes blinking against the sudden light. She could make out the silhouette of a man standing in the doorway, though she couldn't see his face.

"Molly?" She recognized Matt's voice and stepped closer, shading her eyes with her hand. It was him, for sure. She could barely believe it.

"I was down the street at the post office. I thought I saw you come in here."

"I'm just looking around. I might rent it for my shop, Willoughby's Fine Foods and Catering. What do you think?"

"I think that's a classy name." Matt took a few steps inside and glanced around. "It has a lot of light. I like the look of the place from the street, too. Old-fashioned and sort of classic. Or it could be." He looked at her and smiled. "I think you could do a lot with it. I know you could."

"I have a few ideas." Molly stepped closer.

"You always do."

His encouraging words made her feel good, as usual. She liked the way she felt about herself around Matt. That was part of the attraction, she realized. When he looked at her that way, she felt as if he saw the best she could be and anything was possible.

"It's funny to run into you like this," he said. "I was going to call you when I got back to the office."

"Oh?" Molly stopped short, not daring to add, "About what?" It had been three days since their picnic in her living room. She had been hoping to hear from him, all the while warning herself not to get her expectations too high again.

"I wanted to ask you out to dinner actually." He shook his head, smiling with a baffled expression. "But I was almost afraid to. Every time we make plans, some disaster strikes and it doesn't work out."

"Tell me about it." Molly felt a tight, forced smile stretch across her face. She braced herself for another one of those "I think you're swell but looks like this just isn't meant to work out" speeches.

Could he possibly do that to her? She was sure her heart would break.

Something in her expression must have given her away. Matt suddenly stepped closer and put his hands on her shoulders. He stared down into her eyes.

"I was just thinking about you this morning and realized that I've known you for, well, almost four months now, and we've never had a real date. Without any adolescent chaperones, sick children to care for, or Phil showing up, I mean."

Molly took in a shallow breath, unable to look away from his dark, tender gaze. "And?"

She knew she sounded nervous, but she couldn't help herself.

She saw Matt swallow hard, looking unable to answer for a moment. "The thing is, I realized that I'm in love with you, Molly, and we've never even been on a real date." He paused. "Don't you think that's funny somehow?"

His voice trailed off to a near whisper. Molly couldn't answer. She was sure she hadn't heard him correctly, but the look on his face left no doubt. She didn't know whether to laugh or cry. It was all she could do to nod her head.

"Well, what do you think? Did I mess up

totally by being such a jerk and not getting out of my own stupid way? Could you give me one more chance to show you how I really feel about you? How I've always felt . . . but just couldn't figure out."

She paused and took a deep breath. "I love you, too."

The look of relief on his face was astounding; Molly knew she would never forget it. He pulled her close for a long, deep kiss, and Molly melted in his strong embrace.

When they finally broke apart, she stared up at him, unable to believe this was really happening. "Are you sure about this?" she asked quietly. "I mean, I'm just a cook and you're a doctor and everything. We aren't a very good match. . . ."

Matt pulled back, his expression astounded. "Molly, please, don't say another word. I never once thought of you as less than my equal in any way." He grinned at her. "Actually, there are so many times when you're clearly the superior one that I may have to make sure I don't get an inferiority complex."

"But—"

"You're perfect for me." He cut off her objeclions, laughing. "Perfect, period." He pressed his cheek against her hair. "All this time, I've been worried that I wasn't good enough for you. That I couldn't give you enough, give you what you deserve in a relationship."

He leaned back again and looked down at her, a soft smile on his lips. "But I know it will be different with you. I love you so much. I know we'll be happy together."

Molly felt every cell in her body trembling with joy—and shock. This was so much more than she had hoped for. She never in a million years imagined that Matt would have such feelings for her. But it seemed he really did.

She sighed and dropped her head to his shoulder, clinging to him. "I think you're pretty near perfect, too. . . . But I'll let you know if I see any room for improvement."

Matt laughed and held her close, nearly lifting her feet off the ground. "That's just what I expected you to say."

His mouth sought hers, and he kissed her again for a long time. When Molly finally opened her eyes and looked around, she blinked at the sunlight, feeling dazed, as if she were an entirely new person who had woken up in a whole new world.

Tucker was walking the beat on Friday afternoon. Just as he passed the Clam Box, Charlie appeared in the doorway, carrying out a big white laundry bag. "Tucker, how are you doing?" he called out. "Want to come in for some coffee?"

Charlie had never really apologized for the argument he'd started weeks ago. They had barely said hello to each other since.

"No, thanks. I just took my break about an hour ago."

"Ah, come on. Just for a few minutes. What's the matter, don't you like my cooking anymore?"

Tucker gave him a reluctant smile. "What do you mean, 'anymore'? I'm not sure I ever did."

Charlie's face fell, then he forced a smile. A nervous smile, Tucker noticed, as if eager to show he got the joke.

"Okay, then. Suit yourself." He hefted up the laundry bag and tossed it over his shoulder as he headed down the sidewalk to his car.

"See you, Charlie," Tucker called after him.

Charlie raised one hand, his back now turned. "Sure, see you around, Tucker."

Tucker continued walking toward the station house. He guessed that now that Carl was out of the picture, Charlie had decided they should forget their argument and be friends again. It was the same way at the station house. Even Chief Sanborn was now acting as if he had never doubted Tucker's judgment, never pressured him about Carl. It was as if the whole thing had never happened, which made Tucker feel odd and unsettled.

Maybe everyone else could forget that Carl existed now that he had left town, but Tucker couldn't. He refused to. Even if he never saw Carl again, he wasn't going to deny his brother just to keep things smooth and easy. For so many years he had pushed Carl to the back of his mind, almost pretending he didn't exist. He had been embarrassed to admit that he was related to someone like Carl, a convict who had served time in jail. But he couldn't do that anymore. Carl was part of him, part of his family, his history. He could see now that denying Carl was like denying part of himself.

Carl had shown real character in the way he'd pulled himself together, Tucker thought, the way he'd made a new life for himself up in Maine even after being treated so badly down here. Tucker admired that, though he was sure people like Charlie Bates and Chief Sanborn would never understand.

He wasn't sure yet what he would decide about staying on the police force. But he knew his lifelong friendship with Charlie Bates would never be the same. *How could it be?* Tucker wondered. *It would deny Carl and deny so much of me.*

The phone rang early Sunday morning. Tucker had just come in from walking the dog and no one else in the family was up yet. He answered it and heard Reverend Ben on the line.

"Sorry to bother you, Tucker. But I see it's your turn on the fix-it list. Could you come over to the church a little earlier this morning? There's a problem with the side door. It seems to be jammed. It happens sometimes in the warm weather. I'm not sure what to do about it."

"That's all right, Reverend. I know what to do. I'll bring the WD-40 and some silicone spray."

The reverend didn't answer right away. "Sounds good to me, Tucker. Whatever you said."

Tucker laughed in reply. He showered and dressed quickly, then arranged for Fran to come to the service with the children later in her car.

The village green was nearly empty at such an early hour, with only a few joggers loping along the harbor. Tucker parked on the far side of the green and walked toward the church. The tall oak trees were covered with early green leaves, the shade was cool, and the air smelled of damp earth and freshly mown grass.

He found the side door of the church open, but a ladder stood blocking the entryway. *Maybe the reverend called another deacon who got here before me,* Tucker thought with surprise. He stepped up to the doorway and looked around.

"You looking for somebody?"

Tucker turned at the sound of Carl's voice

right behind him. Carl was dressed in his work overalls, carrying a screwdriver and a tiny oil can.

"Carl . . . you came back. Why didn't you let me know?"

Carl shrugged. "I figured you'd find out soon enough. It's a small town. News travels fast, you know."

"Yeah, I know."

Carl walked past Tucker and climbed up the ladder.

Tucker took a few steps back and watched him work. "How long have you been here?"

Carl shrugged. "Day before yesterday. I got a room in that same place where I was living before, and I got my job back here, too. I've been settling in."

"Sure, I understand." Tucker paused. He wasn't surprised that Carl had not called him straight off, all things considered. But he was still surprised that he'd come back to the village.

"Why did you come back? I thought you said you never would."

"Oh, I don't know." Carl shrugged. "I thought some about what you said. I wasn't guilty of nothing. I should have stuck it out here instead of running. The reverend said the same thing to me. He wrote me a letter a day or two after you left. I would have liked to have seen those cops' faces when those kids were picked up in Hamilton. I missed out on that."

"Yeah, you did," Tucker agreed, thinking there would be no lack of surprised looks once people saw Carl around again.

Carl put down the screwdriver. "And I guess it meant something to me, the way you came to find me, to tell me what went on down here. You went the distance for me, Tucker. I don't think anyone's ever done that before."

Tucker didn't know what to say. He looked away from the ladder, relieved that Carl couldn't see how his words had affected him.

"You were right, too. I have a good job here, better than up in Portland. And I got ties, family ties. For better or worse, as they say. So . . . here I am."

Tucker watched him climb down the ladder. Carl kicked the doorstop away and tested the hinges. The door opened and closed smoothly without sticking.

"You fixed that pretty good. Better than I would have."

"It needs to be planed a little on the bottom. I'll get to that tomorrow. I didn't want to take it down today with the service and all. The reverend likes the church to look nice on Sundays."

Tucker met his brother's dark eyes. "I'm glad you came back, Carl. I'm happy to see you."

"Likewise, I guess." Carl's voice was gruff. He coughed into his hand.

Tucker suddenly leaned over and patted Carl's shoulder. It was not quite a hug but certainly more than a handshake. He pulled away and faced him again with a small smile. "Why don't you come by for dinner this afternoon? I think we're having baked ham."

Tucker knew how much his brother liked ham. He doubted Carl had eaten a decent meal since he'd left town.

Carl laughed. "Maybe you should clear it with Fran first. She's probably still counting the silverware from the last time you invited me."

"Don't worry about Fran. She's all right. I think she'll be happy to see you."

Carl squinted at him with utter disbelief. "Sure, when pigs can fly she'll be."

"No, I'm not kidding. People can change, you know."

Carl stared at him a moment, then nodded. "If you say so."

"I do."

Tucker knew he would never doubt that again.

Sophie wasn't sure she could do it at first. But something inside had pushed her beyond her sadness and regrets, beyond her mourning of Gus's death. Maybe it was Gus's spirit, willing her to carry on without him. He would have wanted her to have the Memorial Day picnic at the orchard, just as they did every year for so long now that she couldn't even remember when the tradition had started.

Sophie sat at her dressing table, working on her hair. Through the bedroom windows she had a bird's-eye view of the setup for the party, the long cloth canopies, the tables already laden with food. A number of guests had already arrived and were helping with the last of the preparations.

It was going to be a big crowd this year, maybe the biggest ever. That would be hard to gauge, though, since they never kept records of these things, only photographs. Maybe next winter when the cold set in again, she and Miranda could dig out the old albums and check. But they were far too busy now. Too much work filled every hour of every day to wonder and worry about the past.

Miranda had lit up when Sophie said that the picnic tradition would continue. Sophie knew Miranda would not have argued if the decision had been otherwise, but she could see how Miranda had put her heart into the preparations this week. She found special paper garlands and lanterns to hang from the trees. She gathered pitchers and vases and filled them with flowers. She found a crew of helpers to set up the tables and made phone calls for hours, figuring out the menu and the shifts on the barbeque.

"We'll hold it in honor of Granddad," she had suggested, and Sophie had liked that idea.

Sophie had baked and cooked all of her specialities, her apple pies, Poppy Seed

Cole Slaw, Johnny Cake, and Twice-Baked Beans with Seven Secret Spices.

She stuck one last pin in her upswept hair, smoothing back wisps of faded strawberry blond and gray. She took a necklace from the jewelry tray, a gold heart locket with Gus's photo inside, a picture taken on their honeymoon. She always wore it close to her heart now.

Sophie knew she shouldn't dawdle, fussing over her appearance so. She ought to be downstairs with the guests by now. Still, she felt no hurry. It felt as if Miranda were the real hostess this year, even taking precedence over her aunts Evelyn and Una. That was as it should be, Sophie realized. Miranda had earned that right, the way she fought to save the orchard. Sophie was happy to step back and watch her granddaughter shine today.

Day by day, Miranda was becoming more a part of this place and the orchard, more a part of her. Sophie had not expected their plan to work out nearly so well. But Miranda had been right. She really did belong here.

Sophie rose from her dressing table and gave her reflection a once over. "You'll do," she heard Gus whisper in her ear. "You'll do just fine for me, dear."

She nodded and said a small silent thank you. It was time to go down and join the party.

.

Reverend Ben found he had to park some distance down the road from the orchard. It was always this way when you were a late-comer. He had dropped Carolyn off at the house and now walked alone toward the party. He could already hear the music drifting over the trees and smell the appetizing barbeque. The big yellow house came into view, a grand old Queen Anne, its wrap-around porches filled with lounging guests. A few called out greetings, and he waved back. He was not surprised to see Jessica and Sam Morgan here or to see Sam's sister Molly. But he did take notice of Molly walking hand-in-hand with Matt Harding, his daughter Amanda and the two Willoughby girls trailing behind. They both looked happy, Ben thought, happy and totally at ease with one another. It appeared that Matt Harding had found a way to forgive himself and move on. Ben felt truly pleased for him and for Molly, too, who had certainly weathered her share of difficulties.

Ben walked on, noticing Tucker and Carl Tulley standing together in the shade of a large oak talking to Digger Hegmen. Carl looked fascinated as the old seaman spun one of his many yarns. Ben was glad to see that Carl had come, marveling that Tucker had been able to persuade him.

Strange things had happened around here lately, he realized. Strange and even miraculous. The silent answers to so many prayers.

He walked through Sophie's garden at the back of the house, heading toward the tables and canopies. He glanced across the rows of blooming flowers. Emily Warwick and Dan Forbes sat together on a stone bench. Dan had his arm around her, and they looked as if they were off in a world of their own, more like two teenagers than people in their forties. Ben felt cheered to see Emily so radiantly happy. Only a year ago her life had been so different. She had had no one in her life, just strained relationships with both her mother and Jessica. She hadn't been reunited with her birth daughter, Sara, and had never imagined such a relationship with Dan.

He thought of his own life, how much had happened in such a short time. Carolyn's illness and accident, the birth of their first grandchild, his own crisis of faith, and the return of his son, Mark. He had married Jessica Warwick and Sam Morgan and eulogized Gus Potter. It seemed inconceivable that so much had happened in such a short time, and yet it was all just part of the steady, unexceptional stream of life.

The distant view of the village below captured his attention. Ben stopped and stared out at the town and harbor. It looked like a miniature village from this distance, a Christmas decoration in a shop window. Sometimes it seemed as if nothing ever changed here, and yet the village was really more like the sea, with so much churning under the surface.

What would the coming year hold for him and everyone here, he wondered. Only God in his heaven knew the answer to that. Ben only knew that acceptance was the key—acceptance, faith, and compassion. *To live without fear and to trust in God's love and in his promise to take care of us.*

Today was a time for celebration, a well-deserved rest from the daily routine. There would be music and dancing, eating and laughter. When darkness dropped like a heavy curtain over the horizon, a hush would fall over the crowd as everyone settled back to watch the fireworks light up the sky over the harbor.

Ben knew he, too, would watch and marvel at the sight, knowing all the while that mere fireworks could never match the majesty of the natural world, the miracles God sent us everyday in a grain of sand, a clap of thunder, or the petals of a flower.

Still he would end the day content and smiling, like all the rest, thankful for the simple pleasures of this life and the endless blessings of this single day.